MAY CONTAIN MURDER

Books by Orlando Murrin

Knife Skills for Beginners

May Contain Murder

MAY CONTAIN MURDER

ORLANDO MURRIN

JOHN SCOGNAMIGLIO BOOKS
KENSINGTON PUBLISHING CORP.
kensingtonbooks.com

This book is a work of fiction. Names, characters, businesses, organizations, places, events, and incidents either are the product of the author's imagination or are used fictitiously. Any resemblance to actual persons, living or dead, events, or locales is entirely coincidental.

To the extent that the image or images on the cover of this book depict a person or persons, such person or persons are merely models, and are not intended to portray any character or characters featured in the book.

JOHN SCOGNAMIGLIO BOOKS are published by

Kensington Publishing Corp.
900 Third Avenue
New York, NY 10022

Copyright © 2026 by Orlando Murrin
Previously published in Great Britain by Bantam, an imprint of Transworld Publishers as *Murder Below Deck*

All rights reserved. No part of this book may be reproduced in any form or by any means without the prior written consent of the Publisher, excepting brief quotes used in reviews.

Without limiting the author's and publisher's exclusive rights, any unauthorized use of this publication to train generative artificial intelligence (AI) technologies is expressly prohibited.

All Kensington titles, imprints and distributed lines are available at special quantity discounts for bulk purchases for sales promotion, premiums, fund-raising, educational or institutional use.

Special book excerpts or customized printings can also be created to fit specific needs. For details, write or phone the office of the Kensington Special Sales Manager: Kensington Publishing Corp., 900 Third Avenue, New York, NY, 10022. Attn. Special Sales Department. Phone: 1-800-221-2647.

The JS and John Scognamiglio Books logo is a trademark of Kensington Publishing Corp.

Library of Congress Control Number: 2025943543

ISBN-13: 978-1-4967-5197-3
First Kensington Hardcover Edition: January 2026

ISBN-13: 978-1-4967-5199-7 (ebook)

10 9 8 7 6 5 4 3 2 1

Printed in the United States of America

The authorized representative in the EU for product safety and compliance is eucomply OU, Parnu mnt 139b-14, Apt 123
Tallinn, Berlin 11317, hello@eucompliancepartner.com

I suppose what I believe is not that the cards can tell you anything you don't already know, or that they have magical answers to your questions, but that they give you . . . they give you the space to question . . .?

The Death of Mrs. Westaway, Ruth Ware

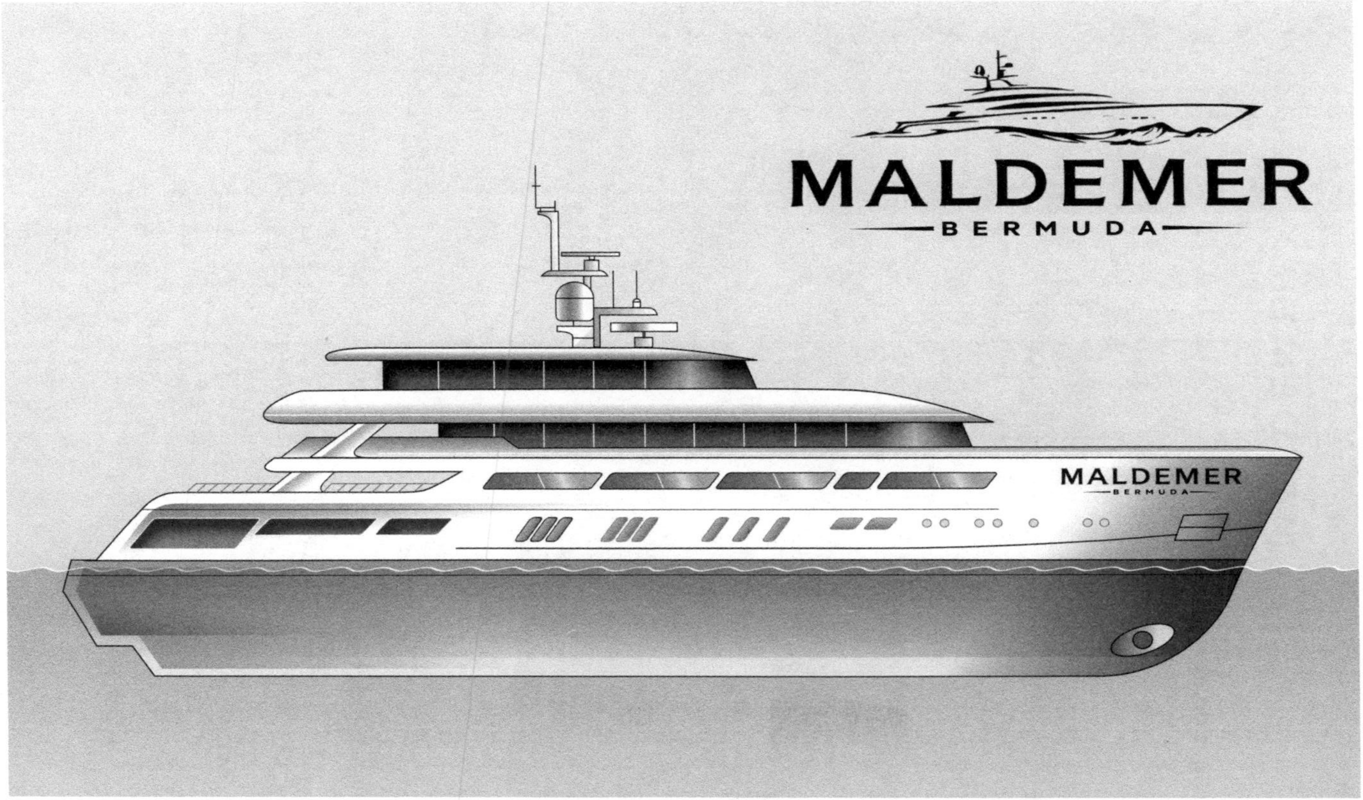
MALDEMER
BERMUDA
MALDEMER
BERMUDA

MALDEMER
— BERMUDA —

Navigation deck

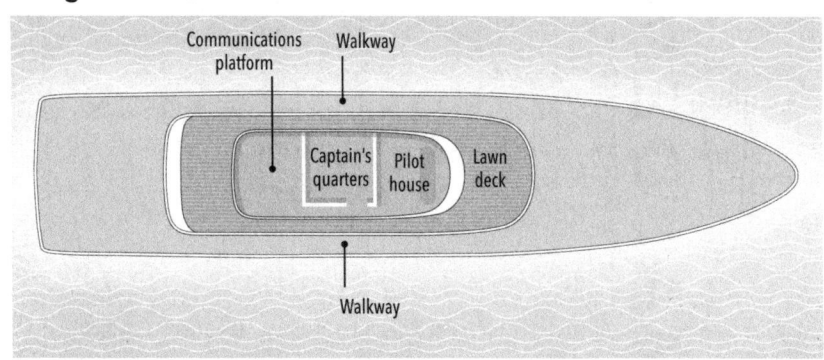

- Communications platform
- Walkway
- Captain's quarters
- Pilot house
- Lawn deck
- Walkway

Sky deck

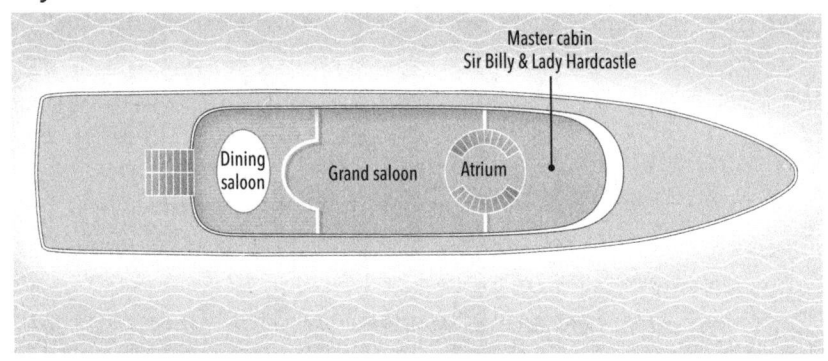

- Dining saloon
- Grand saloon
- Atrium
- Master cabin — Sir Billy & Lady Hardcastle

Panorama deck

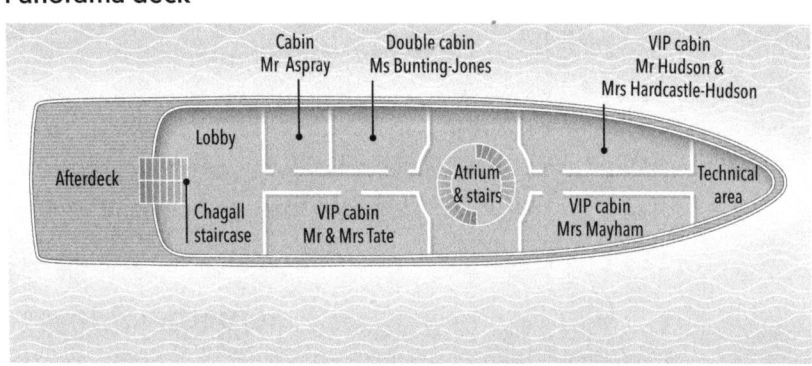

- Cabin — Mr Aspray
- Double cabin — Ms Bunting-Jones
- VIP cabin — Mr Hudson & Mrs Hardcastle-Hudson
- Lobby
- Afterdeck
- Chagall staircase
- VIP cabin — Mr & Mrs Tate
- Atrium & stairs
- VIP cabin — Mrs Mayham
- Technical area

MALDEMER
BERMUDA

Beach deck

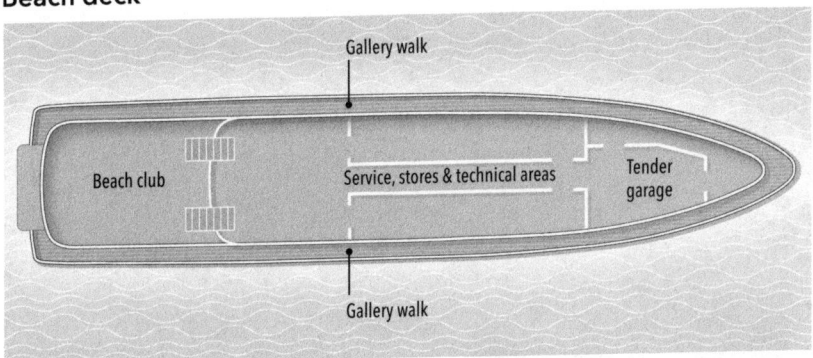

- Gallery walk
- Beach club
- Service, stores & technical areas
- Tender garage
- Gallery walk

Service deck

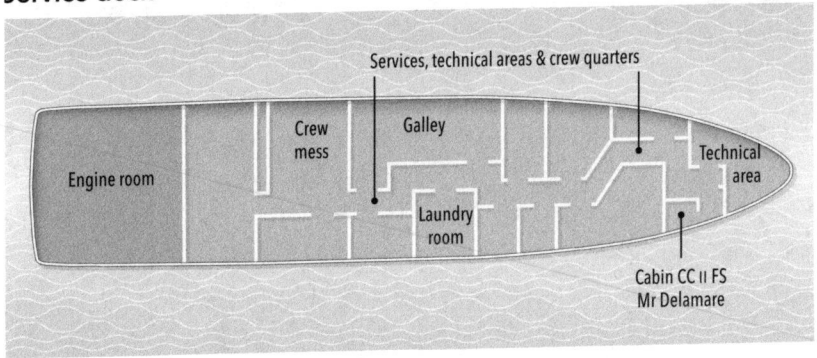

- Engine room
- Crew mess
- Galley
- Services, technical areas & crew quarters
- Laundry room
- Technical area
- Cabin CC II FS Mr Delamare

Bilges

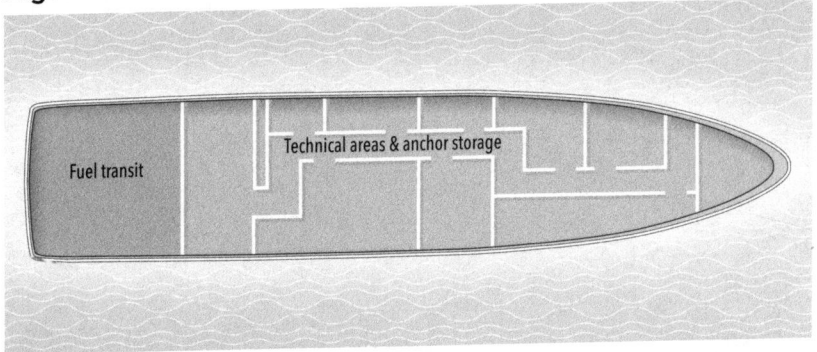

- Fuel transit
- Technical areas & anchor storage

PORT OF LONDON AUTHORITY
DEPARTURE CLEARANCE DECLARATION

YACHT NAME: M/Y *Maldemer*
EMBARKATION POINT: Tower Millennium Pier, Tower Bridge, London
DATE: Sunday 6/10/24
DESTINATION PORT: St. Boniface, near Anguilla, West Indies

PASSENGER LIST

NAME	PROFESSION	PASSPORT	RESIDENCE
Sir Billy Hardcastle *and* Lady Hardcastle (Xéra de Sully)	CEO – *and* his wife	UK France	Belgravia, London SW1
Mrs. Marje Mayham	CEO, MM Artists' Agency	UK/USA	Sunset Blvd, LA, USA
Mr. Blue Aspray	Executive Assistant to Mrs. Mayham	USA	Elm St., LA, USA
Mr. Shane Hudson *and* Mrs. Elise Hardcastle-Hudson	Executive Coach – Interior Decorator	UK	Knightsbridge, London SW1
Mr. Russell Tate *and* Mrs. Judith Tate	Financier *and* his wife	UK	Hurley, Bucks

2 / ORLANDO MURRIN

| Ms. Karol-Kate Bunting-Jones | Canine Steward | UK | Isleworth, Middlesex |
| Mr. Paul Delamare | Chef/Food Writer | UK | Belgravia, London SW1 |

CREW LIST

RANK	NAME	PASSPORT
Captain	ROMER	EU
1st Officer	ADNEY, Aimee	Barbados
Chief Stewardess	ROGERS, Challis	Australia
Chef	(Awaiting conf.)	(TBC via agency: Elite Yacht Chefs, London E1)

CHAPTER 1

For the hundredth time, I wish I'd never agreed to come along. It sounded like a fabulous idea—Atlantic cruise, all expenses paid—and of course I love spending time with Xéra, my dear, kind friend. But from the second I stepped aboard I knew it was a mistake. I don't have the right clothes, or conversation, or even attitude for a superyacht. As for my fellow passengers, well, they're not my kind of people, not at all.

It probably doesn't help that they all know I'm a last-minute addition to the party, invited along by Xéra—let's be honest—on a whim. The official line is that I'm helping her with her current project, but I suspect she felt she needed an ally, a familiar, friendly face. The others are all her new husband's family, plus various hangers-on.

The wedding was a small high-society affair—I wasn't invited—and I'm not yet sure what to make of Sir Billy. And the project in question is a memoir of her family business, which isn't normally my kind of thing either; I scratch a living in the food world, so I'm more at home with recipes for Bonfire Night or how to spatchcock a chicken. On the other hand, she's serious about it and has a mainstream publisher interested; to say nothing of the generous advance on offer to me. This is apparently being paid by Billy (Xéra rather charmingly pronounces it as *Bee-yee*), though I have yet to see a penny.

I dress nervously, looking at my watch every few seconds. I don't want to be first to arrive for dinner, making it look like I'm desperate for a drink, nor do I want to be late and make an entrance (like last night). Especially not when I'm wearing the same clothes as yesterday and they're all dressed to the nines.

Of course, I wouldn't be here at all if it weren't for my disaster back home. The house was flooded and the insurers have moved in these huge drying machines, which roar away morning, noon and night.

When she heard, Xéra was straight on the phone. Would I care to join her and her new husband on a private cruise to the Caribbean—a sort of honeymoon voyage, with a few close friends? They'd find me a nice little cabin and we could get stuck into the writing with few distractions.

Normally the idea would fill me with dread—cooped up with a shipful of the wealthy and entitled—but it seemed like the answer to a prayer. What's more, Julie—my best friend and colleague at *Escape* magazine—said I'd be mad to turn it down, and I trust her judgment. So it is that I find myself aboard Motor Yacht *Maldemer*, bobbing about off the coast of Cornwall, wishing I were anywhere but here.

If it weren't for Xéra, that is. Socially, we're chalk and cheese: she a Parisian socialite, usually to be spotted on the pages of *HELLO!*, on the slopes at Aspen, or at the latest Mayfair restaurant opening; while I eke out a living with poorly paid magazine work and just about manage to make ends meet.

Nevertheless, we've enjoyed a long and tender friendship. She was an old friend of Marcus, my late partner, and the first of his friends to whom he introduced me; he was a lawyer, and she'd originally been a client. When I erupted into Marcus's previously heterosexual life, the news was greeted generally with embarrassment, coldness or—much, much worse—fervent declarations of rainbow solidarity. Xéra, however, greeted me with a shrug and a smile, and offered her hand in friendship. It was as warm as her heart and beautifully manicured.

Since he died, one year and eleven months ago, she's kept faithfully in touch, phoning often and sending thoughtful cards. And whenever we meet, she insists on presenting me with choice, expensive gifts. Arriving in my cabin last night, I found a small, beribboned orange box containing a whistle on a leather strap—eighteen-carat gold from Hermès. When I thanked her she said it was for "calling taxis"; it probably cost more than my monthly retainer from *Escape*, and judging by its pitch, is really for summoning gundogs.

I'm jolted from my daydreams by a ping from my laptop. Since embarking yesterday afternoon, the Wi-Fi signal has been frustratingly intermittent, but my inbox has started flashing. I know at once who it must be from, because I set up a special email address for the voyage and only one person has it: Julie, the mere thought of whom makes me glow with warmth and affection.

I open the message to find a photograph of a tarot card (her latest obsession) plus a line of question marks. I guiltily remember that I promised her a full report after we embarked, and tap out a hasty reply, making an effort to sound more upbeat than I truly feel.

From: Paul Delamare/Aboard *M/Y Maldemer*
Monday 7:21 p.m.
Subject: Sorry!
To: Julie Johnson

48°08'06.0'N 10°50'51.9'W (about 320 nautical miles west of the Scilly Isles, sea level)

Hi Julie,

It's all been such a rush—and now you'll have to forgive me, I've precisely six minutes till I need to head up to dinner.

Thanks so much for waving me off—love the nautical outfit. Wish you'd been there when Tower Bridge opened for us and we sailed through, unforgettable even in the pouring rain.

The yacht! No photographs allowed . . . but it's unbelievable. I haven't done the full tour yet but it's all Baccarat chandeliers, marble staircases and priceless artworks, including a real Miró in the dining saloon.

Xéra's as blissful as ever and a joy to be with. I wish you could see this stupendous necklace she's been given by the new hubby. I'm not sure what to make of Sir Billy yet; he seems a bit, well, uncouth.

All the guest cabins are full so I've been allocated a cubby-hole in the crew quarters. A bit of a squeeze, but good for below-deck gossip. It's not a great vibe among the crew—they're whingeing that the cruise was booked at the last minute and they're terribly short-staffed. But don't worry, I'm not offering to muck in. I shall be staying strictly on the other side of the service door this trip.

One minor disaster is that while I was boarding the water taxi, my duffel bag somehow fell in the water. They managed to hook it out before it sank but it was totally waterlogged, and I'm still waiting for my things to come back from the laundry.

Apart from that, I haven't a care in the world. Ten glorious days of sea and sunshine in Xéra's charming company . . . It's going to be such a treat and thank you for persuading me to accept the invitation.

Love you, Paul

P.S. I'm guessing the Hanged Man tarot card is to punish me for leaving you dangling?

CHAPTER 2

Tonight's dinner is a sit-down affair, and I find myself placed at the very bottom of the table. The suspicion crosses my mind that I might have been invited not just to provide moral support for Xéra, but to even up the numbers. Furthermore, the young woman to my right, whose name card is inscribed "Karol-Kate," isn't a real guest at all, she's a dog handler, brought along to look after a fluffy little animal perched beside her.

"Bichon Frisé?" I ask. She grunts in the affirmative.

I don't approve of spoiled dogs—it's not fair on them—and I note with approval that this one, whose name is Colefax, isn't fed scraps from the table. Between courses, the pair leave the dining saloon for what I assume to be a comfort break, because the handler returns with the corner of a black doggy poo bag sticking out of her pocket. Gross!

I listen in on conversations around the table—not difficult, as the voices are loud—and chip in as best I can. Someone makes a disparaging remark about the salmon—which is, there's no denying it, tragically overcooked—and I meekly suggest that we should give the chef a day or two to settle in, as it's always a challenge to cook in an unfamiliar kitchen. The lemon tart that follows has a familiar look about it—Marks and Spencer's Gastropub range, if I'm not mistaken—then finally, a surprisingly decent cheeseboard. After this has been polished off—the men hacking themselves ungainly chunks with no regard to how fine cheeses should properly be cut—I observe Sir Billy whisper something to Xéra, and she disappears.

There's something imperious in his manner—a man used to ordering other people about—and after this he stands up abruptly and marches into the adjacent grand saloon, in which florid surroundings we are served after-dinner coffee in dainty gilded cups.

There, the chit-chat continues. You can tell that everyone would really like to say goodnight and go to bed, except that—as in the presence of royalty—it would be impolite to do so before our host and hostess give the signal. Sir Billy, having loosened his collar, keeps looking round, impatient for his wife's return.

A minute later we hear a distant scream. I've come to realize the atmosphere aboard a chartered superyacht isn't as hushed or polite as you might expect; except that this cry isn't because there's no slimline tonic, or a favorite lipstick has gone missing, but one of genuine horror.

The guests decide to ignore it for the time being and resume conversation, but there it is again! Now the room falls quiet and we look at one another in alarm. Sir Billy jumps up just as Xéra bursts through the doorway.

"*Mon dieu!* Help me, someone!" The prisms in the chandeliers tinkle in discord as she staggers across the room, ashen-faced and with her shining dark hair in disarray. "*C'est disparue! Where has it gone?*" She holds up a coral suede jewelry box, shakes it pointlessly and, convulsed with tears, drops it to the floor.

I know what should be in that box because she showed it to me just a few hours ago: her bridal gift from Sir Billy—her historic necklace, known as the De Lage Treasure.

I leap up to comfort her, only to find myself bulldozed aside by Sir Billy, purple in the face.

"What the hell?" he bellows, seizing her by the arm. "Well, where's it gone?"

She looks around the circle of guests in mute appeal—they sit in stunned silence, as if turned to stone. She puts a hand to her heart: "It was there this afternoon, *chéri*—I showed it to Paul in my boudoir."

Sir Billy shoots me a venomous glance then continues, in a low voice tinged with menace: "Tell me you put it back in the safe, darling, like I explained you must."

Although there are mutterings of concern at her announcement, my fellow passengers look surprisingly serene; the effect of Botox, no doubt, that scourge of the furrowed brow or wide-eyed alarm. Not Xéra, however—who appears to have aged ten years. Besides the shock of her loss, I can see something else in her eyes: could it be fear?

"Very well," growls Sir Billy, making a slow survey of the room. "That necklace will be found, if we have to rip the yacht to pieces. And when I discover who stole it . . ." His gaze settles unmistakably on me. "I'll have him keelhauled!"

Chapter 3

The captain is summoned by intercom, and strides in a minute later with the chief stewardess in tow and a practiced flick of his lustrous black hair.

"Please explain the happening," he says, calmly authoritative despite his imperfect English. His colleague, an eye-catching redhead with CHALLIS—CHIEF STEWARDESS embroidered across her top pocket, picks up the empty jewelry box and shows it to him.

"Madame's necklace?" says the captain, with a frown and another toss of his hair. "When has this happened?"

"I showed it to Paul while we were having tea this afternoon, Captain Romer," stammers Xéra. All eyes swivel toward me accusingly—including the boot-button eyes of the Bichon Frisé, ensconced on the lap of the dog handler. "Then I placed it in the top drawer of my dressing table—it was there when we left for dinner."

"The first place a thief would look," throws in Sir Billy.

Xéra ignores this. "Everyone wanted to see it and I was planning to show them after dinner."

"There was no sign of any disturbance in the cabin," protests Challis, in a broad Australian accent. "Cross my heart—not when I went in an hour ago, anyway."

"What were you doing in there?" barks Sir Billy.

"Turning down the bed."

"In the middle of dinner?"

"When else am I meant to do it?" she returns, with a flash of her green-as-glass eyes, then remembers herself. "Whenever there's a lull—for instance, when you're eating—I do the cabins."

"Ours was locked, presumably?"

"Of course. I unlocked it using my—"

The captain holds up a hand, displaying an ostentatious chunk of tantalum and gunmetal on his wrist. It's an Urwerk—how much do they pay superyacht captains, for heaven's sake? "An immediate search of the yacht I will launch. We are not a large vessel and we will all night continue, no problem, until it is found."

"What about the police?" says Sir Billy. "This needs to be done by the book. No stone unturned."

"If you mean the British police, sir, we are presently in international waters. But *Maldemer* can to port return if you wish. The nearest—"

"We're not under British jurisdiction, is what he's getting at," cuts in a pompous male voice—this is Sir Billy's money man, Russell. There's something unsavory about him, with his overhanging belly, sallow complexion and smeary rimless glasses. "Plus we fly under a flag of convenience, which is another complication."

"As long as you're sure about that," says Sir Billy. "We mustn't cut corners. Let's start the search immediately. You lead the way, Captain, and Russell and I will follow you, making notes as we go. I don't want anyone to be able to say the boat wasn't scoured from top to bottom."

"Are the guest cabins to be searched as well, sir?" asks Challis.

"Let's do those first," says Sir Billy, with an obvious flick of his eyes in my direction. "Until we find that bloody necklace, no one's going to bed."

Chapter 4

The search party stomps off, Sir Billy in the lead, leaving his guests to tend to Xéra's shattered nerves; not exactly in the honeymoon spirit.

I go to the bar, select a bottle of Rémy Martin Louis XIII Age Inconnu and pour Xéra a glass. In normal circumstances I'd join her—esoteric cognacs are very much my thing—but at times like this, it pays to stay sharp.

Being robbed is one of the hazards of being rich, and it's by no means a first for Xéra: in the fifteen years I've known her she's had her handbag snatched in Barcelona, a brand-new Mini vanish in Monaco and been held at gunpoint in the car park below her apartment in the Avenue Foch. But losing something as priceless and historical as the De Lage Treasure is in a different league.

"That *huge* pink diamond," says Sir Billy's daughter in a languid voice, slumping down on the sofa. Elise is ash blonde and in her early thirties, with a creamy complexion and cool blue eyes; she describes herself as an interior decorator, though I can't see her nailing picture hooks into the wall, or up a ladder hanging curtains.

"It wasn't a diamond," I say, matter-of-factly. "It was a Padparadscha sapphire."

The others glare at me but it's what Xéra told me: an exceedingly rare and exotic lotus-pink sapphire, originally from Sri Lanka.

"Sort of piece that really belongs in a museum," Elise continues, picking an imaginary speck of dust off her silk trousers. Hardly the sort of comment to console her traumatized stepmother, though it's true: Sir Billy bought the Treasure privately through some dubious-sounding middleman, much to the annoyance of the V&A. She then adds, as an afterthought: "Though I'm sure it looked lovely on you, Xéra dear."

Next, it's the turn of Elise's husband, Shane. "Not safe anywhere these days," he says, slightly slurred. Shane Hudson is a famous and recently retired tennis player, who Marcus and I once saw lose at Wimbledon (very graciously). As befits someone who's spent his life in the fresh air being admired by fans, he's buff, tanned and confident, with reddish-blondish stubble—that unusual hair color known as strawberry blond. All these beautiful people make me feel very ordinary and out of my depth. "Still, don't worry, Xéra, they'll have it on CCTV, whoever did it," he says, leaning back and suppressing a yawn.

Xéra stays silent and frozen-faced, staring into the middle distance.

Shane pours himself another brandy (his third, by my count), produces a pack of cards from nowhere and sets himself up a game of solitaire. Meanwhile, another guest, a well-groomed American in his late twenties called Blue, makes his way to the keyboard of the grand piano and starts fiddling with his cufflinks.

Yesterday evening this young man, who evidently models himself on Jake Gyllenhaal, let slip that he played and was "persuaded" to the keyboard: you could tell he was itching for it. Once again, he's overdressed—tonight in a midnight-blue tuxedo and open-neck dress shirt showing a smooth, tanned chest.

"Give us something soothing," suggests Elise. "You know—soft and jazzy."

Shane shoots his wife a glance, then snorts and slaps down a card.

"Don't you think it might seem, well, a little frivolous?" I offer. Last night's performance was decidedly toe-tapping, culminating in a fancy arrangement of "One" from *A Chorus Line*, complete with hand-crossing and up-and-down glissandi.

"Oh, go on," says Elise. "We can't just sit here staring at the carpet."

Requiring no further encouragement, the Jake-Gyllenhaal-alike drifts into a soft and moody selection; he's no Bill Evans, but I guess it's better than listening to one another breathing. Half an hour later, he's still at it. I pick out "Three Times A Lady" and see him flash a suave smile at his ring of female admirers.

At which point Shane rouses himself from his brandied slumber, stares glassily at the pianist and mouths the word "smoke."

It's after one o'clock by the time the search is abandoned and we're allowed back into our cabins. Chief Stewardess Challis catches me at the door to inform me that Sir Billy and the captain wish to interview me after breakfast.

"That's outrageous!" I say. "Why have I been singled out?"

"You were the last to see it. Apart from Madame, of course."

CHAPTER 5

I tread my weary way below deck and along interminable narrow corridors to my micro-cabin, which is in the bow of the yacht. Officially I may be a guest, but it doesn't feel like it.

Along the way, I replay what was happening during dinner, when the larceny occurred. Only three people left the dining saloon: Elise, to "powder her nose"; Blue, the young American, to fetch a wrap for someone who complained she was sitting in a draught; and dog handler Karol-Kate, so the dog could do its business. None was absent for more than five minutes, giving precious little time for the thief to sneak into the master cabin, locate the jewels, hide them and return looking cool as a cucumber.

As for the crew, they come across as totally professional, and I have no doubt they're exhaustively vetted before being let loose in this kind of environment. If one of them was stupid enough to steal the necklace, they'll surely get caught.

I'm at the last bend when I collide with a large obstacle propped against the wall. Something about it looks familiar, and the letters "CC 11 FS," plus a sticky label bearing my name—misspelled, of course—confirm my suspicions. It is indeed the door of my cabin, rudely wrenched off and dumped in the corridor.

I don't know why it upsets me so much that no one can ever get my name right: it's Dela*mare*, not Dela*mere* (which is a service station on the M4). I'm lucky the river police let me aboard, because the boarding paperwork didn't tie up with my passport. Pure carelessness.

It gets worse. I click on the light to find I've been ransacked. Both bunks have been stripped and the mattresses shoved in the shower room. Worse still, my laptop—my only contact with the outside world—is lying on the floor at an odd angle (as if someone's tried to snap it in half) and flashing violently.

Blinking in disbelief, I gingerly lift away the debris, like an archaeologist unearthing a precious artefact, and transfer the wounded device to the spare bunk. Somehow an email has made it through, and now unfurls across the shattered screen.

From: Julie Johnson
Monday 9:12 p.m.
Subject: In the drink
To: Paul Delamare/Aboard *M/Y Maldemer*

Horrified to hear about your luggage nightmare. Not sure you want to hear this, but after waving you off at the pier, I swear I caught sight of JONNY jumping on a bus. You don't think . . .?

I popped into Jubilee Cottage on the way home and some leaves have fallen off your money plant. Don't be alarmed—Declan says it's normal for this time of year. He sends his love.

I also checked your bank account, and sorry, nothing's been paid in.

Today's tarot draw suggests to me that you have fallen within the orbit of a powerful, possibly ruthless,

QUEEN of SWORDS.

woman. With my astrologer hat on, I think she may be a Libran.

J. X

P.S. How do you do your coordinates? Cool.

P.P.S. Don't let yourself be dragged into helping out with the cooking. You're there as Xéra's guest, not galley slave.

P.P.P.S. What do you mean no photos? I thought the whole point of being on a superyacht was to plaster it all over Instagram?

CHAPTER 6

Declan is my best friend's new beau, a rugby-playing copper who's been weaseling his way into her life over the past few months. It started innocently enough with drinks and movie nights, but now it's *Declan this, Declan that,* until I'm sick of the sound of him. I admit he's easy on the eye, and very charming when I'm around, but there's *no way* he's good enough for Julie—and since when is he an expert on houseplants?

This is a new interest of mine, sparked off by the gift of an indoor climbing plant—a hoya—last autumn. It took off and now I have something growing on every windowsill. I'm worried I'll find them all dead when I get home, and have given strict instructions to Julie not to overwater.

On which subject, it's too much of a coincidence that Jonny was skulking around Tower Bridge when my luggage went into the river. Jonny Berens is my stepson, only a couple of years younger than me but a source of ongoing rancor, seeping poison into my otherwise quiet life, and I have no doubt he was behind this latest act of malevolence.

Julie's always urging me to cut loose from him, but I promised Marcus, his late father, that I wouldn't. And then there's his mother: if anything, Olinda is even more troublesome than Jonny. I can see why she might resent me, but I didn't "steal her husband," and certainly not to get my hands on his money.

There's another complication, too—a legal one. I live in a tiny house off Bourne Street called Jubilee Cottage, nicknamed "the smallest house in Belgravia," which was left to me by Marcus. I say "left," but owing to an oversight on his part, I only have a life interest in the property, after which it will revert to the Berens family. They've done their best to oust me, and I've borne it with as much patience and dignity as I can muster. The arson attempts, the glued locks, the broken windows . . . I'm convinced it was Jonny who caused the flood in my basement, though I'm unable to prove anything.

What saddens me most is that I'm not sure how long I can keep going. Even running a place as modest as Jubilee Cottage is beyond my means, with a never-ending stream of bills and charges. Things are even tighter than usual at the moment, and I'm relying on my advance for working on Xéra's book to get me through. I decide to update Julie on the evening's happenings.

From: Paul Delamare/Aboard *M/Y Maldemer*
Tuesday 1:31 a.m.
Subject: Drama
To: Julie Johnson

47°50'43"N 14°00'22"W (about 360NM west of Brittany)

Catastrophe: Xéra's necklace—the one I told you about—has vanished, stolen.

They're saying it's worth a million! Bought from some dodgy chum of Sir Billy's called Luiz Mateus (as in rosé), who they refer to as "Big Lew" (sounds like a boxer). The thief will never get away with it—it's absurd to think they can keep it hidden on a yacht, for heaven's sake . . .

Although having spent a day among the Hardcastles, I wouldn't be surprised if one of them nicked it out of pure malice and dropped it overboard.

In the meantime, now that we're officially a crime scene, may I call on your research skills?

First of all, Sir Billy's money man—Russell Tate. All I know is that he used to fund-manage for a bank, and is now "head of the Hardcastle Family Office," whatever that means.

I'm also a bit suspicious about a flashy young American by the name of Blue Aspray—as in hairspray, to which he is no stranger. He's personal assistant to Sir Billy's sister Marje Mayham—flew over from LA with her—and plays the piano. (Like most amateur musicians, doesn't know when to stop.)

The coordinates are thanks to a miracle of modern technology: tap the Compass app on your phone and they come straight up. We also have GPS, so if you draw a line between the bottom corner of Ireland and the top of Spain, and go left a bit, that's where we are.

The houseplant situation sounds a bit worrying, but I wouldn't get Declan involved. I don't see him as the green-fingered type.

Miss you. XXX

P.S. I noticed Aspray snapping away with his iPhone when he thought no one was looking. I'm tempted to report him.

Adrenaline still coursing through my veins after the evening's sequence of calamities, I'm unable to drift off to sleep. When I finally do, I'm woken by a noise coming from above my head. Not this again! Same as last night: *Bump*. Pause. *Bump bump*. Pause. *Bump*. I'm the only person berthed in the bow of the boat—is it something mechanical?

I roll over, trying to ignore it, then remember that silly story we used to frighten ourselves with at school, about the girl who discovers a psychopath escaped from the local asylum is banging her boyfriend's severed head against the roof of their car.

I check my watch: 3 a.m. The hour Horatio describes to Hamlet as "the dead vast and middle of the night." If this happens again tomorrow, I'll get up and investigate.

Chapter 7

After a few fitful hours of sleep I'm awoken by a lurch in the boat's motion—we've picked up speed. Thanks to GPS I can see we've reached a deep stretch of ocean called the Porcupine Abyssal Plain; two miles below us, sea cucumbers, starfish and sea anemones eke out their existence in Stygian gloom. I also note we've crossed a time zone, and put my watch back to six thirty, at which point I hear a rap at the door. Because it's only propped in place it falls open to a crisp white uniform—it's the first officer, Aimee Adney.

I'm unused to beautiful young women accosting me in bed and instinctively grab my bedclothes to cover myself up. Bar the captain, Aimee is the most important member of the crew, exuding an air of confidence and competence. She's so gorgeous it's a pleasure just to look at her, but her most winning feature is her radiant smile—it's impossible not to warm to it.

"You know you mentioned you'd been a chef?" Although Xéra introduced me as a food writer, the guests managed to winkle it out of me that for many years I worked in Michelin-starred kitchens, and hinted that I might like to cook dinner one evening. No way.

"We're hoping you can do us a huge favor." She tilts her head becomingly. "I hate to ask, but would you mind cooking the guests' breakfast? It's just that the Irishwoman's sick, and because we're so short-staffed, we haven't got a fallback."

I have yet to meet "the Irishwoman" but I do know, from below deck tittle-tattle, that she isn't a chef at all: the voyage was planned as a "delivery"—to get the yacht to the Caribbean for the winter season—and she was booked to cook for the crew, not guests. Judging by the two meals I've eaten so far, she's discovered a cache of posh ready meals in the freezer; it's anyone's guess what'll happen when they run out.

"Just this once?" Aimee adds, widening her eyes in supplication.

"But my clothes aren't back," I say desperately. "I haven't got anything to wear."

"Don't worry—leave it to me. See you in the galley in ten minutes."

As I shower, my head spins with unpleasant thoughts. What if the chef is going to make a habit of this, and I'm stuck in front of a stove for the rest of the trip? As a chef, you need a constitution of iron—you can't just bunk off because you have a headache or don't feel up to it.

I shave quickly and try a few tentative smiles in front of the mirror, remembering that I'm meant to be enjoying myself. By the time I emerge, I find a laundry basket has appeared as if by magic on the lower bunk. My washing, back at last.

But what's this?

For a second, I hope and pray that they've given me someone else's clothes by mistake, then I start to recognize flashes of familiar pattern or trim. Here are my favorite stripy socks—a Christmas present from Julie—shrunk to the size of a baby's mittens. A pile of T-shirts that would be a tight squeeze for a toddler. And no, this cannot be! My best cashmere jumper—the most precious thing in my wardrobe, so soft, so light, so luxurious—reduced to fit a teddy bear, the wool pilled and matted.

This is terrible: I rake through the heap of mangled and maimed garments with a sinking heart. Is there anything here I can salvage? I try on one of my cotton shirts—these had been cunningly placed on top of the basket, to deceive the eye—and by sucking in my stomach and chest, manage to do up the buttons. I grab some denims and lie down on the floor—no mean feat in such a small cabin. Somehow, I manage to zip them up and cover up what I can with yesterday's pullover.

I've taken the trouble to be friendly toward the crew members I've met so far and asked to be treated as one of them, so I set off in the direction of the galley in the hope of a cup of tea and some sympathy. My route takes me through the crew mess: a low, windowless space adjacent to the galley, painted in kindergarten colors and furnished with banquettes. Although designed as a place for yachties to hang out and chillax, it feels more like a fast-food restaurant, designed to make you leave as soon as possible. I find Challis eating a bowl of cereal. She looks up and whistles. "Very Harry Styles," she says. "Aimee—come see. Paul's got a new look."

"How amusing," I say. "You need to get your washing machine checked."

Aimee appears at the door and beckons me into the galley.

"I don't normally look like this," I assure her, wondering how I'm going to survive the next ten days.

"You're a guest—you can dress how you like." Then she adds with a smile: "And don't mind what Poison says: underneath, she's harmless."

It takes me a moment, then I get it. Poison—Challis. Ha! "You don't understand," I protest. "All my clothes have been ruined. Someone must have put them in at the wrong temperature."

Her smile melts, as if the sun has suddenly gone in. "What are you saying?"

"Erm, I don't want to get anyone in trouble . . ."

"Why . . . that is *not* the sort of thing that happens aboard *Maldemer*. I'll find out what happened and sort you out with something to wear."

"Thanks, Aimee." I feel a sense of relief wash over me. Things are going to be all right.

Although I swore I wouldn't get roped in to cook—both to myself and to Julie—I inevitably feel a rush of adrenaline as I walk into the galley. I've cooked aboard a yacht before, but nothing like this: two double ovens plus microwave, a pair of American-style fridge-freezers, triple sink with waste-disposal unit, dishwasher and garbage compactor (can't wait to have a go with that). One of those brilliant Thermomix machines that cooks and stirs at the same time, and a Bamix blender, pro model with all the accessories. Masses of cupboards and drawers with natty little button locks so they stay shut in a storm. A small island, brightly lit, with six-ring induction hob and steel rail round the edge to stop things from sliding off.

When I started out cheffing, I remember how terrifying it was to be confronted with a strange kitchen and equipment you've never seen before, but it's something you get used to. Now that supper clubs and pop-ups are becoming the norm, we're all getting more versatile.

"Do I just cook what I feel like or is there a menu?" I ask.

Aimee looks surprised. "The guests can order anything they like. Take a look at the Guest Preference Book—the chef will have put it somewhere safe." I find it in the knife drawer—a folder jammed full of laminated pages—and flick through. Yikes! Pages and pages of tick boxes, lists and ratings; every guest's tastes, whims, likes, dislikes, intolerances and allergies picked over in forensic detail.

Elise will eat red peppers but not green. No onions for Sir Billy. Blue doesn't care for cinnamon in savory dishes. Two of the guests are nut-alert, and Sir Billy's sister specifies "no *hidden* nuts" which I presume is a dental issue. Et cetera, et cetera, et cetera. How am I meant to remember all this?

A quick inspection of fridges and cupboards establishes that at least there's no shortage of raw ingredients. I start off by getting a batch of maple and pecan granola in the oven then slice melon, pears, strawberries, grapes, and a couple of kiwis into a vibrant fruit salad. I place a selection of frozen pastries—croissants, almond croissants, pains aux raisins—on baking sheets, whack them into the oven at 350°F fan and set the timer. Racing round the kitchen on full alert, I find, to my surprise, I'm having fun. I haven't cheffed for a while but it's as exhilarating as ever.

Breakfast is served in an area at the stern of the yacht dubbed the beach club. It's a remarkable feat of engineering—at the press of a button, the rear section can be swung out at water level and lowered to form a floating swimming pool, enclosed by pontoons.

The transformation is effected thanks to countless cables, winches, cleats, and capstans. These are fascinating to someone with an interest in chandlery (such as myself) but invisible to the naked eye, being cunningly concealed behind the eye-catching décor, on a Tiki theme. Think bamboo screens adorned with wooden masks; ukeleles and surfboards; glass fishing floats suspended from the boarded ceiling. The focal point is an aquarium set in the wall, complete with real lobsters, which stare out dolefully from among plastic shipwrecks and neon seaweed.

It's a long way from the galley, which is in the center of the yacht and two decks below, and Challis and the unlucky deckhand assisting her race back and forth with trays and carts laden with eggs Benedict, wild mushroom omelettes (no salt or pepper) and bacon butties.

Interspersed with shouted food orders and the bubbling of the espresso machine, Challis even manages to squeeze in a bit of gossip. She was woken up last night by a further emergency—a guest complaining about an insect buzzing in her cabin, eventually traced to the bathroom cabinet and an electric toothbrush she'd forgotten to switch off.

"Let me guess—Sir Billy's daughter," I say.

"No—the sister!"

Sir Billy's sister—and guest of honor on the voyage—is none other than Marje Mayham. When Xéra sent me the guest list, I thought I recognized the name, and a quick check online confirmed her as an (extremely) successful Hollywood talent agent. Like the rest, she's immaculately groomed, with a steel gray bob and glossy nails, and is evidently used to ordering people about, in a grating transatlantic accent.

"That's only the half of it," continues Challis, licking her lips. "Want to hear about her sleeping arrangements? That young man of hers—"

"If you're referring to the American, he's her personal assistant," I say primly. "I don't think it's any of our business—"

"Don't be an idiot—his heart's off somewhere else, you mark my words. All I'm saying is, he gets sent in an hour ahead to seal up all the blinds and skylights with black-out tape so there ain't a crack of light. Then she slips into this sleeping suit—kind of like a padded silk onesie—with a hood and holes for her nose and mouth. Like that movie where the sheila gets cut in half by a garage door." That'll be *Scream*, if I'm not mistaken: I don't mind the occasional horror movie but it's not a favorite.

"On a more serious note, Challis, do you think Sir Billy meant it when he said I would be interrogated about last night's theft?"

"Oh, yeah," she says, with a hint of malice. "They'll give you a shout when it suits 'em. In the meantime, you're to stick around."

"Um . . . we're on a yacht. I don't have much choice, do I?"

CHAPTER 8

At ten o'clock, a peal of clangorous bells rings out on the public address system, informing us that it's time for muster drill. This was scheduled for yesterday, but Sir Billy and Russell had it postponed because of an urgent meeting on Zoom. When I arrive at the lawn deck, where the exercise is to take place, I find I'm first to arrive.

Maldemer has several al fresco areas where guests can drink in the sea air and views. At her stern is the afterdeck, set out with low tables and loungers, where you can read or sunbathe, or simply gaze at the wake of the yacht as we slice through the ocean. Then there's the gallery walk—a walkway running round the perimeter of the yacht between the panorama and beach decks, complete with benches and lookouts.

Not many superyachts, however, boast an actual lawn, complete with nodding daisies and croquet hoops. I sit down on the grass, which is soft and springy to the touch. How did it get here? I wonder. Did they sow seed, or lay turf? Who waters and mows it? Such is the folly of man.

The sky today is azure—almost cloudless—and the sea the shade of midnight, spangled and crested by flecks of foam. I survey the horizon and we are totally alone: no land, no boats, no nothing. I feel a soft breeze on my cheek and listen to the gentle lapping of waves. The air tastes much cleaner and sweeter out here. *Now* I understand why rich people own superyachts. I notice the sward has been marked up with white lines, like a school playing field. At first I wonder if they're for some deck game—can you play quoits or shuffleboard on turf?—then realize they form an enormous H. I don't care for helicopters but I can see they're a convenient way for the super-rich to pop to the shops if they run out of shoes or handbags.

I'm thus musing when something catches my attention: a huge bird gliding astern, apparently following the yacht. It has long slender wings in two shades of gray, spanning nearly a meter, and a white body with a yellow beak. Its flight appears effortless, serene.

Birds fill me with awe and wonder: they've been around millions of years—the only known descendants of dinosaurs—yet still we understand so little about them. What distant place have you come from, and where are you heading? The Horn of Africa? The Falkland Islands? I watch enraptured until suddenly the creature banks and wheels, then disappears back the way we came.

Ten minutes late, my fellow passengers arrive and I check them out under the revealing morning light. Marje Mayham looks pallid and sticky, presumably thanks to liberal use of SPF 100 sunblock; her silver bob, on the other hand, remains immaculate. Her piano-playing assistant removes his leather loafers—Tod's, I suspect—to reveal a pair of sockless, perfectly groomed feet, which remind me that Julie told me to invest in a pedicure. I wish I'd listened.

Elise has tucked her long blonde hair into an enormous straw hat and Shane is donning a baseball cap. He has that fair English skin that burns easily, as he must surely know from his time on the tennis court; he is fidgeting with his hands, probably wondering when the bar opens. The Bichon Frisé is scampering about, off his leash.

Also present is Russell's wife, known by the others (behind

her back) as Little Grey Rabbit. She looks even more out of place than usual this morning in a raincoat and headscarf (as if she's nipping out to the supermarket). To everyone's surprise, she steps forward and gives a little cough to command attention. For a second I think she's going to thank me for making breakfast, but no: either they're an ungrateful bunch or no one told them. Instead, she announces in a timid voice that Sir Billy and her husband are once again unable to attend the drill, and we're to go ahead without them.

There's no sign of Xéra either, which I could have predicted, as she's never seen before mid-morning.

We're milling about awkwardly, waiting for the first officer to arrive, when I manage to dredge up from my memory Little Grey Rabbit's name.

"Can you see a ship on the horizon, Judith?" I ask, beckoning her to join me at the taffrail and pointing to starboard. "You look to me like someone with good eyesight." It's only a ploy, but I can tell she feels as out of place as I do and is relieved to break out of the circle.

"How can you tell?" she asks, with a shy smile.

I observe her carefully under the Atlantic glare. She's in good shape for her early sixties, slim and with fine unlined skin—an "English rose," as my parents might have said. With her springy gray-brown hair and eager expression, she's in fact more squirrel than rabbit.

"I'm glad to see you're properly dressed for sea conditions," I say companionably. "We're crossing the Atlantic, not island hopping in the Aegean."

She smiles again. "Thank you for saying. Russell says I should have bought some new things for the trip. He's right—I feel a bit frumpy."

"Not at all. But my mother used to be a whiz with scarves— may I?" Before she can object, I step forward to loosen the knot under her chin, then arrange the scarf to sit higher on her head.

"Oh really, Paul," she says, with a giggle.

I stand back to see the effect. "Let's try a bit of Jackie O." I push the scarf back, so it frames her face in an oval shape. "And this." I flip up her collar and cinch in the belt of her raincoat. Although I say it myself, the effect is rather dashing: I point out her reflection in the mirrored window of the pilot house and she laughs.

"How did you do that? You're a magician."

"Just years of watching Mum. And if I really could do magic, I'd conjure myself up some more clothes."

"I couldn't help noticing you're rather oddly . . . Well, that you don't look very comfy. Did something happen?"

"Disagreement with a washing machine—nothing that can't be rectified," I add, though I don't see how. She gives my hand a little squeeze, and I feel I've made a friend.

We're suddenly interrupted by an unholy squawking from above. It isn't the graceful bird I saw a few minutes ago but an enormous beady-eyed seagull, circling purposefully over the Bichon Frisé.

Someone tries to shoo it away, which only serves to excite the dog, who starts jumping and yapping. Birds have a remarkably keen perception of color and it can't help that the little fellow is kitted out in a fluorescent orange life jacket.

Suddenly the gull swoops, beak open wide, eyes focused. There are gasps and moans of dismay from the guests and a bloodcurdling yowl from the dog. It seems the merciless creature is within an inch of snatching up the unfortunate mutt when an apparition in green—none other than the dog handler—rushes forward and beats away the predator with her bare hands.

"That is one lucky dog," says Blue, once the calamity has passed. "Coulda got snatched or lost an eye."

"Watch he doesn't fall overboard," announces Marje in her braying accent. "Make a tasty snack for a shark."

After drill, I hang back to talk to the dog handler and congratulate her on saving Colefax's life. Karol-Kate is what used to be described as the "tomboy" type: yesterday it was a jaunty boiler suit, today she's sporting a lurid green polo shirt and white jeans: a sprig o' shamrock and she wouldn't look amiss in a St. Patrick's Day parade.

"You know it's unlucky to wear green at sea," I say, by way of conversation. "Just joking."

She grunts—not an unfriendly sound—and follows the dog as he circles the deck, busily wagging his tail and snuffling. I trail a few steps behind, attempting to make conversation. Having had the finger of suspicion firmly pointed at me by Sir Billy, I feel it won't do any harm to gather some information on my fellow passengers to try and identify the real thief.

"I wonder if there's any news on the necklace," I say. "Terrible to think it must have happened while we were chatting away at the table."

She quickens her pace but I keep in step. "They should get Colefax to hunt for it," I say. "Assuming they haven't found it already." The dog looks round at me and wags his tail.

"Bichons are water dogs, not bloodhounds," she replies tartly, hurrying him along.

"Are you on a schedule? I thought dogs liked to stop and sniff, not be rushed."

"It's all planned," she says, pointing to her wrist. I know all about Apple Watches because Julie has one, and insists on telling me how many steps she's done. "Three times round the boat in the morning, then the opposite way in the evening."

Dour as she may appear, Karol-Kate takes her responsibilities seriously. Last night at dinner she explained to me that she's set up an elaborate alarm schedule on her device. Apparently when it goes *yip yip!* it's time for a bathroom break; *grrr!* for a training session; *woof woof woof!* for din-dins; and *owOOOO!* means walkies.

"Do Elise and Shane walk him sometimes—or do they leave it all to you?"

"They're more into playing than walking. Shane's fond enough of him, but Elise . . . she only picks up the lead as an excuse for a smoke break." Rather bluntly put, though I'd rather that than subterfuge. "But we get along just fine, don't we, young man?" The animal looks up with his bright button eyes and nods, though I may be imagining that.

"Is he missing his sister?" I ask; apparently Colefax is one of a pair.

"It'll be Fowler's turn next time," she replies. I get why an interior decorator might choose it, but it's an unfortunate name for a dog.

I change my line of questioning. "What do you make of the other guests?"

Grunt. "Don't have much to do with them."

Dog and handler circumambulate once more—another thirty-two steps—and are about to head off when I stop them.

"I keep meaning to ask, Karol-Kate, is this what you do for a living, look after dogs on yachts?"

She laughs. "Hardly! I'm treating this as a subsidized holiday, same as you. I don't have a dog of my own, so this is the next best thing. And while we're on the subject, I think it's best for people in our position to keep our heads down. I'd quit playing the private detective if I were you."

Chapter 9

Suitably chastened, I set off to meet Xéra. We've agreed to devote two hours every morning and afternoon to working on her memoir, and because Sir Billy and Russell need the privacy of the master cabin for their urgent business discussions, we've diverted today to the grand saloon.

She arrives politely late, in a cloud of fragrance and bearing an ancient attaché case in soft fawn leather. She famously wears a "private" chypre by Guerlain, created exclusively by the perfume house for her mother, and now her. From nowhere materializes a pot of tea—lapsang chinbara, courtesy of Mariage Frères—and a plate of macarons, which have been dusted with iridescent icing sugar to match the décor. Xéra glances at them with disdain.

Impeccable makeup cannot disguise the fact that she has had a bad night. There are shadows under her eyes and today their usual rich brown is almost black with misery and strain. "Bee-yee's beautiful gift—this priceless treasure. The value is not interesting to me, but its beauty and its provenance . . . Who could do this to us?" she asks.

The pendant Padparadscha at the center of the De Lage Treasure once belonged to Xéra's ten-times-great-aunt, who was none other than Madame (later the Marquise) de Pompadour, mistress of Louis XV. It can be seen displayed on that lady's powdered bosom in a lesser-known portrait by Boucher, the "marquise cut" (elliptical with rounded corners) having been created in imitation of her beautiful bow lips.

The greatest tragedy, though I don't say this to Xéra, is that unless it's found speedily the necklace will doubtless be broken up and the Pompadour Padparadscha recut; it's not as if it can ever be seen in public again.

"Bee-yee was so proud to give it to me, he wanted the world to know. I was planning to wear it to the Met Gala in May. But Paul, *chéri*, I tell you a secret, between ourselves: I pay for half. This is the modern way, no?"

There were rumors Liz Taylor chipped in for the diamonds that Richard Burton "bought" her, but I don't like the sound of this—not at all. Tactfully, I change the subject.

"I seem to be in Sir Billy's bad books. Surely he can't believe I had anything to do with it?"

"It must be . . . how you say? *An inside job*," she replies. "We were all at dinner—no one left the table. But you must please forgive Bee-yee—he is quick to anger. I wish that you will be friends."

I think it unlikely. Indeed, my first glimpse of Sir Billy Hardcastle—a good Yorkshire surname which he likes pronounced *harksle*—was inauspicious. To be accurate, I smelled him before I saw him, thanks to the hosed-on Hugo Boss aftershave.

It was our first afternoon, and Xéra and I were catching up on all the gossip, when in barged a tall, sturdily built man in an artfully constructed Savile Row suit. He looked twice the size of his tiny, bird-like wife, with thinning blond hair and a long-ago broken nose he'd not bothered to have reset, and was dragging a huge Louis Vuitton cabin trunk.

"And you are?" he'd said, appraising me with ice-blue eyes. "I wasn't expecting my wife to smuggle another man into her boudoir while we're still on honeymoon." We dutifully laughed. I offered to give him a hand but he waved me aside.

If you enjoy watching old Hollywood movies, as I do, you'll

have observed various phenomena that do not correspond to real life. One is known as Doris Day parking: a vacant space that miraculously appears where and when the star needs it. Another is Hollywood luggage; in moments of crisis, clothes are flung into suitcases—hats, shoes, dresses—but when it's time for the actor to exit, they're light as air. It's probably as well for Sir Billy's back that his Louis Vuittons—for there were three of them—appeared to be of the Hollywood variety. Presumably he's planning to do some serious shopping on the island of St Boniface, the tropical paradise to which the Villa Hardcastle lends its luster, and where we'll land in ten days' time. (Not having been invited for that part of the trip, I'll be flying straight home.)

Xéra had looked on indulgently, as befits a new wife. "Relax, *chéri*, you're on holiday." She straightened his tie and smiled up at him. At which point he'd leaned forward and planted a noisy kiss on her cheek.

Maybe I imagined it, but as he did so Xéra recoiled a millimeter or two, whether in surprise or . . . something else, I couldn't quite tell.

Telling your life story can seem a forbidding task, so at my suggestion, we're breaking it down into manageable chunks. Xéra is from the most illustrious of family backgrounds—French aristocracy on her father's side, her mother an Indonesian beauty photographed by Patrick Demarchelier for *Harper's Bazaar*—but today we've agreed to talk about the business.

I interview her the old-fashioned way, using a spiral-bound shorthand notebook with lined pages, across the front of which I've inscribed in proud capitals:

XÉRAPHINA ASMARA DE SULLY

LADY HARDCASTLE

I jot down that she is wearing white jeans and a sailor-striped top: the epitome of diminutive Brigitte Macron chic. As a backup, I record our talks on a natty little voice recorder purchased for the occasion. Who knows? One day we could turn it into a podcast.

Chapter 10

P D: *The business—Pâtisserie Pompadour—when exactly was it founded?*

X D S: September 1890, at the end of La Belle Époque, by Floris de Sully. He was my great-grandfather.

P D: *So it's been—was—in the family for how many generations?*

X D S: Four.

P D: *Quite a legacy. Business acumen must run in the de Sully genes.*

X D S: I wouldn't say that. The men are charming and handsome, but not necessarily . . . Let's just say, they're attracted to smart women, who can spot opportunities and make things happen.

P D: *Are you suggesting the men in your family were dim-witted compared to the women?*

[LAUGHTER]

X D S: I prefer to say, natural aristocrats.

P D: *. . . who always married brainy women.*

X D S: I would say they chose beauty as well as brains.

[LAUGHTER]

P D: *Tell me more about your mother, Luna de Sully.*

X D S: Maman's family came from a little village in western Sumatra called Pariangan, which looks out over Mount Marapi. I've visited many times to meet my Minangkabau relatives and it is where my charitable foundation will have its headquarters.

P D: *A charitable foundation? I'll be interested to hear more about that.*

X D S: La Fondation Luna de Sully—I named it for Maman.

P D: *Perfect for our last chapter. Now, how did your mother and father meet?*

X D S: Grandpapa was the Indonesian ambassador to France, so Maman was born and brought up in Paris—in the sixteenth. Let me show you a photo of my parents.

P D: *For the purposes of our tape recording, you're opening a calf leather attaché case, with something engraved on the lock.*

X D S: My mother's initials.

P D: *LdS. And here's a folder made of beautiful Florentine paper—hand-marbled, I'm guessing.*

X D S: It's the family archive. Voilà—this is the one.

P D: *Oh, my goodness. What a gorgeous couple—they look like models, or film stars. When was it taken?*

X D S: It's here on the back: "*Apollon et Luna, Paris, Juin 1974.*"

P D: *At Versailles, is it?*

X D S: No, the Élysée Palace. Louis XV gave it to the Marquise de Pompadour—it was called the Hôtel d'Évreux in those days. We think of it as the *maison de famille*.

P D: *Some family pad.*

[LAUGHTER]

X D S: In fact, the marquise had no surviving children, so the de Sullys are descended through her maternal line.

P D: *May I borrow the folder overnight? I'll take great care of it.*

[PAUSE]

X D S: Yes, if you wish. We go through it together next time.

P D: *You were saying that you took over running the business when you were thirty. Was it just the one pâtisserie then— in the Rue du Bac?*

X D S: By then we had branches in Honfleur, Lyon and Nice. Then five years ago came the big push—openings in Vienna, Geneva and New York. All within six months— imagine.

P D: *London too.*

[PAUSE]

X D S: That was before.

P D: *Round the corner from Panzer's—I remember going there and loving it.*

[PAUSE]

P D: *But you decided to close it for some reason?*

[LONG PAUSE]

X D S: We were talking about the business going international.

P D: *What prompted you to sell it?*

X D S: It felt like the right moment. For personal reasons.

PAUSE]

P D: *Maybe we can come back to that.*

X D S: Maybe.

P D: *OK, let's move on. Would you say you were more interested in the business side, or the pâtisserie operation?*

X D S: *Chéri*, you know I would never eat a pastry, but don't write that down!

P D: *I think people will guess you don't eat a lot of cream cakes and doughnuts! Are we going to include recipes in the book?*

X D S: I'm still thinking about it. I don't want to take away from the seriousness of some of the things I have to say, but the publisher told me recipes would sell copies.

P D: *There's one in particular readers would give their eye teeth for.*

X D S: But of course.

P D: *It would be an enormous coup to publish it—it's been such a closely guarded secret.*

X D S: I wouldn't say that. That American woman—

P D: *Julia Child.*

X D S Anyone would think she invented it!

P D: *Then this is our chance to set history straight.*

[PAUSE]

X D S: Maybe you are right. Now ask me something different.

[PAUSE]

P D: *Do you miss the business now you've sold it?*

[PAUSE]

X D S: Very much so, but it was the right thing to do. Maybe . . . I would have preferred to wait a little longer. But we will not put that in the book. Bee-yee—he would not like it.

[PAUSE]

P D: *How did you meet?*

X D S: It is such a sweet story. We were introduced in New York by his sister Marje.

P D: *Really? I had no idea—*

X D S: Marje is an old friend of mine—I thought you knew? Then, a week later, Bee-yee and I found ourselves traveling back to Europe together on the *Queen Mary 2*. The pâtisserie sale was going through at the time . . . problems, problems, problems . . . and Bee-yee was wonderful—so strong. I couldn't have got through it without him.

P D: *Xéra de Sully finally settling down and getting married, after all those carefree years. We were amazed.*

[LAUGHTER]

P D: *How do you know Marje? You, er, seem to come from different worlds.*

X D S: We were keynote speakers at a conference in Reykjavik fifteen years ago. When I am in LA I stay with her, and she stays with me in Paris. We switch between the Chateau Marmont and Hôtel Costes.

[LAUGHTER]

P D: *It must be lovely for her—now you've joined the family.*

X D S: They are very close—brother and sister. I made myself a promise not to come between them.

P D: *Long trip for her, all the way from the West Coast.*

[PAUSE]

X D S: Don't write this down, but she came because she wishes to speak of important business with Bee-yee. He likes to be needed. To be the center of things. And now I must go to him. *À bientôt, chéri.*

[MWAH, MWAH]

CHAPTER 11

I feel a little short-changed—barely an hour's work done—but close my notebook and switch off my recording device. I'm about to follow her out when I remember something I wanted to check in the library's little reference section. I'm not sure what John Fairweather's *Calamities at Sea* is doing here but I soon alight upon what I'm looking for: *Guide to Sea Birds of the North Atlantic*.

I flick through the dog-eared little volume looking at the pictures, mainly in black and white: gannets, petrels, shearwaters, terns. I'd give anything to see a blue-footed booby—like a duck in fancy dress—but I'm looking for my chap from this morning, and that's not him. With apologies if *he* turns out to be a *she*.

I'm at the last chapter ("Vagrants") when I find what I'm looking for.

> Atlantic Yellow-nosed Albatross (*Thalassarche chlororhynchos*): normally resident in the southern Atlantic and Indian oceans, occasional frequenter of the North Atlantic and Caribbean. First UK record: Somerset, 2007

As I suspected—a mollymawk! According to sailors' superstition, they carry the souls of dead mariners and bring good luck, protecting ships from harm and bringing fair winds. Unless, like Coleridge's grizzled old salt, you're reckless enough to harm one.

I can't wait to tell everyone—it will perk them up. With any luck the bird will continue to follow the boat and we'll see him (or indeed her) again.

I'm putting the book back in place and gathering up my things when I hear a door slide open in a far corner of the grand saloon. A figure I can't make out against the dazzle of the morning light hurries out. Has someone been listening and watching? I wonder who—and why.

Interviewing is an art. Simultaneous translators may have to listen and talk at the same time, but interviewers have to ask questions, listen to answers, plan what to ask next and keep an eye on the time—all at once. Somewhat befuddled by the recent session, I decide on some fresh air to clear my head and head to the afterdeck.

Leaning into the breeze, I marvel at the yacht's sculptural quality; her smooth sleek form, slicing effortlessly through the waves, and icy whiteness, as if she was freshly minted this morning. Not all superyachts are white: popular alternatives are turquoise, red, aqua and purple—or bronze-, silver- or gold-trimmed if you fancy a bit of bling. In my opinion, however, you can't beat the classic white.

Above water, four decks of shameless luxury; below, three turbo-charged V16 Rolls-Royce engines (each 2,650 horsepower) connected to jet drives, offering an effortless cruising speed of fifteen knots, a comfortable twenty, and a top speed of thirty-one. The phrase "expense is no object" doesn't do the yacht justice: within this hull expense has been very much the object—the more the merrier.

I'm interested to note she flies the Bermuda ensign—a variant of the British Red Duster—which is something of a curiosity to vexillologists. It's comprised of a red field with the Union flag in the upper left corner and the Bermuda coat of arms diagonally opposite: a grinning lion holding a picture of a shipwreck in its paws. Reassuring to think that the yacht falls within the maritime jurisdiction of the United Kingdom, and that in theory a Royal Navy battleship could be sent out to protect us if things go wrong.

I look up to see the captain in his pilot house and behind it *Maldemer*'s communications platform: two shiny white globes and a large square receiver dish, mounted flat like a table. I've no doubt it's the very latest, so I'm surprised it delivers such erratic results.

I'm soaking up the view when I feel the yacht's engines slow down, and—to my surprise—I hear shouting. It seems to be coming from the beach club below, so I lean out over the stern to see what's happening. A pair of fishing lines stream out behind us and I remember that a fishing session was threatened last evening at dinner. It's not my thing—I feel sorry for the fish, and hope they don't catch any.

Luck is not on my side—nor that of marine life—because shortly afterward there is a whoop. I lean over the stern to see Sir Billy reeling in a magnificent streak of metallic blue and silver. What happens next can only be seen from my viewpoint: one of the deckhands, a young woman with freckles, seizes the fish and clubs it on the head. While she is distracted, one of the guests walks past her and brushes her bottom. She reels round—still unseen by the others—only for him to lean in and touch her breast.

Appalled, I yell "Oi!" at the top of my voice. The bulky figure of Russell looks up—oh my goodness, he wears some kind of hairpiece—and turns hurriedly away. The young woman also spots me, then races down a hatch bearing the fish away. The whole incident is over in seconds but leaves me feeling angry and uncomfortable.

I shuffle down to my cabin, pondering again this nameless underclass living somewhere in the depths of the boat. I arrive to find my cabin door has been crudely repaired and flashing across my TV screen is a message reading: *Please report to galley.* It could be worse: at least I haven't been summoned to the pilot house to be waterboarded by the captain and Sir Billy . . . or at least, not yet. On the other hand, it looks like I'm on lunch duty. This is just what I didn't want to happen.

A pleasant surprise awaits me, however. Laid out over ice on the steel workbench is the yellowfin tuna I saw being brought aboard only minutes ago. After a brief consultation with the Almanac of Allergies and Intolerances, I decide to serve seared tuna steaks with tataki sauce, for those that will eat them, and California sushi rolls, for those who won't.

Japanese cooking moves at a different pace from Western; each procedure is executed calmly and patiently before moving on to the next. I inspect the fish—whoever gutted it has made an expert job of it—and improvise a rolling mat from baking paper. I place rice in the electric rice cooker imported from Japan. At one o'clock I announce to Challis that lunch is ready, the foghorn is blasted and guests are summoned to the afterdeck.

The table has been laid in the Japanese style, with a silk runner down the center, lacquer bowls and chopsticks on silver rests. Somehow, she's even pulled together an ikebana centerpiece, complete with orchids, leaves and twigs.

"*Meshiagare*," I say, with a polite *eshaku*, as the guests start to arrive, then leave them to enjoy their feast. My route back to the galley takes me past the grand saloon, where I spot a whispered exchange taking place behind a potted palm. Seeing me, the conspirators start, then scuttle off in different directions. Marje and Karol-Kate—an unlikely twosome, I reflect.

CHAPTER 12

An hour later I report to the grand saloon.
It's the first chance I've had to examine the décor in detail—described sniffily by Elise as "Parisian bordello on Ecstasy." A teeming mass of hand-crafted exotic flowers in shades of cream, pink, red, orange and peach LUCITE® is suspended over the bar. Underfoot, a vast Persian rug seethes with cherubs, cornucopias, mythological creatures and more vegetation.
Fluted plasterwork columns have been artfully positioned to create curtained-off niches and booths. One is laid out with playing cards, a chess set and backgammon; another for letter-writing; another is concealed by crushed velvet drapes in a piercing shade of violet, which can be drawn back to reveal a small stage complete with a glossy black grand piano. A Fazioli, no less; arguably the finest in the world. Yet another is a library-in-miniature—which is where I'm now sitting, waiting for Xéra to join our afternoon session. Because once again she's late.
My mind wanders next to the strange scene I witnessed before lunch. Marje and the dog handler—what on earth could those two have found to talk about?
My speculations are interrupted by a deckhand scurrying

past—one I haven't seen before—bearing a beribboned basket of fruit and berries. It's what I call "hotel fruit": brightly colored, buffed to waxy gloss but tasteless and unripe. If the contestants of *Love Island* were transformed into fresh produce, this is what they'd look like.

Seeing me, Flower Lady tries to flee, but I jump to my feet and extend my hand. "How do you do?" I say primly. She shrinks away.

Marcus was of the opinion that you should know "hello," "please" and "thank you" in as many languages as possible, so I take a wild stab at her nationality and try Greek. "*Geiá sou!*" She frowns in puzzlement, so in desperation I dredge up my one word of Bulgarian, "*Zdravete!*"

Before I can dig myself in deeper—I hope she understands I'm just trying to be polite—she transfers her basket to one hand and performs a formal curtsey. I bow in return, at which point Xéra enters, gives us a quizzical look and Fruit Lady hurtles out.

Xéra smiles when I explain my gauche attempt at civility; judging by the woman's dark coloring, she thinks she's more likely from Turkey or the Middle East. After this we settle down and she thanks me for preparing lunch: despite the gracious smiles and pats on the arm, however, I can tell something is wrong. What fresh calamity has occurred, on top of the loss of the necklace?

I ask her how Sir Billy's morning went and she shrugs: "Bee-yee does not like to be ordered round by insurance companies. They demand him we return to Southampton but he refuse."

She sighs then continues, "I understand that there has been a problem with your clothes."

"Um, well, you could say that. Do I look totally ridiculous?"

"You are normally so—fastidious. *Soigné*, as we say in French. The beautiful *antillaise* told me what happened."

"Aimee—the first officer. Yes, she promised to sort it out." I'm glad she remembered—I must be sure to thank her.

"I don't wish you to wear crew clothes, so I will ask the men if they have anything they can lend to you," she says. "Billy, he is too big and tall, but this Blue, for example, he is a *dandy*. He will have many, many clothes. Elise will see if Shane has some spare things too."

I murmur my thanks, though tucked out of sight, my toes are curling at the thought. "They make a very—striking couple, your stepdaughter and her husband."

She looks at me carefully and lowers her voice. "Shane drinks too much, everyone knows this. But why does Elise let him? As we say in France: it takes two people to make one alcoholic. May I tell you something in confidence, *chéri?* Bee-yee say he is stopping their allowance."

"It's not something to be done in haste," I suggest.

"I am against it. I think it unwise. This Russell Tate—he is behind it."

"I wouldn't have thought it's up to him," I say. "If financial people had their way, all our money would be tied up and we'd never get to spend it." I say this speculatively, as someone without any cash to tie up or otherwise.

"I hope the family will talk together, Bee-yee, the children and I, without Russell. If it is not too late."

At this point she stops and stares into the distance, lost in thought. Normally a study in calm, I watch her restlessly tap the arms of her chair.

I continue, "I'm glad you're going to be living in London now. Are you looking forward to it?" Since I've known her, on visits there she's camped out in a succession of serviced apartments in Mayfair and Park Lane, very different from being a proper Londoner.

"Making my home in Eaton Place—of course. But there has been a small misunderstanding." She explains that she was looking forward to redecorating the flat, but without consulting her, Bee-yee has invited Elise to do it.

"He's probably trying to spare you the hassle," I say, emollient. Though I certainly wouldn't want a stepdaughter foisting her taste on me.

She looks straight at me. "*Chéri*, I do not intend to be treated as . . . *femme potiche*. "Trophy wife," you say? We will make that clear in our book."

Point taken.

"Now where did we get to this morning?" I commence.

"Your leetle recording machine—we will not use it this afternoon," she announces, folding her arms. At this rate the book's never going to get written, but never mind. Then she leans forward and asks: "How is Julie?"

"Still being tyrannized by our crazy editor-in-chief. Oh—and she has a new obsession. She did an online tarot course and I'm her guinea pig."

Xéra sits up. "Then you must tell her the story of my cards and ask her opinion."

"She'll be fascinated," I say.

"I first went to a tarot reader fifteen years ago, in Neuilly. Something difficult—terrible—had happened. I will not speak about this, but she looked at my cards and said all would be well, and I would enjoy great success in my business. All this was true.

"After I met Bee-yee, I returned to Neuilly. I felt I was at a crossroads, as you say. I wanted to know if it was time to follow my heart."

"I assume the cards said yes," I say.

"I don't know the English names but I write them down for you. Now, please send Julie my love and tell her she is beautiful." I do so, constantly, though she refuses to believe it.

Although we've made no progress on the memoir, Xéra checks her watch and announces time is up.

"Before you go . . . I hope you don't mind my mentioning it," I say. "You're upset. Is there anything . . . ?"

She looks straight at me and lays her hand on mine. "Thank you, *chéri*. Don't worry. But you are anxious also, I think."

I hesitate.

"Tell me," she says, raising one eyebrow.

"It's been hanging over me—Sir Billy suspecting me of being a thief."

"Would you like that I have a word with him?"

"Well, if it isn't too embarrassing. Then there's something else too. I hate to bring it up but there's a problem with my writing fee—do you know why it might have been held up?"

She freezes infinitesimally, something being computed behind those fathomless dark eyes, then nods and murmurs that she will look into it for me. With that, she makes a graceful exit.

CHAPTER 13

Finding myself with an hour on my hands I didn't expect, I rummage in my pocket and withdraw a fold-out plan of the yacht's layout, which we were handed on arrival. I'm hoping an unhurried tour of the amenities will take my mind off things and dispel the vague sense of foreboding hanging over me. I feel bad about laying guilt on Xéra when she's obviously got worries of her own, and wish I'd never complained about her husband, or my financial woes.

When the yacht was moored up alongside HMS *Belfast* at Tower Bridge she looked surprisingly small. Once you're aboard, she's vast. This is partly because to get anywhere involves an oblique journey—up, down and sideways—and partly because wherever you're heading seems to be at the other end of the boat.

I start at the very top of the yacht, on which is perched the pilot house, with the communications platform tucked behind it, and the lawn deck. I spot Captain Romer at the wheel munching a cookie—he seems to exist on a diet of sugary snacks and candy—and give him a cheery wave. Apart from him, I'm the only one about: the guests are enjoying a siesta.

Next down is the sky deck, where the yacht's most glamorous (and ostentatious) spaces are located, including the master cabin, accessed via its own gilded staircase; the grand saloon, as featured in every magazine from *Architectural Digest* to *HELLO!*; and the dining saloon, done out London club-style, with mahogany paneling, parquet floor and button-back chairs.

Everything is the finest craftsmanship, hand- or custom-made, and—something I only just notice—everything is attached to the floor. Chairs, tables—even the piano—are bolted down tight. Obviously the Waterford crystal and Ginori porcelain can't be, so there must be some other solution for them if we're hit by a Force 8.

Below that is the panorama deck, which consists of the guest cabins, lobby and afterdeck, which is a polite name for what is properly called the poop deck (after the French *la poupe*, meaning stern). The lobby is effectively the hub of the yacht, an exercise in Italian modernism, fitted out in chrome and crystal, with suede-lined walls, cream leather banquettes and wall-to-wall sheepskin carpet. The Chagall staircase, named for the Russian master's stained-glass panel displayed in the stairwell, leads down to the beach deck, at sea level.

No floor plan can, however, begin to convey the full sensory overload of being aboard this floating palace: the feeling of being enveloped in color and texture; the tinkling of distant harp music, emanating from nowhere; the heady scent pumped out by vast bouquets of lilies, roses, and peonies.

At one point I encounter a pair of deckhands, scrubbing and polishing, who—without looking up or acknowledging my presence—vanish behind a concealed door. This gives me an idea.

All the hatches and doors aboard *Maldemer* are open and shut by electronic keycards; not just for safety reasons, in case (God forbid) the hull is breached or fire breaks out, but to ensure guests and crew stick to their own territory. Because my berth is in the crew quarters, mine is programmed to admit me below deck, which puts me in an unusually privileged position. I flash my card at the keypad beside the concealed door, and it slides open.

A short exploration reveals that secreted behind all this

magnificence—and purposefully omitted from the floor plan—winds and twists a complicated, invisible network of service areas, passages, companionways, back stairs, hatches, gangways, technical areas and oubliettes. The yacht's countless mirrors, I now realize, are one-way, and the intricate paneling that lines its corridors studded with spyholes and listening devices.

What a creepy environment in which to work! In order to ensure guests get all the sunshine and views, the crew lives as if on a submarine, entirely under artificial light. Forget tempered air and hand-painted wallpaper—back here it's all neon and vinyl, with industrial steel flooring. There's no sound insulation—I hear the steady rumble of the engines—and conflicting smells fill the air—cleaning fluids, frying, laundry.

In no time I become hopelessly lost. After innumerable twists and turns, and many a blind corridor, I decide to drop a deck and see if I can find a way through from below, then another and another. Finally, I reach what must be the bottom of the yacht. It's dark and eerily quiet down here, apart from—what's that? A moaning sound, low and pitiful. There it is again!

I grope my way to the small door from which noise seems to be coming, which is painted red. It's locked, but it's not one that opens by keycard. I put my ear to it and listen hard.

The sobbing stops and I hear a weak voice—the voice of a young girl—intone a few unrecognizable words, as if in prayer. Who's in there?

It breaks my heart to hear such helpless misery—in flagrant contrast to the sickening opulence above deck—and my hand reaches out to tap on the door, offer comfort or solace to the person within. But something stops me: I daren't get involved; I'm in enough trouble already.

With a sad shake of my head, and muttering a few words of prayer of my own, I creep away feeling guilty and unsettled.

Chapter 14

Back in my cabin, my mood sober and still puzzling over what I just witnessed, I open the folder entrusted to me by Xéra.

Slipped into the back of it I discover an onion-skin envelope, yellow and flaking with age, with "Maudie!" scratched in Xéra's curlicued script across the front; judging by the force employed (the letters slash through the delicate paper) she must have been in a passion when she wrote it.

The envelope contains a sheet of paper of the same vintage, folded in four. Across the top are the words "Gâteau Reine de Saba" (named after the biblical Queen of Sheba), and underneath, written out in the Ronde script—one of the glories of the French educational system—with corrections, additions and marginalia presumably added over the years, is the recipe for the Pâtisserie Pompadour's celebrated chocolate cake.

This is the recipe she and I were discussing this morning, a version of which Julia Child included in *Mastering the Art of French Cooking* and demonstrated in her TV show, *The French Chef*, in December 1965. This, however, is the original version, never shared by the de Sully family, and a secret even more coveted than the formula for that steak sauce they make at Le Relais de Venise.

Who was Maud? I wonder. A pastry chef? Or one of the

smart de Sully womenfolk, responsible for passing on this precious palimpsest?

My TV screen jumps to life and Challis's face looms up, to tell me that our chef is back in the saddle and I won't be required to make dinner.

I feel oddly disappointed. Despite my initial determination not to find myself dragged into kitchen duties, I can't deny the thrill of being in front of a stove; it feels as if I'm in my natural habitat. On top of which, long experience has taught me that kitchens are places where information is traded, confidences exchanged. Perhaps a clue will emerge about what happened to the missing necklace.

With this in mind, I present myself at the galley and offer to lend a hand. It will justify my hanging out there for an hour or two, and I have an idea that may brighten up the evening for poor Xéra.

Now that we finally meet, I find that the Irishwoman is something of an oddity: about my own age, with a narrow face, high forehead, dyed brown hair and large hoop earrings. Earrings are discouraged in professional kitchens, especially large ones like these that could get tangled up with whisk beaters, or short-circuit the stove.

As if that's not enough, she wears an *eyepatch*. At one time these were fairly common—a badge of honor for retired soldiers and sailors—but nowadays you rarely see them, unless on a Marvel movie villain or Disney pirate. It's extremely disconcerting.

"So you're the cheffy fellow?" she declares, pausing at the door of the walk-in freezer and looking me up and down with her remaining eye. "I'm Bernadette." She wipes her hand on her apron and seizes mine. "I hear you made a grand breakfast this morning."

"I'm glad you're feeling better," I say, adding some noncommittal comment about her cooking.

She laughs heartily: "Get away with you! I wasn't hired to cook hoity-toity. Just basic meals for the crew. I never claimed I could do the haute cuisine?" She speaks with a pronounced southern Irish accent, ending with an upward lilt so everything sounds like a question; when she's not saying anything, I notice her lips continue to move, as if she's mumbling.

"I wondered if you'd like me to make dessert tonight," I venture. "Help out, till you're fully recovered."

"You're a darling," she says, squeezing my arm and coming up so close that I'm enveloped in a gust of gin fumes. "And you can call me Bernie?"

CHAPTER 15

Aware that Bernie's indisposition might have been gin related, and it would therefore pay to keep an eye on dinner preparations, I throw myself into my cake. There's nothing like baking to focus the mind, even something as comparatively simple as this, which is basically made from dark chocolate and ground almonds. The almonds, incidentally, don't add a nutty flavor, just lightness and finesse to the crumb.

Although maybe a century old, the recipe requires no adaptation and I follow it meticulously. I take care that my butter is *en pommade* (literally, like ointment) and that my egg whites are whipped to *pics mous* (soft peaks). I deliberately undercook the cake, so it is just on the point of setting in the center. (No one has ever explained to my satisfaction why chocolate bakes are always better slightly underdone, but it's evidently not a new discovery.)

I leave the Reine de Saba to cool on a wire rack. At this point it doesn't look like anything special, but in due course I'll apply its glossy chocolate glaze and chocolate curls, arranged like the hours round a clock. Because, as Julia Child puts it, "Even a queen looks like anybody else till she gets her crown on." I'm aware that the dessert will be unsuitable for the no-nut brigade—including Marje, because they're hidden—but they can have ice cream.

I'm making a start on the washing-up when Aimee arrives to fix herself a cup of coffee.

"Thanks for telling Lady Hardcastle about my laundry problem," I say. "She's going to have a whip-round among the guests to find me something to wear."

"No problem," she says, smiling warmly. Then adds, fiddling with an epaulette, "It won't happen again."

"Any update on the necklace?" I ask.

She shrugs. "It's not as if we're an ocean liner—we've searched the yacht top to bottom. There's literally nowhere left to look."

"It can't have disappeared into thin air," I say. "Sounds obvious, but have you checked no one's wearing it?"

This makes her laugh. "Where did you get that from—Agatha Christie?"

At this point Bernie announces she's going to the cold store to gather the finishing touches for tonight's feast. Aimee's about to leave too when I hand her the mixing bowl.

"It's the best bit," I say. That's another thing about chocolate cake—the uncooked batter tastes so good.

"Yum," she says, licking her finger.

"I was wondering—who has access to Xéra's cabin?" It's struck me that in the rough-and-tumble of stripping beds and ripping doors off, no one has thought to apply intellect to the problem.

She shrugs. "Only the Hardcastle family—Sir Billy and Madame. His sister, Marje Mayham. His daughter, Elise. Plus crew members who need to get in to service it."

"Which crew members?" I hand her a rubber spatula, so she can scrape up the last of the batter.

"Normally it would be all the housekeeping team, but on this trip that means Challis. If she needs help from the deckhands, she lets them in and out. It's possible the Hardcastles left the door open by accident, of course," she continues, "but if so, Challis would have noticed."

"Not if the thief closed the door behind them."

"Not possible without the right keycard—the door won't lock." And that's all she's prepared to say. "I hope from now on guests will do as instructed and keep valuables in their safe. One security breach per voyage is quite enough."

"And am I still to be grilled by the captain and Sir Billy, or have I been let off the hook?"

"I heard from Romer that Madame put in a good word for you. Said you were the most honest person she'd ever met and they were using you as a scapegoat."

Thank you, my dear friend.

"Why don't you stay and have your coffee here?" I say. "I could do with the company." While I weigh the chocolate for the glaze into a Pyrex bowl, she sits down at the island and pulls out a copy of *SuperYacht World*.

"Job hunting?" I ask, and she laughs. After a pause, I continue, "I'm curious. What's it like—working on yachts?"

"Thinking of joining us—are you? Fancy yourself as a yachtie?" Then she continues, thoughtfully, "Well, it's more a way of life than a job. And it doesn't suit everyone. For a start, it's very hierarchical—as I'm sure you've noticed—and you have to live by the rules."

"You mean, like, no high heels?"

"That's for guests. I'm talking about below deck—the crew. We wear deck shoes, obviously."

"What else?"

"Subtle things you wouldn't notice if you didn't know. For instance, crew members mustn't use the words *no* or *not* when addressing a guest. Then you must always smile, act cheerful. No alcohol or smoking. No tattoos, piercings or facial hair. No jewelry, no perfume—" she rolls her eyes—"though not everyone obeys that one. No mobile phones except in crew cabins. No swearing. Only ever speak English."

"That one must be tough on the deckhands," I say. She continues flicking through her magazine. "Do you all get on below deck, or is it like on that TV show, where you're all at one another's throats?"

"I think you'll find that's scripted. But if you're referring to Poison, she's harmless enough when you get to know her. Underneath we're all the same—crewing is a means to an end. I come from Barbados and there weren't many opportunities for me there. It's a great life for a few years, then you burn out and it's time to stop."

"But you get to see the world first."

"You certainly see the inside of lots of different yachts. I joined *Maldemer* a couple of years ago, so I think of her as my home." A dreamy look comes into her eyes. "One of my ambitions is to open up the engines, though I don't expect I'll ever get the chance."

"Would you like to be a captain one day?"

"If I'm honest, I prefer being first officer. I've always found the technical and engineering side more interesting than schmoozing guests. Romer loves being the front man."

"You're a good combination."

"Between you and me—I got him the job," she says, then seems to regret it.

"Really?" I say. "I would have thought—"

"Don't tell anyone I said that." She studies me with her large brown eyes. Things being different, I would find her irresistible, with her open, honest face and laughter bubbling under the surface; so different from, for instance, the guests upstairs, always looking around for a more interesting or advantageous conversation across the room.

"How often does the owner use the yacht?" I ask cautiously. Before coming away, I tried to find out who the owner was, but they were hidden behind a smokescreen of offshore trusts and shell companies.

"Never—don't even know who they are."

"Why have a yacht and not use it?"

"Don't ask me. As an investment? To hide away their money?" She laughs and tosses her head.

I leave a hopeful pause, but if Aimee knows anything else she's not telling me.

"So how many more years will you do? And will you go back to Barbados when you've had enough?"

"It all comes down to money," she says. "I like not paying tax. And let's just say—I have plans."

I'm applying the finishing touches to the Queen of Sheba when Challis dashes in, rummages in the fridge and pulls out a purple and orange can: Passiona, the Aussie favorite.

"That's a beaut," she says, nodding approvingly at the cake. "Worthy of the Pâtisserie Poompah-loompah. I don't say this often about guests, but your Xéra is a real lady. When she smiles, it's like the sun's come out."

"I think the theft has knocked her for six," I say, tweaking an errant chocolate curl. I fold the recipe up carefully, return it to its envelope and slip it in my pocket.

At which point Bernie returns and starts opening and shutting cupboards. "Anyone seen my *fines herbes*?" she mutters. "I'm sure I put them in the cupboard?" She pronounces the "*fines*" bit as in Ralph Fiennes and "*herbes*" as very much plain old "herbs," so it takes me a while to work out what she means.

When she frowns there's a tendency for her eyepatch to slip; part of me is dying to know what's concealed behind, though you should be careful what you wish for.

Chapter 16

Every evening the captain sets the scene for dinner with a short, rehearsed speech about cruising speeds, tides and weather conditions; as usual he looks as if he's just stepped off the ironing board.

When he's finished, Marje puts up her hand. "Where did the ship come from, before picking us up in London? Did you sail up from the Med?"

"Not at all, Madame. The Andaman Islands," he says. "Off Thailand."

"So you must have come up the Red Sea," she says, eyes round with admiration. "Any pirates?"

"For them we were ready," he replies. If he had a moustache, he'd twirl it.

After this, to our great surprise, he announces he'll be giving a cocktail demonstration and steps behind the bar. Marje and Elise squeal with delight and hop onto bar stools; though what they'd really like is for him to take his shirt off.

Blue bossily takes charge of the iPad controlling the music system. The boat is permeated by an invisible network of speakers, tweeters and subwoofers, and the usual insipid twangling sounds are replaced with the voice of Diana Krall.

I give Sir Billy a wide berth and plonk myself down next to

Judith. Her outfit is safe but unexciting: a floral dress with a dark pink jacket. Ladies' fashions aren't my expertise—apart from scarves—but I'd ditch the jacket and add a bit of sparkle; even a brooch would do it.

"Not into cocktails?" I ask her. On cue, the captain does a high pour and his audience obligingly gasps; next thing he'll be doing that ice-throwing trick. Cheap.

"I prefer a glass of dry white," she replies. "This St.-Véran is excellent—you should try it."

I do as she suggests, and trade in the Condrieu I'm drinking (and not particularly enjoying) for the white Burgundy. She's right: it's clean, fruity and fresh, just how a Chardonnay should be and so often isn't.

"I don't have much luck with wines from the Rhône Valley," I say; Marcus always advised against them.

"With the honorable exception of Châteauneuf-du-Pape," she adds. "Maybe we could ask for a wine tasting tomorrow."

Ha! A woman after my own heart. "Have you met any of the other guests before?" I ask.

She shakes her head and says confidentially: "Never. I'm not a great socializer, but Russell wanted me to come along."

"I know what you mean. Apart from Xéra, I feel a bit, well, out of my depth." We clink glasses—we're sheep among wolves.

I start to ask about her impressions of the yacht when Sir Billy starts shaking his tumbler in the air. "It's all paid for, so we might as well drink it!" While Challis chases off to find the vodka, he gestures over his shoulder toward the captain with his thumb: "And *he's* paid to drive the boat." We laugh dutifully.

The cocktail turns out to be a blue concoction called a "Poseidon Adventure" (very poor taste to anyone who's seen the film). Once it's dispensed, Romer gives a deep bow, scratches his crotch for the benefit of anyone interested and leaves.

So far I've been shy about introducing myself to Marje, but

seeing she's now on her own, I decide to grasp the nettle. Promising to catch Judith later, I join the Tinseltown legend at the bar.

"I read an interesting piece about you," I say, as a friendly opening. "A profile in the *Sunday Times*, a couple of years ago."

"Oh, that," she says. "The garbage about how I started in the mailroom—that was someone else. But waddya expect? Writers . . ." She dismisses my profession with a flick of be-ringed fingers.

"Ha! I'm sorry you feel like that—I'm one myself," I reply.

"Yeah, Xéra told me."

Conversation is not exactly flowing, but I battle on. "I normally write about food. It's a bit more of a responsibility, writing someone's life story—especially as I'm Xéra's friend."

She eyes me again. "Which has to make it easier, right? So cry me a river! And you got the coffee shop angle to fill a few spare chapters."

"Well," I say, "I wouldn't exactly call Pâtisserie Pompadour a coffee shop—more like an institution. You know Colette uses it as the setting for one of her novellas?"

Marje raises a disdainful eyebrow and tosses her head; her steely bob rearranges itself perfectly.

"I meant to ask. How much is my brother paying you for this . . . project?" She says it with a sly smile. "Because whatever he offers—insist on double."

"We already agreed on a figure," I say stiffly. Julie's always telling me I'm a terrible negotiator and it's time I found an agent.

"Read the small print," Marje warns, serious-faced. "Or he'll stitch you up. Can't help himself. Runs in the family."

Chapter 17

We file into the dining saloon, where a log fire is burning. There are so many clever imitations about but this one's for real: poker, firelighters, kindling, a tidy pile of logs, flames and crackling noises.

There's a convention that when a yacht is at sea (rather than in port), guests dress for dinner. Well, they've risen to the challenge. Xéra is exquisite as always in a little black Givenchy dress and Tahitian pearls; I wouldn't be surprised if she didn't also have a hand in Sir Billy's choice of outfit, a green velvet smoking jacket worn with tapestry slippers—the acme of gentlemanly elegance.

Elise is in midnight blue—a crêpe dress with a ruffled skirt that would move wonderfully on a dance floor—and Shane has also chosen well, in a waistcoat and open-neck shirt that show off his fine chest and shoulders. I see now that he's four or five years younger than Elise, or looks it.

Not for the first time, I wonder at the sheer effort it must cost the super-rich always to look so coiffed and svelte; what armies of couturiers, stylists, beauticians, orthodontists, manicurists, personal trainers and therapists they must retain. When Xéra tosses her head, her dark hair wafts into place like an attendant cloud. On the other hand, her mood hasn't lifted; her eyes flick nervously from guest to guest, as if in search of something.

I notice Blue look at her through narrowed eyes, then pull out a surreptitious pencil and jot something down. It would seem I'm not the only person aboard the yacht keeping an eye on his fellow guests.

As I did last night, I find myself placed next to Karol-Kate. Colefax sits beside her on a pile of well-plumped cushions, closely monitoring proceedings.

For starters it's prawn cocktails with lemon slices that appear to have been cut with a hacksaw. Karol-Kate, who's a vegetarian, has a mound of tomatoes, avocado and mozzarella dolloped with pesto, which she's chewing with a circular motion.

"Tasty?" I ask. She nods, also in a circular motion. I remember a geography lesson in which we learned the different ways ruminants eat: cows by pulling up tufts of grass with great long tongues; sheep with their teeth, *nibble-nibble-nibble*. I half expect her to moo.

"Pleased with your cabin?" I ask, trying not to sound resentful. I'm annoyed to have discovered she has a guest cabin while I slum it in steerage.

She finishes her mouthful before replying: "Mine or the dog's?"

Gulping back outrage, I tell her, "I'm right in the bow of the yacht—almost at water level." She looks unimpressed. "Choice of bunks, too. When you look out of the porthole you feel as if you're swimming." The porthole is lozenge-shaped, so you can see the sea or the sky but not both at the same time.

"You'll have to give me a tour," she says, although I'm not sure she'd get through the door.

I ask Judith, sitting on my other side, about her cabin. "It's actually a suite," she explains. "Russell asked for it specially. He needs very little sleep, so it means he can get up and do his own thing without disturbing me."

"Does he read?" I ask. I rather envy insomniacs—I could do with a few extra hours in the day myself.

"No, he's brought along his jigsaw."

"Oh, of what?" I can't have one in the house—they're too addictive.

"The Battle of Trafalgar."

"Appropriately nautical."

"And he loves stargazing, so he's hoping for some clear nights." I glance across the table toward him. A brisk walk or a session on an exercise bike would do him more good: from his blotchy skin and bags under the eyes I suspect he's diabetic.

I ask Judith about her family; as Marcus used to say, always goes down well. One daughter, living in Swiss Cottage. "Any grandkids?" Women of Judith's age are *obsessed* with grandchildren.

"Sadly not," she replies with a shake of the head. "My daughter is barren."

"What's that you're saying, Judith?" cuts in her husband from across the table.

Puzzled by this odd choice of words and the couple's sharp exchange, I switch attention to Xéra and shoot her a friendly smile. Instead of leading the conversation in her usual way, my friend hasn't said a word so far.

"Thanks for recommending that book," I call across. She's a tremendous reader, and at her suggestion I'm enjoying *Toilers of the Sea* by Victor Hugo. It's set in Guernsey, which we passed on our way down the English Channel. "What's your holiday reading?"

"Montaigne's *Essays*," she replies absently. "I find them . . . consoling."

I'd be interested to hear more—there's a famous one about cannibals, I believe—but we're interrupted by an *owOOO!* from Karol-Kate's watch and she disappears with the dog.

"Did he do this thing?" I ask companionably when she returns.

"No, this is just walkies. The great thing about Colefax is, he's regular as clockwork."

While the guests attempt to mop up their runny fish pie, Challis goes out to fetch more wood for the fire.

"Someone stop that woman putting on more logs—place is like a furnace," declares Marje, even though last night she was complaining the opposite and sent Blue off to fetch a pashmina.

Elise joins in. "I hope you're going to pull them up about the food, Daddy. Seven-star luxury is what they promised, not frozen peas and soggy mash."

Marje agrees. "And what happened to the spa treatments? One of the reasons you come on a cruise is because of the onboard beauty services. All *we* get is a tube of exfoliator and a couple hot stones left outside your door if you ask nice." I've noticed that when she's complaining, as she often is, her adopted American accent comes on stronger.

Shane, loosened by another refill, finally finds his voice, albeit a rambling one. "I would say . . . Ha! I would say that I would rather be . . . rather be cruising round the Caribbean than sailing there." He looks pleased to have got this off his chest, at least until Elise digs him in the ribs.

This could go either way, but Sir Billy decides to play the gracious host. "I'd like to raise a toast to my beautiful girls. My lovely new wife Xéra—" *chink*—"and Elise, my golden girl." *Chink chink chink.* Xéra pins on a smile and reaches across her husband to take his daughter's hand. I hope Elise realizes how lucky she is to have Xéra as a stepmother and not the jealous, manipulative type.

When the moment arrives for dessert, the lights are dimmed, the doors swing open and in struts Challis, bearing aloft a platter topped with a glittering silver dome.

My eyes are on Xéra—I hope a surprise will lift her spirits—but when the Gâteau Reine de Saba is revealed, the opposite happens. She looks around in confusion, rises unsteadily to her feet and stumbles out, muttering something about feeling unwell. Marje hurries out after her, looking solicitous. I rack my brains as to how I might have caused offense but remain baffled.

Understandably, after this, no one fancies dessert, so we retire to the grand saloon for coffee. While Shane cruises the bar, Blue places a pair of candelabra on the piano and subjects us to another of his pianistic blitzkriegs.

When he's finished, Elise pipes up with a request. "Do you know that one from *Cats?*" She starts singing, in a thin, high voice "Midnight," in the style of Elaine Paige.

Lloyd Webber isn't my favorite composer—by no means—but something about this particular request begins to nag away at the back of my mind.

Chapter 18

I'm worried about Xéra. Losing her nerve like that tonight—triggered by a cake, of all things—is a side of her I haven't seen before. The theft must have really rattled her. I make my way below deck and head for my cabin, with that wretched Elaine Paige song going round and round in my head.

When I finally arrive at my quarters, I flip open my laptop and find an evening bulletin from Julie. Plus—what's this?—a new correspondent.

From: d.a.armstrong98@met.police.uk
Tuesday 3:10 p.m.
Subject: Strictly confidential
To: Paul Delamare/Aboard *M/Y Maldemer*

Dear Paul:

Our mutual acquaintance Julie Johnson furnished me with your Email; while your being at sea. I am writing with her permission. But am not at liberty to disclose the contents of this message. Which I am writing in my Official Capacity.

Ms. Johnson shared a Recent Email received from you recently. In which you referred to a LUIZ MATEUS.

A Red Notice has been issued against LUIZ MATEUS by Interpol.

(In case of being unfamiliar with terminology: a Red Notice is the highest level of International Arrest Warrant.)

Please contact me IMMEDIATELY if you can obtain Further Information on this person of interest. Without undertaking personal risk. My direct telephone is +44 7447 417490. In the Unlikely Event you may encounter this person of interest in person, do not approach him, is the official advice.

I am currently in process, of procuring a Physical Description of Mateus, in case useful. To forward to you in due course, when available.

Declan Armstrong, (Acting) DCI

From: Julie Johnson
Tuesday 7:14 p.m.
Subject: Shocking!
To: Paul Delamare/Aboard *M/Y Maldemer*

I can't believe it about the necklace. Terrible thing to happen. Poor Xéra must be shattered. No one seriously thinks you could be involved, do they?

My background research has been hit or miss, I'm afraid. According to the *LA Times*, Marje Mayham Artists' Agency has been losing clients and is "seeking reinvestment." Probably means she's only worth ten million dollars rather than thirty—my heart bleeds for her.

"Family Offices" are nebulous entities formed to manage private fortunes. (In other words, help the rich avoid tax and other responsibilities, and screw everyone else.) Till a couple of years ago this Russell character was a wealth manager in a private bank, then left in a hurry. I've put in a call to my friend at the *FT* in case there's more.

Blue Aspray—not a whisker. A made-up name, surely?!

I also took the liberty of looking up your tennis player. Wait for this: two years ago, Shane Hudson was given a suspended sentence for GBH after a fight outside a pub in Wilton Row. It was really hushed up—my cuttings people found it buried in a law report.

Declan asked for your email address so he can contact you regarding some "confidential business." He won't tell me what it is, but it must be important, as he types very s-l-o-w-l-y with one finger. (You know how I love surprises so if it's dinner at Noble Rot or a trip to Paris don't tell me! And good to see you two getting on better.)

I dropped in at grant.zooms.appear this morning (see what I did there?!). Your cute next-door neighbor popped his head out of the window asking about the noise. I explained about the flood—he didn't seem to know anything about it.

You've received an official-looking letter from a legal firm in Shoreditch. Do you want me to open it?

JUDGEMENT.

Just one card today. This card is generally regarded as a wake-up call, or warning: keep your eyes open, something is about to happen. A transformation of some kind, though unlikely to be for the good, I'm afraid.

J. X

From: Paul Delamare/Aboard *M/Y Maldemer*
Tuesday 10:27 p.m.
Subject: Day of Judgment
To: Julie Johnson

46°41'32'N 20°56'35'W (way out in the Atlantic)

Good to know Jubilee Cottage has its very own what3words, but if you don't mind I'll stick to good old-fashioned coordinates.

As for this tarot lark—turns out you're in good company. Xéra had her cards read a while back and drew Le Pendu, L'Excuse and Le Pape. Mean anything to you?

I'll bear in mind the Judgment card but I've quite enough drama already on this cruise. If the cards really want to be useful, maybe they can tell us who stole the necklace.

Something a bit odd. When I mentioned the London branch of Pâtisserie Pompadour—it was off St. John's Wood High Street, but closed rather soon after opening—Xéra was distinctly cagey. I feel awkward raising it with her again, but can you shed any light?

While you're on a roll with the research, it would be interesting to know about this Captain Romer character. (I don't know if that's his surname or first name, nor can I tell from his slightly murky accent what nationality he might be.) Which reminds me, I have a new cocktail for your collection. I'll save it till I get back.

Also, I've found out the dog woman's name and it's Karol-Kate Bunting-Jones (quadruple-barrelled, obviously the new thing).

I'm not expecting anything from a lawyer. Please let it be a bequest from a rich aunt I never knew I had. Open it!

P.S. Please tell your Acting DCI chum I received his email. What a peculiar writing style.

P.P.S. Can't believe you met my neighbor. Twelve years and I haven't.

Just as my finger hovers over send, the Wi-Fi drops out. Behaviorists have a name for this torturous game of punishment and reward—"intermittent reinforcement"—and I'm not surprised it drives lab rats to distraction.

While continuing to jab at buttons, hoping the signal will reappear, I mull over Julie's discoveries. I feel guilty about asking her to undertake time-consuming research on my behalf because she's under such pressure at the magazine at the moment; for the last six months she's been covering the deputy ed's maternity leave (with no increase in salary, needless to say) which means she's treated as editor-in-chief Diabolical Dena's personal serf and dogsbody.

As usual, she's dug up something interesting: there's only one pub in Wilton Row, and it's a famous haunt for guardsmen from Knightsbridge Barracks, a short walk away . . . hmm.

As for Declan's pompous warning about Luiz Mateus, I sense he's trying to impress me. Mr. Big Shot, with pals at Interpol. He should have read my email to Julie properly—I never suggested Big Lew was a passenger or connected to the theft; just that he helped Sir Billy buy his wife a piece of jewelry, and as far as I know there's nothing illegal in that.

After that, I get out Xéra's folder and flick through the jumble of photographs. Most of them are labeled, but there's no mention of anyone called Maudie.

I nod off while looking at them, only to be awoken by the familiar bumping. I check my watch: just gone midnight.

Praying I'll be able to find my way back, I wind my way through a labyrinth of electrically operated doors and hatches, and up three companionways, until finally I step out into fresh air.

It feels appreciably warmer than when we set off from London because of the miracle that is the Gulf Stream, and the air has that salty, faintly sulphurous ocean smell which apparently comes from plankton. The reflection of a halfmoon oscillates in the inky water, and I hear the gentle slap of *Maldemer*'s hull moving through it above the soft purr of engines.

After last night's burglary, it would be highly suspicious to be caught creeping about in the dead of night, so I slink noiselessly along the gallery walk, keeping close to the bulkhead and pausing in shadows and recesses. I'm directly above my own cabin—I can tell by the curve of the hull—when I arrive at a half-open door marked TENDER GARAGE.

Most superyachts have a "mini-me" powerboat tucked away in the hull, to be craned or floated out for excursions and gadabouts, so this is where ours is kept.

The lights of the garage are off, but a soft light is emanating from the tender itself, as well as rhythmical bumping and what I blush to describe as the sound of *grunting* and *moaning*.

I approach silently, remaining in the shadows, and see a figure perched on a chair, peeping in through one of the tender's portholes. His portly physique is swathed in a voluminous toweling robe, and so transfixed is he by the spectacle inside that he's unaware of my arrival.

It's our insomniac friend Russell. And I can clearly see he's taking great *pleasure* from the show. I've certainly seen more than enough, so I slip back out onto the deck, shivering despite the balmy air.

CHAPTER 19

It's morning and I'm woken just before eight by the foghorn blast and my television springing to life: it's an announcement from the captain.

"Good morning, esteemed guests. It has been reported to me that the albatross seen yesterday has returned and the lawn deck is currently circling. Best greetings."

As fast as I can, I leap into my clothes, hit send on my laptop (my email to Julie whooshes out) and race up to the lawn deck. Judith has beaten me to it. In one hand she holds a rolled-up magazine, with the other she points down to the afterdeck, where Karol-Kate can be seen pulling bits of bread out of a paper bag and tossing crumbs into our wake.

The dog handler has tethered Colefax to the taffrail and for some reason the little dog has worked himself up into a fury, jumping up and down and yapping left and right. While trying to keep him in order, Karol-Kate gives me a friendly wave.

We're joined shortly by Blue, in crisp white jogging gear, and Elise, wearing a short white dress of some lacy material; the two greet each other perfunctorily and take up places at opposite sides of the deck. Russell arrives shortly afterward, and I try to put last night's spectacle out of my mind as I mumble a greeting.

It's a fine morning, with a warm breeze. Although the sun is behind us, the water is bright and glittery, and we have to shade our eyes with our hands.

The only thing is: there's no bird.

We look and look. Elise thinks she sees something flapping in the water but it turns out to be Karol-Kate's now-empty paper bag, which I hope is biodegradable. Blue produces a pair of binoculars—probably part of his spy kit. Colefax continues his furious barking, and Blue yells down at Karol-Kate to shut him up because he's scaring off the bird. Still no albatross.

We're just about to give up when a bloodcurdling scream fills the air. We turn to one another in horror, then someone points to Colefax, who is howling and starts shaking from head to toe.

The hatch behind us shoots open—it's Challis, white as a sheet and gasping for breath. "Paul, right now—emergency!" she gasps, grabbing me by the arm and dragging me after her. My heart pumping furiously, I hurtle down a succession of staircases to the beach club, where a diminutive figure is slumped across a table.

"She's choked," shrieks Challis. "You're a chef—do something!"

Oh my God, it's Xéra! I kneel down beside her, take her hand, which is cold, and look into her face—a weird parchment color. Her lips are ghostly blue, gleaming with spittle where she has regurgitated a yellow and brown goo. There's an unnatural sickly sweet smell in the air.

My mind spins. Obviously I'm familiar with the Heimlich maneuver, but it's no use if someone's unconscious. I tell Challis we're going to try CPR. We lift her lifeless form to the floor, embark on a series of chest compressions, alternating with rescue breaths.

Every few seconds I tell myself that she's started to breathe, or that her eyes have flickered, but I'm fooling myself.

"We mustn't give up," I shout.

Eventually, I have to stop to catch my breath.

"Let me have a go," she says, and embarks on her own futile attempt.

Finally, we abandon hope, exhausted. I look up and see we're encircled by a gaggle of horrified guests, with Colefax huddled on the floor in front of them, whimpering.

I feel myself hit by a wave of grief, and the tears start to fall.

Xéra—my friend through so many years, and Marcus's, too; beautiful, generous, capricious, clever Xéra, who lit up the room when she entered it, and sprinkled it with largesse, love and joy. Xéra is dead.

Chapter 20

Captain Romer and his first officer arrive and call for calm. Sir Billy having missed the whole episode, the captain sets off for the master cabin to break the news to him. Meanwhile, Aimee sends the other guests to wait in the dining saloon, and Challis covers Xéra with a respectful tablecloth.

Numb as I am with shock and horror, I feel a whoosh of adrenaline pump through my system and examine the scene, my senses on hyper-alert.

On the table, the mangled remains of a slice of Gâteau Reine de Saba, and a smeared pastry fork.

Sticky chocolate crumbs, and more of them scattered over the floor.

A tall latte glass, on its side; a pool of milky coffee dripping over the edge of the table.

On the floor, a long teaspoon encrusted with sugar crystals.

I inspect the chair on which Xéra was sitting and spot something poking out from the crease in the upholstery: it's a chopstick, or half of one, to be precise.

I go to fetch a paper napkin from the buffet, so I can take a better look at the chopstick without contaminating potential evidence. The breakfast spread appears exactly as it should, including the plate of last night's chocolate cake, elegantly sliced.

At which point, my ears are assaulted by an unearthly roaring noise. Challis and I look at one another in dismay and the towering, bear-like form of Sir Billy crashes into the beach club.

"Where is she?" he bellows. "What have you done to her? No, no, no—it cannot be. Oh, my darling, darling . . ."

And with this, he pulls back the shroud and throws himself, sobbing, on Xéra's lifeless form.

Ten minutes later, in front of the captain and first officer, and alongside Xéra's body (now transferred to a massage table, which has been wheeled in for the purpose), we outline recent events.

Challis describes setting up breakfast as usual at seven, then coming back just before eight to put the finishing touches to the buffet. At this point she noticed a figure slumped at a table and did a double take. At first, she thought they must have fainted, or possibly—on account of the mess—suffered a seizure. She shook Xéra to try and wake her up; slapped her on the back; then sprinted up to the lawn deck to find me. At this point in her account the shocked stewardess clutches my arm and goes into paroxysms of sobs.

"And how did you know I'd be up on the lawn deck?" I ask.

"Everyone was up there, weren't they? The announcement about the albatross?"

"And why me?"

"I thought you'd know what to do. And you were her friend."

She's right, of course, except we were too late. I think back with a shudder to Julie's tarot card, Judgment, which has been so cruelly delivered.

"It was a tragic accident, that happened," says the captain solemnly.

"Such terrible luck there was no one around when it happened," adds First Officer Aimee.

There's something wrong about this—I feel it in my bones. Reeling with shock I may be, but I know this was no accident, and that Xéra wasn't alone when she died. I try to tell them this but find the words won't come out—just mumbled gibberish—and Challis is instructed to sit me down in a quiet corner and give me a glass of brandy.

Chapter 21

Half an hour later there's another foghorn blast and it's announced over the public address system that we're all to assemble in the grand saloon immediately. I stumble to my feet—they don't seem to be properly attached to my body—and make my unsteady way there, grateful that yachts are so well provided with handrails.

The fairground decoration seems grotesquely inappropriate, but at least Blue has had the decency to change out of his shorts. The guests choose to sit as far away from one another as possible, like a poorly attended cinema matinee.

Missing are Sir Billy and his sister. Marje is comforting him in the master cabin, which is adjacent to the grand saloon and from which we can hear sporadic banging and howls of grief.

Do they realize Xéra was murdered, or am I the only one?

The captain, unable even in these circumstances to resist the dramatic flourish, strides in, sweeps back the violet curtains and steps onstage. I'm surprised Blue doesn't jump to the piano and give him four bars in.

"Honored guests, it is with sorrow that I must Lady Hardcastle's decease confirm," he announces, his syntax betraying the depth of his emotion. "The crew of *Maldemer* express our most sincere condolences to the family of Madame in this terrible time." He gives a deprecating little cough and glances round to see how it's going down.

Is now my opportunity to tell them? I raise my hand, but the captain glares at me and looks away, with a disdainful shake of his curls.

"At such times, we follow international maritime protocol. We have reported the accident to Falmouth Coast Guard and after consultation with *Maldemer*'s agent, have referred the matter to the—" here he produces a slip of paper from his pocket—"Autoridade Marítima Nacional in Portugal. They advised us to divert to nearest landfall, and therefore we have set a new course south, toward Ponta Delgada in the Azores.

"We have our cruising speed increased, and taking account of approaching weather conditions, estimate our arrival time to be in forty-eight to seventy-two hours. I regret to inform you the charter cruise will terminate there and guests will return to your home countries making onward flights."

"Can't we stay on the boat?" protests Blue. "If you're going that way anyway?"

"That is not an option, sir. Once the death with the Portuguese authorities registered has been, *Maldemer* will continue to the Caribbean with crew only on board. These are instructions from the agent. Are there any other questions?"

"Well, it's up to Daddy," says Elise in a choked voice. I notice Shane sitting several yards away from her, drink in hand. "Whatever Daddy says."

"Sir Billy is, naturally, grievous," says the captain. "I informed Mrs. Mayham of our plans and she will communicate them to him when the time is right."

Blue sneaks away his Moleskine—what a time to be taking notes—then raises his hand. "How are we expected to get from Ponta Whatever to Los Angeles? What are the arrangements?"

The captain gives him a scornful look. "Our priority is our

late guest and her immediate family. I am sorry for your inconvenience."

Blue doesn't think much of this. "Marje *is* Sir Billy's immediate family. I'm just asking because she'll wanna know. Jeez, what a fuck-up." Everyone turns to stare reprovingly at him. "And how about you fix the goddamn Wi-Fi?" he adds. This goes down better; I notice Elise and Karol-Kate nodding in agreement and even Shane seems interested in the answer. "How're we meant to get ourselves outta this mess with no internet?"

"There has been an, erm, intermittent fault with the Starlink system," the captain replies, on the defensive. "The first officer is in charge of satellite communications and has been trying to solve the problem. Unfortunately, service cannot be guaranteed."

"Great!" replies Blue. "How are you driving the boat?"

The captain looks puzzled. "What do you mean?"

"Well, if you haven't gotta signal, howya know where you're going?" Then, in a tone heavy with sarcasm: "And how did you speak to the Portugal autori-*DA-DA?*"

"There is no cause for concern," says the captain. "Our navigation and pilotage systems are in perfect order, the problem is specifically with the guest Wi-Fi."

"And another thing," says Blue, his blood rising. "What's happening with the onboard CCTV? It's not as if she'll be needing it now, but the least you could do is find the lady's necklace!"

The captain tuts at this lapse of taste. "We have had a technical problem with the security surveillance system. The CCTV is still inoperative, but I repeat, the first officer is investigating."

This is met with much discontented muttering, after which Elise jumps in with her customary insensitivity. "My father thought he was chartering a super-luxury Atlantic crossing, but it turns out we're in the hands of imbeciles." This sets Shane off laughing, which the rest of us ignore. "The sooner this nightmare is over and we all get home, the better."

She seems to have forgotten that one member of our group will never go home again. No one here cares about Xéra, just themselves.

As for me, I am filled with shame to think that some of the last words I spoke to darling Xéra were those which bad-mouthed her husband and chased up money. My mind flashes back to the terrible events of last year, when I argued with an old friend—a colleague from my cheffing days—then he went on to die in horrific circumstances. Has someone laid a curse on me?

Russell, who has been silent till now, stands up at the back and announces in a low, serious voice: "I would respectfully suggest that we try and remain calm. This is an extremely upsetting time for everyone, especially Sir Billy's family." I'm tempted to add—what about *Xéra's* family? Then I remember I'm the closest thing that she had on this ill-fated voyage.

Judith, nodding, adds in a low voice, "Calm and dignified, as she lived her life." It's a surprisingly astute comment, from someone who hardly knew her, and I appreciate her thoughtfulness; although I notice Russell glare at her and she looks down meekly.

During this exchange, Colefax has been whimpering pitifully. Bichons Frisés are an empathetic breed, and can read a room better than most humans. Shane goes to the dog and pats him on the head, then takes the lead and disappears. This triggers the meeting to break up, and the captain sets off back to the pilot house.

As I watch the guests file out, a chill creeps over me: we have a killer in our midst, and it may be any one of them. Perhaps it's for the best that I didn't make a grand announcement in front of everyone—it's for the captain to handle this.

I follow him up to the pilot house, take a deep breath and march in.

Chapter 22

First Officer Aimee is at the wheel, stern-faced. She sees me first. "Oh, it's you. Would you mind coming back later?"

"This can't wait," I say. The captain, by now settled into his own pilot chair, swivels round to face me.

"Look," I say. "Everyone's talking about this being an accident, saying that Lady Hardcastle choked to death while she was eating breakfast on her own."

"Naturally. That is what happened," says the captain.

"As I said," adds Aimee regretfully, "it's such bad luck she was on her own when there are things we could've done to help. Heimlich, for a start."

"I'm well aware of that," I say, trying not to flare up. *"But it wasn't an accident."*

They turn to me in surprise, then say in unison, "What are you talking about?"

"I can assure you beyond a shadow of a doubt that someone did this to Xéra—Lady Hardcastle. It wasn't an accident. *She was murdered."*

The captain studies me for a moment. "That you feel emotional does not surprise—"

"Of course I'm emotional! But you have to listen to me—"

"Perhaps allow him to explain," says Aimee to her colleague. Then to me, in a soothing tone: "What makes you think this, Paul?"

"It's all wrong—can't you see? I mean, just for a start, what was Xéra doing up at that time in the morning? She never showed herself—in any circumstances whatsoever—before ten-thirty or eleven—"

"This is nothing," interrupts the captain, with a shrug. "She probably awoke early because of the time change. It is not so unusual."

"Rubbish! It was an absolute rule of hers. And you must think I'm an idiot—or you are—because the time change would mean she woke up later, not earlier."

He sniffs.

"Another thing: her idea of breakfast was an espresso, or preferably a *ristretto*. I know her—I *knew* her: that was all that ever passed her lips till lunchtime."

"All very circumstantial," mutters the captain. "Not in a courtroom would this be—"

"Will you listen?" I cry, abandoning any grip I might have had on myself. "Xéra would never touch a slice of chocolate cake. Not if it were forced down her—" I gulp, unable to finish my sentence.

Aimee now adopts a conciliatory tone. "If you're suggesting she had an eating disorder, which I think you are, then—"

"Oh, please!" I shout. "I'm saying nothing of the kind. Look, I swear to you that someone lured her to the beach club this morning, on some pretext or with some threat." I sob as I say this—can't help myself, remembering the mess at the scene and the upset coffee. "She was attacked, held down and cake forced down her throat. Xéra's a fighter and she won't have given up easily—but they were too strong for her.

"You, Captain Romer, are in charge of this vessel. Lady Hardcastle—Xéra de Sully—was murdered. I don't care if it's not the nearest jurisdiction, but this is for the British police to investigate. We must turn back immediately. I *demand* it."

CHAPTER 23

Captains don't like to be told what to do, and he turns away to indicate the matter is closed. This infuriates me all the more and I find myself pleading, raising my voice—I even stamp my feet. It doesn't work. The captain plainly doesn't want murder on his watch, nor a hysterical guest in his pilot house.

If I hoped that Aimee, who comes across as intelligent and reasonable, would support me, I'm disappointed. My theory is crazy and I'm forbidden from rumor-mongering among guests and crew. I'm to remain silent. She reminds me that aboard ship, the captain's word is law.

"You can't do this," I declare. "You're obstructing justice."

"There are measures we can take," says Aimee, her previously benign expression turning hard and unfamiliar. "You would be most unwise to disobey Captain Romer's orders."

Like a dog who's been kicked, I make my way sullenly to the door. Is there anything I can salvage from this disastrous interaction?

A thought flashes into my head. "This Wi-Fi business," I say, wheeling round. "When will it be fixed?"

Aimee glares at me. "If you're planning to make trouble—"

"I have another emergency going on at home and there are people I need to speak to," I reply haughtily. This is kind of true, though what I'm really thinking is that if I'm forced to investigate this on my own, I'm going to need Julie's help.

Aimee shrugs dismissively, so I continue. "If you ask me, you're turning it on and off deliberately, because Sir Billy has fallen out with the charter agent, probably about the bill, and they're putting the screws on him. Am I right?"

Again, no response.

"I'm sure satellite communications don't come cheap," I add, "but how much does switching them off actually save? I notice you haven't *switched off* the champagne and caviar."

"It's more a question of principle," says Aimee, adopting a conciliatory tone, in the hope of heading off another screaming match. "The agent feels an element of inconvenience might, um, expedite matters. I'm sorry, but it's outside our control."

I feel overcome by a sudden wave of exhaustion. "OK," I say, "just tell me when I can get online, that's all I need to know."

The captain turns to exchange glances with Aimee, and I get the sense an olive branch is about to be offered.

"If you agree not to make trouble regarding . . . what happened to Lady Hardcastle, then maybe we can help you out," says Aimee slowly.

"On condition that this also with the other guests will not be shared," adds the captain.

"If I were you," Aimee says, looking me straight in the eye, "I'd try going online at six in the morning. It's when we change watch."

"Is that the best you can do? For crying out loud!"

"You could also try ten in the evening. But don't forget, we're crossing time zones."

I've never been any good at anything mathematical or mechanical—I was the despair of my doctor father—but time zones I can manage, thanks to my trusty Audemars Piguet wristwatch and its world time dial.

"And now, if you will excuse us, we have work to do," concludes the captain.

"I'll catch you later," I add; Aimee rolls her eyes. "You said we're heading for the Azores?"

"Our course is already set," he declares. "Due south." With a stiff little bow—I'm surprised he doesn't click his heels—he waves me toward the door.

Chapter 24

Anger boils up within me. I can taste it in my mouth, hot and rank.

They refuse to believe Xéra was murdered, and I've been forbidden from causing a fuss. The only way Xéra is going to get the justice she deserves is if I fight for it—yet I'm stuck in the middle of the Atlantic, with poxy Wi-Fi and enemies wherever I turn.

I must start gathering evidence and information at once, before the trail goes cold. When we reach the Azores in three days" time, the whole affair will be hushed up. The super-rich have ways of smoothing over embarrassing or scandalous situations and then no one will ever know what happened.

As if that's not enough, there's something new worrying me. The captain just said in front of me that we were headed "due south." Even I know that a compass is 360°, and therefore *Maldemer* should rightly be heading toward 180°.

Why, oh, why, then, did the electronic compass in the pilot house—unmissable and highly magnified if you were standing where I was—read *239°?* Where are we really going, and why the deception? And how is this connected—as it must be—to this morning's tragedy?

My head whirling, I hurry to the beach club . . . but dammit!

I wanted to take another look at the crime scene, only Challis has got here first. She's cleaned and (judging by the smell) disinfected the whole place with her usual superhuman efficiency. The crumbs and the spillage have disappeared without trace, even down to the broken chopstick. Xéra's body has now been covered by a brocade throw, and she lies under the stern gaze of a pair of Moai statues.

Bernie appears, looking baleful. She has been tasked with seeking out a cold store to stand in for a morgue until we reach the Azores. As Xéra was my friend, will I help her find something suitable?

On our way down to the galley she plies me with questions about what happened. I get the sense I'm being pumped for information and wonder if she too has suspicions there's something very wrong here.

We decide the cold stores adjacent to the galley are unsuitable: no chef wants to reach out for a slab of bacon and find themselves holding a dead hand. Next, she leads me to another cold area, away from all the rest, down its own corridor and directly beneath the master cabin. The door is marked REFRIGERATION ZONE. Neither of us has been inside because (unusually for *Maldemer*) it's padlocked, rather than opened by keycard. To my surprise, the chef produces a hairpin from somewhere, jiggles it about and the lock springs open.

"Girl Guides," she says, giving me an exaggerated wink.

We were hoping the store was empty, but someone has overbought on supplies and decided to dump them in here. It seems wrong to stash a cadaver among a lifetime's supply of "Assorted Dry Goods," so we laboriously lug the variously labeled drums and bags and boxes—everything from bicarbonate of soda to bread flour, plus a dozen highly pungent, shrink-wrapped packs of spices—through to an adjacent space marked PANIC ROOM, which in a lighter mood I'd find amusing.

I've heard of these in rich people's houses, but never been in one before: imagine a large steel-walled service elevator, with a door a foot thick and prison-style bunks. You'd think they could supply some books or board games, in case you were stuck in there for a while.

As we labor, Bernie keeps up a stream of chatter, describing the death rituals of rural Ireland, which sound like one elaborate drinking game. After a while I stop listening, preferring instead to think about Xéra and remember the times we enjoyed together.

When Marcus was traveling—which he often did for work—she'd phone me up and say she had a spare theatre ticket or was going to a party . . . was I free? Occasionally we would be joined by Julie—Xéra loved hearing the gossip from *Escape* magazine.

Of course, Marcus was the golden thread that drew us together, and it was only after he died that I discovered the true depth of her kindness and loyalty. The simple, heartfelt voicemail messages when I was too grief-stricken to pick up the phone, and small thoughtful gestures, such as sending lilies of the valley on the first of May—his birthday. It squeezes my heart to realize how very much I'll miss her.

We set the thermostat of the cold store to 39°F—it's only a guess but seems about right—and three deckhands arrive from nowhere to assist Bernie in transferring Xéra's body to her provisional chapel of rest.

To add to the solemnity of the occasion, they've donned headscarves. As well as Flower Lady, I recognize the freckled woman assaulted by Russell during the fishing episode. She is murmuring prayers and holding what I at first take to be a rosary, but on closer inspection realize is a prayer rope—black wool with a tassel and four or five red beads.

"Thank you for taking care of my friend," I say to the group, overwhelmed by emotion. "Please be gentle."

Fish Woman crosses her arms to her chest and looks me full

in the face. Did she understand what I just said? I must and shall find out what the deal is with this silent community, but now is not the time.

"Don't worry, Paul, leave this to us now?" says Bernie. "Your friend is in safe hands and we'll be doing everything with proper respect?"

I'm not at all convinced about Bernie's skill in the kitchen, but she seems like the right person to handle this sad task. I remind her to padlock the door when they've finished, and not to lock herself in the Panic Room, then make a quick exit before I'm overcome by the horror of it all and break down in tears.

Chapter 25

Detectives know that the first twenty-four hours after a crime has been committed are the most important for gathering evidence and testimony—and you can never get them back once they've passed. Clues are wiped away and memory fades or distorts.

With this in mind, I write down everything I noticed in the beach club this morning before Challis moved in with her scrubbing brushes. It's thin pickings: the cake, the crumbs, the coffee, the spoon, the chopstick.

Next, I make a list of everyone who was on the lawn deck with me while the murder was being perpetrated: in order of appearance: Judith, Karol-Kate, Blue, Elise, Russell.

All of them thus have a rock-solid alibi; which leaves Sir Billy, Marje, Shane—plus the entire crew—without.

It's what you might call an open field.

One thing that I intend to do at the first opportunity, even though I've been forbidden to do so, is talk to Sir Billy. It's not a conversation I look forward to, and I shall have to tread carefully. But first, I intend to make a return visit to the pilot house.

I take a detour via the galley, where Bernie is busy preparing lunch with the help of Fruit Lady and another deckhand I haven't seen before. (It's like *The Boys from Brazil*—where do they keep coming from?)

As she works, she's treating them to another of her monologues, this time about the banshees of Skibbereen and Clonakilty, beautiful maidens who appear as harbingers of death. I've heard of Clon (as the locals call it)—they make very fine black puddings, and a white variant, too. I'm relieved to say her captive audience betrays no glimmer of understanding, and I interrupt her feverish performance by asking where the cookies are kept.

I place half a dozen in a large rectangular cookie tin—far bigger than is necessary, but that's deliberate—then head up to find the captain, who is sitting blank-faced at the wheel.

"I've come to apologize for earlier, Captain Romer," I say. "I was out of order." I'm a terrible liar—Julie says I start twitching and blinking—but fortunately he doesn't look at me, merely nods. "I've calmed down now. Brought you a peace offering—something to eat." He pretends to study the horizon but I can tell he likes the idea.

I put the tin down on the chart table, remove the lid and place it alongside. "You stay there," I say, "I'll bring them over." I pick up a cookie in a paper napkin and ferry it over to him.

"*Bitte haben Sie einen Keks, Kapitän,*" I say experimentally, summoning the phrase from my A-level days. His accent is difficult to pin down, but something about his syntax and word order—and his formal manner—suggest he might be German.

Who can resist homemade cookies? Certainly not sweet-toothed Romer. He licks his well-formed lips and starts crunching.

He looks up. "*Ich hätte lieber ein Vanillekipferl!*" he chuckles. He's Austrian! A piece of luck indeed: without further ado I launch forth about *Punschkrapfen*, Linzer torte, Esterházytorte and the myriad other cakes and gâteaux of Vienna, which are a guilty passion of mine.

The purpose of this ruse? Quite simply, to distract him.

When I was leaving the pilot house earlier on, I spotted a chart marked "North-East Atlantic and Azores Archipelago" folded up on the table. Thanks to a dexterous maneuver of mine—laying the lid on the chart, then lifting both of them up together—that chart is now safely in my cookie tin, and the captain none the wiser.

Pleased with this feat of misdirection, inspired by a card trick I used to perform called "Follow the Lady," I return to the privacy of my cabin with the tin, remove the chart and lay it out—or rather, as much of it as will fit—on the lower bunk.

As I said, I'm not a numbers person, nor did I bring along a protractor. So it is with knotted brow that I settle down to figure out where we are and where the yacht is heading.

Improvising, I draw on a dot for our current position (according to GPS), line up 239 degrees (according to the Compass app) and (using the edge of my laptop as a ruler) draw a line plotting our course. Well, we're certainly not heading for the Azores, not even Santa Cruz das Flores, the most westerly of the islands. Even allowing for wind and current, we're pointing *much* further west—two hundred nautical miles away, in fact.

Is there a logical explanation for this? Are we heading off course to compensate for weather or tidal conditions? Or is the yacht's navigation system faulty? I need to find some way of warning the pilot house, though I fear once again I'll be whistling in the wind.

Chapter 26

I'm puzzling over this when I hear a rattling sound from the passage outside my cabin and a knock at the door.

It's Challis, trundling a steel cart. She appears to have recovered her composure since earlier on, or maybe she's just too busy to dwell on things; I've never seen someone work so hard or fast. "I didn't know you had a porthole," she says, peering in.

"Are you OK?" I ask.

"The show must go on," she replies. "It's different for you because you were her friend."

Do I tell her that Xéra was murdered? Does she already suspect it? I weigh this up rapidly and decide not, at least for the moment.

"I know what you're thinking—it wasn't an accident," she says.

So I'm not a lone voice in the wilderness. "You think so too?"

"Looked like a crime scene. And there was someone else there who took milk and sugar in their coffee. Poor lady—what a way to go."

"Will you help me find out what happened?" I say. "I told the captain but he wouldn't believe me—told me to keep my mouth shut."

"Sorry, I can't get in any trouble," she replies curtly.

"Look, why don't you come in, so we're not disturbed?" I rapidly fold up the stolen chart and offer her the lower bunk.

"Not really room, is there," she says. "Lucky you, having a sea view."

She's not green-eyed for nothing. A porthole is clearly a status symbol when it comes to crew accommodation and Challis doesn't see why a scribbler slash chef merits one.

"Do it for Xéra. You were saying how much you liked her." I watch as she struggles with her conscience.

"I don't know how I can help," she says.

"Was there anything—anything at all—that struck you as odd this morning?"

"It was perfectly normal. There was a bit of a drama earlier on . . ."

"What kind of drama?"

"After setting up breakfast, we went off to dust and polish the grand saloon, which is a monster job and takes two of us. That's when I got buzzed by the pilot house."

This is a new development. "What was that about?"

"There was a problem in the master cabin. Sir Billy ran a bath and went mad with the bubble bath."

"Was he in the habit of taking bubble baths first thing in the morning?"

"Apparently it was a surprise for Lady Hardcastle, for when she got back. A surprise that went wrong," she adds ruefully.

I wonder if Sir Billy knew his wife was going out, or woke up and found her absent. If true, it sounds like a kind gesture, and sheds a slightly rosier light on their relationship.

"What did Sir Billy say when you got there?"

"I didn't go—I sent the deckhand to mop up. Apparently it was like an Ibiza foam party in there. Me, I headed to the beach club to take off the cling film, ready for feeding time at the zoo."

Not for the first time, I marvel at what goes on behind the scenes of a superyacht to keep things running smoothly.

"Who's normally first to arrive at breakfast?"

"On the first two days, Mr. Glum was an early bird."

"Mr. Tate?"

She titters. "That's what Aimee calls him and his wife—the Glums. But not today."

"That's because he was up on the lawn deck with me, birdwatching. And when you arrived to take off the cling film . . . ?"

"I saw someone slumped over the table straight away." Challis looks slightly green. "Then I realized it was Madame. She was out cold, not breathing. It was the first thing I checked. I'm a first-aider—we all are."

"Why did you fetch me?"

"I told you—you're a chef. I thought you might . . . have some specialized know-how."

"How long do you think she'd been there?"

"How should I know? I do remember touching her and noticing she felt cold, which I knew was a bad sign."

"And the spilled coffee—was that cold too?"

"Of course it was. Ugh! I hope I got it all out of the carpet—nothing more revolting than the stink of spilled milk."

"Out of interest, which guests take milk in their coffee?"

She counts off her fingers: "Sir Billy, Mr. Tate, Mr. Hudson."

"And sugar?"

"Sir Billy, for sure. I don't know about the rest. Mrs. Mayham has sweeteners, though they don't seem to work."

I can't help smiling. "And there was a chopstick—probably from the sushi lunch."

She looks puzzled. "No, I didn't notice any chopstick. Your Japanese lunch was served on the afterdeck. How did it get to the beach club?" She's right. I'd forgotten that. "Look, are you accusing me of slacking? Cos—"

"No, don't worry about it," I say, though chopsticks can't walk; someone must have moved it. "Just one final thing . . . why were you in such a hurry to clear up the beach club if you suspected foul play?"

"You're jokin', right?" she snaps. "Chief stews keep their yacht sparkling and spotless at all times. No murdering bastard is going to mess with my schedule!"

At this point she checks the time and tells me she must run. "But I almost forgot . . . one of the guests took pity and sorted out some clothes for you. That's why I'm here."

She removes from her cart a cotton shirt, two fine-gauge T-shirts (navy and charcoal), a pair of shorts and some swimming trunks, all on wooden hangers. How kind! "And am I allowed to ask who my benefactor might be?" I say.

"Our handsome tennis player," Challis says, adding with a smile, "but hands off—I'm first in line if he wants to practice his ball control."

My interest has been pricked by the spilled coffee. Considering the planning that went into this attack, it seems almost . . . careless. Unless the killer tipped it over deliberately, to confuse and mislead.

My first priority, however, is to check these missing alibis. Reflecting on the bubble-bath incident, I realize that if Sir Billy was busy flooding his bathroom, he can't simultaneously have been murdering his wife. But what if he did it as a cover—and slipped out while the deckhand cleared up the mess?

And then there's Shane.

I pull on his shirt, which feels beautifully crisp on the skin. It's strange wearing other people's clothes, however good a fit, because they *smell* different. I'd bet you anything Shane uses that murderously expensive laundry in Pont Street where the shirts come back swaddled in tissue paper and scented with lavender and sunshine. On the few occasions I've frequented it, I've had fun spotting famous names on the neat bundles of laundry awaiting collection.

The shirt's a double cuffed affair, requiring cufflinks, so it's lucky I keep some in my sponge bag. When I retrieve them I realize with a pang that they're the antique gold pair given me by dear Xéra after I moved in with Marcus; one side representing a clove, the other a cardamom pod, attached by a tiny chain. "Symbols of love and compassion," she explained, looking at me intently.

Marcus and I may have had our ups and downs, particularly at the beginning, but Xéra was always there, a warm, loving presence in our lives; now I've lost her too—gone forever—and I'm suddenly engulfed by a wave of grief and despair.

If only Julie were here . . . just to feel her healing presence would make things better. Instead, I splash cold water over my face, tidy myself up in the mirror and head off in search of human company, to lift my melancholy mood.

Five minutes later, I enter the grand saloon—and guess who's at the bar?

Chapter 27

"Shane," I say. "I'm so sorry. Terrible for everyone."

He pats me on the back, in the way of sportspeople. "Join me," he says. "Brandy and soda?"

"Don't mind if I do," I hear myself reply, sounding like a maiden aunt. "Though I'll have whisky."

It's far too early for me, but I make my drink—unlike him, I actually add soda—and settle down next to him. There's a gentle tinkling sound from the LUCITE® blossoms overhead which I notice for the first time are illuminated by concealed color-changing lights. A lot of trouble and expense to somewhat vulgar effect, though of course I'm not *Maldemer*'s target market.

"By the way, thanks for sending over the clothes," I say.

"Anytime," he says.

"Is Sir Billy still in his cabin?" I ask.

"Auntie Marje is playing gatekeeper." He laughs: it's not funny so it must be some sort of reflex. "Lise tried to see him and was told to piss off."

"Everyone's upset," I say. Adding after a pause: "Where were you when you heard the news?"

He shoots me a glance, somewhat glassy. "In bed." He laughs again.

We sit there for a minute, saying nothing. I observe him flex his wrists and squeeze an imaginary tennis ball with his right hand.

"I saw you on Number One Court, you know. Playing against Rafael Nadal."

"Ha! Can't win 'em all."

"Two lefties slogging it out . . . it was an exciting match."

He shrugs.

"Do you miss it?" I ask.

"I make the most of the skills I learned: I'm a motivational coach nowadays. Us sportsmen are at quite a premium."

"Must help pay the bills," I say innocuously.

He takes a swig of drink. "If you say so."

"I expect Elise is in high demand, too," I say. "People always need decorators in a property boom."

"If you say so," he says for the second time. Then adds, thoughtfully, "Not cheap, living in Pavilion Road."

"Pavilion Road? Why, I live just the other side of Sloane Square."

Normally people are amazed to hear I live in Belgravia—they'd more likely think Catford or Hounslow—but Shane smiles. "So we're practically neighbors."

"Does Elise have her studio there?" I ask. The houses in their street look like mews cottages but some of them are huge, with swimming pools, conservatories and garden rooms out back.

"Showroom at Chelsea Harbor—not that she spends much time there." Since I first came to London this area has metamorphosed from grungy no-man's-land into a "design destination." Julie tells me that interiors shops commonly charge a 66 percent mark-up, but even so, how do they pay the rent? My theory is that they're a front for money laundering, though you'd get in trouble for saying it.

Shane continues: "I say we'd be better off selling up and going to live somewhere cheap and sunny."

"I guess Sir Billy likes to keep his family close by," I say, coaxingly.

He studies me, weighing up how much to tell me. "Billy's always been good to us, but recently . . ." It's bad form to encourage an alcoholic, but I top up his glass.

"Xéra is—I mean she *was*—a sweetheart, don't get me wrong," he continues, expanding to his theme. "I wish I'd got to know her better. But it seems a bit of a coincidence the moment she comes on the scene, Lise is told our allowance is going to be 'tapered.'" He shakes his head, laughs, and adds: "Polite way of saying, no more moolah."

Is Shane mistaken, or lying? It was Russell who stopped the handouts—Xéra told me so. "Maybe your father-in-law's having to tighten his belt," I continue, leading him on. "Business, finance, it's so unpredictable."

"Billy's a Yorkshireman," he says. "Loadsamoney, just doesn't like parting with it. Ask Auntie Marje."

"What do you mean?" I ask, playing the innocent.

"He bailed her out a couple of years ago, and we never heard the end of it. Let's say, he likes his pound of flesh. This time . . ." There's a pause. "Sorry," he says belatedly, "you must find all this family stuff boring."

"Not at all."

"Whatever. You seem different from the rest. I get a good feeling about you."

Julie has a friend who's famed for her powers of seduction. She won't share all her secrets, but one is to circle the face of her target with her gaze, lingering on lips and eyes. Precisely what Shane's doing to me now.

"Is the dog enjoying his holiday?" I ask to change the subject, picking up a paper napkin to fiddle with.

"Ha! I swear Billy hired that freaky dog handler just to spite me."

"Oh, she's OK," I reply, noticing with dismay that I've turned the napkin into a pile of shreds. I start on the next. "She's very good with Colefax."

"Hmph," he says. Then, looking straight into my lap: "Tell me about you."

Whoa! Did that just happen?

"Oh, you know, pen for hire," I gabble, thinking fast. "I'm only sad that Xéra's book will never be written now." I peer at my watch. "Heavens, is that the time? I'm late for something. See you later!"

I studiously ignore the heap of shredded paper on the bar top. Enough to line a hamster's cage.

As I stand up, he catches me by the arm. "Shirt looks great on you, by the way."

At which point, without a backward glance, I flee the grand saloon.

CHAPTER 28

I'm out of practice with people hitting on me; in fact, everything about the dating scene brings me out in a cold sweat and always has. Assuming that I haven't misread the signals—which might as well have been delivered by singing telegram—dishy Shane, all muscly physique and manly stubble, is into guys as well as girls.

I should of course be flattered. Julie's always assuring me I'm in great shape and have a lovely smile, but that's just to boost my confidence. All that ever mattered was that the man I loved felt the same about me. Now Marcus has gone, I accept I'll never feel that way about anyone else, ever again.

Which brings me back to Shane. A few things make me feel uncomfortable here. To start with, it's very poor taste—my dear friend has just died and I'm still in shock. Secondly, he's *married*; to Xéra's *stepdaughter*. (Not good; not good.) And if he's looking for a shipboard dalliance, why me? Is my sexual orientation so glaringly obvious? Why not try it on with the gorgeous captain or oleaginous Blue? I'm not interested in sex, either now or for the foreseeable future.

No matter how great the temptation.

My next stop is the crew mess. One of its walls acts as a giant noticeboard, plastered with rotas and lists. Among them are bossy posters printed in red and yellow: *READ THIS, IMPORTANT! WHAT YOU NEED TO KNOW.* An alarming photomontage shows a dummy being brought to life by a defibrillator.

As anticipated, Aimee arrives shortly afterward for her midmorning coffee and plonks a large ring-bound file down on the table.

"Flat white as usual?" I ask. She nods. "Sorry about, well, my tantrum in the pilot house earlier."

"Feeling better now?" she asks.

"Not really. It's still sinking in."

"Captain Romer and I . . . we're just doing our job."

"I appreciate that." I insert a pod into the coffee machine, lower the arm and there's a hissing sound. "Glad you've brought along something exciting to read."

She grimaces. "I'm checking procedure. What are you up to?"

The true answer would be gathering information, but I don't tell her that. Instead, I continue, trying to keep things light, "I hope it isn't a regular occurrence, guests dying."

"It's something we have to be prepared for," she says laconically. "At least we're not on a sailing boat in the middle of the Atlantic. There was this guy who died suddenly on one and the only place they could put him was in a rubber dinghy, towed behind."

"They didn't bury him at sea?"

"That's a bit of a myth—you don't just drop bodies in the ocean nowadays. In any case, we're tangled up with different authorities here. We embarked from London, flying under the Bermuda flag, and we're landing the deceased in an Autonomous Region of Portugal." Aimee checks no one is within earshot, then says: "It's a good thing you were mistaken about what happened to Lady Hardcastle, because that would have caused terrible complications."

I busy myself frothing milk.

"Does one of you have to be in the pilot house all the time, or can you leave the boat on autopilot?" I ask her, wobbling the *schiuma di latte* onto our coffees.

"One sugar, please. Mind if I ask why you want to know?"

"Just casual interest. Don't tell me if you'd rather not."

"We're very tight on security, like all superyachts. So if you're thinking of jumping in when we're not looking and seizing the helm—"

"Not after that drubbing you gave me earlier on!"

She chuckles. "I was going to say—we may have an open-door policy, but don't be fooled. It's one thing to have guests popping in for a chat, but if it ever came to it, the pilot house is built like a fortress: iris recognition, deadlocks, bulletproof glass, panic alarms, the lot. An intruder wouldn't stand a chance."

Aimee's laughter is good for the soul: a rich, musical sound accompanied by a sidelong glance from her dancing eyes.

"But to answer your question, yes, theoretically *Maldemer* is perfectly capable of piloting herself. If we came near an obstruction or another vessel, that would trigger an automatic course adjustment and an alarm would sound. In practice, though, we rarely leave the wheel unattended, and never by accident. The captain and I take it in shifts. As there are just the two of us with a licence on this crossing, we need to be as flexible as possible."

At this point Challis saunters in to fetch clean towels from the laundry. She's evidently treated herself to a squirt of fragrance from a guest's dressing table—Marje's Amouage, if I'm not mistaken—and it trails heavily behind her. I'm inclined to agree with Bill Holden in *Sunset Boulevard*, when he describes tuberose as "not my favorite perfume, not by a long shot."

She rather pointedly slams down her basket of cleaning products on the table between myself and Aimee, sighing, "Wish I had time to sit and chinwag."

Aimee bats it back to her. "Come and join me on the night shift. Gossip all you like then." Challis huffs out.

"That must be torture," I say. A couple of years ago I stayed up all night to cook Christmas dinner for a TV breakfast show: I feel her pain.

"Oh, it's not that bad. There's always stuff to do—paperwork, equipment checks. If I get really desperate, budgets. Access logs to be signed off."

"Access logs?"

"The keycards automatically record who's been where when. It's just a formality—it's not as if we're keeping tabs on people."

My ears prick up. "So you should be able to tell who went into Xéra's cabin and lifted the necklace?" I say. "And who was in the beach club this morning when she was attacked. Sorry, died."

She ignores this. "I'm afraid not. The charter was organized in such a hurry that no one activated the system, though of course we've done it now. And we don't track guests; in fact, I think that would be illegal. It's only crew activity that's monitored."

"That must include me," I say, half-jokingly. "Mine's a crew keycard, because of my cabin."

"You have extended access to cover most of the guest facilities—I know because I programmed it myself. But why this sudden interest in systems and procedures?" She adds, with an upward glance, "If you'll take my advice, I wouldn't stir things up. Romer meant what he said."

"As I said, just casual interest!" I continue, in as casual a tone as I can muster, "By the way, who sets the boat's course?"

She looks at me oddly. "Joint effort, really. Captain Romer decides our route, I enter the numbers into the navigation hub. He's not a details man, so I do the technical stuff."

"So would you work out the compass bearing or would he?"

"Not sure why you're asking, but it's all done by computer nowadays," adding with a laugh, "we don't use sextants and draw lines on charts, if that's what you're getting at." She stands up. "Thanks for the coffee—I can tell you're a pro."

"Just before you go, are you sure we're heading for the Azores? It's just that . . . I'm worried that we're off course."

"Why on earth would you think such a thing?" she says over her shoulder.

"Erm . . . the GPS on my phone. It's probably set up wrong—I'm sure you and Captain Romer have everything under control."

She turns round and studies me for a moment, then smiles, as if amused. "If we weren't so short-staffed, I'd invite you up to the pilot house and give you a lesson in navigation. Ocean currents, wind direction, weather systems . . . there's a lot more to it than people imagine. Besides which, if our captain wants to take us to the Azores via the South Pole, we have to trust his judgment. I certainly do."

Chapter 29

A muttering from the direction of the galley informs me that Bernie's arrived to prepare lunch. I decide the prospects of a decent meal will be improved if I offer to help. "Anything I can do?"

Perhaps unconsciously, she's decided on a funeral-style buffet spread: the sort of cold but filling finger food that goes down well after you've been scattering soil on a coffin or watching someone take the final curtain call at the crematorium. Much as the guests at most such events are a mix of elderly and youthful, old-fashioned and modish, so is Bernie's menu: triangular sandwiches, sausage rolls and deviled eggs rub shoulders with skewers, dips and bruschetta.

The rule with hand-held food is the smaller the better, and I fear a lot of this is going to end up dropped on the floor. "I love cutting things up, if that's helpful," I offer.

While I swiftly reduce some oversized wedges of pizza, she attacks a tray of Scotch eggs. "Never mind?" she says, surveying the rubble of egg and sausage meat. "Stick 'em back together with mustard, why don't we?"

Challis breezes in. "Jeez! That's a heap of food!" she says, which I wouldn't take as a compliment. "I'm laying up in the dining saloon—thought we'd give the beach club a break, for obvious reasons. Dunno if anyone's free to give me a hand?"

She obviously means me, which suits me fine. I can keep on the move and zone in on interesting conversations rather than being stuck beside the dog.

We ferry dozens of platters and salvers along endless passages and up companionways, and not for the first time it occurs to me that *Maldemer* could do with a dumb waiter to help transport food and tableware from place to place. It's the sort of old-fashioned tech I love, along with servants' bells and speaking tubes.

Eventually the feast is all arranged on the vast mahogany sideboard that lines one wall of the dining saloon. A foghorn blast announces that lunch is served and in they troop, including, to my surprise, the captain, who takes up a position by the door and stands there like a sentry.

All talk, naturally enough, is of this morning's terrible discovery. Apparently, Elise was once at a cocktail party where someone had a canapé go down the wrong way: one of those roast-beef-and-Yorkshire-pudding miniatures so beloved of party caterers (which I think silly).

With trademark insensitivity, she re-enacts the choking scene for us and I see everyone nervously scanning their plates for potential hazards. Karol-Kate, evaluating the crudités as too high risk, starts cramming in hummus and guacamole with a spoon. Russell alarms us by throwing a coughing fit, prompted by one of the mustard-laced Scotch eggs, after which Judith lays down her knife and fork, though she's hardly eaten a thing.

After ten minutes, to everyone's surprise, Marje walks in. Elise jumps up to hug her, Blue fusses around pointlessly and the rest of us look on with pity. All the usual acid-edged animation has drained from her face, leaving it gray and drawn. Even her silver bob seems to have lost its bounce.

"Shall we send a light lunch to Sir Billy in his cabin?" asks Challis.

"Can if you want but he won't eat it," Marje replies, seating herself between Russell and Blue.

"Poor, poor Daddy," says Elise. "My heart's breaking for him. Is he feeling any better?"

"They found him some diazepam," she says. "Quite a medicine chest Captain Romer's got, if anyone needs anything." This sets Shane off on one of his inexplicable laughing fits, and I notice Elise shoot him a look. For my part—after what happened earlier—I'm trying to avoid meeting his eye.

"I was hoping to see Sir Billy later," says Russell. "If at all possible. There are things we need to discuss before, well, the news gets out."

"Not now. If he wants to sleep, we must let him," says Marje.

"I was thinking—Xéra's family," ventures Judith, with a sad shake of the head. "Her people should be told at once. Poor things."

Apart from some distant cousins on her mother's side, I know that there's pretty much no one. I'm about to volunteer this information when Marje cuts in.

"It'll be looked after, don't concern yourself."

This seems to be all she's prepared to say for the moment, so general conversation tentatively resumes. Elise asks if anyone knows anything about the Azores and it turns out Blue has been there.

"I wrote a story about it," he says, with a little smile; even if you liked him, you'd have to admit it's a smug, self-satisfied little smile.

"What, you mean like a short story?" asks Elise.

"A fairy story?" adds Shane—and he's off again. There's nothing wrong with his laugh per se, so much as the times he chooses to give way to it.

"Tell them about it, Blue—the time you wrote for *Wanderlust*," says Marje, which gets Shane chortling again. "When my assistant's not fetching coffee, he's a big-shot writer."

The young man refuses to rise to the bait, and replies loftily: "This was in fact for a newspaper. It was a few years back and

I wrote a travel piece about São Miguel. I was there for two days and the first one it was too foggy to see anything."

"I'd love to swim with dolphins," says Karol-Kate, toying with one of her dungaree straps.

"You'd fit in better with whales," ripostes Marje. And . . . she's back on form. *Ouch!* "Can't have been much of an article, Blue, if you only had one day to research it."

"There were lots of pineapples," he says, ignoring this.

"And São Jorge cheese," I throw in. The guests look surprised—if you're waiting tables you tend to disappear into the wallpaper. "Cow's milk," I add. "Semi-hard."

"That's Blue, from what I heard," says Marje, and the others obediently titter. She's one of those unfortunate people who vents her anger or anxiety by gratuitously lashing out at the nearest person, and I wonder why Blue puts up with it.

This once, in fact, he doesn't: he rises to his feet abruptly, causing his chair to squeal on the parquet. "I've lost my appetite," he says sourly, and sulks off to an armchair in the corner, to pout with his notebook.

The Azores having turned into a sore subject, everyone is relieved when we move on to something less contentious. Mr. Glum wants to know if he and his wife can pay their respects to Xéra's mortal remains. Judith twitches as if it's news to her they would want to—I can think of more amusing ways to spend a sunny afternoon. Once again, I pipe up, informing everyone that visits are out of the question.

"I presume there will be a post-mortem," says Judith.

"I didn't think we had a doctor aboard, let alone a pathologist," replies Marje dismissively.

"I think my wife means, when we get ashore," says Russell stiffly.

Marje shrugs. "It's up to my brother. And at the moment he isn't making any sense at all."

"Let me know when I can go in and see Daddy," says Elise,

laying down her napkin. "I'm going up on deck for an hour," she announces. "Shame to waste the sunshine."

"Don't forget I need to see Sir Billy too," says Russell. "On matters of great importance. Judith and I will be in the grand saloon."

I have no doubt that Shane will be heading for the bar, so I avoid his eye and help clear the table. Marje hangs back after the others have departed.

"Hey!" she says.

"Me?" I reply.

"Who'd'ya think? Report to my cabin. Now."

Chapter 30

Goodness knows how *Maldemer*'s designers came up with the concepts for the guest cabins, but Marje's is on a space theme, with pale-blue walls, supernova ceiling and shafts of light falling in unexpected places.

"You think this is peculiar, you better see the bedroom," she says, pressing a button. A wall slides away to reveal a vast zero-gravity bed, apparently suspended above the floor. Unhappy as I am in my microcabin, I'm glad I'm not expected to sleep on that.

"Take a seat," she says, indicating a sofa apparently made of brushed steel. "You were first at the scene this morning."

"No, I wasn't," I reply, trying to retain my dignity as I slip and slide on the metallized leather.

"OK, you and the maid. Anything strike you as odd?"

Although even thinking about it gives me the horrors, I describe the sequence of events to her as dispassionately as I can: Xéra cold and lifeless, slumped over the breakfast table, coffee and crumbs everywhere. Not being sure why I've been summoned to this interview, I keep quiet about the fact that it wasn't an accident.

"So you slept through it?" I say.

"I was woken up by that foghorn. Why do they have to sound

the damn thing every ten minutes? It's driving everyone crazy. Then that voice yammering on the loudspeakers almost frightened *me* to death."

Is she speaking the truth? If only I had access to a lie detector. She continues. "What I'd like to know is: necklace is stolen Monday night, Xéra dies Wednesday morning. Must be connected, don't'cha think?"

I'm evidently being pumped for information, so reply stiffly: "If you have a theory, I'd speak to Captain Romer about it. He's the one in charge, at least till we get ashore."

"It's hard to take him seriously," says Marje. "He'd be kicked out of a casting session for playing it too broad."

"In any case, what do you mean? Are you suggesting Xéra was so shocked by the theft she didn't swallow properly?"

"Don't play dumb. I'm suggesting someone gave her a helping hand. And you think so too."

We eye each other. "Why do you say that?" I ask.

"Rich woman marries successful businessman. People get jealous—people eager for money."

I think about this for a moment. "Can I trust you, Marje?" I ask.

"Depends," she says—an honest response.

"I can tell you for a fact that Xéra was murdered. I reported it to Captain Romer and was silenced. Someone needs to tell Sir Billy."

"So tell me your theory."

After I've explained about the coffee and cake and the timing, she says: "You're making sense. Poor Xéra . . . We had our differences but she didn't deserve . . . I never . . ."

I have a habit of rushing in to fill conversational gaps (I can't help myself) but on this occasion, I bite my tongue. I hope she'll finish what she's started to say but she doesn't.

"Look, I'll speak to Bill as soon as the moment's right," she concludes, motioning for me to stand up and walking me to the door. "Tell me if you find out anything, and vice versa. And before I forget—tell the darned maid to go easy on my perfume. I can smell her at the other end of the ship!"

Wondering whether I've made a mistake confiding in Marje—when, like Shane, she has failed to provide a convincing alibi—I make my way to the galley to check for developments. Unfortunately, I've upset Challis.

"Don't worry, I've cleared the dining saloon unaided," she says. "Enjoy yourself, hobnobbing with the guests?"

She rattles a shopping caddy laden with racks full of tiny bottles, applicators and sponges. Apparently she's found red-wine stains—invisible to the naked eye—on the Persian carpet in the grand saloon and this is her mobile stain-removal kit.

I'm about to remind her that I am on this accursed voyage at the personal invitation of the late Lady Hardcastle and her husband, and only helping out below decks from the sheer goodness of my heart, but the words come too late; she's already flown out of the door.

"She's hot-tempered, that one," says Bernie.

"Seems good at her job, though," I reply.

Bernie harrumphs, about to impart some juicy morsel of gossip, then there's the sound of something scratching at the door and in bounds Colefax, followed by Karol-Kate. "Dogs in the kitchen?" I say.

"Oh, this one's allowed, the sweetheart?" says Bernie, scratching him behind the ears. "Who's a clever liddle-bickle diggy-doggy, den?" Animals would stand a better chance of understanding if we didn't talk such rubbish to them.

"We've changed our circuit so that now we come through here," says Karol-Kate cheerfully.

"Let's see if Auntie Bernadette can find a little something for Colesie-Wolesie?" coos the chef, producing a treat from a plastic box. It mystifies me that anyone would make dog biscuits dog-shaped, though I guess humans eat gingerbread men. And jelly babies.

While Colefax crunches away, Bernie reaches into a cupboard and produces another plastic box, this time containing flapjacks.

"You said they were your favorite," says Bernie, offering them to the dog handler, whose eyes light up. "Take another for later, why don't you?"

"I'm glad I've caught you, Karol-Kate," I interrupt. By the look of them, the flapjacks were left in the oven too long, so she's stuck here chewing whether she likes it or not. "About this morning—I'm still trying to get my head around it. When you and Colefax were doing your early walk, did you happen to bump into Xéra?"

Eventually Karol-Kate's jaws grind to a halt, and I mean that literally.

"No," she says, swallowing hard.

"But I thought you did a complete circuit of the boat, including through the beach club?"

"We don't go through the beach club anymore. Like I said, we've changed our route."

"Since yesterday?"

She blinks and looks away. "Colefax doesn't like the lobsters and I'd rather not see them waiting for the chop, so we go round the long way." I don't like seeing them kept in tanks either, but it seems a coincidence that she chose today to change her route.

She jingles the dog's lead and he hops to attention. "Say bye-bye to Bernie."

The chef bends down to chuck the animal under the chin and he licks her hand. As she straightens up, the little chap takes a fancy to her ankle and starts worrying her trouser leg. "Stop that, Colesie!" cries Bernie. Karol-Kate bends down to pick up the dog but he wriggles away.

Things spin rapidly out of control. Colefax gets the turnup

of Bernie's trousers between his teeth and starts pulling while she retreats behind the island, more or less obscured from view by a rack of pots and pans. There's a ripping sound—they don't make cheffing gear like they used to—and the trouser leg splits at the seam . . . to reveal an elasticated ankle holster.

It's over in a flash, and Bernie—unaware of what I saw—instantly restores herself to order. I'm reminded, however, of that scene in *The Wizard of Oz*, when Toto pulls back the curtain in the Emerald Throne Room to reveal the wizard is a fake. So who exactly is Bernie and why the holster?

Karol-Kate leads the dog away, and while Bernie washes her hands—I should hope so too—she chats on lightly about dogs she has known over the years. When she at last draws breath, I ask her if I may pose a question. There's something else I've noticed . . .

"Go on?" she says, continuing to wipe her hands on the kitchen towel though they must surely be dry by now.

"Why are you wearing your patch on the other eye today?"

Her hand flies up to her left eye (where it normally is). "Oh, that!" she says. "Don't you be worrying now. Lazy eye, they call it?"

"So it's a treatment prescribed by your ophthalmologist?"

"That's it, yes." She nods her head vigorously.

"And you switch eyes? I hope I don't sound nosy."

"First of the month," she says, still nodding. "Regular as clockwork."

"You won't believe this, but I thought it was a disguise, maybe." We both laugh heartily.

I know there are occasions when amblyopia is treated by means of an eyepatch, but I can't imagine why you'd alternate eyes. Plus, according to my diary, today is the fifteenth of the month. And probably even more disturbing: why does a ship's chef carry a defense baton and pepper spray strapped to her leg?

Chapter 31

After lunch is the quiet hour, when guests retire to their cabins to read a book or take a nap. Not me.

With all this hidden network of service passages at my disposal, why not make use of it—do some prowling round, without people knowing? It's possible my movements will be recorded on Aimee's access log, but so what? It's not as if I'm stealing things or killing people.

Elise's announcement that she was heading to the afterdeck was somewhat obvious, almost as if she was hinting for someone to join her there. From a spyhole behind the bar, I see her stretched out on a sun chair the size of my sitting room. Because we're heading south it's appreciably warmer—and sunny—but not yet the weather for sunbathing; there's also a stiffish breeze, made stronger by the motion of the yacht. She gets a chiffon scarf out of her bag and wraps it round her neck.

She checks the time on her iPhone, then puts in her AirPods and fiddles about to find something to listen to. She toys with her pack of More Menthols before tossing them aside. Minutes drift by; if this is what private detectives have to put up with, it must be a very boring life.

Next, she tosses aside the AirPods, puts on her huge Balenciaga sunglasses and pretends to doze. A couple of minutes later she checks her phone again and looks about expectantly. I have a strong suspicion I know who she's waiting for, but I can't wait around indefinitely, so therefore give up.

Following a succession of very narrow passages—lucky I'm not claustrophobic—I creep up a level to a one-way mirror that affords me a panoramic view of the grand saloon in all its fussy magnificence. No Shane at the bar for once, but Russell and Judith perched on a window seat with a tray of tea. They remind me of those elderly couples you see at National Trust properties, eking out a long afternoon with a cuppa and a scone, sitting in silence.

On Judith's lap is a piece of tapestry, with tails of colored yarn, but she's not sewing, preferring to look out to sea instead. He holds a newspaper—must have been saved from Sunday—and I realize they're doing the cryptic crossword.

"A-P-P-L-E," says Judith. I rub my ears to hear better.

Russell smiles and slowly fills in the letters. "Well done. Nineteen down. Five letters. E blank blank L blank."

Julie's always trying to get me to take an interest in crosswords but I haven't the patience. She teases away at problems whereas I expect inspiration to strike and get bored when it doesn't.

"What was the clue again?" asks Judith.

"Bird dog losing its head."

"E-A-R-L-Y? Though I don't see how we get there."

"That would mean twelve down is a three-letter word starting with Y."

"E-A-G-L-E—that's it," she says, clapping her hands.

"If you're sure, darling."

"Dog—beagle. Loses its head—take off the first letter."

Russell gives her knee an affectionate squeeze and writes it in. "My clever girl."

This scene of cozy domesticity takes me slightly by surprise. So far on the voyage, the Russell I've witnessed is rather more the overbearing husband, patronizing Judith and putting her down. Maybe he's one of those men who likes to appear macho in the eyes of others . . . or perhaps he likes to keep his wife on edge, by being sometimes affectionate, other times hectoring. (Which is an insidious form of coercive control.) I'll never understand the dynamics between married couples, nor, I expect, experience them for myself.

He's moving on to the next crossword clue—I'm rather looking forward to it—when a figure noiselessly enters the grand saloon. Thanks to all the drapes, screens, sculptures on plinths and flower arrangements, there's no shortage of nooks and hiding places for the visitor, but from my vantage point I don't miss a thing: I watch Blue pick his way across the Persian carpet toward the pair, evidently moving within earshot.

"Speaking of eagles," Judith continues, "I wonder if we'll get to see Paul's albatross."

Blue, lurking in the shadows, pulls out his notebook and jots down this mesmerizing comment. Meanwhile Judith holds her needlework up to the light. It's a narrow shape, a purse or spectacle case perhaps.

"We must keep our eyes peeled," replies Russell, then mutters something else in a low voice that I can't make out. They chuckle. Next time I'll bring a glass to hold to the wall, though I can't believe I'm missing much.

I hear a click and see my fellow spy has dropped his propelling pencil onto a table: it rattles and rolls its way across its lacquered top before plopping onto a rug. Judith looks up suddenly and Russell staggers to his feet.

"Who's there?" he calls.

Blue, having retrieved his Rotring, stands up and beams at them. "Howya doing? Forgot my pencil—came to get it."

I'm tempted to jump out of my hiding place and shout: *LIAR!*

"Why don't you join us for a cup of tea?" suggests Judith. "It's lovely sitting here."

"Gee, thanks. Sure." I see him roll his eyes as he turns away to fetch himself a cup and saucer from the bar. He comes to sit down beside them. "I was up on the lawn deck—damned dog tried to bite me."

"You surprise me," says Judith. "I was petting him yesterday and he seemed a sweet little fellow. Were you teasing him? Cats enjoy being teased, but not dogs. Makes them spiteful."

"I was not," says Blue. "He seems to have taken an instinctive dislike to me." Perfectly understandable, I'd say.

"They make nice pets, Bichons," continues Judith. "Poodle family, you know. Love chasing and making mischief. My daughter's was a bit barky—"

Russell harrumphs. "Finish your tea, Judith," he says bossily, back to his old self. "Then I'll take you back to the cabin and go and check on Sir Billy. I'm sure he'll want to see me as soon as he gets up."

After they've said their goodbyes, I watch Blue scribble scribble scribble, then he makes his way to the piano where he dashes off a few scales and arpeggios. It's what my piano teacher at school would have called "gap-toothed"—uneven, with missing notes—but it is, after all, just a warm-up.

He stops and takes a deep breath. From the bass of the piano growls a slow, insistent ostinato, joined presently by the plangent melody of the "Marche Funèbre" from Chopin's Second Piano Sonata. Apart from some fudged octaves, it's a decent performance.

After this, he produces a piece of sheet music from nowhere and goes into another, even sadder piece: "Dido's Lament," by Purcell.

> *When I am laid, am laid in earth,*
> *May my wrongs create*
> *No trouble, no trouble in thy breast;*
> *Remember me, remember me, but ah! forget my fate.*
> *Remember me, but ah! forget my fate.*

This is what is known in the business as a three-hankie number, played with such restraint and sincerity that I'm tempted to break out of my hiding place and hug him. Instead, I dab a tear from my eye and realize I've been wrong: *somewhere* inside Blue there beats a living heart.

Once the performance is over, he folds up the score, placing it on a table beside the piano; then closes the lid of the Fazioli, lowers the fallboard and walks out.

Curious, I slide out of my hiding place into the grand saloon and pick up the sheet music he left behind. Written at the top in schoolboy hand is "Blane Aspern, LaGuardia." Not quite the same as Blue Aspray, but too near to be a coincidence . . . and what's his connection to an airport?

Chapter 32

Assuming Blane and Blue are one and the same person, why did he change his name? Of what relevance might it be, and does Marje, his employer, know?

Frustrated that my investigation seems to be uncovering more questions than answers, I follow him at a safe distance and watch him disappear inside his cabin. Shortly afterward, there's the whoosh of another door opening and I see a bulky figure emerge. It's Russell, with purpose in his step.

I let him pass my vantage point in an alcove, then track him up the gilded staircase to the door of the master cabin.

Each cabin has a windchime hanging outside the door, so that visitors and crew members can make their presence known by jingling, rather than vulgar buzzing or knocking. Russell evidently finds this beneath his dignity, and shakes it violently, causing a jagged discord to fill the air. Nothing happens, so he thumps the door itself, then finally, in a fit of bad temper, kicks it and gives up.

Instead of rejoining Judith and her gros point in their cabin, he now heads for the lobby. I watch him pad across the sheepskin, pour himself a large gin, no tonic or ice, and plonk himself down at the bar.

"Is this seat free?" I ask chirpily.

He looks at me—can hardly say no—and nods.

Russell is part of Sir Billy's inner circle and however disagreeable the idea, there are some questions I need to ask him.

I pour myself a whisky—the second today I absolutely don't want—and am knocking back a glug when I'm hit by what feels like a sledgehammer.

"Olinda asked to be remembered to you."

Ough! My head explodes. Fortunately, the glug was a modest one but I've managed to achieve 360-degree coverage with it: whisky up my nose, Russell's glasses dripping, and the bar counter looks like a Jackson Pollock.

"*What* did you just say?" I gasp, grabbing a wad of napkins to blot up the splatter.

"Olinda Berens—friend of mine," he says, producing from his pocket a portable spectacle-cleaning kit: a miniature spray and two grades of microfibre cloth. Without his glasses he reminds me of a panda, one who's been chowing down on too many bamboo dinners.

"I hardly know her," I say desperately. "Only met her a couple of times."

So much is true. The first occasion was at Marcus's funeral, when she threw a glass of Pinot Grigio in my face, and the second and only other, she took off a shoe and hurled it at a solicitor's clerk.

"Small world. Anyway, I happened to mention that you were ghosting Lady Hardcastle's memoir—"

"I'm not *ghosting* anything," I snap back. "I'm Xéra's literary editor and collaborator, and in any case, I'm surprised you thought it appropriate to talk about a business arrangement. Client confidentiality and all that." I continue through clenched teeth: "But since we're on the subject, is there someone I can talk to about that? We agreed half the fee was payable on signature and it hasn't arrived."

"Thirty days," he says glibly.

"Overdue," I reply.

"And regrettably, in the circumstances, I imagine it will need to be renegotiated."

Chapter 33

I pour myself a new whisky, which stings like hell on account of the earlier assault on my sinuses, and count to ten. I must focus—stay in control.

"I know you've asked to see Sir Billy urgently," I say. "I need to do the same. There are things I must tell him."

"His first priority is to his business affairs, so that must come first. We need to make some adjustments to his portfolio, on account of the, er, tragic news."

"Have the authorities been informed about Xéra's death?"

"Why do you ask?" he says.

"It sounds as if you're hushing it up so that you can sell a few shares in a hurry, which would be highly improper."

He glares at me. "No public announcement has been made, if that's what you're getting at. Captain Romer is adamant things should be kept discreet, to avoid a circus when we land at Ponta Delgada. I know Sir Billy will agree when he—when he makes an appearance."

"And obviously the theft of the necklace and Xéra's death—they're connected in some way."

"One was a theft, the other a fatal accident. Who's been putting rumors about?"

"Oh, no one in particular," I say. "Of course, it was shattering for her to have lost something so historically important—and to feel in some way responsible."

Russell rubs his chin. "You're in something of a privileged position with regards to Lady Hardcastle's private thoughts and reminiscences, thanks to this book-writing thing. If you're thinking of "monetizing" them, to use the current expression, by going to the newspapers with tittle-tattle, I would strongly discourage it. Sir Billy is no stranger to injunctions, gagging orders, SLAPPs and so on."

"How dare you suggest I would?" I protest. "Since you're such an expert on contracts, maybe you should take a look at what happened with the sale of Pâtisserie Pompadour—check Xéra wasn't shafted. She told me all about how it was rushed through, against her better judgment."

Russell looks at me carefully, as if there's something in my egregious tactlessness that he reluctantly admires. Then he pats me on the back in a schoolmasterly way, pours himself another gin and attacks again.

"Olinda said you were implicated in that big murder case in Belgravia a year or so ago—the one in the cookery school. I remember reading about it."

"Then you've been misinformed," I snap back. "I was called as a witness."

"Seems a bit of a coincidence. But don't worry, I'm not planning to tell everyone; it might make them feel a little, well, uncomfortable. It can be our little secret."

Ugh! The thought of sharing anything with this horrible man fills me with revulsion.

He smiles and scratches his leg. "I take that as a yes. Which reminds me, something I wanted to ask you." He glances round to check we're alone. "Man to man."

What on earth is it now?

"It must be a lot of fun below deck," he says, blinking slowly. "After dark."

"Erm, not that I've noticed," I reply, squirming on my bar stool. My mind flicks back with horror to the peeping Tom episode at the tender garage.

"Captain Romer and his concubines," he continues, lacing his fingers together. "Crew parties. That pretty little redheaded stewardess." He closes his eyes, the better to conjure some priapic scene.

"What in God's name are you talking about?"

"Just saying, that if there's an invitation going spare," he continues, "I'd be pleased to make a contribution to, as it were, *expenses*." At this point he actually removes his wallet and starts fingering banknotes.

Aargh! What is wrong with these people?

Seeing the look of disgust on my face, he adds lamely: "After all, I am on holiday."

"Look, Russell," I reply, "if you don't already know, although I'm sure the former Mrs. Marcus Berens will have dropped it into conversation, I'm *gay*. So if there really are things happening between crew members—which I sincerely doubt—they steer well clear of me. I also happened to notice you trying to touch up that young woman during your fishing session yesterday. You should be ashamed of yourself—she was young enough to be your daughter. Probably underage, in fact. And if that's all, I have things to get on with."

He follows me unsteadily to the door. I know diabetes can cause balance problems and the gin can't have helped. "Don't go off in a huff, Paul. Have a quiet word with the redhead, and I'll chase up that money you're due. You scratch my back, I'll scratch yours."

Raising myself to my full height, I saunter disdainfully off down the corridor. Unfortunately, the engines put on a sudden spurt and I collide with a flower arrangement.

CHAPTER 34

After a clumsy attempt to reassemble it, I make my way up to the lawn deck and sit down on the grass. It's truly magnificent up here; if it weren't for all the terrible things that have been happening, I'd consider myself the luckiest man alive.

I take a few deep breaths to clear my head after my encounter. The air is cool and salty on the tongue, and I listen to the reassuring gurgle of *Maldemer*'s gleaming hull—all forty meters, four hundred tons of it—splashing through the waves. I look up to see feathery wisps and tufts of cloud floating high above us.

I take an interest in the weather. At home I have a meteorological instrument called a barograph: a brass and walnut affair, with a chart attached to a rotating drum, on which, over a week, a nib records the atmospheric pressure. Obviously meteorologists, with their satellite images and computer modelling data, have the advantage, but you can also tell a lot just from studying the clouds.

These are cirrus—sheets of ice crystals, maybe twelve miles above us—signifying the approach of a warm front. The weather's about to change; I'd be surprised if a storm isn't heading our way.

I hear a yap and turn round. Bang on cue it's Karol-Kate and the dog. She lets him off the lead and he trots over and starts licking my ears, which are one of my ticklish areas.

"Behave yourself, Colefax," cries his custodian.

"I was hoping to bump into you two," I say. "May I join you on your walk?"

"As long as you keep up," she says crisply.

"I expect it gets a bit boring, being on your own with him all day," I say. "Have you had much to do with the other guests?"

She shrugs.

"I noticed you chatting with Marje. I bet she has some tales to tell about Hollywood—"

"We were talking about the dog. Here, boy!"

I don't think this is the full story, but Karol-Kate closes the subject down by producing a ball of socks from her pocket and initiating a game of fetch and retrieve. The dog tosses them in the air and catches them in his mouth, then every so often stops and stares, as if fascinated by something: a blade of grass caught in the breeze, or a sunbeam hitting a daisy.

The canine capacity to be entranced by the little things in life is one of their most endearing traits, and we humans could learn from it.

Karol-Kate decides the game is over and wrestles the slobbery socks out of Colefax's mouth, after which he follows us obediently down the companionway to the sky deck, then down again to the lobby. We're about to set off on the gallery walk circuit when I stop her.

"May I ask you a favor, Karol-Kate?" I wonder if her friends shorten her name, to K-K, for instance. It's such a mouthful. "I know it's off your route, but there's something on the beach deck I want to take a look at, only my keycard won't let me in."

She doesn't exactly leap at the idea, but down the Chagall staircase we go and find ourselves in the beach club.

I remember Karol-Kate mentioning this morning that Colefax doesn't care for lobsters, but I wasn't prepared for the full fury of his reaction when he spots them across the room. Jumping and snarling, he launches himself in their direction.

"Stop it, Colefax!" shouts Karol-Kate, grabbing at his collar in an attempt to reattach his lead. "Come away from there."

"What's got into him?" I say. "He's normally so good."

Eventually the dog is restrained. The crustaceans gaze morosely out of their tank, oblivious to the mutt's foaming mouth and sharp, glittery teeth.

The area I want to see is at the bow of the yacht, so we drag him away from the beach club through a long, gradually ascending corridor that curves along the starboard side of the hull and terminates at the tender garage. I haven't been here in daylight before: a porthole tells me that we're about six feet above sea level, and as I suspected, directly above CC 11 FS.

Karol-Kate touches the keypad with her card and the door swings open.

I see now that it really is a garage. These are the "toys" that come out in Caribbean waters: sea bobs, a jet surfer, inflatables, water skis and diving kit. Colefax's eye is caught by a shark-shaped object, which turns out to be an underwater drone: who knew such things existed?

In pride of place—now revealed in all its glory—is the tender: a huge shiny speedboat, done out in *Maldemer* white-and-silver livery, ready for the hatch in the bow to be opened so she can slide out into the ocean.

Or for fornication in the middle of the night.

The chair Russell was standing on last night is still in place, so I step up and peek through the tender's porthole.

I note a glass containing dregs of wine, and another of some spirit, and an ashtray. There's no doubting the lady—Elise is the only cigarette smoker aboard, and these are the distinctive brown stubs from her More Menthols.

But who was the gentleman?

Chapter 35

At dinner, once again, I arrange things so that I'm both guest and waiter, allowing me to circulate and listen in.

Unlike last night, I feel properly dressed: another beautiful, clean, crisp shirt on a wooden hanger having been delivered to my door just as I finished my shower. The hook skewered the nonchalant message *From Shane*, and today the cotton has been spritzed with a waft of a smoky fragrance. Lonestar Memories, if I'm not mistaken: a smoldering leather floral by Swiss perfumer Andy Tauer inspired by cowboys and campfires. Very *Brokeback Mountain*.

Although this sample of Shane's handwriting consists of only two words it's pleasing and regular, and (for a sportsman) surprisingly cultivated.

I wonder if he knows about Elise's nocturnal infidelities . . . you'd have to be a *very* heavy sleeper not to notice your wife slipping out night after night. And who's she meeting? My money is on Captain Romer. Women are so easily taken in by tall, dashing men in uniforms, even if they've got "CAD!" written all over them. I have a hunch Elise's none-too-subtle announcement at lunch that she was heading up on deck was directed at him, even if he didn't show up in the end. And I can't help also asking—could the dalliance be in some way connected to Xéra's murder?

Champagne is served in the grand saloon. There's no real need for Challis to hold the tray so high in the air—it's not as if she's squeezing her way through a throng—but it somehow adds to the occasion, as do the exquisite hand-engraved champagne saucers. I've done my bit to raise spirits, too: a great big (by my standards) pot of caviar having been discovered at the back of the fridge. It's only Oscietra, but it's the real thing and there's plenty to go round.

When the blini run out, I disappear to the galley for another round of canapés: this time, my signature mushroom tartlets. These are made to a secret recipe which friends and clients have been trying to pry out of me for as long as I can remember, but without success. By the time I return, everyone is clustered around Judith.

"It was quite a few years ago, in fact," says Russell disagreeably.

"Magnus Magnusson was quizmaster—such a sweetheart," she counters, spinning the stem of her glass between her fingers. To general amazement, it turns out she was a contestant on *Mastermind* in the late 1990s. My motto has always been to stick around clever people in case some of it rubs off, so I'm glad we have struck up a friendship.

"Gosh!" says Elise. "You must be so brainy! What was your specialist subject?"

"In the first round," she says, with a self-deprecating little smile, "George Bernard Shaw. In the semi-final I did Queen Elizabeth the Queen Mother, but I'm afraid I only got seven points."

"Ha! Still bloody impressive," says Shane.

"Shane met the Queen Mother," says Elise. "Didn't you, darling?"

As usual, he laughs. "I wouldn't really say "met" her: I was presented to her years ago at Wimbledon. I was a ball boy."

"I bet," says Blue, and Shane throws him a murderous glance.

Marje isn't amused either. "Cut it out, you two! And watch how much you're drinking. Just because Bill's paying your bar bill—"

Before she can finish, in walks Sir Billy, the universal benefactor.

It's astonishing how much a man can change in just a day. His tall, broad form now seems sagging and diminished; the tailored suit hanging on him lackluster. His once proud head is bowed. I half expect to see that his thinning fair hair has turned white.

No one knows what to say. Into the vacuum steps Challis with her tray of champagne, just as Elise moves in for a hug. *Crash!*

The clear-up operation takes a few minutes and helps defuse the situation. Blue wanders over to one of the many mirrors and starts examining himself for shrapnel.

"Scars never did a man any harm," comments Marje, flicking her glass with an acrylic nail to demand a refill. This may be considered polite in the Polo Lounge of the Beverly Hills Hotel but Blue curls his lip before stamping off to fetch the vodka.

Elise sits her father down at a table with a brandy before him and there is much murmuring of condolences. The guests mill around—hoovering up the champagne and caviar—and take it in turns to have a quiet word. Judith sits down beside him, takes his hand and says something in his ear, to which he nods.

Blue summons me with a finger snap to change the music, which Marje has complained is too "light." "Choose something tasteful," he says patronizingly. I'm tempted to stick on Black Sabbath or Iron Maiden at full volume just to see the look on his face, but instead settle for "Bonjour Tristesse," which was a favorite of Xéra's. I know it's a mistake as soon as I hear the introductory violins: Juliette Gréco always puts me in a melancholy mood. And this starts me thinking about the funeral. Will it be held in Paris or London? Up to Sir Billy, I suppose. I hope they go for a quiet, dignified affair rather than anything ostentatious or theatrical.

When everyone else has had their moment with Sir Billy, I take my turn to sit down beside him. Obviously, I'm desperate to talk to him about Xéra's unnatural death—how much does he know?—but not now, surrounded by flapping ears.

"I'm so sorry," I say. "She was an extraordinary woman. I consider it one of life's gifts to have known her."

We sit in silence; I wonder how many tranquillizers he's had.

"There's no need to say anything," I add.

"The necklace—the necklace," he stammers. "I feel terrible about the damn necklace..."

I sense Marje, standing guard close by, stiffen. She shakes her head in warning: *don't get him agitated.*

"Billy," I reply, looking him straight in the eye, "I want you to know Xéra adored her bridal gift—she told me it was the most beautiful thing she'd ever owned. The important thing is that you gave it to her, as a sign of your love. That's all that matters now." A bit mawkish, I know, but true. Of course, he doesn't know that I know he only paid for half of it.

"I never meant to hurt her," he adds. Grief affects people so oddly; I remember being racked with guilt when Marcus died, for tiny things I'd said or done.

Marje decides I've done enough damage and pulls me away. "Don't listen to him," she says in my ear. "He's not making much sense."

Shortly afterward, Challis ushers us into the dining saloon, gleaming as usual with its buffed mahogany, silver and crystal. Instead of the merry crackle of logs and flames, tonight she has gone for a more subdued coal fire. Living in London, it's easy to forget what a real fire smells like, especially an old-fashioned coal one, with its tarry, steam-engine aroma.

We instinctively take different places at the table from before, to make the absence of Xéra less obvious. I find myself sandwiched between Elise and the dog.

Wine is poured—a bone-dry Riesling from the Clare Valley in South Australia, intense notes of apple and grapefruit—and silence suddenly descends. For a horrible moment I think someone's going to make a speech or pay a tribute. Maybe even a poem by Auden—though, please, not that. Instead, unobserved by me because my back's to the door, it transpires it's the captain who has dropped in for his evening pep talk.

"Honored friends," he says, fine-tuning the sleeves of his shirt the better to display his biceps, "I do not wish to detain your dinner, but an update on our voyage I have. Earlier today I reported that south we would divert, in order to reach Ponta Delgada on Saturday morning. I trust this meets your approval, Sir Billy." He addresses this to the drooping figure opposite him, without receiving a response.

I'm tempted to shout out, "Oh no we're not, we're heading way off course!" but I restrain myself.

"As is always, the maritime weather reports we have been observing, and there are warnings of a low-pressure system moving toward us."

That at least is true.

"It is approaching from the southwest and strength gathering. We have the option to increase our speed, but it would be bumpy."

"I don't think my brother would appreciate any powerboat maneuvers," says Marje. "Just get us there as comfortably as you can."

"Madame," said with a deep bow, "I am confident that we will the storm to the Azores outrace."

At this point the captain claps his hands as a signal for Challis to bring in the first course. Every time I see him his manner seems more extravagant; maybe Sir Billy's not the only one on medication.

Chapter 36

Our starter is a truffled duck terrine out of the freezer. This is a sensible choice—all Bernie had to do was remove the plastic, slice it up and make a few bits of toast—but not at all to my taste. Does anyone really like truffles, or more to the point, truffle oil? I've tried my best—even hunted them with the pigs of Périgord—yet find the flavor musty and clinging, like stale garlic.

The conversation is slow, but it can't be said the guests have lost their appetite. I've noticed before that Sir Billy is inclined to take more food than he needs and put too much in his mouth at once. Even when not stricken by grief, he's an "automatic eater"—chomps away without tasting, and fails to extract due pleasure from the experience.

His sister and daughter, conversely, peck like birds. Marje must have read Muriel Spark's *A Far Cry from Kensington* because, like the novel's heroine, she always eats exactly half what she's given. Elise pretends she's tucking in, pushing the food around her plate, but takes teeny-weeny mouthfuls; when finished, I see her secrete most of the uneaten terrine under her knife and fork. Now that it's become so unfashionable to waste food, these two should probably find a different way to keep slim.

Blue eats in the American way, with his fork in his right hand. Not always the tidiest technique, but he takes dainty mouthfuls and chews with his mouth shut. When the main course arrives, it's my time to shine. The freezer has once again come to the rescue, yielding up some very acceptable racks of lamb. There's something a bit dated about a rack of lamb—I seem to remember my mum serving them at dinner parties—but not about a "cannon," which is the eye of the joint, removed from the ribs. Roast it to 131°F, leave to rest for fifteen minutes and you've a meal fit for a superyacht.

While I carve, Challis passes round the *sauce paloise*. This is identical to *sauce béarnaise*, only flavored (lightly) with mint instead of tarragon. At home I make this using my sous-vide, which means it can be frozen and reheated (yes, really); tonight I used the Thermomix, with super-fluffy results.

Seeing the meat brings a glint to Shane's eye. Indeed, there's something of the wolf in the way he smacks his lips and opens his jaws wide. While he chews he's in the moment, savoring the juices and oblivious to the chat around him. A sensuous eater, and—in that way—a man after my own heart.

Thanks to the food and wine, the tension in the room begins to unwind. Sir Billy is making quiet conversation with Russell and Marje, who flank him. Blue has discovered Judith does amateur dramatics, and wants to hear all about the West Hampstead Players, of which it seems she is a leading light. Even Karol-Kate has a glow about her, not least because Bernie has pulled out all the vegetarian stops. Piedmontese roast peppers, followed by portobello mushroom Benedict, adorned with a sloosh of the *paloise* and (not my idea) truffle oil.

"Yum," says Karol-Kate. When she's finished her mouthful, she leans across the dog and says in a low voice, "You know, I like our mealtimes together. What you were saying earlier . . . I do get a bit lonely, if you must know, just me and the dog all day."

"It makes me realize how much Xéra was always at the center of things, making sure everyone felt included."

"I'll miss her," the dog handler replies. "She was the only one who ever spoke to me. I mean, had a proper conversation."

"I'm glad you got to know her a bit," I say, wondering what she's referring to. "What sort of things did you talk about?"

It's hard enough to imagine what Karol-Kate has in common with Marje, let alone Xéra.

"She talked to me about things. You know, really opened up to me."

"When was that?"

Karol-Kate's normally inexpressive face looks momentarily stricken.

"It was the day . . . the day before she died. Me and Colefax were going through the lobby and she was sitting there."

"Was she on her own?"

"Yes. Kind of looking into space."

"Oh." Poor Xéra.

"She said Sir Billy was working in their cabin and would Colefax and I join her for a cuppa? She made us mugs of English Breakfast. It was lovely of her."

"What did she open up to you about?"

Karol-Kate takes another large mouthful, chews it thoroughly and puts down her knife and fork before answering. She reminds me of an annoying boyfriend I once had who couldn't walk and talk at the same time, which made for many a pedestrian collision.

"She told me she didn't want to worry her friends, spoil their holiday. But she needed to tell *someone*."

"What?" I say, unable to contain my excitement. "Something to do with the theft?"

"No!" says Karol-Kate. "Why do you keep going on about the necklace? All she would say was—there had been a letter."

Chapter 37

I appreciate *Maldemer* is bigger than a lot of yachts, but not so much so that you need to post someone a letter. This tantalizing snippet is all Karol-Kate knows, however. I file it away to think about later.

The evening winds up inevitably in the grand saloon, with the violet drapes drawn to reveal the Fazioli on its little stage. It occurred to me that when I heard Blue earlier, he might have been practicing his funeral repertoire for this evening, so I'm relieved when this proves not to be the case, and slightly ashamed of my own mean-mindedness.

"Any requests?" he asks.

"Give us 'Für Elise,'" says Sir Billy plaintively. "For my lovely daughter, the real Elise." She smiles indulgently and takes his hand. There are times when you're allowed to be maudlin.

Blue nods—he was probably hoping for something from Michael Bubbly—and adopts a serious expression.

Da-da Da-da Dah (poignant pause) *da-da-da DAH*. It's a repetitive little piece—not Beethoven's finest hour—and you can't blame Blue for tossing in some decorative flourishes of his own. When the melody meanders in for about the fiftieth time, I look toward Sir Billy and see him weeping silently. Marje stands up and, brushing aside Elise's offer to assist, helps the stricken figure to his feet and out of the room.

Unusually, Shane's the first to break the silence. "Great choice of music."

"It wasn't my idea," snaps Elise.

"Nor mine," says Blue.

"Probably enough for tonight," says Russell, getting stiffly to his feet. "It's been a long day for all. Judith doesn't like late nights so we'll sign off for the evening." His wife obediently follows him out.

"Let's have a hymn," says Shane.

"What's wrong with you tonight?" cries Elise. "Play us one more, Blue. Something *you* feel like playing, for once."

He scratches his head. "Something in honor of Xéra," he says. "I know she loved Sinatra." He strums a few tentative chords then breaks into song; his voice isn't bad, in a croony kind of way.

"Did you and Shane know Blue from before?" I ask Elise, with whom I'm sharing a sofa.

"Not really. Marje says we met in the Hamptons, but I don't really remember."

The song is that soupy number about three guys in love with the same girl, "Three Coins In The Fountain"; eventually it stops.

"You're so talented," says Elise, clapping enthusiastically.

"Epic," says Shane, earning himself a nasty look.

We say goodnight and I set off for CC 11 FS. Something is troubling me. Xéra disliked Sinatra—said he was a mobster and a love cheat—so why lie about it? And is there some particular reason for "Three Coins In The Fountain"? As I make my labyrinthine journey through the boat, I wrestle with this thought until finally I get it. You might say, the penny drops.

Chapter 38

Looking forward to testing my theory later, I check my laptop and the Wi-Fi signal springs to life. An email from Julie sent early this morning pings in. Since then everything has changed.

From: Julie Johnson
Wednesday 7:23 a.m.
Subject: All very strange
To: Paul Delamare/Aboard *M/Y Maldemer*

Declan was staying over and he had a rootle about on the yachting websites. Captains do have to be registered, but no sign of a Romer or Romero or even Romeo. Any other clues? *Maldemer* has a bit of a history: previously registered under the Netherlands flag and seized off Plymouth in 2021. This has tickled D's interest and he's going to see if he can find out more through his buddy network.

I've found a Karoline-Katherine Bunting-Jones— KK Autotuning, Twickenham; she remaps car engines. Declan says she must be very high-powered. Ha!

Love to Xéra—glad she approves of the tarot but warn her I'm only a beginner! The spread she mentioned looks like this:

| THE HANGED MAN. | THE FOOL. | THE HIEROPHANT |

Le Pendu is The Hanged Man—something in her past that requires her to pause, take stock. L'Excuse is The Fool—it represents innocence or making a fresh start. The Hierophant—which the French call Le Pape—is about knowledge/learning/doctrine/dogma. You don't say when she drew these cards but they're quite alarming—look at the images! Danger and darkness everywhere. What did her French reader say?

I'd love the tarot to tell us who stole the necklace, but it's not how it works. The cards don't solve problems or tell the future, they sow seeds in your mind and encourage you to look for answers within yourself.

I've only got time to draw you one card—I'm already late for swimming—so here goes . . .

THE MOON.

This is a powerful card and one to be heeded. Don't rely on appearances—things aren't how they seem. Strange imagery—anything leap out at you?

J. X

P.S. I've an idea regarding your Pâtisserie Pompadour question—leave it with me.

Remembering that I have tragic news to impart and the Wi-Fi may go down at any moment, my fingers fly across the keys.

From: Paul Delamare/Aboard *M/Y Maldemer*
Wednesday 10:22 p.m.
Subject: Catastrophe
To: Julie Johnson

43°31'91"N 28°52'66"W (about 240NM north of the Azores)

Terrible, terrible news. Xéra's dead—choked to death by a murderer. No time to tell you the whole story but I need help. Badly.

I hate to ask a favor from Declan but does he have any friends in forensics?

Here's what happened:

- 7:15 a.m. Chief stewardess leaves the beach club, having laid up breakfast

- At some point after that, Xéra arrives

- 7:55 a.m. Announcement over public address system, guests gather on top deck

- 7:59 a.m. Stewardess returns to beach club and discovers Xéra has apparently choked on her breakfast. She is unconscious and cold to the touch. Stewardess runs to fetch me

- 8:02 a.m. I arrive at beach club. Xéra's face is a yellowish color and her lips are blue. There is a strange smell—a "hospital" smell is the best way I can describe it. We perform CPR for twenty minutes without success

Please may I have a time window for Xéra's death, <u>as accurate as possible</u>? Food appears to have been forced down her throat—how might that be done? Am I correct in assuming one attacker? The boat's Wi-Fi is hit and miss—long story—but this is MAXIMUM URGENCY.

XXX

P.S. I think Blue Aspray's real name might be BLANE ASPERN. He's a snoop of some kind—a private dick? And why would he put LaGuardia after his name?

It grates being forced to call in a favor from Declan but I can see no alternative. It will make him feel as if he's been accepted into our golden circle, while as far as I'm concerned, he remains very much on probation.

Of course, it's my fault for introducing them in the first place. It's a long story, but he works with a detective friend of mine and we all went out for a drink one evening; since then they seem to be joined at the hip.

The thing is, I know she could do so much better. Guys absolutely adore her—she's living proof that men don't just go after stick-thin model types—and she deserves to be swept off her feet by a movie director, or airline pilot, or billionaire. I genuinely admire Declan for having put his terrible-sounding upbringing behind him—he was brought up on the dreaded Beaumont Estate in East London—and I'm sure he's a great cop; but that doesn't mean he's right for Julie. Besides which, as everyone knows, the police force has a shockingly high divorce rate and I don't want to see Julie hurt.

My head churning with my many and various worries, I set an alarm for 3 a.m. and drift off into an intermittent sleep. I wake up as planned and listen. *Bump bump bump.* My suspicions about the love shack in the tender garage were correct.

Chapter 39

I knew it was Elise because of the ciggies, but I was wrong about the captain. Lover boy is none other than Blue, and he's been communicating the time for their nightly assignation via his choice of songs.
"*Three* Times A Lady."
"*One*."
"*Midnight*."
And tonight, again, "*Three* Coins In The Fountain."
I wonder if Peeping Russell stumbled on the lovers by accident, during one of his insomniac rambles round the yacht, or possibly cracked their code before I did; he's a clever one and I wouldn't put it past him. I daresay he's up there now, perched on a chair and peeping through the tender's porthole. I insert ear plugs and manage to sleep.
A few hours later—we've crossed another time zone, my watch goes back again—I'm wide awake to face the day. I've agreed to lend Bernie a hand with breakfast, so I'm glad to find a fresh supply of clothes outside my cabin. It's kind of Shane, though I'll get worried if he starts sending me underwear.
By the time I arrive in the galley, the chef's already at work, chatting away.
"Dangerous habit, talking to yourself," I say.
"Oh, don't be teasing me?" Bernie replies. "If I squeeze the juice, will you make the fruit salad? I can't be doing with all the

slicing? Or—and here's a thought—we could just give it to them as fruit, the way our good Lord intended?"

"These folk are too important to do their own peeling and slicing," I say. I start off by segmenting a couple of oranges, adding a couple of pears, cut in slivers, halved black grapes and half-moons of kiwi. I love the way the colors come together to form an abstract painting. It's the same visual magic that brings a plate of tomatoes to life when you sprinkle on green herbs.

I find myself hesitating over whether to add a grapefruit to the mix, to add pink highlights, then remember the dreaded Guest Preference Book. It's the oddest thing that—of all the fruits—the humble grapefruit should contain some pesky chemical that interferes with a range of everyday drugs.

It doesn't take me long to find out that Russell, as well as being no nuts, is no grapefruit. None of my business, but he's probably on statins; blood-pressure medication too, by the look of him.

"That reminds me, Bernie," I say. "I meant to ask you something about yesterday's breakfast."

"I'd rather put it out of my mind, but fire away?"

"Whose idea was it to put the chocolate cake out on the breakfast buffet yesterday?"

"Seemed a shame to waste it. I hope you don't blame me—"

"Absolutely not, though we should really have put a nut warning on it for Mrs. Mayham and the Tates. Of course, it's irrelevant now."

I wonder if Bernie suspects that Xéra's death was foul play? I haven't said anything, and I can't see Challis taking her into her confidence either.

While we work, as a change from her usual ramblings, I ask her how she got into the yachting business. It turns out she's something of a survivor, having fled to London with a young daughter at the age of twenty-two. A couple of years ago the pair of them visited her husband (violent, ex-military) in Wexford, though the reconciliation didn't go as planned. "He came at me with a knife," she says, snatching one off the bread board and brandishing it like a bayonet. "I was ready for him—he forgot he was up against a professional?"

Professional what? "So, er, what do you do when you're not cheffing?" I ask, curious.

"This and that," she says with a toss of the head. "I started out a nurse—trained at Cork College—but one thing led to another. I worked at Heathrow for many years, but had to stop. Mental health, you see?"

"Oh, that must be so tough," I say, surprised she should want to put herself under further pressure in a busy galley.

"Black moods, panic attacks . . . But I turned the corner—back to my old self now."

"I hope you got all the help you needed."

"I'm off the meds—let's just say I've found my own coping mechanisms."

"This cruise can't have helped, though. Hardly a holiday."

"And that's only the half of it! I said I could do plain cooking, not this *MasterChef* stuff. Only came along at all because I thought the change would do me good—sea air and new faces. I'll be honest with you: when I found out what I'd let myself in for, I had a bit of a meltdown."

"Is that so?" I reply; a gin binge, if I'm not mistaken. "I'm just glad you're over it now. Did you get the job through a crew agency?"

"In a manner of speaking. Now, I think I'm done here, where's Challis when you need her?"

The chief stewardess duly arrives. One would assume breakfast this morning would be served somewhere other than the doomed beach club, but not so. "If the guests don't like it, they can take their food away and eat it somewhere else. It's not like it's a murder scene, with crime tape everywhere and coppers swarming about."

If I had my way, of course, that's exactly what it would look like.

CHAPTER 40

Bernie and I survive the onslaught of breakfast orders; if I were mathematically minded, I'd be interested to calculate how many permutations there are for a full English, taking into account the many possible ingredients, and at least eight ways to cook a breakfast egg. When it's all over, I offer to clear the beach club for Challis, so she can get on with the cabin refreshes. I want the place to myself for half an hour.

Despite the outlandish *South Pacific* atmosphere, it's a heavenly spot, with floor-to-ceiling windows and a vast skylight beaming down sunshine from the afterdeck above. The weather is different this morning—puffy white clouds being buffeted across a bright blue sky—and the sun keeps going in and out, as if it can't make up its mind.

I get the tidying and wiping out of the way, then knuckle down to the real business—a re-enactment. If this were *Crimewatch*, it would be done properly, with one actor playing Xéra, the other the murderer, but I do the best I can.

First, I run it through from Xéra's point of view. Elementary psychology tells me that the fact she chooses a chair at the far side of the room, facing in, means she is first to arrive.

There's no way my friend would be wandering about first thing in the morning without good reason; from which I can ascertain the meeting has been prearranged. She arrives first, breaking another habit of a lifetime, suggesting her mental state is one of extreme anxiety.

Next, her attacker. He or she helps him- or herself to coffee and cake, then joins Xéra at the table, taking up a place on her left (which may or may not be of significance). They make pleasant small talk until suddenly, without warning, he or she jumps up and . . . we know the rest.

I sit blinking back tears, overcome by the cruelty and horror of it all, when the clouds part and the beach club is suddenly irradiated by brilliant sunshine. The glass floats sparkle, the wooden masks smile . . . I wouldn't be surprised if the ukuleles started playing all by themselves.

It also has the effect of waking up the lobsters in their aquarium. I find the idea of keeping living creatures in a tank or cage repellent and can hardly bear to look at the poor things, waving their antennae about pitifully and studying me with sad, beady eyes. I realize with a shudder that these creatures were watching through the glass when Xéra was choked to death. If only they could talk, like Sebastian in *The Little Mermaid*, and tell me who they saw.

You'd expect lobsters to be a cheerful shade of bright red, but that's only when they're cooked. The European variety, to which these belong, are purply-blue with orange whiskers and spotty, greenish claws. And what vicious claws they are too: one for crushing, one for ripping. Get in the way of one of those and it'll take your finger off. They're fast movers, scuttling about on thin legs like underwater spiders.

Some bright spark on *Maldemer*'s design team has attempted to brighten up this depressing spectacle by the addition of underwater decorations. Hence, we have streams of bubbles rising from a miniature shipwreck of the *Titanic*. A dinky little humpback bridge is dwarfed by an inexplicable grove of mushrooms, glowing in yellow and pink. From the gravel rise many fern-like growths, billowing in the gentle slipstream.

If lobsters can register pain—which seems likely, according to new scientific thinking—I wonder how they feel about the setting in which they're forced to live out their final days. Even the gravel at the bottom of the tank isn't any color found in nature, but a rainbow mix of sparkles and scintillations.

I'm locked in a face-off with the largest of the crustaceans when I do a double take. Can it be possible? I go right up close to the glass—which gives Big Boy a shock—and peer in. Is it an optical illusion?

The aquarium is flush to the wall, with all the lighting and electrics cunningly concealed behind. My excitement rising, I inspect the area in search of an access door and find one at last, hidden behind a ceiling-high fiberglass megalith, evidently copied from Easter Island. Luck is on my side—I try my keycard and the lock clicks open. I follow a narrow passage behind the paneling and here I am, behind the lobster tank. Seen like this, rather than as a glorified window display, the aquarium looks as if it belongs in an intensive care ward, festooned with tubes and wires and linked up to a bank of displays and monitors. *Blip. Blip. Blip.*

I make my approach gingerly and dip a finger into the water. Big Boy, his eyes swivelling on their stalks, lunges at me from the depths. Whoa! Near miss.

I weigh up my options. I could fetch a pair of tongs and an oven gauntlet from the galley. Or I could distract my adversary—say, by waggling a tasty finger at him (from the safe side of the glass) while I plunge my other hand into the tank. Whatever I do, I need to act before I attract a crowd of rubberneckers, gawping through at me from the beach club.

Thinking fast, I grab a thermometer from the tank's array of maintenance bits and pieces, lower it into the water by its string, and dangle it teasingly in Big Boy's face. If he had lips, he'd lick them; instead, he snatches it with his left claw and slowly closes in on it with his right. While he tries to crush it in his vise-like grip—hear the squeak of pincer on plastic—I dive my other hand into the water, grope about in the gravel and yank out my prize.

Chapter 41

I hold up the dripping necklace and shake it gently. A shower of droplets cascades onto the surface of the water, causing a thousand tiny sparkles . . . but none so bright as the jewels themselves, which have been glittering under our very noses since they disappeared, among the artificial seaweed and tinted coral. With consummate care I untwist the ropes of gems and establish that the De Lage Treasure is undamaged. I had no idea it weighed so much. How many precious carats am I holding?

When Xéra showed it to me in her boudoir, it took my breath away, but now, under the aquarium lights, it is as if a swarm of fireflies is darting across the ceiling. Three strands are gathered at intervals to form a festoon; I can make out citrines, amethysts and tourmalines. At the connecting points are huge cushion-cut rubies. Forming a delicate tracery between and around the colored stones are hundreds of sparkling diamonds. I feel slightly heady, as if I'm riding a celestial merry-go-round.

Finally, I allow myself to stroke the colossal Pompadour-pink Padparadscha at the base of the necklace. A shiver runs up my spine.

I look around for something in which to carry it, but all I can find is a grubby plastic bag—somewhat fishy-smelling. I place the necklace delicately inside, then make my way back into the light and air of the beach club.

Here, I hesitate. Do I burst in on woebegone Sir Billy, waving the necklace at him in triumph when his dead wife will never get to wear it again? Should I entrust it to his unsavory henchman Russell? It would help if I had the faintest idea who hid the necklace in the lobster tank, and why.

In the end, with Aimee's words ringing in my ears—"*aboard ship the captain's word is law*"—I head up the Chagall staircase and through the lobby, where I almost collide with Karol-Kate and Colefax, causing the dog to start jumping up and down. He must also have caught the scent of something, because, oh, dear, he's going crazy, yelping, snapping and lunging. Before I know it, he's got my plastic bag by the corner.

"Let go, Colefax!" I cry.

"Down, boy!" bellows Karol-Kate. It's no good—he's tugged it out of my hand and is prancing round in circles like it's the county fair.

"Give that back!" I yell, trying to pull it out of his mouth. Karol-Kate produces a small chunk of cheese—Parmigiano Reggiano if I'm not mistaken—and dangles it in front of him. He drops the bag and snaffles it up.

"Must be something very delicious in that bag," she says.

"Fish food," I say. "See you later."

Chapter 42

"Sit down," says the captain sternly as I enter. I'm surprised to see Aimee here as well; normally it's just one of them—like a little Alpine weather house I had as a kid, where the *Herr* or *Frau* pops out, depending on whether it's rain or shine. "There's a matter we wish to discuss with you."

"Erm," I say, wagging a finger, "I think you'll find I'm here to see you, not the other way around."

After considerable back and forth, it transpires that Challis was sent off a few minutes ago to fetch me, but I've arrived independently and of my own accord.

"So, who's first?" I say cheerfully. It'll make a change for me to be hero of the hour; maybe they'll find a cannon and fire a salute.

"Not to *dilly-dally* . . ." begins the captain. I suspect he's got an English phrasebook in his cabin, so he can rehearse useful idioms. "We would like you to explain why a certain item in your cabin this morning was found."

Disaster! They found the chart! "Why are people always poking about in my cabin?" I say, outraged. "Aren't I entitled to a bit of privacy?"

"Routine inspection," says Aimee coolly. "It's standard procedure for crew quarters."

"I'm not crew!" I reply. "Anyway, I only borrowed it."

"I beg your pardon?" she says, genuinely puzzled.

"Your stupid chart. And while we're on the subject, I think there's a problem with your navigation system."

The captain looks at Aimee, baffled. She clears her throat and declares: "We've no idea what you're talking about, but this was found in your possession." She holds up a small plastic evidence bag labeled "CC 11 FS." "Weed," she announces. "Stashed away in your cabin."

She passes me the bag on condition I don't open it. Inside is a small pot, the kind you'd buy in a supermarket, labeled *Fines Herbes*. It's definitely cannabis—it reeks.

"Never seen it in my life," I say. "Though Bernie was looking for—" Oh, my goodness, why didn't I realize? This and gin. The chef's coping mechanism.

"You know what it contains," continues the captain. "As you are a guest, I would normally consult Sir Billy as to what action we should take. Because he remains indisposed, Aimee messaged the charter agent. I've printed out his reply, which confirms that the charter company zero tolerance of drug possession or use has, and you are in custody to be held until we reach port."

"Impossible!" I declare, snatching the paper from his hand. "This is just words on a page—anyone could have printed it out. You have no right."

"Except my authority as captain."

"You're kidding? Absolutely no way! In any case, what do you mean, "custody" . . . ? Let me go and speak to Sir Billy."

The captain shakes his head. "I am sure he will the agent's decision accept."

Aimee shrugs. "We're sorry it came to this," she says. What a turncoat—to think I considered her a friend. The tarot was right again—you can't rely on appearances.

"Look," I say, "I don't know who planted drugs in my cabin

or why, but I *swear* they're nothing to do with me. If you're planning to lock me up in my cabin—"

"Who said anything about your cabin?" replies the captain. "The first officer has a . . . *facility* organized."

"You can't be serious!" I squeal, punching my fists against my trousers. There is a crunching sound, which reminds me that all is not lost: surely when they find out about the necklace all will be forgiven. "You've got this all wrong. Now take a look at this."

"What now?" asks the captain, lounging back in his chair and stifling a pretend yawn.

I pull the shredded bag out of my pocket. "The dog got hold of it," I say apologetically. Aimee puts her hand to her nose. "It's not really tropical fish pellets."

Reluctantly, she takes the bag and slides out the contents. They look at each other, stunned, then at me.

"Well?" I say. "Want to know where I found it?"

"Give us one moment, please." *Whisper whisper.* They're probably working out what sort of reward I deserve. A free cruise, perhaps. Would it be rude to ask for cash?

"If you're hoping that your surrender of the necklace as some sort of "plea bargain" can be used, that is not how things aboard *Maldemer* work," intones the captain. "In fact, it makes us more certain than ever that you a danger to your fellow guests are."

Then he and the first officer stand up and he clears his throat. I'm horribly reminded of old movies when the judge puts on his black cap before pronouncing the death sentence. "Paul Delamere—"

"It's Dela*mare*," I snap.

Aimee rolls her eyes and he continues. "I am placing you under ship arrest with immediate effect. The first officer will escort you to a secure area where you will remain until taken into custody by the Portuguese police."

"You're crazy!" I protest.

"At least you've done the right thing returning it," says Aimee ruefully. "It'll count in your favor."

"STOP THIS NOW!" I shout, jumping to my feet. "You've got it all wrong. The cannabis was planted in my cabin. I didn't *steal* the necklace—I *found* it, for God's sake."

The captain towers over me while Aimee blocks the door. "I recommend you quietly go and as instructed by the first officer," he says.

Aimee adds, "Plenty of time to get your confession straight once you're under lock and key."

Can this be happening? As she escorts me out of the pilot house, dazed, I see the captain hold the priceless piece of jewelry in the air and twizzle it round, enjoying the firework effect. Have I just done something very stupid?

Chapter 43

Aimee insists on staying behind me, which means our conversation—or rather my attempt at it—is punctuated by grunts of *left, right, straight on, down*. They're trying to get me lost so I can't do a runner. Not a bad idea, but where would I run to?
"Don't you want to know where I found it?" I ask her.
"Next left," she grunts.
"Lock it up straight away before it gets stolen again, that's my advice."
"Next right."
If the guest decks smell of freesias and lilies, down here it's drains and machinery. We wind our way along the bilges and stop at a steel door marked ANCHOR CHAIN LOCKER. Aimee locks me inside and disappears.
In more cheerful circumstances, it would be a place of great interest to me. Forming a huge pile in the center of the space are what must be over a hundred meters of chain, one link of which is more than I could lift. You'd think anchor chain—which must get wet, by its very nature—would be rusty, but this one is sparkling stainless steel; it's probably washed and dried by the poor deckhands. Some of the links are painted in bright colors, to indicate to the crew what length of chain has been let out.

One end of it feeds through a hole in the deck above me, where the anchor must be stored. Modern anchors don't dangle about on the side of the hull; they're flush-mounted, released by a trapdoor mechanism. At the other end is the largest shackle I've ever seen, attached in turn to a colossal eye welded into the bulkhead. This is known as the "bitter end," and if ever *Maldemer* ran out of chain—for instance, in the Mariana Trench—it would ensure the anchor didn't disappear altogether.

My only comfort is a plastic chair, and my only contact with the outside world a small hatch in the door at waist level, though it's plainly intended for ventilation rather than communication. And thank goodness for that, because otherwise I'd suffocate, it's so close and airless. As she left, Aimee muttered that the crew will "look in on me" occasionally. How very civilized!

I sit down on the chair—you don't want to get caught up in anchor chain when someone starts the windlasses—and wonder how I'm going to fill the time. I could fiddle with my phone, which they fortunately forgot to confiscate, but it's not very interesting without a signal.

Another option would be to try and escape . . . but what happens after that? I was warned my keycard has been canceled, so how would I get about? It's one thing to hide something small like a necklace onboard a yacht, but a whole person? I'm pondering this when I become aware of a soft noise outside the door and a pair of eyes at the grille.

I kneel down to see who it is, which must give an alarming effect, because the person immediately jumps back.

"I didn't mean to frighten you," I say.

She puts a finger to her lips and hisses, which must be her way of saying *shhh*. It's one of the deckhands—Fish Woman. I know their quarters are at the bottom of the yacht, so she must have heard me being locked up. I don't want to get her into trouble if she's not meant to be here. "Do you speak English?"

We eye each other through the cross-hatching of the grille until I start to feel dizzy. Finally, she whispers back. "Why here?"

"Captain lock me up." I turn an imaginary key and she nods. "Why?"

Unsure how much she understands, I try a combination of words and mime. "Someone planted drugs in my cabin. And after I found the missing necklace, they accused me of stealing it." I draw a shape round my neck and wiggle my fingers to demonstrate sparkles.

Fish Woman looks blank, then asks: "Who are you?"

I could say the same to her. Instead: "I'm a friend of the woman who died." She continues to study me, without giving anything away. "She was murdered. I need to find out who did it." Does she understand?

"These other people—are they your friends?"

So she does speak at least some English. "No," I reply. "It's just me—I'm on my own. But why are you here?"

She points behind her. "We are from down there. Red door."

The locked one I heard sobbing through. I note this.

"Do not talk to us—not safe." Then she adds in an even lower voice, "When we were fishing, the fat man . . . touched me. You told him stop."

"It was horrible."

She crosses herself. "Thank you." Then, after a pause: "You need water?"

I nod.

She briefly disappears and returns with a glass of water and a straw, which she holds to the grille so I can drink a cooling draught. After that she feeds a pleated piece of paper through the mesh, which unfolds into a fan, obviously homemade. I'm impressed by her ingenuity and touched by her kindness.

"I return later," she whispers. "Remember—no one must know." She gives a little bow and disappears into the shadows. It's a lot to take in. I think again of the locked red door. Are these mysterious deckhands simply mistreated staff, or is something even more sinister going on? Forced labor? Some kind of trafficking? I'm sitting back, brow furrowed, when I catch a waft of something. I lean toward the grille and, yes, there's the gentlest of draughts fanning in the aroma. Peering out, I see a perforated steel door across the corridor—is that where it's coming from? My goodness—vanilla! Not the artificial stuff, but proper vanilla—fresh pods.

Bizarre as this is, the spice starts to work its magic. Is there anyone in the world who doesn't find the scent calming and soothing? I can almost taste the voluptuous flavor on my tongue, feel the sweet, soft grittiness of seeds between my teeth.

In terrible situations, you cling to small pleasures, and I've got my nose pressed to the grille, snuffling in the fragrance, when I see a flash of red hair.

"Hey, Challis!"

She almost leaps out of her skin. "What on earth are you doing down here?" She leans down and peers in.

"Thanks for planting the cannabis in my cabin."

I've worked it all out, you see—it can only have been Challis, living up to her nickname. She found out that Bernie had a stash of *fines herbes* and planted it in my cabin to get me into trouble. Out of malice? Jealousy, because I have a sea view and she wants it? A bit of both? Poison by name, poison by nature.

"Oh, that," Challis says. "I felt bad having to dob you in but rules are rules. I certainly didn't put it there, if that's what you're getting at."

"And you just decided to search my cabin on the off-chance?"

"Orders from on high," she says, pointing upwards.

I explain about my incarceration, and she seems genuinely sympathetic.

When I ask her why she's down here, she explains that a guest tried to touch her up while she was swabbing the afterdeck and she dropped her mop overboard. She's fetching a new one from the store.

"Don't tell me—Mr. Glum?" She nods. "I hope you're going to report him."

"Don't worry, I can look after myself. And it's OK, yachties have a saying: *do it for the tip*. In this case, I'm hoping it'll be worth my while."

"Then I'd ask for your money up front," I add, thinking back to my unpaid writing fee.

"I'll let you in on a secret," she says. "Back in Melbourne I have a bank account called "Challis Property Fund." I work on yachts for one reason alone and it ain't the sunshine or seeing the world. This Russell character could be quite profitable for me, plus I've got other irons in the fire, don't you worry."

It's infuriating to be driven to exchange confidences through a hole in the door, like a latter-day Pyramus and Thisbe. "Tell me," I say.

"Of course I'm not going to!" she says. "Let's just say I've been asked to book a speedy getaway out of Ponta Delgada, and it'll be worth my while if I pull it off."

"Good luck with that," I reply. In a flash of inspiration, I wonder if this might be Elise and Blue planning to elope; while I don't know their full romantic history, it seems a bit hasty. "You're not hoping to arrange it online, are you? Because the Wi-Fi isn't patchy by accident . . ."

I explain, and it transpires that Challis, like the rest of the crew, has been kept in the dark about the Wi-Fi situation and continues to blame the equipment for being faulty, instead of the charter agent.

"Well, thanks for the heads-up," she says. "Romer's on duty and I'm heading up there now. Maybe he'll give me half an hour online if I treat him nice." I watch through the grille as she pulls a shiny new mop out of a cupboard and strokes it suggestively. "And if you're still wondering who planted the drugs in your cabin, how about your mate Aimee?"

With this, a saucy wiggle of hips and a flick of Titian hair, she disappears from view.

I don't know why she's got it in for Aimee—and I still believe she planted the drugs—but she obviously knows how to rub the captain up the right way: within five minutes I glance at my phone and the Wi-Fi's on.

Jubilate! An email from Julie, sent last night.

CHAPTER 44

From: Julie Johnson
Thursday 12:50 a.m.
Subject: Thinking of you
To: Paul Delamare/Aboard *M/Y Maldemer*

Just opened your email. I'm truly <u>devastated</u> to hear about Xéra.

Declan's had to go away—something hush-hush—but he's got your questions and knows they're super-urgent. Promise me <u>please</u> not to get involved. Call it female intuition if you like, but I smell danger. <u>Grave danger</u>.

More bad news, I'm afraid. I opened the legal letter.

It's from a firm called Waister Timon Hassall asking questions about the flood. Their client "Jonathan Berens, Esquire" (makes him sound almost respectable) is accusing you of "wilful neglect" of the Jubilee Cottage property. He claims the terms of the usufruct have been breached and an eviction notice will be served in thirty days. They're also demanding that any remedial work should be ceased immediately, pending a report by their surveyor (at your expense).

I checked out the company, by the way, and it's one of those "no win, no fee" outfits. Vultures.

I was thinking about poor Xéra's cards: she was in danger, and they were trying to warn her. I've done a reading for you. I hope it may be of some use.

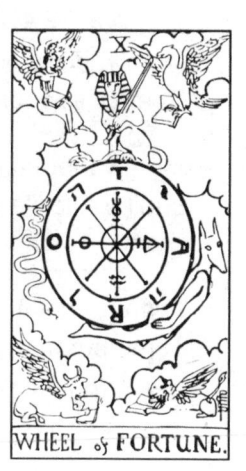

Astrologically speaking, the first two cards represent water signs. (They speak true!) Wheel of Fortune means, literally, all change. Turbulence ahead: be prepared.

J. X

P.S. More yellow leaves, I'm afraid. Someone suggested watering with tea, so I gave everything a dose of Earl Grey. Fingers crossed.

From: Paul Delamare/Aboard *M/Y Maldemer*
Thursday 12:00 p.m.
Subject: Heading home
To: Julie Johnson

42°24'16"N 33°11'68"W

A short reply because I'm on my phone and you know I'm not great with my thumbs. Yes, things are somewhat tense, but please don't worry.

I realize Declan is very methodical and doesn't like to be rushed but can you get him to step on that forensics report?

I <u>knew</u> that letter was bad news. Now I'll have to shell out for legal advice—more money down the drain.

I can hardly think straight at the moment but there's something preying on my mind—Sir Billy. If he's a multimillionaire, he must have made it somehow. Can you do some digging around?

Update on travel plans: we're being chased by a storm but should reach Ponta Delgada at latest by Saturday; I'm not going to worry about flights home till we land. XXX

I continue to feel sorry for myself, then decide some exercise might lift my mood. I walk round and round my tiny quarters in circles till I'm dizzy, then sit sharply back down. As I do so the pocket of my trousers snags on my thigh and brings to my attention that I'm still carrying round Xéra's envelope containing the precious recipe.

I really should have put it somewhere safe. What if it were confiscated, and lost to the world? Hearing the approach of footsteps, I look around in panic and tuck it into a chain link, hidden from view.

"It's your old friend Bernie," a jovial voice declares. "Thought you might be getting lonely?"

"Did they send you to check on me?"

I see a nodding motion at the grille.

"Are you going to let me out? Maybe your trick with the hairpin?"

"A little birdie told me you handed in the necklace?"

"Are they saying I stole it?"

"Let's just say, the chief stew might have heard so from Captain Romer, and you know our Poison—she has to tell the world and his uncle. Thank goodness, we can all relax! As Mam used to say, it's worth losing something for the joy of finding it. Where did you hide it?"

"I'll tell you when I get out," I say sarcastically.

"I heard about the drugs too. I'm sure they'll take pity on you when they know you're sorry."

Unbelievable! She should be the one in prison, not me.

"Favor to ask, if you're not busy?" she continues, then realizes it's unlikely. "I've decided on paella for the guests tonight" she pronounces it *pea-hella*—" and the recipe says use paprika. I've got the sweet paprika, I've got the hot paprika, I've got the smoked sweet paprika and I've got the smoked hot paprika. What do you say I add them all, spice things up a bit?"

"Nope," I grunt. "Just the sweet smoked. Definitely *not* hot."

This woman knows nothing at all about cooking—how did she talk her way into the job?

She patters away, then returns a second later, muttering, "Bernie, Bernie, you'll be forgetting your head next. Here, Paul, I brought your lunch?"

In the circumstances a wrap would be more practical, but

she somehow manages to feed the sandwich through the grille and I reassemble it on my side. Fish paste—who eats that nowadays? That said, I realize I'm hungry and it's all that's on offer. I devour it greedily.

"You'll feel better now?" she says.

Julie's card warned me of turbulent times ahead, and the boat seems to be swaying more than before. Maybe it's the stuffy atmosphere—a lack of oxygen. More likely exhaustion, after the events of the last few days, and then this morning.

A feeling of dread passes over me. Am I being poisoned by carbon monoxide? But then, I relax. In fact, it isn't unpleasant—no, not at all.

I unfold Xéra's recipe and gaze at it. My eyes aren't focusing properly, but what beautiful writing. The word *Maudie!* swims before my eyes, and transforms into a vision of a beautiful mermaid, and then into something horrible—a sea snake.

I fumblingly return the envelope to its nest in the chain link, slump back in the bucket chair and close my eyes. That's better. Oh, how comfortable it is, like a luxurious feather bed. Several feather beds, suspended in the air.

My head nods forward. I haven't felt so sleepy for years. My eyes close, and there's absolutely nothing I can do about it.

Dimly, I hear a scraping sound—someone unlocking the door—followed by the click of the light switch. My eyes flick open too late—it's pitch black.

Next thing I know an arm has been hooked round my throat and I can't breathe. I struggle a bit but there's no fight in me. My eyes spin with phosphenes, I feel myself floating and—I'm out.

Chapter 45

Yaah! I'm savagely shocked back into consciousness. For a millisecond I think I've been thrown from a great height and hit the ground head-first, then a freezing sensation clamps itself around my scalp and slices through my body.

Oh my God—I've been thrown into the sea!

I feel myself bob to the surface, gasp for breath and sink down again. I can't move—I'm paralyzed. Panicking, I concentrate all my energy into my legs and succeed in kicking out.

I burst through the surface, sucking in a lungful of air. My clothes drag me back down and I kick and punch again until I can grab another breath. This time I open my eyes—blurred by froth and salt—and see an immense gleaming white wall towering overhead.

Breathe, I order myself. *Breathe.* It's my only hope of survival. I need to regulate my breathing and work out what to do. Thankfully, whatever I was doped with has worn off—or rather, been neutralized by a massive burst of adrenaline.

I know that if you fall overboard the most urgent thing is to get out of the boat's wake, so as not to be drawn into its propellors—jet engines in the case of *Maldemer*—and so I hurl myself backwards, arms churning in the surf. I look up again to see two man-size flaps in the bow closing, like the power-assisted doors at a supermarket, and realize that's how I ended up here: someone threw me out of the anchor hatch.

I continue to backstroke and reverse butterfly—thank God for swimming lessons—but can't seem to get clear. As well as flailing and thrashing, I now start screaming and launching myself out of the water, dolphin-style, to call attention to my plight. Where is everyone? Why is no one out on deck, looking for me?

Just when my heart is about to burst through my chest, there's a dangerous development. I feel myself begin to turn, feet first, then twist, then spin. The whirlpool caused by the yacht's jet engines is sucking me down, down, down. This is exactly what I didn't want to happen. I feel freezing water slop into my lungs and seep into my ears. Streaks of color and flashes of light burn my eyes, salt fills my mouth.

This is the end, I think to myself. I'll be sliced in pieces by the churning turbines. At least it will be quick.

What seems like minutes later, I bob semi-conscious to the surface and gulp in a vast lungful of air: oxygen has never tasted as sweet.

I briefly take stock. I've somehow survived being shredded, but I have a new problem: the yacht is sailing away without me.

I do a bit more yelling. I can't hear myself over the engine noise and I'm sure no one else can. I wave my arms about as best I can, but it's so exhausting I have to give up. Then I have an idea: with great difficulty, because my fingers have lost all feeling, I unbuckle my belt, slide it off and wave it in circles over my head. The yacht continues to glide away from me.

While dealing with my belt, I'm reminded of my pockets. My fumbling fingers manage to fish out my dingle-dangle *Maldemer* keycard, with Xéra's whistle attached. I know lifebelts come equipped with whistles, so there must be some point to them. Peeeeep. Peeeeep. Peeeeep. Peeeep. Peeeep. It's surely too high-pitched to be of any use—someone should complain to Hermès—but there's nothing else I can think of, so I keep this up. *Peeeep. Peeeep.*

The sloping stern is emblazoned with the name *Maldemer* in huge mirrored lettering. As the yacht recedes, I see the letters twinkling in the sunlight. This gives me a new idea.

I return my whistle and keycard to my pocket—there's enough litter in the oceans already—and pull out my iPhone. I recently invested in a new model, thankfully waterproof.

No signal, but I know it's pre-installed with a mirror app, so you can check your eye makeup's evenly balanced and you haven't got a lump of parsley stuck to your incisor. I open the app and start twizzling the phone above my head; after a while, thanks to a helpful sunbeam, I see my flashes landing on the stern of the boat. In an ideal world I'd employ the SOS signal—*flash flash flash f-l-a-s-h f-l-a-s-h f-l-a-s-h flash flash flash*—but it's impossible to keep in time as I bob about in the water, so I just keep flashing rhythmically until the outsize vessel has shrunk to the size of a weekend cruiser. Then I acknowledge defeat.

By now, I'm acclimatized to the water. It's not as cold as I thought it would be. When I last emailed Julie, we were roughly lined up latitudinally with northern Spain, and I can feel the warmth of the sun on my head, as well as a stinging sensation. At the same time, the waves are big. Up and down I go. Up and down.

I rub my head then look at my hand. Blood—I must have taken a scrape while being dragged out of the chain locker. Inevitably, my thoughts turn to sharks. They're not all dangerous—you'd be very unlucky indeed to encounter a great white out here—but it would put the tin lid on things to see a triangular fin circling in on me.

No, if I am about to die, I will think only cheerful thoughts. Like . . . Julie!

Marcus aside, she's the best thing that ever happened to me—she is light and joy and laughter. I pretend not to take her seriously, but she's right about so many things, and so are her cards. If I had my time again, I wouldn't be mean about Declan either: it's only that I'm jealous of the place he's starting to make for himself in her life. Wish I'd said that when I had the chance.

I can't pretend the last few days have been a barrel of laughs, but I'll miss yachtboard life, too—the personalities, the sea air, even the crazy décor. As for poor Xéra... will they ever find who murdered her? Will someone fight for justice for her when I'm no longer there to do it?

I'm not religious, but something gives me the idea of running through the Lord's Prayer, after which I sing a couple of hymns. Or rather, sing the first line then hum the rest, because I can never remember the words. After that, "Here, There And Everywhere" by the Beatles, and "Here Comes The Sun." I feel the waves moving in time with the music.

By this time, *Maldemer* is a small white square in the distance, with a little white V of wake fanning out behind.

I feel oddly serene. I guess I just bob up and down here until... what? I fall asleep and sink? I'm raised into the clouds by a host of cherubim and seraphim? Maybe I'll soon be seeing Marcus, because wherever he's gone, I'm going too. I feel at peace, and ready.

Chapter 46

I remember my grandparents complaining that food used to "repeat" on them: cucumbers, pickled onions, peppers and so on. Whatever my sandwich was spiked with earlier on seems to be making a similar comeback. I feel sleepy and my eyes are playing tricks. I've lost all sensation in my legs, though I can still apparently move them. And the yacht has changed shape, from a square into a slim white rectangle.

I veer between treading water and floating while I allow my thoughts to drift back to *Maldemer* and the mystery of who threw me overboard. It was planned, presumably by the same person who killed Xéra. Did they think I was on their trail?

The drugged sandwich must have originated in the galley, which points to a crew member; or perhaps a guest and a crew member in collusion. Everyone says yachties are mercenaries, and I imagine an assassination would merit a munificent tip.

By now the rectangle in the distance seems a little larger . . . must be an optical illusion. Strange that I can no longer see the faint twinkle of mirrored lettering on the stern. I blink to focus. My goodness, it's turned and is coming back in my direction.

I would pinch myself, except I'm too numb. Can it be true? Have I been given another chance?

I feel like screaming at the top of my voice and splashing my arms and legs, but I stop myself. My problems are far from over. It's practically impossible to be seen in the water, even when conditions are mill-pond flat, let alone in choppy waves with little licks of foam and sparkles of sunshine attracting the eye in all the wrong directions. Wearing something bright instead of marine blue might have helped me.

I get out my whistle in readiness, and check I haven't dropped my phone. I can make out someone leaning out from the bow like a figurehead, holding binoculars, and a group of people on the lawn deck, waving and pointing. I put my whistle in my mouth—*peep peep peep*—and with great care, because my hands feel so cold and clumsy, remove my phone. As I do so I realize I didn't turn it off, so it must have been mirroring all the time it's been in my pocket. I'm glad it wasn't switched to record because that would make one helluva boring video . . . although unfortunately the battery's gone flat.

I continue whistling as the yacht comes toward me, and waving back to the people on deck, who make no signs of seeing me. By now, *Maldemer* is only fifty meters away. If I had more energy I could swim there, but they still haven't seen me. I try screaming—I've been saving what's left of my voice for this moment—but the engine noise drowns me out.

That, I suppose, is that. So much for a last-minute reprieve. I'm grateful to have already said my goodbyes.

Except . . . Except . . . Except that—if I'm not seeing things in my final delirium, the yacht is now turning in my direction . . . and the figurehead (who I now see is a man) has dropped his binoculars and is racing up to the pilot house . . . and the stick figures on deck are jumping up and down and cheering as if they're at a football match . . . and someone is holding Colefax in the air and jiggling him about . . . and he's yapping and waving his paws . . . and the handsome captain is at his wheel shouting orders into a microphone . . . and the glistening yacht, with a shower of spray, flips round so that I am astern . . . and the beach club jetty lowers itself majestically into the sea . . . and onto it step three figures armed with lifebuoys and a boathook . . . and . . . it's going to be OK.

Chapter 47

I was resigned to death but I've been summoned back from the threshold. Life hasn't finished with me yet, and I will make the most of it, so help me God.

I'm hauled up onto the pneumatic jetty at the stern of *Maldemer* by her crack rescue team: Challis, Blue and Karol-Kate (the latter in charge). They're as wet as I am by the time I'm landed, like a flapping, ungainly fish. Slapped down on the boards, bruised, battered and with a raging thirst, I mumble a few words of thanks to my rescuers and pass out.

I come to on one of the beach club loungers, gazing up at nets and faux-Tahitian fishing tackle. I'm glad I missed the ignominious experience of being carried in, undressed and cocooned in towels, though perhaps my being unconscious made it easier for them. As my vision swims into focus I find Aimee kneeling beside me.

"You are one lucky sonofabitch," she says. Her usually sweet face is furrowed with concern. I'm not the only one shocked by the narrowness of my escape. "The chances of finding you in the ocean—a million to one."

"I—someone . . ." I croak. My throat feels as if I've been swallowing razor blades. I notice the jetty has been drawn up and the doors and windows closed; outside a flag is flapping wildly in the wind.

"What Captain Romer and I can't understand," she continues, resuming her usual first officer manner, "is how you broke out of the chain locker without damaging the door."

"I didn't! Someone came in, tried to strangle me. I blacked out. Then I woke up in the sea."

"Are you sure? But... I don't understand. We assumed you were trying to hide and fell overboard... You mean someone did this to you? That's horrific. Who?"

I shake my head.

She presses both hands to her face in disbelief. "You must have seen *something*. How many of them were there?"

"N-no idea. The l-light went out and an arm came round my throat." I raise my elbow weakly to demonstrate.

"Man or woman? Did someone hold you down while it happened?"

"I—I—I d-didn't see them," I stammer. "N-no way of kn-nowing."

"And you can definitely say you have no idea who did this to you? It's just that—we need something to go on if we're to launch an investigation."

"Bernie brought me a s-sandwich. I think there was something in it," I say. "It made me sleepy."

Aimee shakes her head. "I don't think that's possible. The guests had sandwiches for lunch. A few came back from the dining saloon uneaten, so I asked Bernie to take you down one of those. It certainly didn't look as if it had been tampered with, and why would anyone do such a thing?"

She's right. I'm just not thinking straight.

"Please don't tell me you're going to put me back in the chain locker," I croak.

"In view of what's happened... and the captain took some persuading, I don't mind telling you... no, we're not. Not for the time being." Without further ado she stands up to go. I reach out to her—she's a friend after all, and I could do with some aboard this doomed vessel.

"Aimee, I'm absolutely terrified," I say to her back. "Someone just tried to kill me. Let's look out for each other, right?" She half turns and gives me a thumbs-up.

After she's left, I feel a tear trickle down my face, and soon I'm weeping in earnest. I can't tell whether it's because I feel sorry for myself, all alone in the world; or shock, after so nearly drowning; or gratitude for having cheated death; or a combination of all three.

Fortunately, Karol-Kate arrives with a mug of hot sweet tea, sits down on the adjacent lounger and takes my hand. Gradually I feel warmth and energy start to course through my veins. My life force rallies.

"So, what happened?" she says quietly. I tell her the story of my incarceration on false pretences and being thrown into the sea. She is genuinely horrified.

"Do people really believe I stole the necklace?" I ask.

"Oh that," she says. "The story going about is that you hid it in the fish tank, then miraculously "found" it when it suited you. Otherwise, how would you ever have known it was there?"

"Rubbish," I declare. "Of course I didn't steal it. And I only found it thanks to Colefax."

She raises an eyebrow.

"Do you remember him going berserk, jumping up at the lobsters?" I continue. "I must have registered it unconsciously, that there was something in there that shouldn't be."

"I think we're in for a change of weather," she says, with an abrupt change of subject. She's right: on the starboard horizon is a low bank of pale gray cloud, like a distant mountain range. "I don't like the look of that."

We sit in silence for a few more minutes, then I say, "Thanks for fishing me out of the water—you were amazing."

She gives a modest little harrumph. "Again, it's the dog you should thank. He's the one who saved your life. We were up on the lawn deck enjoying a game of fetch when he started going ballistic. I haven't seen him so excited since . . . well, since Xéra, you know . . .

"He dragged me to the afterdeck, stood at the rail, put his head back and howled—simply wouldn't stop."

"He must have heard me whistling. So what happened after that? Tell me everything."

She describes picking up the dog—which didn't please him at all—and carrying him to the lawn deck. Looking out to stern, she saw a light flashing in the water and reported it to Captain Romer.

"That was me, signaling to the boat."

At this point the first officer arrived and swore it was just sunlight reflecting off the sea. It turned into quite an argument between her and the captain, but in the end he ordered her to turn the yacht around.

"I get the impression he didn't know how to do it himself," explains Karol-Kate. "After that, they turned on this cool device called a Personal Locator Monitor. A siren started screeching and *MAN OVERBOARD* came up in flashing blue lights—it must have been activated by your keycard. After that, everything happened very quickly. We all went out on deck to look for someone in the sea. And Piano Man managed to spot you using his binoculars."

It's a staggering story, containing so many strokes of grace and good fortune that I almost forget someone first saw fit to drug me and shove me overboard to die in the water. I feel a clutch in my throat and blink back more tears, at which point the foghorn sounds and the public address system booms into life: "*Mr. Delamare, please report to the captain immediately.*"

Chapter 48

Karol-Kate offers to help me up to the pilot house. As we climb the Chagall staircase, with its dreamlike images of floating couples and angels in luminous pinks and purples, it comes into my head that I've been spared for a purpose: I will bring Xéra's killer to justice, even if I have to die in the process. Which I very nearly just did.

The captain doesn't invite me to sit down, perhaps out of concern I'll drip onto his upholstery, which is unlikely, enveloped as I am in 900-thread-count cotton toweling. I don't like toweling robes at the best of times—they amplify one's shape and make movement ungainly; one reason (among many) I don't like spas. There's also the easy access/wardrobe malfunction problem, which is why I hope I won't bump into Shane.

Romer starts off with his usual little cough and looks me up and down. Then, in a stern voice: "Following the unfortunate incident, I wish to inform you that you will not be returned to confinement, but you will remain under observation." He seems to have less swagger than usual. His eyes keep flickering to starboard, where the ominous cloud bank is gathering.

"What are you going to do about my being thrown overboard?"

He looks away. "It is common for important guests with

their own security to travel, but Sir Billy chose not to. I don't have a shotgun to lend you, if that is what you are suggesting."

"But you're in charge. You can't just pretend it didn't happen."

He raises a tweezered eyebrow. "All I can suggest is locking yourself in your cabin. Unless you are frightened an assassin will crawl in through the porthole."

"It's hardly a joking matter."

"Please note, I am briefing the guests at eighteen hundred hours, attendance compulsory. One other thing," he adds. "As a result of your . . . adventure . . . we have lost time and the weather system is fast approaching." He points toward the water, where white horses run free. "The chef has requested that in the event we need to consolidate the galley against rough weather, you will assist her tomorrow morning."

"Why should I cooperate when you do nothing to protect me?" I say.

"Because we are very short-handed. In bad weather, of all aboard it is expected—"

I think quickly. "I'll do it on one condition."

"You are not in a position to—"

"I'll help the chef tomorrow as you ask—but I need the Wi-Fi turned on. Now."

"Impossible," he says.

"It'll only take a minute."

He shakes his head—we're at an impasse.

Ignoring me, he removes a metal flask from the cupholder at the side of the control console, unscrews the top and pours himself some coffee. An idea comes to me.

"You know what would go down well with that?" I say, in a wheedling tone. "Some of those delicious Austrian cookies we were talking about."

He involuntarily licks his lips.

"*Vanillekipferl*, for instance. Fresh from the oven."

He flicks me a look then shuts his eyes, dreaming of the

warmth and sweetness of the vanilla, the soft, buttery crunch rolling round on his tongue. "*Mit Puderzucker bestäuben?*" he asks quietly.

I make a motion with my hand, as if sifting fairy dust. "Of course: sprinkled with icing sugar."

He puts out his hand, which I shake, and without further hesitation presses a couple of buttons and twirls a knob. "The Starlink takes ten minutes to initialize, then five minutes you will have to sort out your email. Do not tell the others. Or the first officer."

Unbeknownst to the captain, during this conversation I succeeded in maneuvering myself into a position from which I could see a huge shiny capstan outside the window. Reflected in this, in large numerals (mirror-image, obviously) is our current course on the compass. Something else for me to check when I get to my cabin.

Alas, I don't get very far, because my keycard is dead. Seeing Challis through the doors of the grand saloon, I rap on the glass.

"What is it?" she huffs, letting me in. "Better be quick—I'm in the middle of candle-izing." It's not a word I've come across, but the meaning is plain: every surface is strewn with candles and tea lights, nestling in colored glass jars or arranged on decorative dishes. "Guest birthday," she adds, standing back to admire the display.

I wonder whose—but I'm not sorry I'll miss it. It's a snack, some bottles of Evian and an early night for me.

"My keycard isn't working."

Tutting, she comes to the door. "I'll buzz you into the service area now, but it's going to make life very difficult if you pester us every time you need to go somewhere. Come and find me later. I've a spare I may be able to lend you. And don't drip on the carpets."

I make my way to the galley, knock on the door and Bernie lets me in.

"Jesusmaryandallthesaints!" she exclaims. "'Tis Lazarus himself. How are you feeling?" Fish Woman is at her side peeling vegetables; as agreed we make no indication of recognizing each other.

"Getting there," I reply. "And I'd go slow with those onions if I were you—maybe add a splash of water." It feels trivial to be offering cookery advice after what just happened, but if she takes the base for her pea-hella too far the whole dish will taste burnt.

At this point I feel a clutch of anxiety. I need to be very careful of what I eat in case someone tries to drug me again.

"You had us all scared sideways," she breezes. "What brings you here?"

"Would you mind letting me into my cabin?"

"Door was flapping open when I passed earlier," she replies. "Nice little cabin like that, you'd do well to keep it tidier?"

When I get there, it's a rerun of Monday night, except the door is merely wide open rather than ripped off. I tidy up, plug in my phone to charge and fire up my laptop. True to the captain's word, the Wi-Fi's on, and I've not one but two messages fresh in.

Remembering we're two hours behind, I realize with a chill that they must have arrived while I was in the water, preparing to meet my maker.

Chapter 49

From: Julie Johnson
Thursday 5:10 p.m.
Subject: Are you OK?
To: Paul Delamare/Aboard *M/Y Maldemer*

Declan's sending the forensics results—terrible, terrible. There's stuff you're not telling me, I know it. <u>Watch your back.</u>

First, I've got the low-down on Russell Tate. You didn't tell me he wears a toupee . . . Disappeared from the City eighteen months ago after a Me Too moment involving an intern; by no means the first. The journalists rather miss him as he has a reputation for being "generous with information" if you oil him up with a few G&Ts or dinner at the Coq d'Argent.

Now, Sir Billy. He's evidently had his Google results wiped clean by one of those "reputation management" agencies, so I put it out to the press cuttings agency we use at work. Not much, but here goes:

- At a 2018 meeting of the Parliamentary All-Party Betting & Gaming Group he's described as "a stain on the profession of bookmaking."

- A year later Boris knights him for services to the online gambling industry. (Sleazy even by Tory standards.)

- Houses in London and Yorkshire—the Harrogate one had a big burglary eighteen months ago.

- I reckon Xéra must be <u>at least</u> wife number three.

Absolutely nothing on this Aspray/Aspern character, which is odd in itself. LaGuardia being in New York, I've messaged you-know-who. The things I do for you . . .

Don't think me frivolous, with all that's going on at your end, but I've read your cards. And don't blame me when they come out upside down—nothing to do with my shuffling.

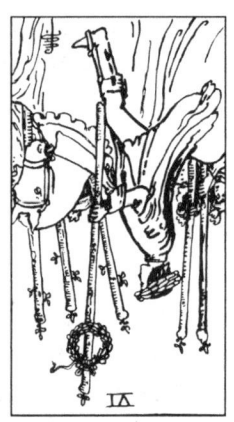

Justice represents truth; here it's reversed, which suggests it's warped, or someone is actively concealing it from you. I think this links to your third card: the Knight of Swords is the private investigator of the tarot deck—clever, fast-thinking, resourceful. Perhaps he's hiding from you?

The Six of Wands often represents health and well-being. Reversed, the opposite. I know I keep saying it, but take care and avoid risky situations.

The idea of tarot is that we work together to understand what the cards say, so may I have some feedback, rather than you pretend it isn't happening?

I drew an extra card and it was Ace of Cups. Cups keep coming up for you—I'd have thought with all those moneyed people round you we'd be seeing Pentacles—and Cups mean romantic attraction. Hmm. Anything you ought to be telling me?

Love you. J. X

From: Declan Armstrong (personal)
Thursday 5:21 p.m.
Subject: UNOFFICIAL Forensic analysis
To: Paul Delamare/Aboard *M/Y Maldemer*

Dear Paul,

Julie suggested I should email you direct. Regarding information I have acquired for you (regarding your recent Unfortunate Event, for which, please accept my heartfelt and deep condolences). Note: I am sending this from my personal email account, this not being official police business, for reason of it being a personal favor, and please Confidential.

My Forensic Examiner friend says: (I summarize) note this is an informal report based on inadequate information

Body cool to touch/lips pale blue (possibly purple tint)/ skin yellowish = death has occurred 15–25 minutes previously. Odor would normally be detectable at +25–30 minutes, so ToD = c. 25 minutes before discovery.

Assailant would need to be stronger/larger than victim in order to restrain them while forcing food down throat. This form of attack would inevitably lead to significant bruising round throat/neck area, visible immediately.

Paul, this is not much but if it is useful; it has been Worthwhile.

As per request via Julie: I apologize for not yet having been able to make a site reconnoiter of deceased's former business premises off St. John's Wood High Street, as previously offered: It is on my to-do list to do, to be done at the first available Juncture.

Warm regards:-

Declan

Writing obviously doesn't come naturally to Declan—he's probably more at home filling out forms about noisy neighbors and double parking—but, in my new spirit of open-mindedness and acceptance, I reply thanking him for everything he's doing. He *is* going out on a bit of a limb for me, in fairness. Later on, I'll go through the forensics notes carefully to make sure I've understood everything. It'll be interesting if he turns anything up at the old Pâtisserie Pompadour site in St. John's Wood, too. Great idea of Julie's to have him scope the place out with his professional eye.

As for my lovely friend, I'm more impressed by her research skills than I am by her tarot readings. (Romantic attraction—as if!) I can well imagine Sir Billy choosing to conceal the source of his wealth as—thanks to Xéra—he climbed a few more rungs on the social ladder. No surprise either that sleazebag Russell has a secret or two to hide. Some wives turn a blind eye, but I'd wager that Judith has no idea what she's actually married to.

Which leaves Blue. Who the hell is he, underneath the fake name(s)? If anyone can find out, it's Julie.

Julie! Where would I be without her? I laugh about her fads and fancies but you'll never meet anyone more diligent or thorough. A few years ago, after a holiday in Lisbon, she announced she intended to learn Portuguese. Like many musicians (she plays the clarinet) she has an ear for languages, and nowadays when we go up to Golborne Road for *pastéis de nata* she chats away like a *tuga*.

We now seem to have entered a "spiritual" phase: last year it was I Ching, then astrology. This coincided with an extremely irritating period when she would only communicate in emojis. And now tarot. What'll it be next?

Before I reply to her, however, there's something I want to check. Working quickly, I open Compass on my phone and mark *Maldemer*'s current position on the chart. In the vastness of the Atlantic Ocean, we are a tiny pinprick.

Thanking my lucky stars the operation doesn't involve a pelorus or sextant, I line up 236°, as observed in the pilot house, and pencil in our course.

According to an inset on my chart the currents in this part of the ocean at this time of year are easterly; I would guess in today's conditions these are more than canceled out by the strengthening wind from the west.

In which case, I can confirm we're definitely going to miss the Azores, and by an even wider margin than before.

But what's this? The line seems to point straight to a tiny triangle. At first, I think someone must have been doodling on the chart, but it's marked in tiny letters: LACUNA. I magnify the image with my phone, wondering if it might be some manmade object—a rig or windfarm—but no, it's a tiny jagged island. Not one I've ever heard of and with no distinguishing characteristics. Is it just a rock sticking out of the ocean? Is it inhabited?

From: Paul Delamare/Aboard *M/Y Maldemer*
Thursday 5:47 p.m.
Subject: Lacuna
To: Julie Johnson

41°13'04"N 37°41'55"W

Lots happening—I won't bore you—but quick question while I've got the Wi-Fi on my side.

Just out of interest: what can you find out about a small island—more of a rock really—called Lacuna, in the mid-Atlantic? No big deal, just idle curiosity.

If you feel like a break from pillow talk, maybe teach Declan some grammar and punctuation? Also the use of capital letters? Joking—I'm grateful for his help, even if it turned out to be a wild goose chase.

Love you.
P XXX

Chapter 50

The foghorn blasts and Challis looms up on my TV screen to summon all guests to an "extraordinary briefing" in the grand saloon. Her Australian accent twists the vowels in "ek-STRAW-din-ree" to make the event sound more exciting than it's likely to be: maybe the captain will arrive in full drag, or Blue and Marje will treat us to an exhibition cha-cha-cha.

My instinct is to curl up and hide, but time is running out on my investigation. Nor dare I risk the captain's ire if I don't show up.

My supply of borrowed clothes has run out, so I have to fall back on my child-size wardrobe. I pick out a shriveled dark shirt and khaki chinos. My thighs look and feel like sausages, so tightly are they encased in fabric, and I squeak my way to the grand saloon.

Because I can only take shallow breaths, I'm hyperventilating by the time I reach the sky deck. Heeding the warning of Julie's upside-down card, I pause to recover: no point in fainting in front of everyone and making a spectacle of myself.

The glass doors whoosh open and I discover I'm last to arrive. Someone wolf-whistles—that'll be Shane—then conversation stops dead. It's not just my appearance that's embarrassing; my fellow guests must be torn between congratulating me on having survived, and shunning me for having stolen the necklace.

I decide to brazen it out and stride into the room with panache, in the style of John Wayne. It's a mistake: there's a ripping sound and I realize the seat of my trousers has split. Thinking quickly, I tug my shirt down at the back but this makes things worse: a button pings off my front, landing softly on the Persian carpet in front of me.

Elise is first to speak. "You look pale," she says. *So would you if you couldn't breathe.*

"Washed out," says Marje. Not that funny but they all go ha ha ha, and the dog starts barking merrily. In a futile attempt to make myself invisible I settle down between Judith and Russell and attempt to cross my legs—more ripping—to await the arrival of the captain.

The swell seems to be increasing by the minute and the wind has started whistling. Russell—top heavy at the best of times—stands up then slams down as the yacht crashes into a wave. After this, he lollops across to the bar, leaving me to entertain his wife. If these two are examples of the joys of married life, you can keep it.

Judith has made an effort this evening with a dab of blusher and a long beaded jacket, rust-colored.

"Happy birthday!" I say, taking a calculated guess. With her bright eyes and stiffly brushed hair, she reminds me more than ever of Squirrel Nutkin.

"It's lovely to spend it among friends," she says, doubtfully. Not for the first time I feel sorry for her—you couldn't exactly call it a festive atmosphere, with Sir Billy steeped in silent gloom and Shane slopping brandy down his shirt.

Judith starts rootling about in her handbag—I half expect her to produce an acorn—and pulls out a rather ordinary birthday card, the sort you'd pick up at a petrol station: "To My Dear Wife."

There's something so pathetic about it: inside it just says "R.," not even "XXX." I get the sense she's reaching out to me, wanting me to be her friend.

"I don't know if it's public knowledge," I say in a low voice, "but I didn't fall into the sea. Someone half strangled me and pushed me overboard."

She blinks nervously. "I thought your neck looked sore." Then she adds, in a serious tone, "You did the right thing, giving back the necklace. Though of course it was very wrong of you to take it in the first place."

"Judith," I whisper, "listen to me. We're all in danger. They're trying to hush it up but Xéra's death wasn't an accident."

The color drains from her face. "What are you saying?" she stutters.

Before I can elaborate, I feel a presence sidle up behind me and realize it's Blue, snooping as usual. I switch course and address her in a loud voice: "If I'd known it was your big day, I'd have bought you a present, or at least a bunch of flowers."

"How kind!" she says, joining in the ploy. "But don't worry, Russell's been spoiling me rotten. And my daughter bought me this."

I know some consider charm bracelets old-fashioned, but I'm not among them. "Come and look, Blue," I say, to his obvious annoyance.

She gives us a swift guided tour—a little angel, pretend padlock, clasped hands, hedgehog, butterfly, silver thruppence, a gold cross. Her birthday addition is an exquisite enamel miniature.

"Antique French," she says proudly. "I can't imagine where she found it."

At a glance it looks like a portrait, then I see it's a holy medal.

"Any saint in particular?" drawls Blue. He's probably hoping for some gruesome martyrdom.

"Are you telling them about your new car?" cuts in Russell, turning away from the group gathered about him. It's odd, but since Xéra died he seems to have increased in stature among the others. Knowing this lot, they're trying to glean info about her will.

"I'm just about to, darling. Yes, there's a new Honda waiting in the drive—"

"We thought Judith could go electric, because she only needs a runaround," he brays.

"What color did you go for?" I ask. Cars are painted such hideous colors nowadays, please let it be something subtle.

"Fireball Red Metallic, so other drivers can see her coming and get out of the way," Russell replies, with a patronizing chuckle. Judging by the look on Judith's face, we both prefer the bracelet charm.

Eventually, the others go away and Judith says to me, in a low voice, "If what you said is true, it's terrible. Have you told Sir Billy?"

"I ... er ... haven't had the chance. And if you really want to know, I'm worried he might be mixed up in it in some way."

"Surely not!" she says, eyes like saucers. "I wish I could think of something I could do to help."

"Well, having you on my side is a start," I say. And Aimee has my back too, I remind myself.

"Were you thinking I should tell Russell? I honestly think we'd be better keeping it to ourselves. He's very protective of Sir Billy and I'd hate to get you into trouble."

It's not something I do very often, but I take her hand and give it a light squeeze.

At which point the captain enters.

Chapter 51

His black hair glistens, his eyes dance, his epaulettes sparkle—but he's definitely not himself. He's brought along a capacious briefcase, from which he lifts two sheets of paper.

"Ahem," he begins, to get our attention, though Sir Billy and Shane prefer to gaze deep into their vodka and brandy respectively. "Warm thanks for your attendance. This is an important meeting for your safety and comfort, but it is purely a formality and there is no cause for alarm."

If you want to strike fear into someone's heart in four short words, *no cause for alarm* is the way to do it.

We steel ourselves.

"I informed you yesterday that there was a storm moving in from the west. I have now had a warning from the Coast Guard as follows—" he refers to his notes—"*Gale force 8 veering southwesterly later, sea very rough or high, visibility moderate occasionally poor.*"

"Don't like the sound of that," says Marje.

"Not what we were promised," says Elise.

"When is 'later'?" asks Russell.

"Thank you for asking a relevant question, Mr. Tate. *If* the storm comes—and *if* it is severe—I would estimate twelve hours, starting tomorrow morning. It is not certain, but we should be prepared."

He flutters his papers and turns to the next page, at the top of which I can make out "Heavy Weather Checklist."

"We have a procedure for such occasions and I will read it out now. It is very important that everyone follows the instructions, yes, so the crew knows where everyone is at all times. Do not wander about or you will be reported as missing." He proceeds to explain that instructions will be issued via blasts of the foghorn.

"Let me guess: twelve blasts means the ship's sinking," says Marje.

"Not *ship*, Madame," he replies, tetchily. "Not twelve blasts, not sinking. If we need to board the lifeboats, we ring the bell." It's not sounding good.

Challis, meanwhile, has entered unnoticed and set herself up at a vacant table. The captain explains that *Maldemer* is provisioned with the latest in sea-sickness medications and that the chief stewardess will make individual recommendations and dispense accordingly.

Without further ado, he upends his briefcase onto her table and wishes us all good evening.

It's not how it's done at my local pharmacy: a jumble of pill strips, patches, boxes, bottles and wristbands, as well as a couple of pairs of funky-looking blue and white plastic spectacles, spill over the tabletop. We form ourselves into a genteel queue, Sir Billy and Marje at the front, Karol-Kate and I bringing up the rear. Same old story: the poor and needy left till last.

I tuck my hands behind my back in an attempt to cover the hole in my trousers. "Would you like to borrow a poncho?" offers Karol-Kate.

"Nice fur," observes Shane, with a lascivious glance at my exposed midriff.

While we're waiting, the guests compare notes on likely remedies, and fail to find consensus.

"Lots of water—no alcohol," says one.

"Tot of rum," another.

"Watch the horizon," says one.

"Lie down and shut your eyes," another.

"Dry toast, nothing else," says one.

"Eat a good breakfast," another.

Elise points out that if you write out the yacht's name in three words—*mal de mer*—it means seasick. "Odd name for a yacht. Like calling your car *Carsick*."

"Except automobiles don't have names," says Blue sourly.

"Captain Maldemer is a character in *Tintin*," pipes up Judith; you'd want her on your team in a pub quiz. Then she adds, turning to me, "And *almost* an anagram of *Delamare*, except you're an *M* short and an *A* over." For once someone's got the spelling right—thank you, Judith.

Elise yawns and continues. "Maybe the owner of the yacht doesn't speak French and they told him it meant something racy, like *Sea Devil*. I mean, people get tattooed with Chinese characters, don't they, then find they've got *Caution Wet Floor* written up their arm."

"Who does own the yacht?" asks Blue. "Anyone know?"

I notice Sir Billy and Russell exchange glances but no one replies.

The queue shuffles slowly along until it's Karol-Kate's turn. Challis hands her a pack of tablets and some calming drops for the dog and that's it, there's nothing left for me.

"That's not fair," I complain. A twenty-pound note is peeking out of Challis's shirt pocket—they've been bribing her.

"Never mind," she replies, checking we're alone and placing the spare keycard she mentioned into my hand. "Just don't tell anyone where you got it and don't go nosing round where you're not meant to."

CHAPTER 52

Thanks to the borrowed keycard I'm able to proceed down through the yacht toward my cabin, where I intend to have an early night. On my way, I feel the scrape on my head beginning to throb and stop off at the crew mess to get someone to look at it. Aimee is there, sitting on a banquette eating an apple, and offers to fetch the medical kit from the pilot house.

She returns with a large padded grab bag, from which she sorts me out a sterile dressing and some painkillers. While she fetches me a glass of water, I rather naughtily rummage through the backpack and borrow something I think may come in useful at some point: a stethoscope.

After that, Bernie offers to knock me up a plate of cheese on toast. The mere mention gets me salivating—I'm suddenly famished—but I daren't risk being poisoned again. "Not just now," I say. She asks me about the bruises on my throat and I pretend they happened when I was being hauled aboard. After what I saw strapped around her ankle the other day, I'm wary of confiding in her.

I lock myself into my cabin and arm myself as best I can—with a pair of nail scissors—then I lie down on my bunk. Because of the thick low cloud in which we're now enveloped, there's not much to see out of my porthole except fuzzy gray and white outlines. The yacht is bobbing about, quite energetically, but it's not unpleasant: like being in a giant rocking chair.

I read through the forensics notes one more time. The main development is that Xéra was murdered *before* we assembled on the lawn deck, not while we were up there. Unfortunately, this means no one has an alibi—any of the guests or crew could have done the deed then appeared when the albatross was announced.

As I suspected, Xéra's attacker must have been a man, to overpower and choke her; but I remain puzzled by the reference to bruising on her throat and neck. I know what this looks and feels like from recent personal experience, but on her there was none: her throat was as pale and translucent as on our first afternoon, when she modeled the De Lage Treasure for me.

As for Julie's discoveries, Sir Billy's unsavory business activities come as no particular surprise. Bad luck that he's suffered two robberies in such quick succession—or is it?

Eyelids drooping, I take one last look at today's draw. This Knight of Swords character has to be me, doesn't it? Maybe there's something in this tarot lark after all.

With uneasy thoughts swirling round my head, I tumble into oblivion, thankful at least to be safely back in my banana-shaped bunk and not sleeping with the fishes.

Chapter 53

Six a.m. My television screen springs to life: a blur of red hair and Aussie upspeak. "You're needed straight away in the galley, Paul. The captain's ordered the whole boat to be lashed and secured."

Overnight, the weather has taken a lurch for the worse: I'm amazed I slept through it. The wind is up and I can feel the yacht laboring through the waves. It sounds different, too: deep growling from the overworked engines and intermittent grunts and squeaks from the superstructure.

I quickly check my laptop. Wi-Fi unavailable: I hope the Starlink hasn't been blown away.

By the time I arrive at the galley, Bernie's hard at work. She's a different person this morning, moving swiftly and efficiently. Everything that isn't fixed down is being stashed in cupboards or drawers or else anchored with bungee cords.

"I want you to see to the food, Paul. If it can jump about, it will. That's fridges, freezers, larders, store cupboards. Imagine we're a tin can that's going to be all shook up—as the King would say?"

I set to work, rearranging, screwing on lids and tops, and packing everything in tight; not as easy as it sounds when the world keeps moving under and around you. "You seem very good at this," I comment.

"It's more my line of work than cheffing," she says. "We had a caravan when I was wee, and I've worked on the airplanes too. If they'd been recruiting in my earlier days, I'd gladly have gone into space. Now if you've finished here, I know Challis could do with a hand upstairs?"

I report to the grand saloon. All the chandeliers, sculptures, ornaments and cushions have disappeared and a large white cloth has been hooked up to secure the hanging flowers, giving a marquee effect. It's an improvement.

I find Challis in the dining saloon, where she's flipped open the solid mahogany paneling to reveal custom-made cabinets behind. Wineglasses are suspended on racks, plates zigzagged with elastic and loose items stacked in foam-lined drawers.

My job is to tissue-wrap the ornaments from the mantelpiece, including an Ormolu Empire clock surmounted by a golden Neptune and sea serpents. One thought leading to another, I find myself asking: "Do you remember which deckhand you sent to Sir Billy when he flooded his bathroom?"

"Odd question to ask!" she replies. "The one with freckles, I don't know her name. And as soon as you finish that, would you mind making a start on the lobby?"

As I reach the door, I notice the boat is starting to heave and shudder quite alarmingly, and I hear three blasts of the foghorn. The captain, reverting to his native word order, instructs that guests should to their cabins retire, and for anything they require, call.

I go to the foot of the staircase and hover about, with the intention of intercepting Sir Billy on his way to his cabin. He pretends not to see me but I catch him at the door.

"Forgive me, but it's of the utmost importance I speak to you. Give me five minutes, please."

He glares at me. "Shove off."

"Please, for Xéra's sake."

This works: after a moment's hesitation, he opens the door and jabs his forefinger, indicating for me to enter.

I haven't been in here since our first day, when Xéra was showing me her jewelry. Louis Quatorze style may be just about bearable as a backdrop for a high society tea party, but in a room pervaded with grief it's ghastly. The sheets of Sir Billy's swan-shaped bed look damp and twisted, and clothes lie in heaps on the Savonnerie carpet. Challis would never allow it, but he and Marje won't let her in.

"What do you want?" he says rudely.

Now that this long-awaited interview is actually happening, I find myself tongue-tied. I need to play this carefully; I want Sir Billy on my side, but he also remains a suspect.

"Erm, I can't begin to say how sorry—so very sorry—I am about Xéra. I offer you my sincerest condolences."

He grunts and sits down. Slants of light fall in through the curtains, which haven't been drawn properly, creating an atmosphere of danger and suspicion.

"You know what, Paul?" he says. I give a nod of encouragement, though soon regret it. "I don't like you. Never did. I don't even like you being in my cabin. So why don't you piss off out of here?"

Gulping back my anger, I stand on my heels and give it to him straight: the full, horrible story of how his wife was murdered, no details spared. All the time, I'm studying his reactions.

Initially, he yawns and taps his fingers on the table, shrugging the whole thing off, then he starts listening. By the time I get to the forensic analysis, you can hear a pin drop.

When I've finished, I ask him: "Do you believe me?" He doesn't reply but a big fat tear rolls down his cheek.

Chapter 54

Before I go, I guiltily offer to fetch Marje or Elise, but he insists on being left alone. Is this how an innocent man would behave? Or is Sir Billy an extremely good actor? As often, I wish Julie were here—she has a way of reading people, seeing under the surface, which I lack.

I report to the lobby, where I'm surprised to find the circular bar (scene of Romer's mixological triumphs) has disappeared—under the floor. Marveling at this clever piece of engineering, I'm set to work dismantling the man-size floral arrangements, which I'm sorry to hear will be dumped in the sea.

Although part of me is annoyed to find myself press-ganged as an (unpaid) member of the crew, from the seasickness point of view it's a blessing. The first rule of avoiding nausea in heavy seas is to keep cheerful and busy. While I was in the galley, I took the precaution of arming myself with a supply of crystallized ginger to chew. And if that fails, I have up my sleeve a failsafe "system" taught by my mother, who learned it from the skipper of a dayboat at Westward Ho!, which for geography fans is the only place-name in the world with an exclamation point at the end.

Forty minutes later, the crew are summoned to the pilot house for an emergency briefing. Challis says that includes me, so I tag along, but I notice on arrival that the deckhands haven't been invited. Surely they should have been?

At the helm is Aimee, looking grim-faced. The waves are now enormous and coming at us from all directions; the electronic compass is swinging wildly. Her technique seems to be to choose a wave, square up to it then ride up and over like an Olympic skier.

The yacht climbs to the top of one particularly monstrous swell only to find there's nothing on the other side; the boat plunges down in a sickening bellyflop, leaving our stomachs at the top. At one point Aimee loses concentration and the sea catches us broadsides. The boat pitches and yaws, and Bernie whispers in my ear, "Hang on for your life—we're about to capsize?"

The captain—shiny in the face, with undertones of green—arrives to instruct us that nine blasts will shortly be sounded. This is the signal for the guests to be escorted by crew members to the grand saloon, because we are about to be hit by the full force of the storm.

Chapter 55

I yank the windchime outside Shane and Elise's cabin, but it can't be heard for all the creaking and banging, so I bang on the door instead, then yell.

Shane pokes his head out and looks me up and down.

"I'm your escort," I announce, then want to kick myself. "What I mean is, I've been assigned to accompany you and your wife to the grand saloon."

"One moment," he says, "I'll check with the boss."

Seconds later the door opens, the yacht surges and they both fall out of the cabin. Elise is in a dove-gray jersey tracksuit, Shane in silk pajamas (cream with gold piping) and paisley dressing gown—rather dashing.

They lurch down the passageway, grasping at handrails, and forget I'm just behind them.

"We'll fix you a drink when we get there," says Elise. "They can't just stop serving because it's a windy day." Shane laughs, as usual. "And don't forget to speak to Russell. If he tries to fob you off, tell him I'll ask Daddy straight out."

At the door of the grand saloon, I hand them over to Challis and set off to collect the next guest on my list—Marje.

From what I can see—and there isn't much of her showing—she's suffering. This must be the sleeping suit Challis was talking about, in ivory padded satin, topped off with a voluminous headscarf.

"Hello, Marje, let's get you to the grand saloon," I say cheerfully. From the mummy comes a moan.

"I've got this," says Blue, brandishing two life jackets and a wad of paper napkins emblazoned with jolly blue sailing dinghies, which I quickly realize are sick bags.

Ignoring him, I put out my arm for Marje and the scarf slips down to reveal she's wearing a pair of novelty spectacles—the ones I spotted on Challis's bric-a-brac stand last night. They're unlike anything I've seen before: clear plastic lenses framed in thin plastic tubes containing colored liquid. When Marje moves her head—about which she has no choice, on account of the rolling of the yacht—the liquid flows and bubbles. If this is intended to prevent seasickness—to provide an artificial horizon, I'm guessing—on me it has the opposite effect. I reach for a chunk of ginger.

On the way up we encounter Karol-Kate and Colefax. You'd think that the dog, having a lower center of gravity, would be able to keep a straight course, but the two of them are ricocheting along the corridor like a pair of billiard balls. The impression is heightened by the fact that they've donned their life jackets—Karol-Kate's bright red, Colefax's bright yellow.

By the time our convoy arrives at the grand saloon the others are settling down for the ordeal ahead.

Sir Billy has arranged himself near the window, eyes intent upon the swirling mass of blue, gray, white and black on the other side of the glass. Now and again a shaft of light penetrates the scene, reminding us that it's not late evening, as you might think, but nine o'clock in the morning.

In the center sits Russell; Judith is as far away as possible, having found herself a wing chair in a distant niche in which she sits, looking resolute.

Blue lounges moodily in a chair near the piano.

We get everyone seated in the nick of time before the sea takes a rapid and severe turn for the worse. From our haphazard lurching, it feels to me as if the mountainous waves are coming at us from all directions, and Aimee, assuming she's still at the helm, has lost control. The groaning of the yacht is joined in counterpoint by the tinkling of LUCITE® as the now invisible herbaceous border over the bar swings and sways. We're being tossed about like a rubber duck in a bath.

Obviously, a boat rises and falls in the water, and can be turned to port and starboard, but there are no less than six different ways it can move in heavy seas. It can rotate in three directions—roll, pitch and yaw. And it can rock in three more: sway, surge and heave. Shutting my ears to the whining, banging and squealing of steel, fiberglass and timber, I set myself the challenge of identifying the different motions. It takes my mind off the implications for us passengers.

An hour goes by, during which it all gets worse, then another. Whatever Challis was handing out last night must be super-potent because the guests sit in a stupor, punctuated only by the occasional groan from Marje.

I continue to slip sugary cubes of ginger into my mouth and decide the time has come to deploy Mum's seasickness cure. It's simple, but requires absolute concentration; one to remember the next time you find yourself in high seas and decide you'd rather be dead.

Sit quietly and monitor your breathing. Now make a start: breathe in when the boat goes up, out when it goes down. Continue, always matching your breathing to the rise and fall of the boat.

This can be used in any kind of sea, however chaotic. You might find yourself doing a great big long breath, and then a super-quick one, then vice versa. It helps the brain interpret what is happening and, equally important, dispels feelings of panic.

I'm enjoying a Zen moment—feeling very much better—when I notice *Maldemer* seems to be rising higher than ever. I extend my in-breath as long as I can, then when my lungs are full, hold it in, waiting and waiting for us to descend.

I'm blue in the face, thinking we must surely have become airborne, when the boat shudders and stops moving. I realize we're riding the crest of a colossal wave, maybe even a tsunami. Everyone looks at everyone else in panic: we're at the top of a roller coaster, poised for the dive drop.

Oh, oh, oh. We're falling, falling, falling—
CRASH!

My eardrums survive this only to be newly assailed by an unearthly shriek. Even Marje is jerked out of her torpor at its suddenness and pitch. Last time I heard such an ominous noise was on the night the necklace vanished.

Chapter 56

All grand pianos are equipped with locks on the wheels so they don't roll about during a *presto con fuoco*; superior instruments such as Faziolis have double castors immobilized by means of tommy bar screws. Aboard *Maldemer*, the engineers have taken extra precautions, each foot sitting in a deep brass drum, attached through cut-outs in the wooden floor to the deck below.

The problem is that during the boat's last free fall and crash landing, two of the piano's three legs have jumped clean out of their fixings, and the huge instrument—over three hundred kilos in weight—is on the move.

Judging by his cry—extraordinary that such a high-pitched sound can have been emitted by a male—my initial thought is it has rolled onto Blue, crushing him alive; instead, I see him leap as if on fire toward the other side of the grand saloon.

We feel the yacht begin to climb again and hear a squealing sound: it's the piano's newly liberated castors grinding their way through the parquet, leaving huge ruts in the wood. At the top of the wave, there's another violent lurch. The lights flicker, and the lacquered black beast slews round, as if rearing on its hind legs, and, with a metallic crash, the last castor (wheels) bursts free from its brass drum.

Sir Billy, sitting near the window, watches in paralyzed terror as the runaway piano careens toward him, splintering chairs and tables in its path. A plaster column smashes onto the keyboard, causing a diabolic discord—all eighty-eight keys struck at once—to ring through the air.

At the final moment, a figure in silk pajamas flies across the room, grabs Sir Billy and discus-swings him to safety. There's an explosion of glass and the grand piano disappears out of the panoramic window.

Chapter 57

"No worries," says the chief stewardess as she steps into the carnage. I'm reminded of Mrs. Miniver, who on surveying her dining room after it's taken a direct hit from the Luftwaffe, drawls that it's not so bad, just needs a clean and tidy.

Taking advantage of a temporary lull in the storm, Challis forms the guests into a line and they're led away to the beach club. "You'll be more comfortable down there," she says reassuringly. "I'll be along shortly to make hot drinks."

The guests out of the way, I fully expect Challis to go into meltdown, gibbering nonsense and rending flesh. Instead, she flips open a console recessed into the wall, presses a couple of buttons and a huge steel shutter rises from the floor, sealing the gaping cavity left by the window. After the raging of the wind and sea, it feels suddenly cozy.

"That's handy," I say, as she busies herself with her broom, clearing up the debris. "But if we've got storm shutters, shouldn't we have put them up earlier?"

By now a deckhand has arrived to help. Fish Woman and I look at each other sidelong but say nothing.

"They're not for storms," says Challis curtly. "They're for terrorists."

Although I've earned a cup of tea as much as anyone else, I

don't follow the guests down to the beach club. By my calculation, it's two hours since the storm hit, and it feels as if it just peaked. Weather patterns being symmetrical, as they usually are, it'll be at least an hour before the guests feel it's safe to return to their quarters.

Tight timing, but I know what I need to do.

CHAPTER 58

Thanks to Challis's passe-partout, I let myself discreetly into Karol-Kate's cabin, which is a double divided into two, with the dog occupying the larger portion. The floor is strewn with books; I can't get excited about *Four-Stroke Performance Tuning* or *Haynes Dog Manual*, but good to see someone still reads George Eliot.

Among them I spot her passport, which really ought to be in the safe. I tuck it under her pillow for safety, but not before noticing that she's thirty-two and quite a traveler: Korea, Canada, Mexico, South Africa. Most countries have given up stamping passports, so for all I know this is the tip of the iceberg. Who knew there was so much money in car maintenance and dog handling?

I check the drawers quickly and the bottom one opens to reveal a tangle of silk, straps and lace. Wow! Are female undies always so—jazzy? I don't know what half these things are, or where you'd put them. I like to keep up to date myself in the underwear department (as Mum used to say, you want to look your best in an accident), but this seems, well, above and beyond.

In the wardrobe I find a collection of leads, toys, brushes and accessories, which I hope belong to the dog, plus a shoebox half full of chocolate bars and crisps. If she wants to fill up on zero percent chocolate and snacks with No Nutritional Value, that's her call.

From the bathroom I learn she's a fan of eco-friendly products, which is just as well because if she spends her working life under a car hood, she's got a lot of carbon to offset. But what's this in the pocket of her toilet bag? A thick wad of bank notes, held together by a rubber band. A slip of paper on top reads: £1k.

Some people still travel with cash—indeed I hear traveler's checks are making a comeback—but Karol-Kate doesn't strike me as the type. What's it doing there?

My next cabin inspection is Blue's, which has been designed on a Disney theme—princess curtains, *Toy Story* duvet and Mickey and Minnie carpet. Ha! He must hate it.

I start with his wardrobe. Honestly, what a peacock! He could easily have lent me a shirt or two in my hour of need, from the dozens and dozens and dozens he's brought along. As for the bathroom: even by American standards, it seems excessive. Pills (including Propecia 5mg, something I'd try myself but for the expense), supplements, styling products, dental kit, the entire Kiehl's skincare range, sticks, sprays, misters and a whole *shelf* devoted to his beard!

It's in the desk that I find what I'm really looking for—his notebooks. There's one labeled *Sir B & X* (that must be Sir Billy and Xéra), another *M. M.* (Marje), another *E. H. -H.* (Elise) and, blow me down, one for me—*P. D.*!

I don't know why I should be so flattered, but it gives me a bit of a glow to be thought interesting enough to have my own notebook. I must try and be more sparkling in his company, rustle up some funny anecdotes.

I don't know how I'll decode them—they're written in some form of cypher or shorthand—but I snap a photograph with my phone of the first pages of *E. H. -H* and (purely for casual interest) *P. D.*, before slipping out into the corridor.

The next cabin I come to has a problem—the door's jammed. I manage to slide my hand in and pull out the obstruction—a twist of belts, scarves and tights—then creep in.

What a disaster zone! When I was last in Marje's lunar module it was immaculate, but now cupboards and drawers flap open and the floor is strewn with clothes, papers, books, toiletries, magazines and shoes. An awful lot of shoes. It's probably Blue's job to tidy up after her, and this is what happens when he takes a morning off.

I clamber my way to the desk, slide open a drawer and rake through. A sheaf of company bank statements. I can't understand them at all, but it's not the sort of reading you'd normally take on holiday with you. Hidden underneath, a creased photocopy.

I don't claim to be a whiz at copiers but even I could do better than this: it's been printed out absurdly small (50 percent?) and crooked to boot. I can, however, make out the logo "WTH" and the words "HIGHLY CONFIDENTIAL." In my experience, documents thus marked are rarely as juicy as they sound, but for some reason "WTH" rings a bell. I flip out my phone and take another snapshot to decipher later; it's only the one page, very short.

On the way out, I check out Marje's coffee table. Julie swears you can tell everything about a person from their reading matter: *The Hollywood Reporter*, *How To Spend It* and *The Art of Simple Living*. Also, two books: *Smashing the Glass Ceiling* and *Dream of a Quiet Life*.

I come away from her cabin wondering if Marje is quite as much in control of her life and destiny as she'd have us believe.

Chapter 59

All this time, *Maldemer* has continued to thrash through the waves, engines surging, buffeted by squalls. As I step into the corridor, I hear a deep grinding sound and the lights flicker. Three cabins to go. I hope the lights hold out.

I let myself into the Tates' cabin, which is on a Renaissance theme. Mythological figures spy on me from the ceiling, and the walls whisper with silk and brocade. Under the desk is a row of bulky leather boxes, labeled:

    Hardcastle Family Office
    Fortuna (PlayWinLive)
    L. M.
    W. H. – Legal/Insurance
    W. H. – Marriage/Will
    W. H. – P. P.
    X. H. – Miscellaneous

All very orderly, all, alas, locked. *W. H.* is obviously Sir Billy, and *PlayWinLive* sounds exactly the sort of hyperbolic name you'd call a betting company. It's curious that Sir Billy has his own *P. P.* (presumably Pâtisserie Pompadour) box. I pull it out and give it a shake: lots inside considering, as Russell claims, all they did was offer a bit of advice. I'm guessing *L. M.* is Luiz Mateus, who sold Sir Billy the De Lage Treasure. Do the pair have other dealings, apart from trading in jewels under the counter?

The desk drawers are empty apart from one, which yields a wallet and purse. I riffle quickly through both—plenty of cash (used twenties), credit cards, organ donor cards, loyalty cards, nut allergy cards (his blue, hers pink—how quaint), library cards... but nothing leaps out.

This being one of the VIP suites, the cabin has two small dressing rooms leading off. I step into the first and jigsaw pieces crunch underfoot. The walls of the second are handpainted in swirls of umber, terracotta, rust and black, and recessed lighting adds to the grotto effect. It's probably as well that Judith doesn't go in much for makeup because you can barely see a thing.

On the dressing table a candle flickers—fortunately one of those battery-operated LED ones. It illuminates a silver picture frame—the folding type, technically known as a diptych, no bigger than a postcard and arched at the top. On the left is a religious figure, probably a saint; the picture on the right-hand side is missing.

I'm fumbling with the flashlight app on my phone to get a better look when I hear my name being called from the corridor outside. My heart pounding like a steam engine, I crush myself behind an alabaster statue and hold my breath.

Chapter 60

The voice gets louder—it's Bernie—then fades away down the corridor. Breathing a sigh of relief, I decide to ignore it for the moment and press on with my mission while I have the opportunity. The next cabin is Elise and Shane's. This consists of (real) brick walls, steel beams and open-plan minimalism in black and white, with the Empire State Building glinting in the distance.

It's extremely tidy, and everything is the best money can buy. Big luxe labels—Fendi, Prada, Chanel—rub shoulders with high-end British—Stella McCartney, Emma Willis, JW Anderson. In the bathroom, it's what looks like the complete range of La Prairie Men alongside Clive Christian and Sarah Chapman. I check their bedside cabinets, which are reclaimed filing chests, mid-century, and filled with the latest hardbacks. Elise is currently halfway through the new Colleen Hoover and Shane a political biography; at least I hope it's that way round.

How much does it cost to fund this sort of lifestyle? If they really did blame Xéra for cutting them off, how far would they go to take her out of the picture?

Finally, I creep up the gilded staircase and let myself into the master cabin. I go first to Xéra's boudoir, where it seems only yesterday we were admiring her necklace. It's decorated on a shell theme—oyster silk drapes, dressing table inlaid with mother-of-pearl and a button-back sofa in aqua velvet. Beyond a porthole—scallop-shaped—churns the ultramarine ocean, stabbed and crusted with silver.

Someone should have come in and packed up her things, because they've all been thrown about, as if no one cares about her anymore. I'm hit with a sudden ache of loss.

Lying on the floor among the usual feminine vanities—jars and bottles and hair adornments—I spot an open laptop (either broken or battery flat), and a letter.

Letters are a rarity nowadays, more's the pity, and this one is only short and unsigned. I'm guessing it's the one Xéra mentioned to Karol-Kate.

At first, I think it's been penned in some strange, secret script, then I realize it's merely terrible handwriting, with the letters joined up erratically or not at all. An Enigma machine wouldn't go amiss, but I can make out:

> Xéra dear ... Look ... sunk. You did promise ... after all, I was the one ... lovebirds! ... old paperwork ... boy ... bail me out ... get it back ... dangerous!

I photograph it.

In Sir Billy's dressing room—cherub theme, powder blue—I find a set of box files and take a look. The documents in the first are smothered in stickers, flags and Post-it Notes—*TO PAY. URGENT. OVERDUE. PAYMENT DECLINED.* And I thought *I* had money worries.

Another contains a sheaf of emails from Opulence Yacht Charters BVI—*IMMEDIATE ACTION, FOR YOUR URGENT ATTENTION*. A quick skim reveals that the wire transfer to pay for our cruise has been "lost in transit." I recall from a Netflix series that "lost wire transfers" are a speciality of international fraudsters: I sincerely hope we won't be made to pay for the cruise if Sir Billy doesn't or can't cough up.

Caught up among the printouts is an A4 sheet with <u>CALL BIG LEW URGENTLY</u> daubed in huge letters.

A third file is devoted to the De Lage Treasure. The insurance claim form (twenty-seven pages long) has been filled out, the declaration signed. Attached to it is a set of photographs, including of the suede box in which it was kept, the inside of the box (empty) and the dressing table from which it disappeared.

Thanks to me, the De Lage Treasure has been recovered and is now in the captain's safe, so they won't be needing any of this. Which reminds me: I still haven't had a word of thanks.

I'm letting myself out of Sir Billy's cabin when I realize the yacht has stopped. We're still rising and falling, but not going anywhere.

I tiptoe down to the lobby—there's no one about—and continue down the Chagall staircase to the beach club, where the guests are stretched out comatose.

On arrival, I'm met by the reek of butyric acid. Challis, God bless her, is handing out hot lemon-scented towels with a pair of tongs, and Fish Woman and Flower Lady are swabbing the floor. Even Bernie has arrived to lend a hand, circulating bottles of water, apples and bananas.

"I came looking for you earlier?" she says. "Thought we'd lost you."

"Oh sorry—did you need me?" I ask.

"Funny smell in the galley I'd like your opinion on?" I promise to call in later and check it out.

I said all along that the secret of fighting seasickness was to stay busy and cheerful, but no one ever listens. Sir Billy and Marje are stretched out on loungers, dead to the world. Elise and Shane are together on a double lounger, hands clasped as if awaiting the Day of Judgment. Even the lobsters look out of sorts, lying listless on the gravel.

Blue sits up and gazes at the spot where the piano used to be, wondering if it was all a bad dream. I wonder whether or not to tell him he has vomit in his beard.

"Think you might want to go find your dog friend," he says. "Haven't seen her since she went out an hour ago."

Surely Karol-Kate hasn't been out on deck in this? I stare at him horror-stricken, then hurry to the door.

"Before you go," calls Blue, "what time's lunch?"

To my relief, I find Karol-Kate on the afterdeck, where she's constructed a hut for herself and the dog out of sun lounger mattresses. They both look very wet and very windblown, but Colefax is wagging his tail and his handler gives me a cheery "Howdy!"

"You survived," I say, with relief.

"That was quite a show," she says. "What I don't understand is why we've suddenly lost power. Either they've cut the engines or something's gone wrong and we've stalled."

Chapter 61

We arrive at the pilot house to find Aimee in conversation with the captain. She's so exhausted she can hardly stand up: her eyes are red-rimmed and her hands shaking. We eavesdrop as she explains to Romer that one of our engines is malfunctioning and the Starlink is down. She's going to run some tests but first she has to lie down for half an hour.

I find it odd that guests are allowed to hang about in the pilot house—after all, you're not allowed to speak to the driver of a train or bus, and visits to airplane cockpits were banned years ago. And let's face it, this news is alarming. What if the other engine pegs out? Horrible visions race through my head—of being becalmed for months and having to drink seawater. What if we end up eating one another?

As Aimee is leaving, Karol-Kate steps forward. "I was wondering if I could offer my services," she says. "I work with engines."

The captain and first officer stare at her with undisguised scorn.

"Dog handling is a sideline," she adds. "I'm a Motor Vehicle Master Technician, IMI Level 4 Diploma."

"Thank you, miss," says the captain. "We will let you know if we need you."

* * *

Although we're not actually going anywhere, normality is tentatively restored aboard *Maldemer*. The waves are still large, we're swaying about, but after what we've been through, it feels smooth as a millpond.

The guests in the beach club open their eyes and realize they're alive. Gratitude doesn't come naturally to this lot, but they're aware of having been through hell and come out the other side. Singly or in couples, they raise themselves and shuffle off to their cabins to wash and change.

In the grand saloon, Challis and her deckhands are finishing the big clean-up. The cushions and flowers are back, the bar is lined with bottles, the ceiling is jingling harmoniously and sandwiches triangulate under plastic film. To disguise the bullet- and bombproof steel shutter now blocking the view, the chief stewardess has draped it with colorful tablecloths in the spirit of an Arabian souk. In what is arguably a step too far, the gap left by the Flying Fazioli has been filled by an enormous inflatable unicorn brought up from the tender garage.

Shane and Blue arrive simultaneously through different doors—not what either of these sworn enemies would have chosen, but too late now.

"You saved Sir Billy's life," I say to Shane. "I haven't seen a flying tackle like that since I was at school."

He nods self-deprecatingly.

"You should join the circus," smirks Blue.

"You too," says Shane, helping himself to a brandy. "Bearded lady."

Elise arrives before the handbags come out and places herself between them at the bar, shortly joined by Russell. Judith enters on her own a few minutes later and takes a distant table. Everyone sips tea and nibbles on sandwiches and chats and feels very much better. It's as if it never happened. Euphoria sparks and fizzes in the air. We have cheated death.

After a while, Karol-Kate appears at the doorway with Colefax on his leash.

"You look wet," says Elise, mistress of the obvious.

"Shall I take him?" says Shane. Karol-Kate likes this idea—she must be longing to change into something dry—and hands the dog over with alacrity. His owner immediately lets him off the leash and Colefax scampers off. Seconds later he returns with a little stick between his teeth, no doubt one he hid somewhere for a rainy day.

Russell looks up and turns pale. "See you all later—paperwork," he mutters as he hurries off. As he does so he glances back at the dog, capering about and shaking water everywhere.

Chapter 62

I approach Judith, sitting on her own with her needlework on her lap.

"Can I get you another of those?" I ask: Sprite Zero, rather her than me. "Ice and a slice?"

"Thank you, I'd love that."

We commiserate about the horrible experience we've been through. After that, she says to me in a low voice: "I can't stop thinking about . . . poor Xéra. I mean, is there any evidence of foul play?"

"That's the problem, Judith—absolutely none. But the circumstances leave no doubt."

"Who else knows?" she asks.

"As I said, they're hushing it up."

"I wish I could help in some way. I keep thinking back to the morning it happened."

"I remember you were already on the lawn deck when I arrived," I say. "Had you been there long?"

"A little while. I like to start the day with a word puzzle. I find it clears the brain."

"And did either of you notice anything unusual?"

"Russell wasn't with me—he was back in the cabin doing his Battle of Trafalgar." My thoughts churn—of course! Russell was last to arrive on the lawn deck—what if he wasn't doing his jigsaw at all, but . . .

"I saw the dog, of course," she continues. "And the American pretending to run laps round the gallery walk."

"What do you mean—pretending?"

"He came out early on, stretching and making loud puffing noises, then disappeared. Half an hour later he reappeared, pretending to look hot and breathless, but he didn't fool me."

While I'm considering this, she picks up her needlework and starts sewing.

"What are you making?" I ask.

"It's for Russell. I don't expect he'll appreciate it." Not for the first time, I feel sorry for this intelligent but oppressed woman; I sense she could have done more with her life. "A bookmark," she continues, inserting her needle at the front and pulling it fully out at the back before continuing. Excellent technique.

Now that I'm up close, I see it's a picture of the night sky, with stars picked out in silver thread and tiny pearls for planets.

"Your stitches are so tiny and even."

"How kind of you to say," she says, opening her eyes wide. "Most people don't notice."

"May I look at the back?" I know that in some circles such a request would be considered impolite, like lifting up a teacup to see if it's Crown Derby, but Judith strikes me as someone who'd automatically sew in her ends. "That's amazing. You can't tell the difference."

"That's the whole point," she says. "It's double-sided, so it won't need backing. I'll make you one if you like."

Gosh! Even something small like this takes hours and hours and hours of stitching; I'm genuinely touched.

"Really, I wouldn't offer if I didn't mean it. What takes your fancy? Checks or stripes always suit a man." She adds, and I can't tell if she's teasing me: "Or perhaps you're more the floral type?"

We sit in companionable silence for a couple more minutes; it's restful being with someone while they're sewing. "You're a perfectionist," I say eventually.

"I take pride in doing everything to the best of my ability," she says. "It comes from my professional life, you see."

"Oh, what do you do?" I say.

"Oh, I'm retired now." Before I can jump in with my *oh, but you're too young to be retired* schtick, she explains: "I used to be a dental nurse. I'm always telling Russell I spent thirty years looking into people's mouths and now I'm stuck listening to what comes out." We both laugh, though it isn't exactly hilarious.

"I can't imagine you're bored," I say. "You have so many interests." She looks flattered—probably unused to compliments. "You mentioned you do am-dram. That must be such fun."

"Oh, only in a small way, the local light operatic society. Walk-on parts or singing in the chorus, but I love it. In another life, it's what I'd like to have done, go on the stage."

"Does Russell act too?" I ask.

"You're joking! He thinks it's a total waste of time. But when I'm in a show, my daughter comes along to cheer me on." Presumably the daughter she described as "barren" the other evening. "Last year I was an understudy on *My Fair Lady* and someone broke their foot. I stood in for Mrs. Pearce—"

"The housekeeper! Then you got to sing—"

Judith breaks quietly into "I Could Have Danced All Night": she has a sweet, pure voice, perfectly in tune.

While she sings, with me humming along in tenor and tapping the table to add a bit of swing, there's a loud rumble from the depths of the vessel and the lights go out.

Chapter 63

"No cause for alarm," booms a voice over the public address system—those words again. "Will Ms. Bunting-Jones please report to the pilot house?"

"Captain needs some help with heavy lifting," quips Blue as Karol-Kate hurries away.

"Nice to have a man about the house," throws in Marje.

Joking apart, the captain and Aimee must be in a tailspin panic if they've decided to take Karol-Kate up on her offer of technical assistance. I'm glad in a way, except it seems somewhat unprofessional. Come to think of it, everything about the captain rings false, from his vainglorious coiffure to the Gucci stripe boat shoes.

Judith lays aside her needlework—not a hobby you can pursue in semi-darkness—and stumbles off to her cabin. I grope my way to a service door and find to my relief the emergency lighting has kicked in. Thence to the galley, where I find Bernie surrounded by eggshells, piled up to resemble those ancient dwellings in southern Turkey, or perhaps the *trulli* of Puglia.

"What's the *craic?*" she says with a grin.

All my life I've wanted to hear this phrase for real. "I'm grand," I reply.

"Box of eggs broke loose! The ones not completely banjaxed I'm breaking into a bowl. Maybe make an omelette."

Crack. Crack.

"Giant omelette," I say.

"If anyone can get the electric working again, it's our Karol-Kate," she replies.

I sniff the air. "I know what you mean about the funny smell. But I'll tell you what it is . . . *chamomile.*"

While Bernie busies herself feeding the eggshells into the garbage crusher—lots of crunching and popping—I kneel down to take a look at a cast-iron vent behind the island. Yes, it's coming up through the ventilation shaft. The wing nuts come off OK, but the vent itself is stuck, so I reach up to the worktop for a knife with which to lever it off.

The ensuing events happen frighteningly fast. The heavy vent crashes onto the tiled floor, I hear a cry from behind me and my arm is jerked back in a vicious twist. Something hard and cold stabs into the small of my back.

"Freeze!" hisses Bernie.

"Ouch!" I shout in fury, trying and failing to wrestle her off me. "What the hell are you doing?"

"Tell me what you're playing at?" she demands, pulling my arm harder and jabbing me with what feels distinctly like a pistol.

"Get off me!" I squawk. "I just bent down to find where the smell was coming from. Let me go!"

She considers this for a moment and the pressure on my arm is released. She slides the gun back under her apron, where I catch sight of a leather shoulder holster.

"What's going on, Bernie?" I splutter. "How dare you attack me for no reason—threaten me with a—"

"Thought you were up to something," she mumbles, and turns away. "Apologies . . . feeling a bit jumpy. Storm shook me up."

My shoulder is pulsating with pain—I swear she's dislocated it. "Why are you carrying a pistol? What's really going on here?"

She puts her hand to my mouth to hush me; from what

Aimee told me about *Maldemer*'s sinister-sounding "access log," I'm not convinced we're ever quite alone, and Bernie seems to think so too.

"I'm sorry," she says sotto voce, then picks up a tea towel and starts twisting it. At this point I witness what is technically known as a face journey, in which a sequence of expressions passes across her features in quick succession: she studies me, then looks away, then her lips start to move, then she shakes her head. Finally, she makes her mind up and whispers: "Paul, I've not been completely straight with you."

"You don't say," I whisper, adding in a booming voice, for ears that might be glued to walls or listening in remotely: "Let's throw the rest of the eggs away, Bernie, we've picked out the best."

"You must promise not to tell a soul," she continues. "Our secret?"

I stare at her. "But seriously—a gun! Who are you?"

She takes a deep breath.

"OK, I didn't join the yacht to cook—that's only a front."

I remain silent.

"Did you guess?" she says.

"Chefs don't usually carry defense weapons strapped to their legs," I reply, politely not mentioning that they also tend to have a flair for cooking. "So, tell me all."

"We need to go back eighteen months, to this big burglary in a village called Kirkby Overblow in North Yorkshire. It's not random thieves after TVs and laptops—they're stealing to order: half a dozen oil paintings, porcelain, valuable watches and a rare coin collection, housed in a Victorian walnut cabinet with pull-out trays lined with red velvet. Sounds like a lot of detail, but I've a reason for telling you." I notice her accent has subtly shifted—still Irish but she's lost the sing-song.

"It's the perfect crime. The owner and staff are away and security cameras on the blink. There's a watchdog tranquillized with a dart—he recovers just fine, in case you're worried. The insurers, Calamitas Protection, have their doubts—it's all *too* tidy for their liking—but they cough up on the claim, down to the last penny.

"Three months ago, someone at Calamitas happens to see a walnut display cabinet in an online antiques auction, and recognizes the velvet lining. It's only the cabinet, but it's a start. Their fraud team get cracking and trace it back to an underling working for an online gambling company registered in Harrogate."

"Don't tell me—PlayWinLive."

She nods. "While that investigation rumbles on, Calamitas discover Sir Billy has purchased the world's most expensive necklace and is taking out insurance with another company. Insurance companies talk to one another, so they put their heads together and can't help wondering if he's going to try and cheat them again."

"Good grief! A common criminal! He arranges for his own house to be burgled, then steals his own wife's necklace."

"Not so common. Those jewels would fetch a mint, especially the big pink one. Get the right bidders, sky's the limit."

"Are you sure about all this?"

Bernie slowly nods her head. "About the burglary, there's a ton of evidence: he's guilty."

"But how can you know that?" I ask.

She reaches into her trouser pocket, pulls out an ID card, peels off her eye patch and declares: "The name's O'Houllahily. Bernadette O'Houllahily."

Chapter 64

The card reads CALAMITAS PROTECTION PLC along the top and SECURITY OFFICER—INVESTIGATIONS UNIT along the bottom. As if to add gravitas to this amazing development, there's a sudden low rumbling from deep below us, followed by the massive clunking of gears. The lights flood back on, air conditioning and refrigerators cough into action. And we're moving.

"So *you're* the Knight of Swords!" The tarot was right.

"What's that?"

"Oh, just I had a premonition," I reply.

"I *see*. So here's the thing: you're the one mixing with the grand folks above deck. I need you to help me prove Hardcastle was the one who took it."

I let this sink in. "I'm really sorry—this isn't what you want to hear—but he didn't."

"But he must have been. It's insurance fraud, pure and simple."

"I was in the dining saloon all Monday evening and Sir Billy never left the room. I've been over and over it in my mind: the only guests who went out were Elise, for a cigarette . . . and Blue, to get something for Mrs. Mayham to put round her shoulders. Oh, and Karol-Kate took the dog out."

Bernie looks disappointed.

"By the way," I say, "are we absolutely sure the necklace is safe now? It could be stolen again."

"Put that out of your mind: I saw Captain Romer lock it in the safe in the pilot house, with my own two eyes."

"Speaking of which—the patch . . . Erm, as disguises go, it's quite, well, original."

"Hiding in plain sight, it's called. I always like to go the extra mile when I'm on undercover assignment. And if there's one good thing to come out of all this, it's that I've got to know you, Paulie."

"Thank you, Bernie—I'm touched. And now I know you're on the right side, we both need to watch our backs." She nods and waves her pistol.

"As you may have guessed, I didn't fall overboard yesterday—I was pushed."

She frowns. "Can you be sure?"

"I think the reason it happened was because I refuse to remain silent about Lady Hardcastle's murder. You do agree it was a murder?"

She touches my arm. "Without examining the scene, I couldn't be sure, but I feared as much."

"And the last thing I want to say is—can you lay off the *fines herbes*? Or at least keep an eye on your stash so it doesn't turn up in my cabin."

"I'm sorry, Paul—purely medicinal. They disappeared from my cabin the afternoon I arrived, so I turned to the gin instead. I'm sorry you were landed with kitchen duties."

"I hope this isn't normal behavior for insurance investigators," I reply, and we laugh.

"Now everything's out in the open," I say, "here's an idea. How about we do a joint mission to find out who's brewing chamomile down there—and why."

"Count me in, but would you do me a quick favor first, Paulie?" she says, opening the fridge. "I'm shy of the folks upstairs, but I've got something special for Colesie. He deserves it, after the day he's had. Will you give this to him?"

Chapter 65

Everyone stops dead when I walk into the grand saloon brandishing a large meaty bone. It's a beef shank, split, with lots of juicy marrow in the center—just the thing to reward a brave dog who's survived a storm at sea, though he'll need to be supervised while he eats it.

They stare at me as if I just killed someone and hacked off a limb to shock them.

"Not necessary," says Blue disapprovingly.

"Really?" says Marje, who is nursing a vodka at the bar, alongside a silent Sir Billy. The glance he shoots me from bloodshot eyes reminds me of an angry bulldog.

Elise informs me I'll find Colefax on the lawn deck with her husband.

"Don't get blood on the carpet," adds Challis.

The thought of being on my own with Shane doesn't fill me with rapture but he's a prime suspect, and I need to keep an eye on him, professionally speaking. I head up to the top deck and step out onto the grass. It's soggy. More than that, waterlogged. I feel an icy chill seep into my shoes and up my socks. There's a time and place for capillary action, does it have to be now?

Shane doesn't see me at first: he's too engrossed with the dog, making him chase and jump. The cloud has lifted and the afternoon light is making everything look silver.

I know some people find male tennis players highly attractive (their masculinity, controlled aggression, fierce concentration, to say nothing of their honed physiques) but in general they don't do much for me. I find tennis the game more interesting than the people playing it.

Not that I'd call Shane your typical tennis pro. Honed he may be, aggressive allegedly, but he has a sharp sense of humor and a pleasant way of talking. I've noticed that indoors he looks fair, it's only outdoors that his hair takes on a reddish sheen. I remember when I saw him at Wimbledon he seemed different from the other players, and I was sorry he didn't win.

"Hi there," I say.

"Oh, hello," he says, stopping mid-throw. "That what I think it is?"

"Compliments of the chef. Is Colefax allowed a bone?"

He laughs, as usual. "Of course. Here, doggy!"

He throws it to the far side of the deck, where it lands with a splash in the sodden grass. Colefax drops his prized little stick and scampers toward it, head down.

We stand side by side and watch the dog for a minute while I work out my line of questioning.

"Good to see your father-in-law up and about," I say.

"S'pose so," mutters Shane.

"You know what you were saying the other day, about things being tough for you and Elise?" I ask. He shrugs and looks away. "Anyone know what's happening yet with Xéra's estate?"

"Bit early for that," he says, surprised by my bare-faced nosiness. "If you're expecting us all to sit around while the will is read—"

"Absolutely not!" I protest.

"In any case, I'm sure Russell has it all sewn up. Or should I say, stitched up . . . Swindler through and through."

There's so much animosity festering within families. As I've said before, it sometimes makes me glad I don't have one.

Our conversation is interrupted by an agonized squeal. The last time I heard that sound was when Colefax was being set upon by a psychotic seagull; now he's running back and forth with his jaws gaping open.

"What is it, Colefax?" cries Shane, rushing to help him. "Is he having a fit?"

The dog looks up at us with huge *HELP ME!* eyes. *DO SOMETHING!* they signal to Shane. *SORT THIS OUT!* they plead to me. He continues this performance, swinging his head from one of us to the other, as if watching a rally.

"He's swallowed something," I say.

"He's in pain!" shouts Shane, panicking.

At this moment, thank goodness, Karol-Kate emerges from the pilot house and comes squelching across the turf.

"What have we here?" she says.

"It's my fault, we gave him a bone!" I say.

"He's dying!" cries Shane. I roll my eyes.

Karol-Kate kneels down, sinks into the mud, and lifts the dog between her knees. "There's a good boy. Calm now . . ." Holding his muzzle gently open with one hand, she feels about at the back of his mouth. Pitiful whimpers fill the air.

Hours seem to pass, though it can't be more than ten seconds, until Karol-Kate quietly announces, "There you go!" and holds something up in the air.

The dog jumps free, snapping his mouth open and shut, joy in his eyes. At first, I think she's pulled a tooth, but it turns out to be a fragment of beef bone.

"Imagine if we hadn't been here," says Shane weakly.

"How did you do that?" I ask Karol-Kate, curious.

"I could tell he had something wedged in his jaw—it was just a case of finding it and removing it. Same principle as a break stick, which is how the police break up dog fights. You insert something behind the molars of the animal and it means it can't bite."

I consider this for a moment and a horrific thought crosses my mind: some form of break stick would be a convenient way to prop a human mouth open, if you wanted to force something down their throat.

Blocking this speculation, at least for the moment, I congratulate Karol-Kate on having so rapidly solved our engine problem.

"Hardly!" she laughs. "Impurity must've got into the feed pipe—too much rocking about—but we flushed it out and she's running nicely now. The FO promised to show me the engine room later on," she adds.

To Colefax's chagrin, we toss the bone overboard. I pick up his discarded stick, splintered and slobbery, wondering where he'd even found one out at sea.

I look at it more closely, and realize it's a chopstick, or at least half of one. I slip it into my pocket to think about later.

Chapter 66

Bernie and I track the chamomile smell to a vent in the deck below, and follow the ducting until I realize with a shudder we're adjacent to the chain locker. I haven't been down in the bilges since my incarceration, and it doesn't feel good.

The vent disappears into a wall, beside which is a small unremarkable door painted pillar-box red. I remember it: the locked door from which I heard that horrible moaning sound.

I knock quietly. It immediately opens a crack and a fearful eye peers out, accompanied by a strong waft of chamomile. From the freckles I can tell it's Fish Woman. Seeing Bernie, she shrinks back in fear.

"She's OK," I say, pointing toward the chef. "She's one of us."

Fish Woman steps out, closes the door behind her and stares at us, frowning.

"We've met before?" Bernie says with a smile, slipping back into brogue. "But were never properly introduced. Bernadette, but please call me Bernie. And you would be . . . ?"

It's hardly the moment for social niceties. "We could smell something," I say, pinching my nostrils to demonstrate. "Are you all OK?" Fish Woman stares at me, unblinking. "We come as friends."

She holds up a forefinger, indicating for us to wait, and disappears behind the door. The sound of low muttering is punctuated by one of Bernie's monologues: "Think of the poor lambs being thrown about in the storm, saying their prayers for the dead and dying . . . Why weren't they brought up to the crew mess, where we could have taken care of them . . . It's inhuman, so it is . . . Forced to live in the bowels of the boat, no light or air . . ."

Finally, Fish Woman returns. "We have problem," she says. "Will you help us?" she asks. Hoping it's not a trap of some kind, I nod and Bernie crosses herself. "Come in. My name is Afet."

"Afet," says Bernie, doubtfully. "Not a name I've come across."

The young woman adds with a downward glance: "It means "mischief." We enter and she locks the door behind us.

It takes a moment to adjust to the light, which is dim and heavy with fog. This is the chamomile steam we detected in the kitchen, and it is emanating from a large brass thurible hanging on a chain straight ahead of us; unlike the ones you see in church, it consists of a glass chamber for liquid, with the low flame of an oil burner below.

The space is in no sense a cabin, more a passageway running between vast floor-to-ceiling tanks made of stainless steel and traced with pipework, dials, valves, wheels and levers. This is *Maldemer*'s fuel bunker, in which are stored the half-million liters of diesel required to convey her, her guests and all her trappings in excess of four thousand miles nonstop across the Atlantic. I'm not sure what Health and Safety would say about the oil lamp, but I let it pass.

Some attempt has been made to turn the space into a home, with strips of carpet underfoot and photographs and posters taped onto the sides of the tanks. Rosettes, fashioned from twisted strips of brown paper, shade the bare light bulbs. One nook serves as a primitive kitchen, with a hotplate and kettle simmering away; another, hung with a curtain, as a washroom, with tap and bucket.

Afet motions us to stay where we are, and lightly claps her hands. To our amazement, out from between the tanks steps Flower Lady, flanked by three other young women, all dressed in simple robes and holding hands.

I recognize one of them, maybe two, but seeing them out of uniform, they're younger than I thought, in their late teens at most.

Our hostess proceeds to introduce the women by name. Flower Lady is called Alisiya, and her colleagues Brilyant, Marija and Ulduz. As each name is called, the owner gives a graceful bow. Then it's our turn. Bernie attempts a deep curtsey, but loses her balance and the girls titter. This breaks the ice.

During this ceremony, I feel burning shame course through my veins that these innocent young women—whoever they are and whyever they're here—should be imprisoned in the bowels of the boat, nameless and ignored, while upstairs we wallow in pointless and wasteful luxury.

We are beckoned down the passage and I realize we're in a dormitory; the spaces between the tanks having been furnished with narrow bunks. One has been draped with a colorful spread and Bernie and I are invited to sit; tea arrives in tiny cups. Afet draws up a stool and her companions cluster round, watching us intently.

"It's all right," I say. "You can trust us." Perhaps as a reflex, Bernie whisks her security ID card out of her pocket and flashes it round; the women look on in polite bafflement. "We will help, if we can. But we need to know what's happening here. Who you are."

Afet considers this for a moment.

"Are you stowaways?" asks Bernie.

Afet translates this for her companions, and a short exchange follows. As far as I can tell, Alisiya remains suspicious of us, while Afet shrugs, as if to say, *We have no choice.*

Finally, she wins her colleague over. Raising her head high, she declares: "We are from Rustavaijan."

Good grief! I rack my brains, rotate an imaginary globe in my head: small country between Russia and Iran, in the Caucasus.

"From fishing village," she continues, pulling in an imaginary net and undulating one hand. That'll be the Caspian Sea: explains why she was so adept at handling Sir Billy's catch the other day. "We are on our way . . . to *America.*"

Chapter 67

All eyes light up at the word, except for mine and Bernie's.

"What do you mean?" I say, suddenly filled with doubt.

"Are you . . . are you hoping to work there?"

"Land of the free," she replies, eyes shining.

Bernie and I exchange glances. "Who organized this?" I ask.

Afet shakes her head and looks down.

"Is it the captain? He must know what's going on."

"No, no. Keep secret!" She suddenly looks frightened. "We pay for voyage, we work. We happy to work. All—" she struggles for the words—"good, no problem."

Bernie and I sit in silence, absorbing this bombshell. I don't know who's behind it or who's in on it, but as I feared, it's plainly a people-smuggling operation of some kind. What destiny awaits Afet and her friends in the United States—or wherever they're really going? Modern slavery? Sex work? One thing I'm sure of: we must get them off this accursed yacht at the first opportunity, and that means the Azores.

Our tea is refreshed and, from scraps and gestures, we piece their story together. It's the age-old clash of traditional values and what they see on television—Turkish shopping channels and American soaps. They are all from the same extended family. Afet describes their odyssey, by bus to the Black Sea and thence to Turkey, where the group boarded *Maldemer* by moonlight.

We could stay all night listening, but Bernie catches my eye. "We've been here long enough," she says. "You said you needed help, Afet. Anything we can do, we will."

We follow Afet to the end of the fuel bunker. To our astonishment, here's another of them: Kifayet. She's younger than the others—early to mid-teens, I'd guess—and lies stretched out in bed. Overhead hangs an Eastern Orthodox crucifix.

"Poor lass," says Bernie, approaching and taking her hand. "What a pretty name you've got."

"It means *enough* in our language," explains Afet, adding, "She's youngest of nine sisters."

I notice that the girl has deep bruises to one side of her face, though she turns her head against the pillow to cover them when she sees me looking. The marks are recent. "I am sorry," she mutters, refusing to meet my eye. I don't understand why she should be apologizing to me but for some reason I feel overwhelming guilt. Who did this to her?

I don't resist when Afet takes my arm and steers me discreetly away, leaving Bernie to whisper privately with the girl.

"Afet, I need to ask you something," I say to her. "It's important."

She looks at me gravely.

"The morning the lady died . . . you were sent to the master cabin to mop out the bathroom." She nods.

"You know who I mean when I say, 'Sir Billy'?" She nods again.

"Was Sir Billy there when you arrived?"

"Yes," she replies.

"Now, think back. Was he there all the time, or did he go out of the master cabin and come back later?"

"He stay all the time."

"Are you sure? If you were in the bathroom, he could have—"

"He say I use wrong mop. He tell me I do it wrong, take too long. He stand watch till I finish."

Chapter 68

If you were looking for someone to stand you an alibi, you wouldn't find anyone more convincing than this earnest young woman. If Sir Billy was in his cabin when Xéra was murdered, then he's in the clear, and I must urgently persuade him to help me.

I'm recalled to the moment, however, by the return of Bernie, in full nurse mode.

"I'd say it's an abscess in her sinus, possibly a fracture," she declares, as we climb back to the land of the living. "Poor girl needs more than a whiff of chamomile. I'm heading straight to the first officer to get a broad-spectrum antibiotic from our medical supplies. I'll say it's for me, and we'll get her to a doctor soon as we land."

It's outrageous that the only way to get medicine for a deckhand—who's been mysteriously beaten up—is to pretend it's for someone else. I make a vow to get to the bottom of that, but first the murder inquiry.

Last time I saw Sir Billy was in the grand saloon so I head straight there. Marje is alone at the bar, scribbling lists and numbers on a little square-lined pad.

"Is Sir Billy coming back?" I demand.

"I'm waiting for him," she says, looking up and making it clear that my presence will not be required.

I ignore this and take a stool further along. The place is strewn with empty glasses and cups; it wouldn't hurt these people to tidy up after themselves occasionally.

"Much happening?" I ask, cautiously.

"Captain *Romeo* popped in to flutter his eyelashes—apologize for the broken engine," she replies, not looking up from her pad. "If it's not one thing it's another."

"Did he give us a new ETA?"

"Tomorrow evening. Last time you see me on a goddamn ship."

"May I?" I ask, reaching over for the ice bucket. As I do so I manage to sneak a look at her notepad, which is covered with crude squiggles; I notice she doesn't join up her letters properly. She sees me looking and snaps it shut.

"That reminds me, Marje, I keep meaning to say. We're not technically a ship. *Maldemer* is a yacht."

"I know that—I'm not dumb. I say it to annoy the captain."

"Well, it annoys everyone else too." Then I lower my voice and ask: "When you called me into your cabin the other day, we agreed to keep each other in the loop, if we found anything out. Have you?"

"You go first," she says, swilling her vodka.

"Well," I say, feeling outmaneuvered, "I told Sir Billy that Xéra's death wasn't an accident, which—by the way—you said you would do. It didn't go down well."

"Whadya expect, you go stirring things up? Question to ask is, who mighta wanted her out of the picture?"

"I can think of a few," I say, like Marje herself, for instance. "And what about the necklace? Who do you—"

I'm interrupted—to Marje's relief, I sense—by the arrival of Sir Billy. He pats her on the shoulder and rebuffs my attempt at a handshake, saying instead, "Excuse us, please. My sister and I wish to talk privately."

"But, Sir Billy—"

The pair traverse the grand saloon and settle in a quiet niche, the one set out for games. Sir Billy must feel at home among dice and playing cards and gambling chips; a slot machine and bingo caller wouldn't go amiss. I'd really like to hear what they're talking about. I knew that medical device I "borrowed" from Aimee's medicine chest would come in handy.

Chapter 69

I hurry to my cabin to collect the stethoscope, then slip unnoticed through a service door and behind the paneling to a position not far from where Sir Billy and Marje sit talking.

Mwamwam, mwaum. Waummwa? Mwaam maamwaaaa. I uncoil the stethoscope with care, plug in the eartips and press the diaphragm—the bit that's always freezing cold—against the wall. *Yesss!*

". . . and after all, Bill, a promise is a promise," Marje is saying.

"Then you should have kept your side of the bargain," says Sir Billy.

"I did, for chrissake! Not my fault it ended up in the hands of Xéra's little dolly boy . . ."

Is she referring to me?

"Look, Marjorie," replies Sir Billy wearily. "When we spoke last year things were going well. How could I know they'd throw this raft of new legislation at us? If I'd realized it would wipe out PWL, I obviously wouldn't have given you false hopes."

"False hopes? All I asked was for you to guarantee a bank loan, and I only need that till the DiCaprio project comes through. Christ, Bill, I'd have thought if nothing else you'd do it in memory of your wife."

"How dare you drag Xéra into it? And, by the way, she told me what you were up to—threatening her, to make her cough up if I wouldn't. Blackmail, pure and simple."

I must take another look at the scrawled letter I found in Xéra's dressing room.

"The fact remains—" says Marje, voice strident now.

"I asked Russell to explore all options and he said that we're maxed out, quite imposs—"

"That snake! You said you were going to fire him."

"I was, Marjorie. Obviously now—"

"OK, in that case what's the update on the . . . you know what? Which Russell swore was "watertight" . . . Watertight my ass. Tell me what's happening."

"If you're talking about the prenup, Russell's had all the papers out and gone through them with a fine-tooth comb."

"Could do with using it on that lousy wig of his," mutters Marje.

"There's a prenup, and there's a UK will, which—assuming she signed it—supersedes her French will, and the respective tax authorities will have to battle it out between them."

"'Assuming she signed it?' For crying out loud, Bill, don't tell me . . . So, while we're waiting a hundred years for all this to sort itself out, how much is there?"

"Erm, it's complicated. Her *notaire* is in Paris, but we decided not to contact him before we officially announce her death. Trust me, everything will be fine, but we must all be patient. And for the foreseeable future, I regret I'm in no position to keep my family in frills and furbelows."

"Frills and furbelows my butt," snaps Marje. "Come off it, Bill. Getting rid of a wife with millions in the bank should solve a few problems, not create them."

"How dare you!" roars Sir Billy—and they're on the move.

I hear the sharp sound of a slap and the crash of glasses and crockery falling. Should I jump out of my hiding place and separate them?

"Never *ever* talk about Xéra in that way!" he bellows. "She was the only . . . For heaven's sake, Marjorie, *I LOVED HER!*"

Racking sobs fill the air, interrupted by a perky Australian announcement over the public address system that "Oi! It's Happy Hour," and cocktails are about to be served.

Chapter 70

I tuck the stethoscope away and hurry back to my cabin. I have work to do.

This conversation, exposing the rot at the heart of the Hardcastle empire, shocks me to the core. I knew it would come down to money—it always does—but I wasn't aware how desperately they all need it, or how urgently.

There's so much information bouncing around that it's time to make a list. Ruling out Sir Billy, the only person with an alibi, I draw up a table of all the males aboard.

SUSPECT	ALIBI	MOTIVE
Captain Romer	Unknown	Unknown
Blue	Pretending to jog	Unknown
Russell	Jigsaw in cabin	To prevent being sacked
Shane	Asleep in cabin	To preserve financial status quo

I decide to rule out Romer and Blue, at least for the time being, because neither had anything to gain from Xéra's death.

I'd like it to be Russell because he's such a monster. He could easily have slipped out of his cabin for ten minutes while Judith was up on deck doing her word puzzle.

Then there's Shane. It's easy to imagine Elise goading him on, telling him to screw his courage to the sticking place; there's something of the Lady Macbeth about her. A forensics team would probably have been able to determine whether the attack was perpetrated by a left-hander, but it's too late for that now.

I'm trying to figure out how the necklace incident, and my near drowning, might fit into these different scenarios . . . when my television springs into life. "Hi, Paul," says Miss Australia. "After all the excitement, dinner has been canceled. We're gonna take trays round to the cabins, so you can have the evening off."

What a nerve! I go along to the galley anyway, and find Bernie laboring over a bubbling pot of pasta, which she intends to make into mac and cheese. A few clever twists later, including the addition of lobster morsels and some chargrilled red peppers (plus a punchy green salad to accompany) and we've produced a supper fit for a superyacht.

After that—because a promise is a promise—I turn my attention to cookies. Properly made, *Vanillekipferl* are tender, moist and light, with cornstarch to add airiness, egg yolks softness and a high proportion of high-quality butter. Last time I came across vanilla was during my ill-fated sojourn in the chain locker, but even Bernie isn't eccentric enough to store it there, surely? I'm relieved to find a jar of pods tucked behind the sugar; you can never beat seeds, freshly scraped from the pod.

I shape the cookies in the traditional way, by rolling the dough into short logs, slightly tapered, then curving them into half-moons. I end up with two dozen. After baking I transfer them to a wire rack, out of harm's way. Once cooled, they'll be rolled in icing sugar, then again before serving.

Next, I make myself a comforting cold sausage sandwich on

white, dab of Dijon, and take it back to my cabin to eat in front of my sliver of sea view. As I eat, I call up the images I took on my phone during my unauthorized cabin inspections.

What, for instance, does Blue have to say about Elise?

E. H.-H.

@ a glnc $_s$'s splt & slf$_s$, bt hr upbr^{gg} ws fr frm ^{p}fct – a wywrd f$_t$r & str^g of stpm$_t$rs. Hr mrg 2 Shane, $_w$o I sspct s bsxual, s un^{c}vn^{nl}. $_s$ ^{c}dns hs drnk^g, h hr smk^g & phlndr^g. Ds h hv any idea abt r afr? H crtnly ^{d}lks m, bt ds h no I'm hdlng n lv w$_t$ hs bt^f wf, & wd gv any$_t$^{g} 2 hv hr as my own? I've nvr flt $_t$s ^{d}prt 2 b w$_t$ smn – I st n my hdeous cbn lng^g 2 gt a glmps of hr, her hr vc. $_s$ ^{p}mss $_t$t t wl al b fn $_w$n w gt awy 2g$_t$r @ $_t$ end of $_t$ crs

I can work out the first few lines—he's clocked Shane as bisexual!—but that's about it. Not for the first time, I wish I'd learned to speedwrite myself. If Julie can learn a language from scratch, maybe it's not too late to learn a new writing system, which could come in useful one day.

Next, I call up the letter I found in Xéra's cabin, which—no doubt about it—is the work of Marje: I recognize the griffonage from her notepad at the bar. Why did she feel the need to write her friend a letter?

By a combination of zooming in with my iPhone, zooming out, examining individual words from different directions and under different lights, holding the script up to the mirror, et cetera, et cetera, this is the best I can do:

Tuesday morning. Xéra dear, So sorry about the robbery, but did you manage to speak to Bill? Look, things are worse than I thought and if I don't get something sorted soon I'm <u>sunk</u>. You <u>did</u> promise you'd put in a good word; after all, I was the one who introduced you two lovebirds! [Several words illegible here] *old paperwork—I'm sure you remember* [more illegible words] *boy.*
   I know that with you on my side, Bill will bail me out, after which I'll make sure you get it back. Give it some thought.
   P.P.S. You know I regard Russell Tate as <u>dangerous</u>! <u>On no account</u> speak of this to him.

What "old paperwork"? What "boy"? This is surely what Marje is blackmailing Xéra about—infuriating that the missing words are the very ones that I really want to read.
   Compared with this, the photocopied document I found apparently hidden in Marje's cabin is a breeze: all I have to do is enlarge it on my phone.
   I scrutinize the WTH logo, which caught my eye earlier . . . Oh, no, what a horrible coincidence! For it is none other than that evil-sounding legal firm Waister Timon Hassall—the "no win, no fee" tricksters Jonny has instructed to try and evict me from Jubilee Cottage.
   The letter is dated January 2011. As well as *Highly Confidential*, it's *Without Prejudice* and *Ex Gratis*; nice touch, that Latin, though I bet they charged extra for it.

   To Pâtisserie Pompadour Ltd
   24 Holborn Viaduct
   London EC1A 2BN

   <u>SETTLEMENT AGREEMENT AND RELEASE</u>
   With this letter we hereby acknowledge receipt of your

payment in the sum of £3,000,000 (THREE MILLION POUNDS) in full and final settlement of the dispute between:

PÂTISSERIE POMPADOUR LTD

and our client:

MR. GRAEME CAESAR MARCH, of Flat 217, Wymering Mansions, Wymering Road, London W9 2NB, United Kingdom.

P.P. Ernest Timon
Waister Timon Hassall
The Pyramid
187 Shoreditch High Street
London E1 6JE

CHAPTER 71

I'm pondering this new information, wondering if the old paperwork mentioned in Marje's letter and this old photocopy might in some way be linked, when an alarm sounds on my phone: 10 p.m., time to jump on my laptop. Thank heavens, the Starlink's up and running: an email from Julie from first thing this morning, plus another which—if it weren't for the time difference—I'd swear came from the future.

From: Julie Johnson
Friday 7:58 a.m.
Subject: Panicking here
To: Paul Delamare/Aboard *M/Y Maldemer*

That's the shortest email I've ever had from you—something's not right. TELL ME WHAT'S GOING ON!

As for Lacuna—I hope you're not serious? I looked it up and three years ago an American yacht disappeared and was found floating off it, and the yachtsmen never heard of again. As you guessed, it's some kind of volcanic rock, sticking up in the middle of nowhere. One harbor, no roads, protected habitat for an endangered scorpion and the Lacunan viper.

Belongs to the Azores. In 2019 an undisclosed individual (i.e. pirate/bandit/racketeer/Tory party donor/all of the above) bought a 20-year concession on it. No pictures on Google Earth (why?) but I'm imagining shacks and shanties. Wild West-Sur-Mer.

I happened to mention it to Declan who says it's a terrible lawless place and why are you asking?

WHAT IS HAPPENING?

I'm not in the mood for tarot, but I thought it would calm me down. It hasn't! The first three cards were so alarming I decided to turn it into a pentagram spread with two more . . . that made it worse.

So: finally the Pentacles show up, and they're in force: money, money, money, money, money. <u>Five of Pentacles</u>, financial collapse or misdemeanor of some kind.

<u>Death</u> may not happen literally—let's hope not!—but expect a reversal of some kind; next to the Pentacles, it could be financial.

<u>The Hermit</u> is always searching for something; whoever he may represent (you?), he's in a bleak, lonely place.

Into the mix let's throw <u>Five of Swords</u> (conflict) and <u>The Devil</u> (not necessarily THE Devil, but something or someone of life-or-death importance) and you are pretty much ambushed by negativity. Even if you don't know it yet.

I'll do my utmost to try and draw you some more upbeat cards tomorrow—I wish I could pick and choose.

<u>Take great care.</u> Email me back immediately when you get this.

J. X

From: Declan Armstrong (personal)
Friday 10:27 p.m.
Subject: Visit to NW8
To: Paul Delamare/Aboard *M/Y Maldemer*

Please find attached: a Voice Memo from earlier today. With Apologies for the Delay, caused by the intervention of urgent matters. I have reformatted the file to make it easier to play: on account of your unreliable Wi-Fi; and the difficulties you have in technical matters. D. A.

Thanks, Julie, for telling your boyfriend I'm an idiot. On the other hand, it means I haven't got to wince my way through another of his literary efforts.

I hit play and hear his familiar growly voice: he has a strong cockney accent, which Julie describes as "charmingly authentic" and which even I enjoy listening to; though I sometimes wonder if he dials it up for our benefit.

"Hi Paul, sorry for the delay, but I finally managed to get meself down to St. John's Wood High Street today to have a butcher's at the ol' pâtisserie."

In the background I hear his feet slapping the pavement; cops always stamp their feet down like shire horses. There's the background boom and rumble of traffic.

"It's me lunch hour and I'm on me way to work, so I thought I'd fill you in straight away.

The premises is off the high street in St. Ann's Terrace and its current tenant is a Mr. [mumble], spelt F-L-U-G-E-L."

Dear me, as in *Flugelhorn*, surely.

"Mr. [mumble] took it over from Pâtisserie Pompom fifteen years ago and runs it as a Viennese caff. It's proper posh, wiv tinted glass and gold paint everywhere."

Ah! I remember it well! The domed ceilings, Pompadour

Pink upholstery piped in gold silk, and "Après nous, le déluge" picked out in stained glass above the door.

"*Here's the interestin' bit. The story is that it closed cos of a birthday party that went wrong—that's all anyone would say. A birthday party that went wrong. And that—*"

A truck goes past, there's shouting and Declan swears. My goodness, for someone with limited linguistic abilities, that's quite a . . . rich vocabulary.

"*Sorry 'bout that, let me just write down that muppet's VRN.*"

Here I imagine him getting out a pad, licking his pencil.

"*Where was I? Yeah, the Pompom lot closed the place all of a sudden, wiv eight months left on the lease. Which was odd, seein' as it had only been open a couple of months.*"

"*And I'm afraid that's it! Sorry I haven't been more helpful.*"

"*Oh, yeah—this is important. Julie mentioned Lacuna. The FCDO advises against non-essential travel to the island. I got a contact at the NCB in Manchester if you need to know more, but it sounds a bleedin' 'ellhole to me.*"

"*If you don't 'ear from me again, it's cos I died crossin' Finchley Road! You take care.*"

I feel a twinge of guilt about Declan—I'm not sure I'd have given up my lunch hour to conduct a wild goose chase across North London for the friend of a friend. I tap out a reply.

From: Paul Delamare/Aboard *M/Y Maldemer*
Friday 10:11 p.m.
Subject: Birthday party
To: Declan Armstrong (personal)

40°69'93'N, 33°33'27'W

Dear Declan,

You have been so helpful and thorough—as has your friend in forensics. Thank you for your voice note—I like listening to your cheery voice. Have you thought of auditioning for *Crimewatch*?

I'm not sure how a birthday party in NW8 fits into the mystery, but I'm grateful to you for your efforts. I owe you a drink.

I keep forgetting to congratulate you on your promotion to "Acting Detective Chief Inspector." Very important-sounding.

Kind regards, Paul

P.S. One day you must tell me what FCDO and NCB mean.

Chapter 72

I try writing a reply to Julie, making it sound as if I haven't a care in the world, but give up. I can't lie to her.

A glance out of my porthole tells me it's turned into a pleasant evening: the calm after the storm. I don't feel like going to bed yet, so I decide to take a turn on deck, have a nightcap and see who's about.

Stepping out onto the lawn deck I see Karol-Kate and Colefax emerge from the pilot house. They've evidently been chatting to the captain.

"Evening, you two," I say. "Saved any more lives? Fixed any more engines?"

"We've been invited down to the galley for a cup of tea. A glass of wine would have been my choice, but Bernie says it's not allowed below deck."

"She's good company, isn't she?" I say, wondering if Bernie whisked off her eye patch for the big reveal.

"She was telling me she's really sharpened up her cheffing skills, thanks to you." And there's the answer to that.

"Karol-Kate, there's something I keep meaning to ask." For some reason she looks slightly alarmed. "It's only a little thing, but I keep going over and over what happened on Wednesday morning, whether I or anyone could have done more to help Xéra."

"Don't torture yourself, Paul. You mustn't. What you did was spot on."

"I'm trying to establish a timeline. You know you were on the afterdeck with your bag of crumbs?"

"Absolutely," she replies. "Judith told me you shouldn't feed bread to albatrosses, but it's rubbish."

"What time was it when you first saw the albatross?"

She looks at me, puzzled. "What do you mean? I didn't see the albatross."

"Oh. Then why did you tell the pilot house you did? And where did the crumbs come from?"

"I never saw any bird, and never said I did. We heard it announced on the loudspeaker and headed up."

"Oh, I assumed it was you. And you just happened to have a bag of bread?"

"We passed a cart on the way with someone's breakfast-in-bed on a tray, and figured they wouldn't miss a bread roll."

"Who do you mean by 'we'?"

"Who do you think? Me and my shadow. Colefax started freaking out—must have known something was wrong." The Bichon looks up at us with round black eyes and gives a slow, sad blink.

I tap my chin. "OK, in that case, where did the bag come from—the one you had the bread in?"

"It wasn't a bag," she says. "I grabbed a napkin off the cart and wrapped it in that."

The story seems watertight, but *someone* must have seen and reported the albatross.

I descend to the galley to collect the *Vanillekipferl*, which are where I left them but a couple short. I pile them concentrically on a plate and head back up to the pilot house.

"Hello, captain." His eyes light up, but I don't hand the cookies over quite yet. "Turned into a lovely evening. I didn't know storms came and went so quickly. Still expecting we'll make land this time tomorrow?"

"Yes, indeed," he says. "Although a minor problem with the navigation system there remains." So much is true—the illuminated compass and most of the other controls are off.

"I was hoping to check something with you, if it isn't too much trouble. It's about the albatross."

"You watch birds?"

"Hardly an expert. The other morning—the day Lady Hardcastle, erm, died—you announced you'd seen the bird and we all went up to take a look."

"I remember."

"We must have been too late, because it wasn't there."

"Did I make the announcement? Yes. Did I see the bird? No."

"Then why announce it?"

He gives me a puzzled look. "Because one of the guests came to the pilot house, very excited, and asked me to put it out on the public address system. I did as asked."

"Who?" I ask, moving the cookies nearer to tantalize him with the butter and vanilla aromas.

He raises a tweezered eyebrow. "Go and ask him your questions. There he is now—walking on the grass."

Chapter 73

I approach Russell at the rail, where he's in the process of lighting a cigar. I notice he's chucked the cap on the grass: the sort of person who throws chocolate wrappers out of his car window.

"Beautiful evening," I say. Under the slanting light his hairpiece looks even odder than usual; maybe it's back to front. "Montecristo?"

He nods.

"No Judith?"

"She does her own thing," he says with a sniff. "I would offer you one—"

"Not for me, thanks." Can't stand them: Marcus used to take a cigar-smoking client to lunch and I had to hang his clothes out of the window when he got home.

"Can I get you a drink?" I offer. Judging by his breath he's had one or three already.

"Rum on the rocks for me—might as well pretend we're in the Caribbean even if we're not going there now."

By the time I return with a laden tray of glasses, bottles and ice, he's looking oddly flushed; I hope he knows not to inhale. "Why don't we sit down and make the most of the sunset?" I say, leading him to a bench. A pinkish sky with a half-moon rising: what could be more perfect?

It's extremely bad form—as well as dangerous—to ply someone with alcohol in the hope they'll be indiscreet, but I'm spared the need because Russell pours himself a triple, knocks it back in one and glugs out another.

"Have some ice," I insist.

"What a tragic week," he says, with an expansive gesture of his arm. "And after Sir Billy was generous enough to invite us all along . . ."

"Such a shame for Judith," I say next. "She told me how much she'd been looking forward to it."

He frowns. "Not really. She's more the stay-at-home type."

"I hardly know her, of course, but she seems very sensitive. Underneath."

"Quite the psychoanalyst," he says. "You seem to understand her better than I do."

Perhaps if he paid her more attention that wouldn't be the case. I continue: "It's a pity you didn't get to know Xéra better. She was a wonderful person. Everyone adored her."

He stirs his drink with his finger then licks it. "I daresay."

"She's been part of my life for fifteen years. What makes it even more tragic is that she'd waited so long for this. All those years of building up the business and living out of hotel rooms, and finally she finds the right man to settle down with."

"From her point of view, very, erm, advantageous, I'm sure."

Ignoring this, I ask: "How long have you worked for Sir Billy?"

"He was a client of a firm I used to be with, then offered me the chance to work for him full-time."

We gaze out to sea for a minute or two.

"How did you think Sir Billy and Xéra were together? As a couple, I mean?" I think back to that interrupted kiss in their cabin the first time I met him. "You didn't get the sense either of them was having second thoughts?"

"Absolutely none of my business. And if you're asking in an underhand kind of way whether or not I approved of the match, same answer. *However*," he says, relighting his cigar, "I can see that the marriage had repercussions for the rest of the family—his daughter and son-in-law, for instance."

"How do you know this?"

He exhales a puff of blue smoke and pauses. "Elise likes a cigarette after dinner, and sometimes I like a cigar, so yes, I admit, she and I have talked." Julie's always warning me to watch out for smokers and their cabals: they plot and gossip while they puff away, scheming the downfall of non-smokers.

"Let me guess," I say. "Elise resented Xéra and felt she was being squeezed out. The old wicked stepmother routine."

"Lady Hardcastle may have come across as kind and generous, but there was another side to her. I suspect she was jealous of my influence over her husband. And she decided that Elise and the tennis player were old enough to start paying their own way."

"Doesn't sound like Xéra to me," I reply. I know for a fact this is rubbish—she told me it was all Russell's idea.

"Perhaps you didn't know her as well as you thought. In any case, Elise found herself with an immediate cashflow shortfall."

"Did she ask for a loan, to tide her over?" Rich people don't beg for money—"loan" is the usual polite fiction.

"Lady Hardcastle was adamant. There was to be: No. More. Money." He gesticulates to drive home his point. Xéra would never stab her forefinger in your face in that vulgar way, not in a million years.

"Well, Sir Billy's his own man now, he can start writing checks again."

"Circumstances have indeed changed," says Russell, picking an ice cube out of his glass and crunching on it—detestable habit.

"How so?" I say.

He examines me again with rheumy eyes. "I had the honor of being involved in certain arrangements with respect to Lady Hardcastle's—*poor* Lady Hardcastle's—will."

Chapter 74

"What does it say?" I ask, refilling his drink to stop him doing it himself: at the rate he's pouring he'll slide under the table.

"If you're angling to find out if anything was left to you—"

"Last thing on my mind. Rumor I heard is that she made a new will in Sir Billy's favor, but you're not sure whether she signed it or not."

He looks up in surprise. "All I'm prepared to say is that yesterday there was a communication from France that we couldn't quite understand."

"If it's in French I can probably help."

He looks at me scornfully. "That won't be necessary."

"Xéra told me about the sale of the Pompadour business, by the way. It sounds to me as if—"

This riles him. "If you're suggesting any impropriety—that Sir Billy exerted undue influence—"

"Your words, not mine."

He sniffs. "Look, Sir Billy is an extremely wealthy man in his own right. It was entirely up to Lady Hardcastle what she did with her own money. Previously, I can't quite remember all the details, she had the idea of funding a project in the Far East."

"It's a foundation, named after her mother. Yes, she had it all planned. I imagine she'll have made provision for it."

"I'll take your word for that. Charity begins at . . . well, you know the saying."

"So tell me," I say, "exactly how much does Sir Billy stand to inherit from his wife of a few days?"

There's a long pause, but he takes the bait. "Not so much as perhaps . . . but enough to . . . The low millions, let us say. Not a life-changing sum."

Rather depends where you're coming from!

Russell continues: "If things play out right. Not as much as . . . But a useful sum for . . . a businessman who knows what to do with it. I can imagine . . . with a sensible spread of investments . . . a long–short equity shtrategy . . ."

Alcohol affects everyone differently, particularly when combined with cigars, and I'm losing him.

"Russell, one last question. What can you tell me about Luiz Mateus?"

He snaps back to attention. "Never heard of him."

"After the necklace was stolen, you were the one who said it had been bought from a middleman called Mateus. "Big Lew" you called him."

"Not me."

"In case it jogs your memory, Elise said that you introduced her at Crockfords and he spent the whole evening looking down her dress."

"Nonsense," he replies.

Pondering why he should suddenly and so vehemently deny the man's existence, I ask if he'd like coffee.

"If you inshisht," he slurs.

"Keep an eye open for albatrosses," I say, casually, as I cross the deck.

"Never sheen one in my life," he replies, with a hiccup. "Wouldn't know an albatrosh if it shat on me."

I go down to the grand saloon and press a few buttons on the Gaggia—I don't know how he likes it, but only savages take milk in their coffee at this time of night.

My mind races. I've got my man! He set up the albatross announcement in an attempt to give himself an alibi. He killed Xéra because she threatened his prestigious position and his hold over the family.

But what next? I could tell the captain, but he'd laugh in my face. I could hammer on the door of Sir Billy's cabin, and we could get Bernie to stand guard over him with her pistol. But it's not as if there's anywhere for him to escape to, and in any case, he's drunk as a skunk.

I resolve to keep calm, not arouse his suspicion, and tell Sir Billy first thing tomorrow morning. Then we can go together to the captain and get the murderer put under lock and key.

Five minutes later, I'm back up on deck with an espresso. Russell is hanging over the railing, gazing into the sea, and I realize tears are sliding down his face.

"Are you OK? Anything I can do?"

I hand him the coffee, which he looks at doubtfully. He takes a sip, makes a face and hands it back.

"I meant to say," he snorts, "thank you for putting in a, erm, good word with the chief stewardess."

Uurgh! That must mean Challis has succumbed to his charms. Strictly for the tip.

Now he starts to weep in earnest.

"What's wrong, Russell?" I say. "Would you like me to fetch Judith?"

He scowls at me, shakes his head and breaks into great heaving sobs. He staggers forward as if to hug me—I shrink away—then collapses back onto the bench, mucus streaming down his face.

He could do with a tissue—a box wouldn't go amiss—but I remind myself this is the man who murdered my friend in cold blood. I mutter goodnight and cross the grass to the hatch leading down.

I thought I heard a scuffling sound when I went down for coffee, and now, as I descend the companionway, I see a shadow slide away down the corridor.

I've no right to complain—I've been guilty of it myself—but who is it creeping round the yacht, watching and listening?

Chapter 75

The exertions of the day finally catch up with me and I put myself to bed, exhausted. I should really rehearse what I'm going to say to Sir Billy tomorrow, but I drift off into an uneasy sleep. I don't believe in dreams as harbingers, but tarot cards keep popping into my head, specifically the one involving dogs and lobsters. A vision comes to me of Judith weeping; as she surely will when she discovers she's married to a murderer.

My tossing and turning is interrupted by a noise. Or rather: lack of noise. It's suddenly gone deathly quiet.

I check my watch—shortly after twelve—and listen hard.

The door to CC 11 FS is a sliding device, activated by keycard. When you lock yourself in—as I did, with great care—a little red light comes on. It isn't on now.

Taking a grip on myself, I climb down from my bunk and flick the light switch. Nothing happens. I try opening the door with my keycard and again, nothing. It must be a power cut, except you'd expect an emergency system to leap into action.

At least I have a porthole: I raise the blind. The moon has set and the sea turned ink-black. I'm trapped down here in the dark.

My heart starts pounding. I know there's a killer aboard the yacht—a double killer if they'd had their way and I'd drowned.

I must think fast.

CC 11 FS is an overflow crew cabin in the bow of the boat—*FS* stands for "Fore Starboard." It's isolated from the rest of the crew: I could scream and shout, but *no one will ever hear me*.

I kick myself for not having brought a proper weapon from the galley. There's no shortage—as I'm always saying, a kitchen is a deathtrap. A knife. A rolling pin. A fire extinguisher. Too late now.

The hairs on my head bristle: that was a noise! A footstep in the corridor. There is no earthly reason for anyone to come to this part of the boat at this hour. Who is it?

A bead of sweat breaks out on the back of my neck and I shiver as it trickles down my spine. My ears adjust themselves with a soft pop and I can hear myself breathing.

There it is again—nearer now. The soft thud of a foot on vinyl, followed by another.

Suddenly I get an idea. Scarcely daring to breathe, I lower my feet onto the floor and gently slide open the door of my closet. I can't think why I kept my wrecked clothes, but it's lucky I did: I pick up the bundle of maimed and shriveled garments and place them under the duvet on the lower bunk, arranging them to simulate a sleeping body. I tuck in the pillow to complete the illusion. All this I do noiselessly, though I'm terrified the banging of my heart will give me away.

Then I squeeze myself into the closet. I feel my neck crick as I slide the door shut, and a stab of pain from my knee, wedged at a peculiar angle.

I'm not safe, but at least I'm hidden.

The steps get nearer and stop outside the door. If my visitor were legitimate—for instance if they'd come to tell me about the power failure—they'd call out or knock.

Instead, I hear a scrabbling sound, a soft click and the door opens.

Who is it? A pinprick of light suddenly beams in through

the fingerhole in the closet door—someone's switched on a flashlight. I twist my head round to try and look out.

The intruder is holding something in their hand, but I can't see what. I move my head a millimeter for a better view—and *bam*! A dislodged coat hanger clatters down beside me. My visitor jumps and drops the flashlight; it hits the floor and goes out.

The next few moments happen in a blur, like a speeded-up film. With a hiss, the interloper jumps at the closet, rattling the door furiously. Inside, I fumble to shield my head with my hands, which are shaking like the clappers at a football match.

Before they can locate the fingerhole to slide the door open, there's a new shock: the most tremendous *SPLASH!* from outside the porthole. My visitor gasps and jumps back, then scrabbles about on the floor for the flashlight and disappears, footsteps pattering off down the corridor.

I wait like a sardine in a can for a full five minutes, then extract myself and shake out my cramped limbs. I clear my bunk and wedge myself in, knees to chin, wide awake.

There's still no power, so with one eye I watch my door, which I've slid shut but can't lock; with the other, my porthole. I fall into a doze until I'm jerked awake by another splash outside the porthole.

I peer out. The sun is starting to rise, and across the sparkling water I see a trail of foam and bubbles. A minute later, more bubbles and an unmistakable gray form glides across the surface, followed swiftly by a companion. Thank you, dolphins, for saving my life.

Chapter 76

I fire up my laptop ready for 6 a.m. Bang on cue, two emails flash up—one from late last night, one from just now.

From: Julie Johnson
Saturday 1:20 a.m.
Subject: URGENT!!!
To: Paul Delamare/Aboard *M/Y Maldemer*

Why haven't you emailed me back?

WHAT'S HAPPENING?

I asked you if you were all right—please reply as soon as you get this. What are you not telling me? I know you replied to Declan, so why are you ignoring me?

While I was hanging about <u>waiting for you to email,</u> I phoned Adrian in New York. The things I do for you! He has a new job—at *Vanity Fair*—and a new girlfriend (which means I was at least spared the heavy breathing *I-miss-you-darling* spiel). I mentioned

Blane Aspern and get this! He's an <u>undercover reporter</u>, based in New York. He did an exposé for them last year called "The Servant Problem," about the exploitation of maids and butlers by Manhattan socialites.

Rumor is he's been appointed editor-at-large for *Alligator*, some nasty new gossip mag. My theory is he's been working incognito for Marje to get the inside track on the LA talent business then saw a chance to write a juicy piece about disgusting superyachts, and the lazy rich people who sail on them. Good on him.

I asked about "LaGuardia" and it's apparently the High School of Music and Art and the Performing Arts. Hence the piano-playing.

You know you have a knack for saying the wrong thing—don't speak to him! Keep your mouth shut!

I drew you a card, though I don't know why I bother as I appear to have been dropped.

Forget <u>Death</u> or <u>The Hanged Man</u>—<u>The Tower</u> is the one no one wants: chaos/destruction/all hell unleashed. Simple as that. Let me know you're all right <u>ASAP</u>.

Yours IN EXASPERATION
J. X

P.S. Popped in at J. C. on the way home. There's no easy way to tell you but your aspidistra thingy has a problem. The tips of the leaves—and I mean all of them—have gone brown. I took advice and it's either too dry or too wet at the roots. What shall I do?

From: d.a.armstrong98@met.police.uk
Saturday 7:58 a.m.
Subject: Fwd: Urgent/confidential—Interpol Red Notice
To: Paul Delamare/Aboard *M/Y Maldemer*

Hi Paul. This is a Message regarding suspicious individual. Which arrived from my colleague at NCB. For information, NCB is Interpol's National Central Bureau.

Yours sincerely,
Declan Armstrong (Acting) DCI

Begin forwarded message:

<u>LUIZ MATEUS, alias of LJUBA MIRSAYEV, male, age 71 / 5'5" / 115 lbs. Appearance: bald, clean-shaven. Distinguishing marks: tattoo of dollar sign on the left pectoral, tattoo of mermaid on the right forearm.</u>

<u>This person is regarded as extremely dangerous and should not be approached.</u>

I admit to a twinge of disappointment. I'd love to be able to produce Mateus/Mirsayev for Declan, to prove I'm smarter than he thinks. Unfortunately, none of the male guests or crew is this old, short or skinny—and it would be a disguise too far even for Bernie. Nor have I found out anything about him, except that for some reason Russell chooses to deny his existence.

While I've got the signal on my side, I compose a short, calming reply to Julie. She enjoys a lie-in on a Saturday morning, so I imagine her reading it as she sips her wheatberry and turmeric smoothie, or whatever it is at the moment.

Then I make my way to the lawn deck to lie in wait for Karol-Kate, with whom I have a matter to discuss before breakfast.

Oh. My. Goodness. This is the life. I look around in wonder at the unbroken blue above and around me and take in deep, slow breaths of clean ocean air. I feel vitality and well-being course through my veins and arteries and despite my lack of sleep, my brain clears.

The cruise has been a catastrophe—cost me one of my dearest friends and almost my own life—but one can't deny *Maldemer* is a magnificent vessel. If I were a billionaire, I'd want one too. Then I remind myself I'm in grave danger. Must stay away from sheer drops and railings. Trust no one.

Karol-Kate arrives on schedule. "Wow!" I say. Today she's wearing fatigues in a funky neon camouflage print which would draw gunfire on a battlefield; perhaps deservedly.

"It's our last day so I thought I'd make an effort," she says, shuffling off to attend to Colefax, who's finished doing his business in a designated corner of grass, shielded by a screen which she erects and dismantles for the occasion.

"He's so reliable—the moment he hears *yip yip*," she says from behind the faux-bamboo. "Once a day, seven on the dot." She insists on showing me the special little chute down which she drops his leavings, appropriately bagged.

"Jolly civilized, that dog," I say. "Shame he got dragged in as accomplice to a crime."

"What on earth are you talking about?" she says, wheeling round.

It's not the first time I've found that if you go to sleep with a problem, you wake up with the solution; even if, as in this case, you hardly slept at all and only then in mortal terror. Because as well as unmasking Xéra's killer, I now know who stole her necklace.

"Why did you do it?" I ask.

She looks at the floor, sighs and says: "How do you know?"

"Let's just say it came to me . . . dogs and lobsters. There was something in the tank that agitated Colefax. Then I remembered the night the necklace was stolen: you took him out, I assumed for a comfort break, and returned with a doggy poo bag sticking out of your pocket. It had the necklace in it—am I right?"

She nods.

"Did you do it for the money?"

"What do you mean?" she replies, looking up sharply.

"Thousand quid in used notes."

"How on earth do you know about that?" she says, eyes flashing. "Anyway, I didn't want their filthy money—it was put in my cabin to incriminate me, in case I got caught. Plus, they threatened to throw poor Colefax overboard if I didn't steal it, and they would have done it, too."

"Who's 'they'?" I ask.

She ignores this. "I regret doing it, but I had no choice. Can we leave it at that?"

"Who put you up to it? You have to tell me."

"I'm sorry, Paul," she replies ruefully. "I can't. They threatened Colefax. He isn't safe until we get ashore."

We're interrupted by a colossal blast of foghorn, then the engines suddenly thrust and the yacht is thrown into a turn.

"*MAN OVERBOARD!*" booms over the public address system. Karol-Kate and I turn to each other in horror.

We hurry down to the afterdeck, where Aimee issues brisk instructions. The other guests arrive, still in pajamas and dressing gowns, and we line up each side, combing the sea with our eyes.

Chapter 77

Even before we've convened in the grand saloon for the latest doleful announcement, the story has whistled round the yacht.

The captain was in the pilot house, enjoying his morning coffee, when someone hammered on the door, in a state of great agitation. Judith had woken up early to find herself alone in bed, and assuming her husband had risen early to enjoy the splendid morning, went up on deck to look for him.

She couldn't find him, nor could a lightning search conducted by the crew. The captain therefore had no alternative but to pronounce Russell Tate missing, and now—presumed drowned.

The over-decorated room, with its overstuffed furnishings and lurid color scheme, looks even more grotesque than usual in the southern sunshine. Judith is slumped in a cocoonlike wing chair in maroon velvet, Challis kneeling at her side, holding her hand. Her breathing is quick and shallow, and the chief stewardess helps dab the tears away as they course down her cheeks.

The captain enters, complete with his signature cough and sleeve adjustments. In fractured syntax he explains that Mr. Tate must unfortunately have awoken in the night, gone for a walk and fallen overboard. According to Mrs. Tate, her husband suffered occasional dizzy spells.

Terrible, terrible, mutter the guests, who must be thinking uneasily: *Two down, seven to go.* And: *Will this Voyage of the Damned never end?*

"Any history of sleepwalking?" asks Elise. "And was he in his pajamas or did he get dressed first?"

"According to Mrs. Tate, Mr. Tate does not require much sleep and it is not unusual for him to go for a walk at night." He nods respectfully toward the pitiful figure in the wing chair. "And yes, he appears to have been dressed."

"Why turn the ship round if he fell off last night?" asks Marje.

"The technical term is 'Williamson Turn,'" the captain replies, with a glance at his nails. "In such cases, you do whatever you can. We have notified the Coast Guard at Ponta Delgada, Madame. That is the protocol in such a situation. And yacht, not ship."

"The fob on our keycard that saved me—the Personal Locator thingy," I say. "Can't you use that?"

"Mr. Tate's keycard was not about his person, it was left in his cabin." This puzzles me—he couldn't have got very far without it—but before I can say anything, Blue cuts in.

"So we still arrive in Ponta-da-da tonight?" You'd think all these shocks would drain him of his usual bloom and bounce, but he looks bandbox fresh, in a striped linen shirt and white shorts.

"Tonight without fail," says the captain.

During this exchange, I notice Karol-Kate whispering with Shane. She now puts up her hand. "Just an idea, in case it would help . . . and of course, only if Mrs. Tate agrees . . . but shall we get Colefax to track where Russell might have gone walking? Where he was before . . .?"

Judith is so distraught that Karol-Kate has to explain it again. At first, she shakes her head, then appears to change her mind. "You're right, thank you for your kindness. Even just to know . . . might be consoling." Then she buries her face in her hands and weeps convulsively. It's agony to witness.

Eventually, Challis leads her gently off to her cabin, shortly to return with a ball of Russell's socks, which has been suggested as the best way to give the dog his scent. I follow Karol-Kate and Shane into the corridor, where they brief the Bichon in a firm, quiet tone, explaining in grown-up English what is expected of him.

Colefax nods—I'm not imagining it—then shakes himself, puffs out his woolly chest and blinks keenly, ready for the off.

Chapter 78

As the search party sets off, I'm alarmed to hear the sound of shouting from the grand saloon. I step inside and it's like *Lord of the Flies*—the remaining guests have turned on one another. Sir Billy is shouting in Blue's face so furiously that you can see beads of spit flying, and Marje and Elise are hissing at each other like a pair of wildcats.

Suddenly, all eyes swivel to me and I see their nostrils twitch. Fresh prey to feast on.

Sir Billy comes at me, poking his finger: "Get the hell out of here, you poncy bastard! This is a family matter."

Marje joins in, her voice jagged with rage. "Prying and questioning, like some goddamn private dick."

Blue pulls his notebook out of his pocket and is about to jot this down when she wheels round and delivers him a vicious slap on the face.

"How dare you!" screams Elise, hurling herself at her aunt. "You leave him alone—you—you—jealous old bitch!" Sir Billy and Blue rush to separate the women and shrieks fill the air.

I count to three, take a lungful of air and boom, in my most masculine voice: "*STOP THIS NOW!*"

Stunned silence falls.

"In the name of God," I declare, "pull yourselves together

and have some respect for that poor woman who's just lost her husband. You're behaving like animals."

After a long pause, Marje mutters, "He's right, dammit," and Elise rushes to her, collapsing weeping in her arms.

Sir Billy looks sheepish and fidgets with his shirt buttons. Blue busies himself picking up cushions and replacing them where they belong. There's an art to plumping a cushion: you whack it on opposite edges, rotate ninety degrees, whack it again, then drop from head height; I'm glad to see him doing the job properly.

"That's better," I declare. "Now we've all calmed down, let's keep it civilized."

A sense of collective embarrassment creeps round the room.

"I'll make breakfast," I say slowly. "Now, would anyone like scrambled eggs?"

Dabbing away her tears, Elise puts up a tentative hand, followed by the rest.

"Good, I'll ask Challis to lay up. And someone please look in on Judith, see if she needs anything."

I make my way to the galley, where I find Bernie and Challis at it hammer and tongs.

"Not you too!" I declare. "Can everyone please calm down?" You wouldn't think I was the type to take command in a tense situation—it's a surprise to me too.

"It's all right for you, Paul, but if news gets out about this, my career's down the tube," says Challis.

"Self self self," mutters Bernie. "There's a lady up there lost her hubby and all this one cares about is whether Sir Billy will forget to leave us a tip."

"As I said, it's part of the—"

"Stop squabbling." They look at me, look at each other, then look down, ashamed of themselves. I step forward and put my arms around their shoulders, which isn't my usual style at all.

"If we're going to get through this, we need to stick together. It's bad enough them attacking one another upstairs."

I explain what's happening and Challis disappears to unpack the dining saloon, which we consider a dignified setting for the Last Breakfast.

"So tell me what to do," says Bernie.

"You can get out those eggs for a start."

There are many ways to scramble an egg, and don't let anyone tell you different. Sometimes I fancy them unctuous and saucy, other times fluffy.

One method is sous-vide; it's a favorite cooking method of mine, in which you vacuum-pack your food and immerse it in water circulating at a precise temperature. The eggs are cooked hyper-gently and flop out of the bag silky smooth, like a thick savoury custard. A Thermomix—a food mixer with heating element—does a similar job, without the use of ocean-wrecking plastic.

Or you could adopt the classic French method and cook them in a bain-marie for fifteen to twenty minutes, stirring constantly; instead of setting a timer, put on Ravel's "Boléro" (sixteen minutes), which will also keep you in rhythm.

Today, however, we'll keep things simple. I divide our rescued eggs into batches of about eight, which is the maximum you can successfully cook in one pan. Season generously, beat lightly (throw in a couple of extra yolks if you've got them), add two tablespoons of full-fat milk and the same of double cream.

Heat a large knob of butter in a large frying pan over a medium-high heat till it foams and subsides (not brown), pour in the eggs and swirl it about, then gently scrape it up as it cooks, using a rubber spatula. When it's mainly cooked, two to three minutes, turn the heat down and fold for a minute more. I like my eggs moist and shiny, but you can continue till pale and fluffy if you prefer.

We're getting into our swing—Bernie on toast duty, me swirling and stirring—and I'm lecturing her on why she should always buy mixed-weight eggs whenever possible (it's kinder to hens), when the door slides open and in steps Elise.

"What on earth?" I declare, amazed that she should venture below deck; then quickly realize she's leading a deputation, of her, Marje and Blue. At first, I fear there's been a new outbreak of hostilities in the grand saloon—Sir Billy lies bleeding on the carpet—but she announces they've come to lend a hand while Challis lays up.

"We'll do the fetching and carrying."

I'm favorably impressed. For once they're not behaving like spoiled brats.

The scrambled eggs have the desired pacifying effect and afterward the guests split up, some to pack for this evening's disembarkation, others bound for the grand saloon and a stiff drink.

That is where I now head, because I have business to do. At the door I collide with Karol-Kate, making a clumsy U-turn.

"Lost the dog?" I say.

"I left him with Mr. Hudson."

"Who are you avoiding, Sir Billy or his sister?" I ask.

"Marje," she replies, boot-faced, and disappears down the corridor.

I make a mental note of this then stride across the grand saloon and plonk myself down next to Sir Billy.

"Do you mind—?" he splutters.

"We need to have an urgent conversation," I announce. "Marje, would you give us ten minutes?"

For a moment she looks dumbfounded, then gathers herself and flumps out of the room. Sir Billy makes to follow her.

"Stay right where you are," I command.

Chapter 79

"A glass of that rather nice Krug," I say to Challis, as it's obvious I'm not going to be offered one. "Then you can leave us to it."

Once we're alone, I turn to Sir Billy. "I'm sorry to jump you like this, but you left me no choice."

He snorts, a farmyard sound. To think of Xéra marrying this graceless bully . . . Still, we're on the same side now and we need to work together.

"I don't expect us to be friends," I say, "but we can at least show civility to each other. If only for Xéra. She would want it that way."

Silence. One of us must break it, but for once it won't be me.

"Xéra . . ." he mumbles finally, his eyes filling with tears. And now it all comes pouring out. "From the day we met, she talked about her friend Paul. How smart and funny you were, how talented. She wanted us to be friends."

A wave of emotion rises within me and my eyes start pricking. "It was Marcus she was close to," I say. "I came later."

"You're wrong," he says. "You were the special one—she told me so. I regret it now, but I made up reasons not to meet you. I felt you were part of the life she was leaving behind, the old brigade. I guess I wanted her all to myself."

"I can understand that." In a funny kind of way, it's how I feel about Julie and Declan.

"She wanted to invite you to our wedding, you know."

"Really? Me?"

"I said I'd rather she didn't."

Another silence.

"It was wrong, I know, but I can't pretend I thought you were the . . . right sort of company for her to keep. Going forward."

Going forward—how I hate that phrase. "What, because I'm gay? Good God, Billy, we're living in the twenty-first century."

"It was wrong, I know. I was brought up with traditional values, I can't change that now."

"Or maybe you just felt threatened by her having a close friendship with another man? Even one who catches the other bus."

He thinks about this for a minute, then looks me in the eye.

"There's something else I should tell you, though. Five or six weeks ago, Xéra said out of the blue that she'd like to write a memoir and what did I think? Now, I don't know the first thing about writing books, but I'd heard you're some kind of a writer. So I suggested you give her a hand."

"That was your idea?"

"I thought it was time I got to know you, to stop feeling jealous. Then the idea of the cruise came up and it seemed like a good way of bringing you into the family, so to speak."

I let this sink in.

"Then why have you been so nasty to me?"

"I never was!" he replies. "I'm just a blunt Yorkshireman, take me or leave me."

"You as good as accused me of stealing her necklace."

Mention of the robbery has an odd effect on him—he glances down. "Oh, that," he says, deadpan. "OK, I could have handled it better. I was upset and you happened to get in the firing line."

Another long pause, then I say: "I also owe you an apology of sorts. I thought at one point it was you who killed Xéra." He looks at me with swimming eyes. "I was wrong, but I think I know who did."

Chapter 80

When I mention Russell's name he falls silent; then—calmly and dispassionately—listens as I lay out my theory.

He shakes his head sadly. "I would never have had him down as a killer. A weak character, and not always honest, but to go that far . . . Anyway, he's past doing any harm now. Someone needs to tell the captain—would you mind?"

"I'm not in his good books," I say, "but yes. And I meant to say—I hope you'll look after Judith in Ponta Delgada—put her on a flight home."

He nods.

"You could even lend her your London car and driver to take her home from the airport."

He raises an eyebrow.

"Xéra would think it proper behavior," I add, and watch a large fat tear drop onto his lapel.

I stand up to go, and reach out to shake his hand. Instead, Sir Billy rises to his feet and envelops me in a fierce bear hug.

I go straight to the pilot house.

You can't hear a thing through the armored glass but I can see the captain and first officer are in the middle of a screaming match, arms flailing and eyes flashing. Suddenly, the captain spits out an oath, turns on his heel and disappears into his cabin; if it weren't a sliding door, I daresay he'd slam it behind him.

Aimee notices me staring at this spectacle and beckons me in.

"What was that about?" I say.

She looks around to make sure we're alone and indicates for me to sit down at the chart table.

"You don't want to know!" she says, and bursts into tears. I get up to console her—I've never known such a day for weeping and hysteria.

"Do you want to tell me?" I say gently.

"Oh, it's just Romer being Romer," she says. "And I'm exhausted by it all. He's discovered we're way off course and he's blaming me. It's pathetic—he doesn't even know how to work the equipment, so of course when something goes wrong it's all *my* fault." This sets her off again; when she's recovered enough and blown her nose, she continues.

"During the storm we were traveling back on ourselves, then there was that wave that knocked out the Starlink and the electronics. After that, engine failure . . . I'm not sure I can take much more of this." More tears.

"So where are we heading?" I ask gently.

Between sniffs, she replies, "Don't worry, we'll get there in the end."

"Can I tell you something in confidence?" I say, to which she nods. "I worked out we were off course a few days ago—before the storm. It looked to me as if we were heading way west of the Azores. I tried to tell you, but you wouldn't listen."

"What do you know about it?" she stammers, blinking back tears. Crying isn't a great look for most people but I have to say she looks as beautiful as ever.

"Let's just say I got hold of a chart from somewhere—"

"So that was you, was it?" She shakes a finger at me. "You're trouble, Paul!"

"And I checked our course. I think Captain Romer, for some reason, may be taking us to an island called Lacuna, where we definitely don't want to go."

A look of bafflement passes across her face. *"La-cu-*what? Never heard of it. What's he up to?"

"You mean, you had no idea? I thought you were in charge of the navigation."

"Not in charge, Paul. I just do the techy side, crunch the numbers."

"I'll be honest with you, Aimee—there's something fishy going on here. The captain's up to something."

She squirms in her seat. "Erm, well . . ." Her eyes flick about the room. "Look, can I tell you this in confidence? Romer and I . . . well, we go back a few years."

"Ah," I say. Captain Romer and his harem.

"I met him in Antibes." She adds, with a downward glance, "Then earlier this year I put him up for the captain's job, even though he's not exactly, erm, qualified."

"Good God, Aimee. You must be crazy. How on earth did you fix that?"

"I'm the only crew member on permanent contract and the charter agent took my advice. Frankly they haven't got a clue—all they want is a quiet life, and for the yacht not to sink."

"But that means we're sailing without a proper captain. This is madness."

These words strike home and she stifles another sob. "Oh, Paul, Paul, that's so true, but I couldn't help myself." She puts her hand on her heart and shakes her head ruefully. "We had our future all planned—settle down, open a bar. Once we got to the Caribbean, he was going to come and meet my folks in Barbados."

She tries to continue but her eyes are welling up. I pull a package of tissues from my pocket and hand them to her. "Are you a big family?"

"Quite a few of us," she says, blinking back the tears.

"You lucky thing—I'm an only child. Brothers and sisters?" I add, hoping to console her with thoughts of loved ones back at home: "What are they called?"

She hesitates, as if surprised I'm interested. "Er, Annette and Adney are the ones I'm closest to."

"All the As."

She forces a smile. "Right."

"So what happened with Romer?"

"I saw an email I wasn't meant to. He's arranged a hookup with some girl in St. Boniface. Can you believe it?"

"Probably got one in Lacuna too," I add, realizing too late it was tactless.

I'm not a big hugger, but once again I find myself locked in an embrace. When she's calmed down, I explain my reason for coming up to the pilot house, at Sir Billy's behest, and the terrible truth about Russell.

She whistles. "Are you sure? I wouldn't have thought he had the strength to—"

"Sir Billy is absolutely convinced," I say, not wanting to go through it all again.

"OK, we'll sort it out. Rest assured, I'll get straight in touch with the Coast Guard and they'll advise on procedure."

After another pause, I say: "I feel better for having talked to you."

"Likewise," she says. She gets up and stands with her back to the door. "Now my advice—for your safety as well as mine—is to tell *nobody* about the navigation problem. I think Romer has been playing dumber than he is, which is saying something, and he's got some plan up his sleeve. I'll have the pilot house to myself till early afternoon. I'll get us back on course and do some poking about, see what else I can find."

"How will you get hold of me, if you need to?"

She thinks for a second. "Here's what we do. If you hear me announce: "It is warm and sunny in Ponta Delgada" over the public address system, that's our signal: you come here immediately. You got that?" She repeats the words.

I give her a comforting hug and leave the pilot house. Maybe I've been missing out—I should do more hugging.

CHAPTER 81

I set off in search of Shane and the dog, to see if Colefax's nose has shed any light on Russell's death. Despite what we now know about him, it makes me uncomfortable to think I may have been the last person who spoke with him before he fell—or jumped. The one person who could shed some light would be Judith, but it isn't the time to question her.

I can't find any sign of them, but I do intercept a secret conversation going on in the grand saloon. Blue and Elise, half hidden by silk curtains, are nursing gin and tonics. For years we were told gin makes people sad; then scientists proved it, and now here's the living proof.

"Hello, you two," I say chirpily. "May I sit down?" I've wasted too much time pussyfooting about on this voyage—I'm going on the offensive from now on. "Been a pretty action-packed cruise, hasn't it? Lots of juicy material for your exposé."

Blue does a double take. "Excuse me?"

"Oh, forgive me, didn't you tell Elise? Blue's writing an exposé about horrible rich people on superyachts for a gossip mag. A theft, a couple of deaths—it's going to be quite the headliner."

Poor Elise looks at him, appalled. "Is this true?"

"He's editor-at-large, so we may even be on the cover," I interject, stirring harder.

Now it's Elise's turn with the waterworks. "Blue! Why didn't you—?"

"Elise, honey," says Blue, taking her hand and kissing it. What a creep. "I was going to tell you everything. But you've nothing to worry about—you and your family and the yacht will be totally unidentifiable—I'm changing all the names."

"Including your own, *Blane Aspern*," I throw in, adding as an aside to Elise, "everything about your boyfriend is false, including his name." Tears turn to sobs.

Blue snarls at me, fists curling: "Why, you . . ." He gets wound up so quickly—would benefit from a course in anger management.

"Anyway, moving on, I wondered why you two are looking so sad. Are you breaking up?"

Their heads go up like meerkats.

"No idea what you're talking about," snaps Elise.

"I heard you were planning to elope once we landed in the Azores. My advice would be—don't. A holiday romance is one thing but you're not at all suited. You're both too selfish."

"I've had enough," announces Blue. He stands up and marches out of the saloon.

Elise stays put. "Fix me another gin, please."

"No," I declare. "My mother told me never to drink alcohol before eleven in the morning, and no spirits till I was forty. Good advice—your husband might heed it, too."

"Keep Shane out of this."

At which point, in he walks.

Chapter 82

Who am I to sit in judgment over people's marriages? Never having tied the knot myself, I'm hardly the expert. One has no idea what's said or done behind closed doors, the laughter or weeping, the shared whispers or skeletons in the closet. As for what goes on in the bedroom—that's anyone's guess.

I suspect the affair with Blue was just a holiday amusement and that Elise dreamed up this crazy elopement idea—assuming it was their speedy getaway Challis was trying to arrange—to take her mind off the crisis she and Shane are going to face when they get home, now that the handouts from Daddy have stopped.

As for Shane, I've rarely met someone so brimming over with sexual tension. I think of the GBH conviction Julie uncovered, and can absolutely imagine him decking a buff young soldier after a couple or three brandy and sodas, in a confusion of lust and self-doubt.

I wonder if Elise knows what goes on? She's not stupid. Maybe she even likes it: never underestimate the allure of conflicted, unpredictable men. If he's as highly sexed as he appears, it's not surprising he spills out of the marital bedroom occasionally, and maybe Elise is pleased to have a break.

"What have you two been talking about?" he asks, sitting down between us and taking his wife's hand.

"You," I reply.

Needless to say, he laughs. In someone else it would be such an irritating habit, but in Shane I've come to like it; so does Elise—I can see her melt under his spell.

"How did it go with Colefax?" I ask. "Did he find a scent to follow?"

"That's the thing about Bichons—they never let you down. We started off at Russell's cabin. By the way, you should've seen it, Lise! Knock-off of the Palazzo Dolfin Manin near the Rialto Bridge, the one with the Tiepolos." A tennis pro who's interested in art history? I *have* underestimated him.

"He played with the socks for a while and didn't want to have them taken away, but then things clicked and he started tracking. There was one false alarm—a waste bin full of crisp and chocolate wrappers—" that'll be Karol-Kate—"but after that he went straight down to the gallery walk, followed it round and suddenly stopped dead."

"To the bow, on the starboard side?" I say.

"How do you know that?"

"Because it's directly above my cabin and I heard the splash."

The splash that distracted my would-be assassin wasn't a dolphin after all, but Russell going overboard.

Chapter 83

When a dish goes wrong in the kitchen, as will happen even to the most experienced cook, the first step is to refer back to the recipe, to check you haven't forgotten an ingredient or missed something obvious.

It is in this spirit that I return to my cabin, to sit down and go through everything methodically.

I get out the table of suspects I made earlier and comb through the photographs on my phone. I study Colefax's chopstick, which I've kept wrapped in a tissue, in case it might turn out to be a clue.

On a fresh piece of paper, I write the word *Russell*, and underneath:

Did he fall?
Was he pushed?
Did he jump?

Inevitably, the thought of suicide turns my heart to ice; my poor dear mother took her life in 2009, something I've never been able to—never *will* be able to—discuss.

It's at this point that I realize one of my documents is missing. Where's the recipe for Gâteau Reine de Saba?

Kicking myself, I remember the last time I had it was when I was incarcerated in the anchor chain locker. I shoved it among the massive metal links. How careless of me, but at least it wasn't thrown overboard with me. Could it still be there?

I set off immediately to find out. I peer in through the grille and *think* I can make out the envelope, tucked in the link where I left it. Lucky we haven't dropped anchor.

I go to the galley to find Challis, who's busy setting up lunch. I don't know about commercial cruises, but this one feels as if it's one endless succession of meals and cocktails.

"Can you let me into the anchor chain locker, please?"

"Really, after what happened last time?"

"I left an envelope there—of sentimental value."

"Oh that. Fed it into the garbage crusher." Seeing my look of dismay, she says, "Just pullin" your leg. I haven't got a key."

I don't feel I can bother Aimee again, so I try Bernie, who's stirring a dark brown mixture bubbling away in a stockpot. "Boeuf bourguignon," she announces. "What do you think?"

I taste and correct it according to my usual routine—which I could do in my sleep. First, correct the *salt* level, without which you can't properly taste what's happening. Next, round out the *flavor*: does it need a pinch of sugar to smooth it out, or a splash of acid to brighten it up (lemon juice, balsamic, mustard, soy sauce, et cetera)? After that, does it need *spicing up* (pepper, nutmeg)? Finally, do we want to enhance *mouthfeel* with a knob of butter or slug of brandy to make it sing when it hits the palate?

This infallible step-by-step—which I devised myself, though the same idea is found in some Asian cuisines, and indeed that excellent tome *Salt Fat Acid Heat*—will prevent your cooking from bearing that most tragic of epithets: boring. If all this is new to you, practice on a risotto and you'll see exactly what I mean.

The lackluster stew needs all I can throw at it: I add sugar, balsamic, a good pinch of crushed chili flakes and a glug of cognac. This is the best I can do: it was no masterpiece to start with, and adjustments won't turn it into one.

"'Tis a revelation," she declares, tasting it with relish. "Now show me this lock."

We descend to the anchor chain locker, where she pulls out a hairpin and tries it in the lock. Try as she might, this time the trick doesn't work.

She leaves me peering morosely through the grille, hoping some *deus ex machina* will come to my rescue. Suddenly, I jump. Something lightly brushed my shoulder. What was that? A bat?

I wheel round to find myself face to face with—Afet.

"Thank goodness," I say, when I've got my breath back. "I need that piece of paper," I tell her, pointing through the grille.

She holds up a finger: "Wait!"

No more than a minute later she returns with a basket of equipment.

"Fishing champion of village!" she says proudly, picking out a hook and tying it nimbly to a line. She pokes a makeshift rod between the bars of the grille and lowers the hook.

Seconds later, I watch with wonder as she slides her slim fingers between the bars to catch the corner of the envelope, then delicately maneuvers it through the grille, as she might tickle a trout in the Caspian. Refusing to accept my profuse thanks, she disappears as magically as she arrived, and I retire to my cabin to see what—if any—secrets the Queen of Sheba might reveal.

After ten minutes of puzzling, a glimmer of light appears on the horizon. I tuck the recipe back in its envelope, fold it in my bedside book for safekeeping and plot my next steps.

Chapter 84

The teak feels warm under my belly as I crawl across the communications platform, trying to keep as low as possible and out of sight of the pilot house.

I remember the first time I came up here, on our first afternoon, watching the guests step off the passerelle to be kissed and greeted by Xéra and her new husband. Everything feels different now, and as if to symbolize our shattered world order, the sleek Starlink receiver damaged in the storm has been crudely patched up with gaffer tape, bungee cords and bits of frayed wire. There's the pungent vinegary smell of glue.

My destination is a rectangle of Plexiglass which serves as a skylight for the dining saloon. I need to check the guests are all at lunch—or at least two of them in particular—so that I can perform an urgent mission. I daren't be seen, so I listen for the voices.

"Anyone would think he was the one who lost a family member." Transatlantic drawl—that's Marje.

"Wheedled his way in, like a spider," flutes a second female—Elise. "I can't imagine why darling Xéra ever took him up as a friend."

A burst of laughter next. "I rather like him. Livens things up," says Shane.

"You know he's been snooping about, doing background checks?" says a male voice. "What a snake." I venture a peep over the frame of the skylight to see the back of his head: Propecia ain't working, Blue.

It's true that eavesdroppers never hear good of themselves, so I'm relieved when the insults are interrupted by the arrival of Sir Billy, followed shortly afterward by Judith. I make my way rapidly to the guest cabin area.

First, I let myself into the master cabin. As when I was last here, it's in disarray. There's that heavy smell of sleep and sheets that need changing—someone should open a porthole, let some air in—and I almost trip over a tray of untouched food.

In the center of the cabin stands the four-poster bed, with cabinets to either side. I check the first cabinet: all three drawers are empty.

In the top drawer of the second I find various sleep aids—including mists and masks—and a book. This is what I'm here for.

Throughout my investigation, I keep coming back to the question: why did Xéra go to the beach club that morning?

She will have been summoned there either in person or by means of a note; she mentioned a letter to Karol-Kate and I'd like to see it. Many women, I know, would tuck such a thing in their handbag, but Xéra refused to carry one. Which is why I've decided to check if she might have placed it in her bedside book—just as I did with my precious recipe.

Here is the Montaigne—an exquisitely printed modern edition, in French, of course. Tucked into Volume 1, Essay IX, I find two things.

The first is an envelope containing an old photograph, postcard-sized, with the top corners trimmed away, of a young boy in a garden. Smiling at the camera, he holds a small dog in his arms—a miniature poodle. Printed along the bottom of the picture: *1/6/2003 – 1/6/2010.*

I'm engulfed by a wave of sadness: poor kid, dead at the age of seven.

On the back, written in black felt-tip, in block capitals:

BEACH CLUB TOMORROW 7:30 A.M. TELL NO ONE.

The second piece of paper is a cutting from a local London newspaper, also from 2010. I read it through once, then again, trying to think how these disparate pieces fit together.

I photograph both pieces of paper on my phone then replace them where I found them.

As I do so, for some reason, I look at the essay Xéra was reading and notice a sentence underlined. *"En verité le menteur est un maudit vice."* This rings some kind of bell in my unconscious, so I snap that too.

Next, I go down the gilded staircase and let myself into the Tates' cabin. I pick up the diptych on the dressing table. The picture on the right is still missing, and the saint on the left appears to be performing a miracle of some kind with a stick or candle. As I click a snapshot with my phone, I hear the swish of a keycard and someone enter the cabin.

Chapter 85

I dash to hide. Peeking through the crack in the door I see . . . a flash of red hair.

What on earth is *Challis* doing here? The bed is made, the cabin spotless, so it's not housekeeping. She goes straight to a drawer and pulls out Russell's wallet. From it she removes a wad of mauve-purple banknotes, counts out fifteen and puts the rest back. She tucks them in her pocket and returns the wallet to the drawer.

"Looking for something?" I say, jumping out from the shadows.

It's a very bad thing to do: hundreds of people a year die from heart failure after suffering shocks like this. Challis screams and falls backwards; as luck would have it onto the bed.

"What the—?" she cries, leaping to her feet again. "You nearly killed me! What are you doing in here?"

"I could ask the same thing."

"Hardly! I'm chief stewardess. I've every right to be—"

"—stealing money from a guest who's just drowned. How low can you stoop?"

"Absolutely no way!" she splutters, the red tide rising in her cheeks. "You've got it all wrong."

"I saw you put those notes in your pocket!"

"If you're talking about this," she says, snatching out the banknotes and waving them under my nose, "I earned it all, every—single—penny." I've never seen anyone go such a bright shade of scarlet—maybe it's a redhead thing. "No one accuses Challis of stealing or cheating. I worked for it. *Three hundred for a rub and tug.* He booked another session—which by all rights I could charge for, but I'm not—and promised to settle up at the end. I'm not even taking a tip," she adds in a tone of outrage.

Well, you have to admire her for staying focused no matter what: client overboard, no worries! A posthumous deposit will do for that ever-growing Melbourne bank account.

"What I want to know is, what are *you* doing here?" she demands. "Looking for another necklace to steal?"

"How dare you? You know I had nothing to do with that! I seem to be the only person on this boat who cares what happened to Xéra, and if I have to rummage about in a guest cabin to find out, I'll do so."

"Not any more, you won't," Challis says, leaping forward and snatching away the keycard I was stupid enough to leave protruding from my top pocket. "Now, get out of here before I report you to Captain Romer—again."

I leave with my tail between my legs.

I head for the grand saloon and tap on the glass doors for someone to let me in, after which I traverse the Persian carpet and settle myself down in the little library.

On the bottom shelf is a complete *Encyclopædia Britannica*—the fifteenth edition, dated 2005 before it went online—in thirty-one handsome volumes (including two indexes). Should I end up in a coma, set me up to listen to this in the morning (read by Simon Russell Beale) and Radio 4 in the afternoon.

I find what I'm looking for in Volume 2 and replace it carefully on the shelf. After which I pick out another tome—*Le Robert & Collins Dictionnaire Français–Anglais*—and turn to *M*.

Once I've finished with the dictionary, I feel new energy

rush through my veins—almost light-headed under the force of the revelations I've just received. How can I have been so wrong and wasted so much time?

   I know what I need to do . . . and I've an idea how to go about it.

Chapter 86

I've made a lot of enemies on this boat, but there are a handful of people essential to my plan. One is in the pilot house, doing her valiant best to steer us away from accursed Lacuna, where the captain for his own dastardly reasons is trying to take us. Another is in the galley, fixing afternoon tea for the guests.

But first I must speak to Sir Billy. I can't pretend to like him or approve of his attitudes, but we are united by a love of Xéra, and now is his chance to show it. I race to his cabin.

He opens the door, sees who it is and greets me cautiously. "Would you mind coming back later? I'm in the middle of something."

"I'm afraid not, Sir Billy. I need to speak to you on business of the utmost urgency."

"Don't just stand there, then—come in."

He studies me carefully as I explain my plan, nodding occasionally, then asks me questions, to check I've thought everything through. It's how the contestants must feel on *Dragons' Den*, only there's very much more at stake today.

Within ten minutes, it's all agreed and we've shaken on it. (For a moment I fear we're going in for another bear hug, but we catch each other's eye and decide not.) Even in the rawness of his grief, he's impressively decisive and practical, weighing up options and calculating chances in a matter of seconds. For the first time I catch a faint glimpse of what Xéra might have seen in him—commanding masculinity and natural authority.

I wish some of his bulletproof self-assurance would rub off on me, because I could sure do with it for what's coming next. It's going to take every ounce of charm and persuasiveness I can muster, and I can't afford to fail.

My legs turn to jelly as I approach my target, and I have to grab a chair to stop myself from falling over. I try the opening gambit I've prepared but my tongue seems stuck to the roof of my mouth.

Do this for Xéra, whispers a voice inside my head. *Get her the justice she deserves.*

I take a deep breath and, haltingly at first, the words flow. My listener hears my suggestion in silence, scrutinizing me closely. I adopt a pleading tone; they hesitate. I weave in some subtle flattery and—oh my goodness!

"If you insist."

My heart pounding, I gallop round the yacht to make a few more hasty briefings. A gigantic blast of the foghorn is sounded, and Aimee's bright tones ring through the air.

"*All guests and crew are to report to the grand saloon immediately on the captain and Sir Billy's orders.*"

Chapter 87

Challis and Bernie have done us proud. The little tables in the grand saloon are laid out with the best china, including elegant gold tea forks and crystal vases of spring flowers—miniature tulips and narcissi. (On a yacht? In October? How can this be possible?) An array of colorful cakes, arranged on doilies, bedecks the bar: I espy fairy cakes (iced in pastel colors), shortbread fingers and—well, I never—rock buns.

The latter have a fatal flaw: exposed bits of dried fruit burn to tar in the oven and then stick horribly to your teeth when you bite into them. I haven't touched one since my grandmother was alive and I'm not going to now.

Someone has mercifully removed the inflatable unicorn and Challis has selected a jazzy playlist to make sure no one nods off before the main event. "Slaughter On Tenth Avenue," "Thriller," "My Heart Will Go On" sung by Celine Dion, hits from *Chicago*; appropriate choices.

The guests filter in and seat themselves around the room: they seem bewildered, as well they might.

"Shame about your piano," I say to Blue, sulking on his own.

I wasn't being sarcastic—or only slightly—but he snarks back: "Shame about your personality."

This playground exchange is interrupted by Marje. "We saw you spying on us through the skylight."

"We all did," joins in Elise. "You've single-handedly ruined this trip, Paul." With a toss of her ash-blonde locks, she turns her back on me.

Unbelievable.

The captain and Aimee arrive, in full uniform; at least no one makes the "Who's driving?" quip, to which cruise-liner captains are subjected every night at dinner. They choose a position near the door and Romer starts checking his watch.

"Are our Rustavaijani friends joining us?" I whisper in Bernie's ear; they're the only ones missing. She and Challis buzz about pouring tea and serving cakes with silver tongs.

"They didn't think they were wanted," she whispers back. "But don't be worrying—Afet says they're busy getting ready for when we go ashore. They've a plan."

"Good afternoon, ladies and gentlemen," I begin. I've taken to the stage, with my audience ranged around. "Sir Billy has asked me to, er, compère this afternoon's entertainment." The word "acrimony" is derived from the Latin for pungent bitterness; you can smell it in the air.

At the table directly in front sit Sir Billy and Marje: he looks solemn, she ready to jump up and swing her orange Birkin at me. To my left are Shane and Elise: he's trying (and failing) to look serious, she's draped across him possessively.

At individual tables sit: Karol-Kate, who has changed into a jazz-print jumpsuit, with Colefax at her feet, watching proceedings attentively; Blue, in a crisp button-down cotton shirt, freshly spritzed with Creed Aventus; and almost hidden at the back, Judith, dressed in purple, being fussed over by Challis and Bernie.

I begin.

"I'd like to thank you all for gathering at short notice. In the first instance, we are here to pay our respects to Russell and offer our condolences to Judith, after this morning's tragic accident. I begged her to join us—I thought it would do her good to be among friends, and us good to be able to show our support."

There's a murmur of doubt from the guests, but when they turn to her, she gives a dignified little bow of the head.

"I know it is traditional to throw a party at the end of a cruise, but on this occasion it hardly seems appropriate to indulge in frivolities. After careful consideration, however, we decided—"

"Who's 'we'?" snaps Elise.

"*Sir Billy and I* decided that it would be fitting to come together this afternoon for a quiz."

A quiz? Has he gone mad? Did I hear right?

Incredulous, they reel round to stare at Sir Billy, who shrugs.

"Ridiculous!" hisses Marje, getting to her feet. "I'm going to my cabin."

"Stay where you are, Marjorie," barks Sir Billy.

"It's insulting to Judith," says Elise. The widow, however, gives another gracious bow.

In the circumstances, their reaction is reasonable, but I have good reason for having arranged things like this. The principal reason, banal as it may sound, is safety: safety in numbers, lest things turn violent, and my own safety in particular.

Another is that this is my last chance to unmask the villain(s)—and, if possible, extract a confession, before we land wherever we're heading and it all gets hushed up.

But why a quiz, for Pete's sake? That will become clear soon enough.

Chapter 88

"Not wishing to interrupt, but will this take long?" says the captain.

"Be over before you know it, Captain Romer," I say, with what I hope comes across as a patronizing little smile; nice to have the boot on the other foot. "Oh, quick question—is everyone happy for Blue to take notes? He's writing the trip up for a gossip magazine. You're going to love reading about yourselves."

"You godda be kidding?" shouts Marje, wheeling round to face him.

"Nothing major," stammers Blue. "Just a feature article."

"Why, you double-crossing... Just wait till my attorneys—"

"I won't use real names."

"Rat!" she cries, lobbing a rock bun at him. "You're fired."

"Go fuck yourself!" he snarls back, picking crumbs out of his facial hair.

Judith emits a sigh at this lapse of taste. "Quite right, Judith," I say. "Which reminds me: we are honored to have in our midst someone who excels at quizzes, games and puzzles of every kind—a *Mastermind* semi-finalist in 1998, no less. Judith has agreed to keep the score." At this fanfare, she attempts a brave little smile.

"Let's start!" I declare, clapping my hands. "Here's an easy one. Who stole the De Lage Treasure?"

Sir Billy leaps to his feet, erupting with rage. "Why, this isn't what you—?"

"Hold your horses, Sir Billy. Slight change of plan, that's all."

"I'll—I'll—" he splutters.

"Trust me, I know what I'm doing. Now, everyone, any guesses?"

The only sounds are the faintest tinkle of resin blossoms from above the bar as the boat undulates on the waves and a crunching sound from the captain, who's found the shortbread fingers.

It's uncomfortable sitting in silence, and eventually Elise breaks it by saying: "Those deckhand people. Obviously. I knew it was them from the beginning—that's why they're not here, I take it."

"Wrong! And they're not here because they knew they weren't wanted," I say.

"Garbage!" trumpets Marje. "The announcement said everyone assemble immediately. Gone into hiding, I bet."

Ignoring her, I continue. "Since the voyage started, has a single one of you spoken to these so-called 'deckhands'? Said please or thank you—even acknowledged their existence?" They all stare at me. "As far as you're concerned—and that includes Captain Romer and even, I'm afraid, our first officer—they're invisible and irrelevant. And now you expect them to turn up and bow and scrape so you can throw accusations at them?

"They had nothing to do with the necklace's disappearance, nor with any other misdemeanor aboard *Maldemer*, so put that out of your heads. The necklace was stolen by Karol-Kate, but as it's now been returned, Sir Billy has agreed not to press charges."

The guests turn and stare at the dog handler. "It's not what you think," she protests. "I'm not a thief—I was forced into it. I wanted to throw it over the side, or put it down the garbage crusher, but the jewels were so beautiful . . . the colors! The way they sparkled! I've never touched anything like that before."

"Appealed to your feminine side, I guess," says Blue, spiteful as ever.

"So who made you do it?" I ask.

The dog handler shakes her head sadly. "I'm sorry, Paul, I told you. I'm bound by oath."

"Then let me say it for you. It was Marje Mayham."

Marje leaps up and her eyes start to glow, as if someone's lit her fuse and she's about to shoot sparks. "You, you—"

"Sit down," I say. "You're not going to jail, even if you deserve to. And before you lash out at Karol-Kate, I worked it out for myself. The night it was stolen there was some monkey business going on at dinner. You sent your toyboy out for a pashmina that you didn't need so you could slip Karol-Kate Sir Billy's keycard."

"Don't drag Bill into this," cries Marje.

"I also saw you plotting with Karol-Kate behind a potted palm in the grand saloon, and after the necklace was discovered, there seems to have been a falling-out. I imagine you didn't want it found."

"I never touched that vulgar piece of trash," snarls Marje. "It was far too good for Xéra."

A blatant contradiction, but I let it pass. "Why don't you admit you were jealous of your sister-in-law?" Silence. "So, you bullied and blackmailed Karol-Kate into stealing it from her. You threatened to throw Colefax overboard if she didn't do it."

Shane and Elise gasp with horror and the dog growls and snarls at Marje, straining on its leash.

Marje ignores it. "The dog woman should have listened to me. I told her to hide it somewhere *intimate*. In other words—" said with a sneer—"somewhere no one would ever look. And now she can damn well give me back my thousand pounds!"

I'm still reeling from the mental image Marje has conjured, but Karol-Kate hits right back.

"No way! It's going to charity," she declares.

"That's not the end of the necklace story, I suspect." (I say this with a glance toward Bernie, who taps her nose.) "But we must now move on to something much more serious."

My audience sits stunned. What next?

"Question number two. Who killed Xéra?"

"What are you talking about?" says Elise, breaking the silence. "Who says she was killed?"

"Come on, Elise. If you haven't worked it out, everyone else has. She was attacked and choked to death."

"But that's horrific!" declares Elise. "If you knew that, why didn't you tell us?"

"Maybe if you weren't so wrapped up in yourself," I fire back, "you'd have put two and two together, like the rest of us. And the reason there was no big announcement is that Captain Romer insisted on hushing it up."

"It was only a rumor," the captain sniffs, straightening his epaulettes.

All this time I've been strutting about on stage, like an actor delivering a soliloquy. Now, I jump down and plonk myself on the edge as if about to tell a bedtime story. I admit this isn't my idea: it's borrowed from Judy Garland, who ended her 1951-2 Palace show every afternoon and evening by singing "Over The Rainbow" with legs dangling over the apron.

My audience is a mere nine—as opposed to seventeen hundred—and I sadly have no sixteen-piece backing orchestra; but the air is crackling with anticipation. "I take it you all pass. So let me tell you."

Chapter 89

"The time will come for the police to interview witnesses, for forensics to examine the victim's body, for lawyers to fight it out in court. All this is complicated by the fact Xéra was a French–British–Indonesian tri-national, in international waters, aboard a yacht flying the Bermudan flag. My bet, however, for what it's worth, is that the murder trial will be held at the Old Bailey."

Dead silence.

"The origins of this crime go way, way back: by no means as far as the De Lage Treasure (the recent theft of which is entirely unrelated, by the way), but still, many years. Let's jump, however, to the morning of Xéra's death.

"She has been summoned to a secret early morning meeting by means of an old color photo with *TELL NO ONE* written on the back. The picture terrifies her, for reasons I'll come to later.

"In the beach club, without warning, an arm closes around her throat and she is pinned to her chair. It's not an arm *choke*—which is what I was subjected to when I was attacked the day before yesterday—but a *hold*; so she remains conscious, and unbruised."

Sir Billy buries his head in his hands.

"Next, her mouth is propped open. Shane and I witnessed first hand how this can be done yesterday, when Colefax got a piece of beef bone stuck in his jaw. Vets put sticks behind the molars of animals to stop them biting, and dentists use bite blocks during long dental procedures. You simply wedge something at the back of the jaw and the mouth is propped open. In this case, the thick end of a chopstick, set aside from the sushi lunch, was used.

"You may wish to cover your ears for what I have to say next. Panic-stricken, her heart beating frantically, Xéra sees something from the corner of her eye. A plate of chocolate cake comes into view. A lump of it is put in her mouth then forced down her throat using a pastry fork. And another, and another . . . until her trachea is blocked."

The grand saloon sits in traumatized silence.

"At this point, they make their one and only mistake. The chopstick falls onto the chair and Xéra pushes it into the crease in the seat. I like to think she does it deliberately, hoping it might incriminate her assailant, but maybe it's an accident. In any case, clever Colefax somehow finds it and adopts it as a toy. I later found him playing with it on the lawn deck, and I have it safely stored away as evidence."

Tears stream down cheeks. Elise buries her face in Shane's shoulder. I give them all a minute to recover.

"I'd like to say the worst is over," I resume, "but now we must go back to June 2010, and another tragic event." It's estimated that no more than one in ten of us can move our ears, but I swear I sense one pair twitch in my audience when I mention that date.

"What I'm about to tell you, I've put together thanks to several sources. I'm not proud of the fact that my investigation required me to enter guest cabins without permission, but—"

"Permission granted, albeit after the event," grunts Sir Billy, mopping his eyes with a handkerchief.

I give a polite bow and continue. "Fifteen years ago, something terrible occurred in the recently opened London branch of Pâtisserie Pompadour, from which Xéra never recovered.

"Thanks to a miscellany of documents I came across in various cabins, I've been able to piece together the story. In Xéra's, I found a letter from Marje referring to the tragedy, and a copy of a legal contract pertaining to it. On a subsequent visit, I found a photograph of a boy who died in 2010, and a newspaper cutting from the same year. The newspaper doesn't name the Pâtisserie Pompadour, but I know that's where it happened because a friend visited the former premises a few days ago and spoke to the current owner. A lot of loose ends, but they all tie up.

"Let me read out the news report," I say. "From the *Ham & High*, 12 June 2010."

Children's Party Ends in Tragedy

Last week, a seven-year-old boy (who cannot be named for legal reasons) died in a St. John's Wood tearoom at his own birthday party.

Having walked from Maida Vale with his parents, the boy was served with drinks and food and shortly afterward became pale and breathless.

His parents rapidly identified the problem as anaphylactic shock caused by something the boy had eaten, but discovered that each thought the other had brought the child's Epi-Pen, and were thus unable to deliver a life-saving injection of epinephrine. Medical assistance was called immediately but by the time paramedics arrived, it was too late.

Horrible, horrible, the guests mutter. Even Blue is moved, shaking his head and stroking his beard.

"How could such a thing happen? The child, who was highly allergic to nuts, had been served a slice of the pâtisserie's signature Gâteau Reine de Saba. Unless you saw the closely guarded recipe, you'd never know it contained nuts; of course, now there are laws about such things and one hopes it could never happen again, but at the time, it could and did.

"Obviously, no amount of money can even begin to recompense a parent for the loss of a child, but the boy's mother and father, perhaps naively, perhaps egged on by a rapacious grandparent, fell into the hands of one of those *have you been involved in an accident that wasn't your fault?* outfits and sued Pâtisserie Pompadour.

"The lawyers couldn't believe their luck when the pâtisserie paid out the three-million-pound claim, in full and on the dot.

"In a fit of passion, Xéra took the historic recipe for the fateful chocolate cake and scrawled on the envelope, in writing that cut through the paper, *MAUDIT*.

"At first, I misread this as "*MAUDIE*" and thought it referred to a person—the letters e and t are easy to mistake in some French scripts. My memory was jogged by seeing one of Montaigne's essays earlier today, which reminded me that *maudit* means *damned* or *accursed*."

The guests look at one another sorrowfully, then Elise puts up her hand and asks in a timid voice: "It's a terrible story, but I still don't understand what it's got to do with Xéra's murder."

"Until yesterday, there were two people among you who could have answered that," I reply. "Today, there's only one."

CHAPTER 90

There's a rustling from the back, and a figure rises slowly from her chair and steps forward. The artificial flowers above the bar shrink from her approach, tinkling in fear. Sir Billy stifles a sob, the others gasp in astonishment.

It is Judith. Maybe it's the purple velvet that has sucked all the color out of her face, but she's chalk-white. Her icy eyes are staring and her mouth is stretched in a rictus smile. In the center of the grand saloon, she stops dead.

"Our guest of honor," I say. "It's hard to resist a good old-fashioned quiz, isn't it?"

"You think you're very clever, don't you?" she growls. "But none of this can be proved. None of it, you hear me?"

"Don't tell me—Russell killed Xéra and you knew nothing about it?"

"Correct." She laughs—a dry, coughing sound. "I'll score you a bonus point."

"You won't get away with this, Judith. You're in it up to your neck." I'm bluffing—I need to secure a confession. "The boy who died. Who was he?"

She stares at me with Gorgon eyes, saying nothing.

"You must have had a reason for keeping that photograph of him in a silver picture frame, alongside your favorite saint."

"Don't bring St. Blaise into this, blasphemer!" she hisses.

"Would that be the same St. Blaise who miraculously saved a young boy from choking circa 316?" Thank you, *Encylopædia Britannica*; also for the detail that his emblem is a taper, which in all the pictures looks just like a chopstick.

Judith stares at me so fiercely that the hairs on the back of my neck prickle and stand up. I can't believe the change in her. She always seemed so timid and overshadowed by her bombastic husband. Or maybe that was how she chose to be seen and we obligingly took her at face value.

"Tell me about the child," I demand.

"No idea what you're talking about."

My mind races.

As Marcus always said: *Women of Judith's age are obsessed with grandchildren.* This boy was her *grandson*! And the clue I previously missed is that the poor kid shared the same life-threatening nut allergy as both his grandparents: this sort of allergic reaction is often hereditary, especially if it occurs on both sides of the family. It's the missing piece of the puzzle.

Chapter 91

Everyone listens dumbfounded as I explain the invisible chain linking Xéra, the Pâtisserie Pompadour and the accidental death of Judith's grandson.

"Did Xéra have any idea who you were?" I ask Judith.

A gleam enters her eye. "Not until . . ." She stops, remembering herself.

"Not until you confronted her in the beach club, you were about to say."

She glares at me in silence.

I continue: "Why did you tell me your daughter was "barren" if you had a grandson?"

"His name was Gideon," she spits. "After his birth, my daughter was told she could never be with child again. God in all His wisdom chose to grant her an *abnormality*. Gideon was our only and dearly beloved grandchild. And hear this: he died in *my* arms."

"So let me get this straight," I say, fixing her with my eyes, unable to believe this is the same person as the nondescript woman I took pity on and befriended. There's no hint of remorse in the steady way she stares around the room, taking in our incredulous, appalled expressions—only hate. "All this time you've been stalking Xéra, waiting to take revenge?"

An odd look passes over her face, as if she's going into a trance. Then she intones, in a low, clear voice: "Fifteen long years I waited—in the Wilderness: it was God's will. Then He put the Pompadour woman in my way."

"In other words, Russell weaseled his way into a job with Sir Billy?"

"It was a sign!" she replies, turning her pale eyes toward the ceiling.

"Xéra disposed of the family business she loved rather than risk being responsible for another terrible accident like Gideon's death. Wasn't that enough for you?"

"There is such a thing as divine justice." Now her lips start to mumble inaudibly—probably verses from Ezekiel.

It is said that when Elena Ceausescu was captured by Bucharest demonstrators on Christmas Day 1989 and led in front of the firing squad, she stank like a polecat. She was wearing a full-length sheepskin at the time, which can't have helped, but it's what I smell now. A miasma of rage, selfrighteousness and fear creeps through the grand saloon, mingling with the scent of jonquils. Marje gags into a tissue.

"So, what about Russell?" I demand. "Is he still alive? Have you taken away his insulin and stuffed him into a cupboard?"

This appears to jolt her back to reality.

"I know nothing of Russell or what he did," she says blandly, as if reading from a script. "You all saw us—we weren't close. We led separate lives. I don't know what he may have done and cannot be held responsible or implicated in any of his actions."

"That's what you want us to believe, but you were playacting—something you've had plenty of practice at. You and your husband looked happy enough doing the crossword together, when you didn't know I was watching."

She curls her lip.

"The great thing about forensics nowadays," I continue, "is

that they'll be able to verify all of this." For the first time I see doubt flicker in her eyes—but I still need her to *confess*.

"Look, Judith, we know there were two people involved." I'm bluffing, of course. "Your DNA will be all over the chopstick."

She stares at me.

"And there were fingerprints all over the pastry fork," I continue. Unfortunately, the fork in question was put through the dishwasher by Challis, but Judith doesn't know this.

She stays silent.

"Who knocked over the latte glass?"

"That clumsy . . . I've no idea what you're talking about."

I keep up the pressure. "You realize that if Russell held her while you forced the food down her throat, that makes you the murderer and him a mere accomplice?"

Her eyes appear to lose focus. "He was weak," she says dismissively. "I watched him lose control when he spoke with you last night on deck. He imagined he had the upper hand in our marriage. Pathetic! I knew all his wicked ways . . ." She sweeps the room with narrowed eyes. "I knew about *you*!" she cries, pointing at Challis, innocently refilling teacups. "Whore of Gomorrah!" The chief stew turns beetroot.

"Is that why you pushed him overboard?" I persist. "Don't repeat that lie about him going walkabout—he wouldn't get far without his keycard."

"He was drunk. He had balance problems." A contemptuous smile on her face, she makes a motion with her hand, as if pushing a revolving door. The guests gasp.

"He wanted to confess so you had to get rid of him?"

"The fool! His use to me was over." The Fool—wasn't that one of Xéra's tarot cards? "Even as he held the woman down, he begged me to be merciful!" she says, with that distant look on her face again. "Why should I show mercy? She deserved our retribution, every last *crumb* of it. It was right that the cake that killed my grandson should kill her too."

Egad, she's speaking in tongues! "That's it!" I cry. "You've confessed, in front of witnesses! Note it down, Blue, every word." His speedwriting flies across the page.

Judith eyes the door then suddenly makes a sprint for it.

Does she intend to hurl herself overboard and join her husband at the bottom of the ocean? Or make a hole in the side of the yacht and set light to the engine room? We'll never find out, fortunately, because during this outburst Karol-Kate has quietly maneuverd herself in front of the door and is standing there immovable as a sarsen at Stonehenge.

"Stop right there," says Bernie, tossing aside her patch and springing forward, pistol in hand.

"She's an undercover insurance investigator," I tell the astonished guests in a stage whisper. The erstwhile chef and dog handler swiftly overpower their kicking, screaming, biting adversary and click on manacles, after which Colefax joins in the fun, jumping up and nipping at Judith's bare ankles.

"Get thee behind me, Satan," she hisses, kicking out at the dog, which excites him further.

At this, Bernie produces a zip tie and—after checking it's structural—cinches Judith's ankle to one of the plaster columns. This sets Judith off shrieking such obscene oaths and curses that even the Book of Revelation would blush. Finally, they're forced to gag her.

If this hellish vision is what The Hierophant looks like when crossed, Xéra's tarot reader did well to warn against her.

Chapter 92

I clap my hands for silence. "Our entertainment is almost over, but I have one final question. This one is for our captain."

He snaps to attention.

"A third crime occurred on Thursday, when I was almost strangled in the anchor chain locker and thrown into the sea. Naturally, I thought it must somehow be connected to the necklace, or to Xéra's death, but I was wrong. My would-be assassin was a hijacker, who realized that I had found him out."

This new disclosure stretches the already extended credulity of my audience. *Hijacker? What's he talking about?*

"So, '*Captain*,'" I demand, drawing air quotes with my fingers, "where are you taking us, and why?"

He looks baffled; his brain scrambles for verbs to misplace. "What do you mean? We're for the Azores heading."

"That's what you've been telling us for the last three days, but it's a lie. Does the name 'Lacuna' mean anything to you?"

With a toss of his head, he gets to his feet. "I will not have my authority challenged. I am returning to the pilot house."

"Admit it—you threw me overboard. And one more question."

"Technically, you're out of questions," remarks Blue, who's been faithfully noting all this down.

I shoot him a look and finish: "Why have you hijacked the boat?"

"I never threw anyone anywhere," says Captain Romer, genuinely flustered. "And what is this about hijacking?"

"Thankfully, there's one senior officer we can trust, and she's been doing her best to steer us away from Lacuna—which, in case you haven't heard, is a criminal hellhole: the money-laundering, drug-running and piracy capital of the Atlantic." I'm laying it on a bit thick here, but it's got their attention. "So, I'm afraid we've outwitted you, Captain Nobody.

"Ladies and gentlemen, I proudly present our hero of the hour, who will, with the assistance of security guard Bernadette Houllahilly, take the helm and steer us to safety . . .

"Er, where's she gone? Has anyone seen Aimee?"

The grand saloon's hundred and one loudspeakers, concealed in soft furnishings, plasterwork, ice buckets and oil paintings, emit a gentle click and we hold our breath. Colefax freezes and Judith stops clawing at her handcuffs.

"*Ha ha ha ha ha! Ha ha ha ha ha! This is your NEW captain speaking! Ha ha ha ha ha!*"

She's turned the volume to eleven—we clap our hands to our ears to try and muffle the sound of cackling.

"*It is warm and sunny in Ponta Delgada!*"

Aimee must have slipped out through a service door and hotfooted it up to the pilot house. But why? Has she gone mad?

"*Paul Delamare—please report immediately to the pilot house. Ha ha ha ha ha!*"

"That went well," snipes Blue as I march out of the grand saloon with Bernie, leaving Karol-Kate to stand guard over Judith. We file across the sheepskin-floored lobby, up the companionway and out onto the lawn deck. Bernie takes charge, pistol in hand; as we approach the pilot house she tells me to stand back. She's going in. She hammers on the glass with the butt of her pistol.

"*Ha ha ha ha ha! Drop the gun, GI Jane—it's bulletproof!*"

"This is—unexpected," says Captain Romer, appearing behind us and shaking his head sadly. "But the first officer is right: the pilot house is—" he gropes for the word—"impregnable."

"*Ha ha ha ha ha!*"

I wish she'd stop that noise.

Inside her fortress, Aimee stands at the wheel. She's stripped off her uniform to reveal an extremely flattering bikini in sugar pink, and is waving at us gaily as if it's a sunny Sunday in St. Kitts and we're all having fun. Now she flips a switch and Rihanna's "Don't Stop The Music" starts blaring out.

Aimee shrieks in hideous descant, gyrating like a madwoman and smooching with her life jacket. She snatches up a bottle of rum and takes a swig, then seeing us all peering in at her, goes to the microphone and cries in a mock-playful tone: "*Hold on, folks, I'm opening her up!*"

There's a tremendous roar and we're all hurled backwards, clutching at railings. Aimee pumps the throttle and the yacht's engines scream to superthrust. An inhuman screech rings out.

"*Lacuna ahoy!*"

Directly ahead of us, a forbidding gray rock rises from the sea. Although there isn't a cloud in the sky, a shadow seems to hang over its jagged outline. A wisp of smoke rises from the top, as if someone is burning a fire up there or sending us a signal: *Stay away!*

"How long've we got, Captain Romer?" I ask.

"Ten minutes," he replies.

The bow has lifted and we're cutting through the water like a giant dagger. Is Aimee planning to drive *Maldemer* onto the rocks and drown us all? At least it'll be quick. Or will we be taken ashore as prisoners, thrown into a dungeon without food or water, to die slowly among the indigenous scorpions? Maybe she'll make her escape and leave us drifting in the Atlantic, hoping to be spotted by a passing ship.

I can't believe I was taken in by her. It's so obvious now: the false acts of friendship, and (God, I now realize) beating up a defenseless child for making a mistake with my laundry. She must have been the one who framed me with the cannabis when I started asking too many questions, then choked me unconscious and threw me overboard. The sob story about Romer . . . when all the time she's been plotting our course to this godforsaken rock.

I feel my phone buzz—I notice other guests also reaching for their pockets. It's a text!

"There must be a mast on the island," declares Shane. "Ha! Come look, Lise—Fowler's sent us a video!"

I tap on my inbox, hoping I won't be landed with a £15,000 roaming charge, and scroll through. Dozens of messages of increasing urgency—*Answer my email! Important! Extremely important!! What's happening?! Where are you??? Reply to me IMMEDIATELY!!!! EMERGENCY!!!!!*—plus just one that isn't from Julie. I click on it.

As if I needed my pill to be made more bitter, this is what I read:

From: d.a.armstrong98@met.police.uk
Saturday 8:40 a.m.
Subject: Fwd: Urgent/confidential—Interpol Red Notice
To: Paul Delamare/Aboard *M/Y Maldemer*

Begin forwarded message:

An associate of MATEUS/MIRSAYEV has been issued with an International Arrest Warrant. ANNETTE ADNEY, also known as AIMEE ADNEY, female, origin Barbados, age 27 / 5'5" / 127 lbs. Appearance:

Bajan (Barbadian Afro-Caribbean), black hair, brown eyes, no (known) distinguishing marks.

This person is regarded as extremely dangerous and should in no circumstances be approached.

Annette Adney. Aimee Adney . . . all the As. Julie's always telling me I trust people I shouldn't, and don't trust people I should—and once again I got it wrong, wrong, wrong.

Chapter 93

There's someone back in London who cares enough about me to send a thousand texts of concern; if only for her, I can't just sit here and let this happen.

"Captain Romer, is there any way of stopping this boat?"

He thinks for a moment, which is a first, and slowly shakes his head; his blue-black locks sparkle in the sunshine. "From the pilot house I regret only."

"Is there any other way of cutting off the engines?"

He shrugs again.

"It's worth a try!" cries a voice from behind me. Karol-Kate, who has evidently entrusted watching the Bride of Frankenstein to someone else, has come up to see the unfurling catastrophe for herself; she now beckons me to follow.

The two of us speed down several decks until we're standing in front of a steel door marked ENGINE ROOM. The pulsating heat and thrumming sound make me feel nauseous, but at least there's no oily engine smell. That's Rolls-Royce for you—makes you proud to be British.

Karol-Kate swipes her keycard and nothing happens; she tries again. Alongside the keypad is an emergency button in a glass box with a little hammer hanging to one side. For years I've longed to use one of these—even considered faking an emergency on a train to do so—and now's the moment. The glass tinkles to the ground, I press the button, a siren sounds, the steel door shoots back. It was worth the wait.

Inside is not at all what I expected: instead of clashing pistons, whirling cogs and spinning belts, the V16s are encased in sleek bodywork bearing the Spirit of Ecstasy logo and encrusted with consoles, buttons and flashing lights. Karol-Kate's eyes widen in wonder.

"How do we stop it?" I bellow.

"Isn't it beautiful!" she shouts back, transfixed.

I feel let down by Karol-Kate in my hour of need, but I have an idea. Years ago, I bought a sleek Italian mincing machine, which arrived with no instructions and as far as I could tell, no on–off switch. I looked everywhere: on it, under it. In it. Finally, I decided it must be movement-activated or infra-red or telepathic and phoned the manufacturer in Turin to ask.

"*Molto semplice*," replied the voice. "Is on, is on. Is off, is off." In other words, plug it in to make it work, pull the plug out to make it stop.

Taking a *molto semplice* approach to our current predicament, I leave Karol-Kate to keep watch over the engine room and race down to the bilges, where I hammer on a low, narrow door painted bright red.

"Afet, we need your help!"

The fuel bunker, which currently doubles as the deckhands' living and sleeping quarters, is a complex piece of engineering, with pipes running in all directions like steel spaghetti. I tell the deckhands we need to close everything down, and within seconds they're swarming over the tanks, scaling ladders, legging one another up, dangling from pipework. Some of the feeds are worked by buttons, others levers, and there are wheels too, lacquered in bright colors.

They're strong, fit young women—used to physical effort, unfazed by machinery—and they know the meaning of teamwork: I can imagine their grandmothers in days of yore singing away as they repaired nets and gutted fish. Harvard Business School could learn from them.

In a matter of minutes, everything has been switched off, with the exception of one wheel, painted neon orange and labeled EMERGENCY DEFAULT FEED. Try as we might, this one will not budge.

In the kitchen, the way to separate stuck tins or dishes in extremis is to heat them with a chef's blowtorch; in an adaptation of that technique, I seize an oil lamp dangling from the ceiling.

It isn't a good idea to play about with fire near fuel tanks, but needs must. I grab a cloth and remove the chimney of the lamp, then turn the flame to max and play it over the valve; brass having excellent thermal conductivity, it heats quickly and the metal expands. I clamp the cloth to the scorching metal and squeeze and press.

Still stuck.

I look at my watch—our time is almost up. It'll be like *Titanic*, trying to fight our way out as the water gushes in around us. I decide to give it one last shot. Afet holds the flame under the valve and I clench the wheel with all my strength. The cloth keeps slipping, so throwing it aside, I use my bare hands.

The wheel is so hot that my flesh sticks to it, like a pork chop hitting a screaming hot skillet. Pain shoots through my body, but yes, it moved! I keep turning and a barbecue aroma fills the air.

Finally, Afet, gesturing with horror at my burned and bloodied hands, drags me off the wheel and plunges my hand into a bowl of cool water, while the others, armed with cloths, pile in and finish turning till we hear a gurgle, and the valve is closed.

The effect is instant. There's a creaking sound, then a puttering, then the engines die. It's suddenly, eerily quiet.

Unfortunately, we're not safe yet: the yacht's still traveling under its own momentum, and our hull may yet be ripped from beneath us by a reef or rocky outcrop.

"Come with me," I order Afet, as the women bind my hands

with makeshift bandages. "Yes, all of you. Come with me up into the light."

Like the Pied Piper, I lead my Rustavaijani friends up through the ship. At the service door leading out to the lobby they hold back, fearful to enter, even those who have been above deck before, cleaning or waiting.

"Is it safe?" asks their leader.

"Trust me," I insist. From the creamy luxury of the lobby I take them up to the lawn deck, where they blink in the sunshine, like moles that have been burrowing in the dark.

Challis bounces up from nowhere. "Will these ladies be requiring lifeboats?" At this point she sees my hands: "What happened there?"

"Nothing serious," I say, though I've never known such pain.

She disappears briefly and returns with a sealed plastic bag containing cold water.

"No ice?" I say.

She rolls her eyes. "Keep your hands pressed against it. Trust me." Then, turning back to the Rustavaijanis: "Now, ladies, follow me."

By now, *Maldemer* has stopped moving, although vicious-looking rocks poke through the surface of the water here and there, and Lacuna the Dread is only three or four hundred meters ahead. I'm trying to work out what to do next when, to my horror, an ominous rumbling sound fills the air. Has Aimee found a reserve tank, and restarted the engines?

No—it's coming from overhead.

I look up to see a huge camouflage-painted helicopter, emblazoned FORÇA AÉREA PORTUGUESA, circling overhead. It's a Merlin EH-101. Good grief! They've sent in their fabled 751 Squadron. A man leans out of the cockpit window and gesticulates furiously, then gets out a megaphone and screams in a metallic voice, *"Saia da porra do caminho!"*

The big *H* on the grass is about to have its moment.

Chapter 94

Eight figures, dressed head to toe in midnight blue and with POLÍCIA MARITÍMA written across their backs, leap from the helicopter and kneel down in formation.

"Whoa!" I shout, dropping my water bag and waving my bandages. "Don't shoot! I'm innocent!"

The commander jumps out of line and screams in my face: *"Onde está Mateus?"*

"Luiz Mateus? Not here." Another steps forward to translate, and I tell her Aimee—Annette Adney, or whatever she calls herself—has barricaded herself in the pilot house.

It takes several gunshots and a coordinated shoulder charge but eventually they gain entry. After that they smash through the door leading to the captain's cabin—more mess and destruction—but no Aimee: she got away.

"That was a close call," I tell the translator after the others disappear to search for the fugitive. "But who told you we had a problem?"

"Interpol was alerted by British police. They tell us last known coordinates of yacht and destination Lacuna."

She asks where she'll find "Sir Hardcastle" and I lead her down through the yacht to the lifeboats, where guests and crew are patiently waiting in line. I don't know who put Karol-

Kate in charge, but she appears to be conducting an inspection.

"You can relax," I tell her. "The cavalry has arrived."

"No rush," she says. "I'm going to teach them a shanty."

"Anyone seen Sir Billy?"

"We thought he was with you," she replies.

Turning to the translator, I say: "I think you should know that these young women are being trafficked." I indicate the Rustavaijanis, standing in dignified silence, and she makes a note of this. "Also, the yacht is being used as a cover for a smuggling operation."

Hearing this, she summons a couple of her colleagues by radio and I lead the posse to the bilges, and the perforated door I noticed opposite the anchor chain locker. One of them shoots the lock open to reveal a capacious cupboard stacked with shrink-wrapped black blocks. When one is peeled open, a lush fragrance billows forth.

"There!" I declare, proud as Punch. "I think you'll find that's Grade-A Madagascar vanilla, being illegally imported to the United States. Worth thousands. Probably stolen, or produced by child labor, or both."

The officers look at me, unimpressed.

"*Narcóticas?*" says one of them hopefully.

Suddenly I remember something else. "Follow me."

I lead them up a deck, past the padlocked refrigeration zone where poor Xéra lies at rest, and stop at the door marked PANIC ROOM. It's wide open.

"Take a look at this lot," I say, flicking on the lights to reveal the packages of baking supplies we innocently moved in here a couple of days ago. Except they've disappeared.

I'm spared having to make an embarrassing apology because an officer's radio starts buzzing, then another, then they all start: it's as if we've stepped into a beehive.

"*Se apresse!*" cries one of the other officers. "*Rápido! Ur-*

gente!" another. We race up through the yacht and onto the lawn deck, where we hear a colossal sploosh followed by a mechanical roar. Through a choking fog of gasoline fumes we see *Maldemer*'s tender erupt out of the bow of the yacht, like the chestburster in *Alien*.

At the controls is Aimee, Sir Billy alongside her.

Slung in the cockpit behind the pair are three enormous Louis Vuitton trunks. Empty on arrival, I would wager that the "Assorted Dry Goods" with which they're now filled are in fact cocaine and crystal meth.

Chapter 95

The officers fire on the getaway boat and Sir Billy takes the wheel so Aimee can shoot back. The officers yell at me to take cover so I miss the bit where she is hit in the shoulder and Sir Billy raises his handkerchief in surrender.

A few seconds later, the Merlin lowers an officer aboard the tender and steers it back alongside *Maldemer*, after which Aimee/Annette and Sir Billy are escorted onto the helicopter under close guard, joined shortly by Judith. A guard offers Aimee a sling for her arm, but she spits in his face.

As the chopper rises overhead, I get the opportunity to wave my bandages at my ex-companions, but they don't wave back.

After this, we give statements to the translator. I ask her to be gentle with the deckhands, who have already made themselves popular by stowing the tender and restoring the place to order, as well as serving tea and snacks.

"I've been thinking," I say. "Mateus's real name is Ljuba Mirsayev. Is he Rustavaijani, by any chance?" She nods. "Makes sense. If you can unravel all the shell companies and offshore trusts, you'll find he owns this yacht. And Aimee works for him."

I ask her if we're going ashore at Lacuna and she laughs. "Nothing there except a few crazy islanders," she says. "Also, no jurisdiction." Another loophole in international law the United Nations should be doing something about.

* * *

Farewell cocktails on the lawn deck are a more democratic affair than previously: surviving guests, crew, stowaways and law enforcers sip and mingle in the soft evening sunlight as we cruise toward Ponta Delgada, where we will receive a hero's welcome. Relief and gratitude flood through my veins, lubricated perhaps by the buprenorphine Bernie found in the medical kit to hold my burns at bay.

Best of all, I've spoken—actually spoken!—to dearest Julie. Launching an international air-sea rescue operation is a first even for her; she burst into tears when she heard my voice, which set me off too.

Captain Romer, the old charlatan, is at the helm, although I believe someone from the Portuguese military set a course for him. The windows of the pilot house having been blown out, a becoming draught teases his raven locks, causing him to run his hand frequently through them like a shampoo ad.

I look down to the afterdeck, where Shane and Elise are gazing at the sunset, hand in hand, with Blue sitting on a banquette nearby, scribbling notes. Bernie and Karol-Kate, their friendship cemented by our miraculous escape, stand side by side gazing out to stern. In honor of the occasion, Bernie's put on her big hoop earrings, which twinkle in the sunshine.

"Looking for albatrosses?" I call down, and they laugh. "Sorry to spoil the moment, but could you give me a hand, Karol-Kate?"

"Call me Ki-Ki," she calls up, looking bashful, or a close equivalent. "All my friends do."

"I'll hold Colesie," says Bernie.

"Back in a mo, Bern," says Ki-Ki.

Five minutes later, the dog handler and I emerge onto the afterdeck carrying four buckets. There are times when it comes in useful to have your hands protected by bandage mittens, and now is one of them. I lift the first lobster out of the bucket, he clacks his pincers in the air with joy and gratitude and I drop him gently into the sea, where he belongs.

When we've done the same with the others and the applause has died down (and Colefax, nose in the air, has finally stopped yapping), there's a blast of foghorn and the captain's voice booms out.

"*To Ponta Delgada, where it warm and sunny is!*"

CHAPTER 96

THE FOLLOWING WEEKEND

"I'm a lousy judge of character," I tell Julie. "I go too much on first impressions, take people at face value."

"Don't change," she replies, gently touching my hand, which feels good even if it makes me wince. "That's why everyone loves you—because you're naturally kind and trusting."

In honor of our reunion, she's wearing a new outfit—a wrap dress in a rich modern tartan, which flatters her curves and makes her hazel eyes and glorious brunette hair shine like lanterns.

I tried to persuade Declan to stay, but he wouldn't. He drove Julie over from Putney Bridge in his new BMW—an upgrade, now that he's been promoted from acting to actual DCI—from which, to my amazement, he produced a huge gardenia smothered in fragrant blossom and a "Get Well Soon" card.

It's good to be back at Jubilee Cottage, warm and cozy. The drying machines have departed and I've salvaged what I can of my houseplant collection. I enjoy watching plants grow, I've discovered, but they're not like people: they can be replaced. A (not strictly legal) wood fire, laid and lit by Julie, crackles in the grate and I've cracked open a bottle of a rather acceptable Californian red called the Whole Shebang.

She has demanded the full, unabridged story. Being addicted to true-crime programs on TV, she wants to know every detail of the murder plot that (despite her protestations) she played such a large part in unraveling.

"What gave you the idea for the quiz?" she asks.

"I knew I had to get Judith to confess in public, and it was all I could think of to lure her along. Thank goodness she took the bait. She's a warning to me: be careful around very clever people; you never know what's going on in their heads. Of course, it hardly matters now—she's boasting about the murder to anyone who'll listen. She sees herself as some kind of avenging angel."

"If I were on her defense team," says Julie thoughtfully, "I'd argue psychosis: highly intelligent woman controlled over many years by coercive, unfaithful husband."

"I don't think you're being entirely fair to Russell," I say. "I can't help feeling just a little bit—"

"Oh, not that again, Paul," she says, rolling her eyes; apparently, I have an infuriating habit of feeling sorry for people who don't deserve it.

"And you're convinced Sir Billy loved Xéra, despite everything he did?" she continues. "Including stealing her bridal gift?"

It's come out—as it inevitably would—that it was he who strong-armed Marje into stealing the De Lage Treasure, promising her a share of the money raised from breaking it up and selling the jewels, as well as the insurance payout.

"Yes, although he's also in love with money."

"I simply cannot understand what she saw in him."

"The day we understand love is the day we'll understand the human race. He hid from her that he was in desperate financial straits, which made him easy prey for a devil like Mateus."

"To think he's still on the loose," says Julie ruefully. "The forces of justice should be chasing him, not hounding Rustavaijani asylum seekers. Any news on that?"

"I wish them a happy ending with all my heart, but we're dealing with reality. The publicity hasn't done any harm, and they may get to America yet—if they still want to go. At least we've saved them from Mateus. Afet has promised to stay in touch, by the way."

"How long will Sir Billy get?" asks Julie.

"Fraud, human-trafficking and narcotics offenses. Several years at least."

"You must be the only person in the whole world who'd believe a ton of white powder on a yacht that just arrived from the Andaman Islands is nothing more than flour and baking powder," she comments.

It's true: another example of my taking things at face value.

"And Aimee? Or rather Annette?"

"Cruel and ruthless. Throwing me overboard was attempted murder, plus more serious narcotics offenses and human trafficking charges. And, oh yes, GBH, for assaulting the poor deckhand."

"What about Judith?"

"Double murder, mandatory life sentence. Quite right too."

"On a more cheerful note, what happened to our handsome tennis player?" asks Julie.

"He and Elise will be OK. They can sell the Knightsbridge pad and set themselves up in one of those chic coastal towns to which impecunious Londoners retire, living off the difference. There's probably a local swingers' club they can hook up with—they'll be very popular. Especially Shane."

"And the dog handler?"

"Ki-Ki! I hope it works out for her and Bernie—Calamitas are giving her a great fat bonus for exceptional service."

"What about Marje? Her agency still on the rocks?"

"Not from what I heard. Robbery, murder, helicopters—LA is all over her and a production company has optioned the story. On the other hand, I will never forgive her behavior toward Xéra. Conniving in the theft of the necklace and blackmailing her—how scheming."

Julie shakes her head sadly. "And what about the smarmy journalist? I hope he got his comeuppance."

"Oh, Blue's not so bad—not when you get to know him better."

"Uh-oh," says Julie. "Here we go again."

"Well," I say, somewhat sheepish, "you remember I photographed a couple of pages from his speedwriting notes?"

"What's that got to do with it?"

"One of the pages was about me. And I had it translated by this nice speedwriting expert."

"And? What does it say?"

My bandaged hands fumble hopelessly with my laptop; Julie takes pity on me, taps in my password and opens up the email.

> *Dear Paul,*
> *I'm delighted to help you with your speedwriting mystery. I know you're a writer because I've seen your name in* Escape *magazine (even made a couple of your recipes!) so do think about learning speedwriting—it's a useful skill. I've typed out the excerpt you sent me:*
> *P. D.*

^{i}g^g crctr cltvtd & nwlg^b. I fnd hm sm$_w$t ^{c}trdctry – $_c$rm^g 2 ur fc bt w$_t$ a drk sns of hmr. Also, h's tngd by sdns: Marje tld m $_t$ lv of hs lif dd a cpl of yrs ago & u cn tl h's nt ovr t. A cpl of fny trts. F ^{c}vrs^n stps, h's alwys $_t$ one $_w$o hs 2 lp n & fl $_t$ gp. (t's sm syclgcl nd) & typcl Engl$_s$mn h hsn't $_t$ 1st idea of hw atrctv h s! H's alwys 2 bsy wry^g abt $_w$t ppl r $_t$nk^g 2 ntc $_t$ wy h's b^g lkd at. Endr^g, I gs. I nd 2 w$_c$ hm crfly bcs I $_t$nk $_t$r's m$_c$ mr g^g on $_t$n

And here's the translation:

P. D.

Intriguing character, cultivated and knowledgeable. I find him somewhat contradictory—charming to your face but with a dark sense of humor. Also, he's tinged by sadness: Marje told me the love of his life died a couple of years ago and you can tell he's not over it.

A couple of funny traits. If conversation stops, he has to leap in and fill the gap. (It's some psychological need.) And typical Englishman: he hasn't the first idea of how attractive he is! He's always too busy worrying about what people are thinking to notice the way he's being looked at. Endearing, I guess.

I need to watch him carefully because I think there's much more going on than—

"There!" exclaims Julie. "Isn't that just exactly what I'm always telling you?"

Chapter 97

"Your turn now," I say. "How the heck did you manage to mobilize the Portuguese Air Force?"

"Don't exaggerate—it was the Maritime Police. And I know he's not your favorite person, but it was Declan."

"I never said—"

"Oh, Paul, he's tried so hard! He knows how close we are, and he's so anxious to make a good impression . . . You *intimidate* him. And by the way, I looked up what you said about most police marriages ending in divorce and it's rubbish."

My mind flashes back to when I was floating in the Atlantic, certain I was going to die: I regretted being mean about Declan then, and I'm going to try harder from now on. "I'm sorry, it's only that I want the best for you."

"That's the whole point," she continues, "he is the best. Kind, thoughtful, funny . . . plus he has a serious, worthwhile job, unlike you and me." She could also add that he always looks so marvelous, something I haven't allowed myself to acknowledge before now.

"I'm sure you're right," I admit grudgingly. "But it's a pity he can't write a coherent sentence."

"Oh, Paul . . . He begged me not to tell you—he's embarrassed, particularly among educated people like you. But he's severely *dyslexic*. He gets his emails checked by someone in their communications office, who corrects the spelling and puts in the punctuation."

The communications office? For once, words fail me.

I learn how Declan, in between doing his day job, alerted Scotland Yard and Interpol's National Central Bureau to the fact that most-wanted international crook Luiz Mateus was connected in some way to a superyacht crossing the Atlantic to St. Boniface. This caused cogs to start turning. When Lacuna was mentioned—Mateus had long been suspected of using it as his offshore HQ—they became seriously interested.

Julie—using the opportunity to practice her Portuguese—had a long conversation with the Maritime Police in Lisbon. *Maldemer* was sailing "under the radar" (with her Automatic Identification System turned off) but thanks to the coordinates I supplied, they were able to plot our course and, when the moment came, send in 751 Squadron.

Since Declan came back from Ponta Delgada, he's been infuriatingly discreet, but I gather some kind of a confession has been extracted from Annette/Aimee. Her plan was to land *Maldemer* at Lacuna—where she could not be arrested—and send guests and crew off in a leaky old fishing boat to Santa Cruz das Flores (the westernmost of the Azores). At least she got the chance to open up the engines as she always dreamed, because it'll be a long time before she steps onto a yacht again.

Our so-called captain was a cocktail barman in Antibes, who picked up his peculiar English while crewing on posh yachts in his spare time. He's somewhat naive, having agreed to play along with her ruse without any idea of what she was really up to. At least now we know why he looked his happiest shaking martinis.

I've opened a second bottle and Julie's updating me on what's been happening at the magazine.

"Am I out of a job?" I ask.

"Quite the opposite," she replies. "Dena . . . Well, you're not going to like it, but she's had a big idea." I groan. "You know how she's always saying every crisis is an opportunity? She wants you to do a cover feature for our New Year issue about—"

At this point there's loud rapping at the door and I take custody of a large rectangular parcel; as usual, Julie tells me off for giving the guy a tip, but I feel sorry for delivery drivers. Attached to it is a card—Nancy Lancaster's Yellow Room in Avery Row, circa 1950—written in a flowing hand:

Dear Paul,

I was hoping we might be able to meet up, as we're virtually neighbors, but Lise and I have started packing up the house, so it's not going to work. (Don't know where we'll end up—Lise fancies Hastings, I say Morocco.)

Lise was going through Xéra's things and came across these family letters and photographs in a folder marked "BOOK." I thought you might like to have them.

I couldn't help noticing a little package tucked in with them. Xéra obviously wanted you to have it.

As you know, I'm not the expressive type, but I wish we might have met in different circumstances and become friends. I hope you feel the same.

Warm regards to a lovely guy,
S. XXX

Because of my incapacity, Julie unwraps a familiar old attaché case of soft fawn leather, the lock engraved with *LdS*.

"Oh, my," I say, deeply touched. "It's the family archive,

going right back." With any luck I can finish Xéra's memoir—perhaps we can even mount an exhibition at the Fondation Luna de Sully in Pariangan, to celebrate its opening.

With great care, Julie lays the contents out on the table. Letters, cuttings and recipes. Lots more photographs: Xéra's handsome great-grandfather, grandfather and father, and their beautiful, brilliant womenfolk. Xéra as an infant, a young girl and a radiantly beautiful young woman. It's impossible not to shed a tear.

As Julie puts the yellowing photographs and flaking letters back, I spot something wedged into the bottom of the case, which must be the mysterious "something" to which Shane referred: a brick-like package wrapped in brown paper, inscribed *Paul* in Xéra's extravagant script and dated last Wednesday—the very morning she died.

I look at Julie dumbfounded then nod for her to unwrap it.

Inside is a huge wad of cherry-red banknotes fastened by a thick elastic band, with a note on top.

Darling Paul, your fee plus a small extra token of my appreciation. Put it toward the Grosvenor Estate standing charges. X

Julie insists on counting them out, and I watch transfixed.

I'm not the sort of person who sees a £50 note often, and they add up very quickly. "That's five hundred . . . That's a thousand . . ." And so it goes on.

We'll never know for certain, but did she have a premonition before she died, and decide to look out for her friend?

That would be so like Xéra—how blessed I was to have her in my life.

"I've something else to thank you for," I tell Julie when she's stashed the windfall in the cash box I keep under my bed.

"You mean my tarot readings?" she says eagerly.

"No, I mean—"

"Remember, I warned you up front about the Queen of Swords and the star sign Libra? Judith's a Libran—it was her birthday. Just saying."

"You're right, all very thought-provoking. But what I most want to say is—thank you for saving Jubilee Cottage."

It's true. While in friendly conversation with the neighbor I have consistently ignored for the last decade, Julie noticed something interesting: he has a discreet little CCTV camera mounted above his front door.

For legal reasons, the coverage does not extend to my basement (I should hope not) but the footage from the morning my basement was flooded shows the slouching figure of stepson Jonny approaching Jubilee Cottage with a hose coiled round his arm, and departing ten minutes later without it. I've informed my insurers as well as Waister Timon Hassall, and trust they'll follow it up with him.

"There's a lesson for you there—always keep on friendly terms with your neighbors," says Julie. "By the way, you seem to have hit it off with the seafaring dog," she continues, watching for my reaction. "Any more thoughts about getting one of your own?"

"They're a bit of a tie."

"I'll look after him when you go away."

I shudder. "Like you did the plants?"

Looking thus to the future, we raise our glasses and drink our customary toast.

"*To new adventures!*"

TEN WEEKS LATER

From *Escape* magazine, January issue, page 5.

PAUL DELAMARE GOES TO SEA

Escape readers will be aware that our intrepid food editor-at-large, Paul Delamare, was recently awarded a King's Gallantry Medal for his bravery aboard a yacht hijacked in the Atlantic last fall. We are proud to present an exclusive menu created by him for *Escape*, inspired by the ocean and his heroic voyage.

POSEIDON ADVENTURE

This cocktail celebrates the original popular disaster movie The Poseidon Adventure (1972), set aboard a ship struck by a tidal wave.

It was created by Austrian mixologist Romer Schnapps, who was aboard the hijacked vessel and played a part in its rescue. Schnapps has subsequently been awarded his country's Grand Decoration of Honor and opened Romer's Ruin, a cookie-and-cocktail bar in Marseillan, on the Côte d'Améthyste, SW France.

Garnish with a maraschino cherry, to represent Shelley Winters going into the drink, in both senses, and accompany with the film's hit song, "The Morning After," in the version sung by Maureen McGovern.

4 dashes Angostura bitters
1 measure blue Curaçao
1 measure vodka
about 4 measures lemon-flavored soda, such as Sprite®
   or 7-Up® (or seltzer water, for a less sweet drink)

Serves 1

Put three cubes of ice in a martini glass and splash with bitters. Shake the Curaçao and vodka in a cocktail shaker with ice, then strain into the glass. Add lemon-flavored soda or seltzer to taste, stir gently and serve.

Note: a traditional cocktail measure is 1 fl. oz., or 2 tablespoons. If you use a proper old-fashioned jigger, the small end will yield one measure (1 fl. oz.), the larger end, two measures (2 fl. oz) or 4 tablespoons. In a shocking example of shrinkflation, modern jiggers have shrunk to ⅚ fl. oz. (1 tablespoon plus 2 teaspoons); if you use this, your drink will have the correct proportions but be on the mean side, so compensate accordingly. A dash of an ingredient such as bitters is technically ⅛ of a teaspoon but usually interpreted as a short, sharp shake.

MUSHROOM AND ONION MARMALADE TARTLETS

This deceptively simple canapé was a favorite aboard M/Y *Maldemer*: for many years I've been begged to share the recipe. Guests will never guess that the crisp shell is white sandwich bread, and not an elaborate pastry.

If you can only buy thick sliced bread, roll it slightly thinner with a rolling pin before using. You will need a 12-hole tartlet pan, with holes 2½ inches in diameter.

Makes 12 canapé-size tartlets

2 tablespoons olive oil
1 onion, chopped
1 tablespoon white granulated sugar
2 cups thinly sliced mushrooms (clean before slicing)
1 garlic clove, minced
2–3 tablespoons finely chopped fresh thyme
12 slices of thin-sliced white sandwich bread
sufficient butter for spreading on the bread
1 scant cup shredded Gruyère or sharp cheddar, for sprinkling

Heat the oil in a generously sized skillet, add the onion, and sauté over moderate heat for 7–8 minutes, till softened and golden. Stir in the sugar and some seasoning, turn up the heat and add the mushrooms. Sizzle for 5 minutes, stirring occasionally, till you have driven off any moisture and the mushrooms are golden. Stir in the garlic for another minute, till fragrant, then turn off the heat and stir in most of the thyme (save some for sprinkling). The mixture can be refrigerated at this point, in which case give it a good stir before using.

To make the tartlet bases, cut 12 disks out of the bread using a 2½–3-inch cookie cutter or the rim of a glass of a similar size. Butter one side and stick buttered side down into the tartlet pan.

When ready to bake, heat the oven to 425°F/400°F fan. Divide the mushroom mixture between the tartlets and top with a sprinkle of cheese. Don't be too tidy about this—any cheese on the pan will form a lacy edge to the tartlets. Bake for 10–15 minutes till golden and bubbling. Sprinkle with reserved thyme and serve.

MAC 'N' CHEESE SURF AND TURF

A luxurious pasta dish incorporating juicy morsels of seafood and chunks of salty bacon, enlivened with the classic French *fines herbes*, in dried form.

You can add another cheese instead of the processed cheese, if you prefer, but Velveeta® contains sodium citrate, which will give the dish its characteristic gloss and creaminess.

Serves 6

2 cups dried macaroni, or elbow macaroni
6 slices thick-cut bacon
a little vegetable oil
3½ tablespoons butter
heaping ¼ cup all-purpose flour
scant 3 cups whole milk)
2 packed cups shredded sharp cheddar
5 Velveeta® processed cheese slices (or if slicing from a Velveeta® block about 3½–4 oz.)
1 scant cup (about 6 tablespoons) finely shredded fresh Parmesan
1 teaspoon dried *fines herbes*
grated zest of half a lemon
½ teaspoon mustard powder
½ teaspoon onion powder or granulated onion
pinch of hot red pepper flakes or ground cayenne pepper
12–16 cooked, shelled large or jumbo shrimp

FOR THE TOPPING
8 oz. (about 2 large) fire-roasted sweet red bell peppers, from a jar, drained and sliced

⅓ cup panko (Japanese breadcrumbs) or regular breadcrumbs

2 tablespoons finely shredded fresh Parmesan

Cook the pasta in a large pot of boiling salted water according to package instructions (typically 8–10 minutes). Drain and rinse under a running faucet, then shake or stir occasionally as it dries, so it doesn't stick together.

In the same pot (no need to wash) sauté the bacon in a little oil (halve the slices if they don't fit and cook in two batches if necessary) till brown and crisp, then remove to a plate or board lined with paper towel and using scissors snip the bacon into strips.

In the same pot (again, no need to wash) add the butter, flour, and milk and bring to a boil, whisking constantly with a wire whisk until thickened and smooth. Simmer for 3–4 minutes, stirring often, until smooth. (You will seem to have a lot of sauce, but this is correct.) Stir in the remaining ingredients, except the shrimp, and taste for seasoning, then stir in the bacon bits and cooked pasta.

Spoon half the mixture into a 12 × 8-inch, 2½-inch deep baking dish or casserole (about 3 quarts capacity), add the shrimp and herbs in a layer, then the remaining pasta mixture. Top with the sliced bell peppers, arranged in diagonal lines. Mix the panko breadcrumbs and remaining 2 tablespoons shredded Parmesan and sprinkle this on top.

Put in the oven at 350°F/325°F fan for 20–30 minutes, till piping hot and bubbling round the edges; there's no need to preheat the oven but it will save you five minutes if you do. If you wish, finish by placing under a hot broiler for an additional 3–4 minutes, to brown the top. Allow to cool for five minutes before serving.

SALAD DELAMARE

As a glamorous accompaniment to the mac 'n' cheese, I've created this variation on the classic Caesar salad. Not wishing to sound controversial, I find classic vinaigrette too sharp and/or sweet. Years ago, an esteemed food writer told me the secret was to add a little water, "to delay the vinegar hitting the palate before the oil"; don't believe it. My version is glossy and slightly thick, and the method described here is how to achieve it.

Serves 6 as a side, or 4 as a light entrée

2 small crisp lettuces, or a mixture of crisp salad greens and Belgian endive

FOR THE CROUTONS
1 tablespoon rapeseed oil
4 slices smoked streaky (belly) bacon
2 tablespoons butter
3 slices medium-sliced white bread, crusts removed, cut into cubes
1 large garlic clove, papery skin removed

FOR THE DRESSING
5 anchovy fillets in oil, drained
4 tablespoons mayonnaise
1 tablespoon Dijon mustard
4 teaspoons Worcestershire sauce
zest and juice of quarter of a lemon (you'll need 2–3 teaspoons juice)
⅔ cup rapeseed oil

TO FINISH
¼ cup finely shredded fresh Parmesan

Tear the lettuce into bite-size pieces in a salad bowl and refrigerate till ready to serve.

Heat the 1 tablespoon of rapeseed oil in a medium skillet. Add the bacon and cook until golden and crisp, then remove from pan with a slotted spoon to a paper towel-lined board (leaving the juices and oil in the pan), slice thinly and set aside.

Add the butter to the skillet, allow to melt then stir in the bread cubes and garlic. Bread varies, so if the cubes look dry, add more oil and/or butter, so that they are just saturated. I like to cook croutons low and slow, shaking and turning often, till just golden and crisp; adjust your heat accordingly and keep an eye on them. When done, set aside (leave them in the pan) and remove the garlic.

For the dressing, finely chop the softened garlic with the anchovies, or put them both through a garlic press (anchovies stick in some presses, but not in my Kuhn Rikon version). Transfer to a large jar or bowl. Using a mini whisk or fork, whisk in the mayo, mustard, Worcestershire, and lemon. Now start adding the oil: at first, add it slowly—literally, a drop at a time. After about a quarter of oil is in, start adding small glugs and watch it emulsify. When half is in, you'll find you can finish by adding it in a thin steady stream. Taste for seasoning—it should be assertive. If it is sharp or rough, a pinch of salt will soften it. The dressing can be made in advance.

When ready to serve, toss the lettuce with the bacon bits and the Parmesan. Pour over most of the dressing and tumble the leaves till glossy and coated; add more if necessary (or refrigerate for another time). Serve at once scattered with the croutons.

GÂTEAU REINE DE SABA

Perhaps the most elegant of chocolate cakes, first served by Pâtisserie Pompadour in 1909. This recipe, the original, is from the archive the late Xéra de Sully, who tragically lost her life during our ill-fated voyage to the Azores, and is shared with permission of her estate. Another version was popularized in the United States by Julia Child. De Sully's memoir, *The Icing on the Cake*, written in collaboration with me and including never-before-seen photographs and tried-and-tested recipes, will be published posthumously next year.

Serves 8

FOR THE MERINGUE
3 egg whites
pinch of fine salt
¼ tsp cream of tartar
1 tablespoon superfine sugar
1 teaspoon white wine or cider vinegar

FOR THE CAKE
4 oz. bittersweet (dark) chocolate (at least 60% cocoa solids), broken into small pieces or chopped
¼ cup ground almonds
heaping ¼ cup all-purpose flour
2 tablespoons cornstarch
1 stick (8 tablespoons) butter, softened
¾ cup superfine sugar
1 teaspoon pure vanilla extract
¼ teaspoon almond extract
3 egg yolks
2 tablespoons rum, brandy or coffee

FOR THE GLAZE

4 oz. bittersweet (dark) chocolate (at least 60% cocoa solids), broken into small pieces or chopped
¼–½ stick (2–4 tablespoons) butter, as needed (see method)
1 tablespoon rum, brandy or coffee
sliced almonds, well toasted, to decorate (optional)

Butter an 8-inch loose-bottomed cake pan (about 1½–2 inches deep), and line the base with a disk of parchment paper.

Melt the chocolate for the cake in a heatproof bowl set over a pan of hot water or just give it 2–3 minutes in the microwave. Leave to cool.

For the meringue, put the whites, salt, and cream of tartar in the bowl of a stand mixer, or use an electric hand whisk. Whisk till beginning to stiffen, then add the sugar in two batches. When the mixture is stiff and meringue-like, beat in the vinegar and set aside. If you are using a stand mixer and have a spare bowl, use it now, otherwise transfer the beaten whites to a fresh bowl, and rinse the bowl ready for the chocolate mixture.

For the cake, mix the ground almonds, flour, and cornstarch in a small bowl. Cream the butter, sugar, and vanilla and almond extracts using a stand or electric hand mixer, until light and creamy, then beat in the yolks, followed by the cooled chocolate and rum or brandy.

Gently fold in a third of the meringue mixture using a large metal spoon, then half the flour mixture, then repeat, finishing with remaining meringue mixture. There should be no lumps of egg white or flour visible. Spoon the mixture into the prepared pan and lightly spread it out to the edges.

Bake in a 350°F/325°F fan oven. There is no need to preheat—in which case it will take 25–28 minutes; if you do preheat, it will take 22–25 minutes. Rotate halfway through cooking time if necessary. The cake is cooked when a toothpick inserted about 2 inches from the edge comes out clean, with a few crumbs attached. The center of the cake should feel slightly soft to the touch but not liquid.

Run a palette knife round the edge of the cake, then allow to cool for ten minutes. Invert onto a rack, discard the parchment paper, and leave to cool completely—about an hour. You can make a day ahead and wrap if convenient.

Melt the chocolate for the glaze with ¼ stick (2 tablespoons) of the butter and rum (as before) till smooth. Chocolate varies, so if it's too thick to pour, melt in the extra butter. Put the cake (still inverted) on a rack with a sheet of baking parchment underneath and pour the glaze over it, smoothing the top and sides. Decorate with almonds if you wish.

When set, remove to a cake plate. If you refrigerate this, the finish will go dull, so best kept in a container at room temperature and served within a day or two.

VANILLEKIPFERL

These melt-in-the-mouth crescent-shaped cookies are Austria's answer to the shortbread cookie, and especially popular during Advent. It is believed the shape symbolizes the victory of the Holy Roman Empire over the Ottomans after the two-month Siege of Vienna in the summer of 1683. A similar confection—ghorabie—is a delicacy in Rustavaijan.

Viennese cooks take great pride in shaping them elegantly, so don't rush this stage of the process. You can substitute finely chopped almonds for the chopped hazelnuts, if you like. I prefer toasted nuts, but for a paler cookie, you can leave them untoasted.

I don't normally bother to preheat my oven—it's a waste of energy—but the timing here is critical, so turn the oven on while you shape the cookies.

Makes 24 small cookies.

½ cup finely chopped toasted hazelnuts
¾ cup ground almonds
¼ teaspoon fine salt
1 cup plus 1 tablespoon all-purpose flour
1 stick (8 tablespoons) best-quality unsalted butter, such as Vital Farms (or if using imported, which I recommend, ½ 250-g bar French Beurre D'Isigny), softened
3 tablespoons superfine sugar
½ teaspoon pure vanilla extract
seeds scraped from 1 vanilla bean
sifted confectioners' sugar, for dusting

Mix the nuts, flour, and salt in a small bowl.

In a stand mixer, or using an electric hand whisk, cream the butter, sugar, and vanilla extract until pale and whippy, scraping down the sides of the bowl with a spatula. Beat in the vanilla seeds then add the flour and nut mixture and beat until the mixture just comes together.

Handling the dough lightly, remove from the bowl, weigh and divide into two pieces of equal size. Roll each portion between your fingers into an even cylinder 9½ inches long, then slice into 12 disks, to form 24 cookies in total.

Turn the oven to 350°F/325°F fan. Line two cookie sheets with parchment paper. Take the first disk and shape it into a sausage, 2¾–3¼ inches in length, tapering slightly at each end (but not too much or the tips will scorch in the oven.) Curve it into a semi-circle then place on the lined cookie sheet. Don't worry if it crumbles—just smooth it together. Repeat with the remaining disks, arranging them 1¼ inches apart, though note these are not cookies which rise very much.

When you've shaped all the cookies, bake for 16–19 minutes, rotating the sheets halfway through cooking time, if necessary, until the cookies are still pale, but just beginning to show signs of going golden. Let cool on the sheets for 3 minutes.

Wait till the cookies are completely cool then tumble in sifted confectioners' sugar to cover completely. Store in an airtight container for up to a week, re-dusting with more confectioners' sugar if necessary, before enjoying.

Author's Note

"Natasha's Law" came into effect in the UK in 2021, requiring full labeling of ingredients on all prepacked food for direct sale. It is named after Natasha Ednan-Laperouse, who died tragically in 2016, aged fifteen, from an allergic reaction to sesame seeds. The sesame seeds were an ingredient in a sandwich-shop baguette, but had not been mentioned on the packaging. Her parents continue to campaign on behalf of children and adults with food allergies, and the results of the Natasha Clinical Trial, an investigation into the efficacy of oral immunotherapy using everyday foods, are expected in 2027. Find out more or donate at the Natasha Allergy Research Foundation website: narf.org.uk.

For those interested in making Paul's recipes (which are real recipes, triple tested) you will find photographs of the finished results at orlandomurrin.com, as well as the rationale for not preheating your oven and choosing mixed weight eggs (see also the British Hen Welfare Trust website: bhwt.org.uk). In classic cuisine, *fines herbes* comprise finely chopped parsley, chives, tarragon and chervil; if using dried, I recommend purchasing from steenbergs.co.uk, which also offers a seasoned version for vinaigrette and the more robust and grassy *herbes de Provence* (which include lavender). In the US, visit penzeys.com.

If you're drawn to the idea of speedwriting, Blue uses the BakerWrite system, a flexible, intuitive approach using the letters of the alphabet which increases writing speed by 30–40 percent. Shorthand is still used by some journalists (Pitman or Teeline), but the days when a reporter could scribble on a scrap of paper in their pocket with the stub of a pencil and the results be used as evidence in court have, alas, gone forever. The highest speeds of all are achieved on stenotype machines, which are still used in the High Court and for TV captioning.

370 / AUTHOR'S NOTE

Men's fragrances Creed Aventus and Andy Tauer's Lonestar Memories are available from Les Senteurs at 71 Elizabeth Street, London SW1W 9PJ (round the corner from Paul's Belgravia cottage). Amouage can be purchased at Selfridges and Harrods in London. In the United States, these scents can be tracked down online, for instance at luckyscent.com.

You can trace *Maldemer*'s course across the ocean by tapping the coordinates into Google Maps—though don't expect to find Lacuna at 39°23'10"N 31°09'50"W. If—like Julie—you are looking for an easier way to find out where you're going, I'd recommend what3words, a geocode system which divides the surface of the Earth into 56 trillion 3 metre squares, each identified by a unique (and easily memorized) three-word combination.

ACKNOWLEDGMENTS

There are many different strands in *May Contain Murder*, and I'd like to thank the numerous friends, colleagues and experts who have generously helped with information and advice.

First, my publishing team: I consider myself profoundly lucky to be published by Transworld, and to have as editor the insightful, inspiring and ever-courteous Finn Cotton. My publicity is managed impeccably by Patsy Irwin, marketing by Lucy Upton and sales by crack team Deirdre O'Connell, Tom Chicken and Cara Conquest.

Having started out as a sub-editor myself, I know details matter. I'm indebted to the eagle eyes of proofreading supremo Vivien Thompson and her team, including copyeditor Fraser Crichton and proofreader Clare Hubbard. Thank you also to Irene Martinez for the splendid cover and Sebastian Humphreys for reading the audiobook with such flair and humor.

It is a pleasure to work with the most amiable, efficient (and coolest) agent in the business, Oli Munson; also at A. M. Heath (and also all of the above), Harmony Leung. For her invaluable help on the manuscript, imagination and urbane wit, thank you Lynn Curtis.

Having been brought up in the Channel Islands, I spent my youth messing around on boats. We never ventured into the Atlantic, thank God, so I was fortunate to be put in touch with Herbie Dayal, who shared his first-hand experience of Atlantic yachting, storms and all. Sailor-chef Sam Kilgour gave me an insight into how it really feels to cook in a superyacht galley. The International Maritime Organization steered me through the intricacies of law on the high seas.

The recipes were put through their paces by food editor and

stylist Angela Nilsen, who also took the mouthwatering photographs of the dishes to be found on my website. For recipe inspiration, a call-out for Julia Child, from whose recipe my Queen of Sheba cake is adapted, and Christie Dietz, who taught me the finer points of *Vanillekipferl*. Fish specialist CJ Jackson (@fish_boss1962 on Instagram) advised on catching and preparing yellowfin tuna. The recipes were adapted for American readers (from the British metric system) by Julia Charles.

The Poseidon Adventure cocktail was created exclusively for *May Contain Murder* by mixologist and cinema historian Jenny Hammerton. Jenny has written several books about famous movie stars' recipes and tipples, including *Cooking with Joan Crawford* and *Murder, She Cooked*; you can find her @silverscreensuppers, or visit her enormous archive of star-spangled recipes at silverscreensuppers.com.

I was introduced to the world of tarot via an online course by Daisy Waugh at idler.co.uk. My friend Titania Hardie, expert on folklore, magic, symbols and divination, helped me choose the cards for Julie and interpret them. The images are from the Rider Waite Smith deck (1909).

For the speedwriting examples, I thank Joanna Gutmann. Joanna offers live online and self-learning programs in minute-taking and speedwriting with an inclusive, hands-on approach which makes learning both fun and involving. joanna-gutmann.co.uk – *fl fre 2 gt n tc f u hv any?s*. For information on shorthand and stenography, I'm grateful to Andrew Roberts. I write using a Contour RollerMouse Red Plus Wireless and Matias Notebook Pro Keyboard supplied by keyboardco.com in Stroud, Gloucestershire. My website, orlandomurrin.com, of which I'm inordinately proud, is managed by Heather Brown (heather-brown.com).

Colefax, the Bichon Frisé, was modeled on much-loved Ted, who sadly died during the course of my writing this book.

Thank you, Laura Washburn Hutton, for sharing him and your insights into this fascinating and adorable dog breed: I am sure Ted is continuing to chase socks in doggie heaven.

The cure for seasickness (page 214) really does work; I learnt it from Liz Glaze, who herself learnt it as a schoolgirl, from a sailor who served during the war. For help with Xéra's French, I'm grateful to Stephen Mudge; for Latin, Noonie Minogue; for Bernie's Irish accent, to Alison Dunne and my cousin Clare Skardon; and for advice on the finer points of tennis, my sister-in-law Sharon Murrin. Thank you, Katie Allen, for wading through the correct edition of *Encylopædia Britannica* on Paul's behalf.

Finally, this book was written against the backdrop of a blissful and often hilarious domestic life. It is handy indeed to have a professor of English literature at my beck and call (my husband Robert), and Benjamin and Maxim the cats to ensure that we don't take life too seriously. *Nil domo dulcius.*

ABOUT THE AUTHOR

After being flung into the culinary limelight as a semi-finalist on *UK MasterChef*, Orlando Murrin edited various British magazines, including *Woman & Home* and *BBC Good Food*, and founded *Olive* magazine. He then switched track to become a chef-hotelier in South West France and Somerset.

He has written six cookbooks and received an Outstanding Achievement Award from the British Guild of Food Writers, its highest accolade. A popular guest on TV and radio, and at food and literary festivals, he is also a regular podcaster and podcast host.

From his grandfather, a famous detective who rose to become a crack MI5 interrogator, he inherited a fascination with crime and mystery. He lives in domestic bliss in Exeter, Devon, and has written culinary crime novels: *Knife Skills For Beginners* (shortlisted for four major awards, including the McDermid Debut Award) and *May Contain Murder*.

You can find Orlando on Facebook and Instagram @orlandomurrinauthor, and @orlandomurrin.bsky.social on BlueSky. His website is www.orlandomurrin.com